CHRISTMAS WITH THE SPITFIRE GIRLS

Yorkshire, 1944. The end of the war feels tantalisingly close, but Air Transport Auxiliary girls Bobbie, Viv and Mary have plenty more flights in their beloved Spitfires yet.

Risking their lives doing their bit for their country, this Christmas they're determined to have some festive fun. But as they set about bringing good tidings for all, a stern and mysterious new flyer in the form of Peggy arrives.

Mary has a wedding to plan before her fiancé is sent away, but then makes a devastating discovery so shameful she can't tell the other girls. Bobbie's beau issues an ultimatum, and Viv is wondering whether she wants a man at all . . .

With the big day around the corner and hope of peace on the horizon, can the girls find joy and love this Christmas after so many years of war?

JENNY HOLMES

CHRISTMAS WITH THE SPITFIRE GIRLS

Complete and Unabridged

MAGNA
Leicester

First published in Great Britain in 2020 by
Corgi Books
an imprint of Transworld Publishers
London

First Ulverscroft Edition
published 2022
by arrangement with
Transworld Publishers
Penguin Random House UK
London

This book is a work of fiction and, except in the case of
historical fact, any resemblance to actual persons, living
or dead, is purely coincidental.

A catalogue record for this book is available
from the British Library.

ISBN 978-0-7505-4929-5

For the courageous few:
the surviving heroes and heroines
of the Second World War.

1

'Make hay while the sun shines — that's my motto.' Viv Robertson twirled in front of the long mirror in her bedroom at Burton Grange. She was dressed to impress in a red satin dress with a sweetheart neckline and a cinched-in waist. Her thick dark hair refused to conform to the current fashion for sleek, smooth tresses and instead tumbled down over her forehead to frame her delicate features with a mass of shiny curls.

Her fellow Atta girl, Bobbie Fraser, stood in her black lace petticoat, trying to decide between green silk and russet-brown crêpe de Chine.

'Definitely the green silk,' their friend Mary Holland advised from her position by the bay window. She was trying on a pair of black high-heeled shoes that belonged to Viv. 'It suits your colouring.'

Bobbie held the green dress against her pale skin. 'I wish my hair wasn't so ginger,' she said with a frown.

'Your hair's sandy, not ginger,' Viv soothed. 'And it does what it's told — which is more than can be said for mine.' A second twirl and a flare of red skirt and white petticoat confirmed that she was almost ready to dance the night away with the RAF boys at nearby Aireby training camp.

'You're sure you don't mind me borrowing these?' Mary was pleased with Viv's peep-toed evening shoes. They made her legs look more shapely and gave a

1

sophisticated impression to match her off-the-shoulder dress in purple jersey knit.

'Feel free,' Viv assured her as she snatched the brown dress from Bobbie and threw it on the bed. 'Get a move on, Roberta McFlirta. At this rate all the decent dancers will be snapped up by the time we get there.'

Bobbie slid into the strapless green dress. 'Zip it up for me, then,' she told Viv in her soft Scottish brogue. The boned bodice gave her slight figure a more womanly outline and she responded shyly to the whistle of approval from Viv and the smile and wink from Mary.

'Not bad,' Viv said with a grin. 'Now that only leaves make-up and hair.' She swept to one side her bottles of perfume, hairbrushes and powder puffs to make room at the dressing table for Mary and Bobbie to sit down. 'Slap it on nice and thick, girls. The aim is to knock those RAF boys clean off their feet when we finally make our entrance.'

Mary and Bobbie knew from experience that Viv's exaggerations had to be taken with a pinch of salt. It was the Canadian girl's way of letting off steam after another strenuous week of ferrying fighter planes and heavy bombers from factory to RAF base, or from a maintenance unit in the Midlands to secret airfields in the south. It would be the same with the jitterbugging when they got to Aireby: vivacious Viv would be first on the dance floor, loving the attention and making everyone smile. But her pilot friends knew Viv's flip side: the gritty, determined, fearless flier who had grown up in Vancouver and made her way to this remote corner of Yorkshire to do her bit and help win the war.

'More lipstick,' Viv advised Mary. Then, 'Perhaps a

touch more eyeshadow,' she recommended to Bobbie.

Bobbie hesitated. 'Are you sure? I don't want to look like a clown.'

'Honey, that's impossible.' Viv picked up a bottle of red polish and gave her nails a quick extra coat while she waited. 'You're the perfect English rose.'

'Except that I'm Scottish.' Bobbie gave a peal of laughter. She'd been born into money on a Highland estate north of Loch Lomond, complete with grouse moor and salmon fishing.

Mary put down the lipstick then studied the over-all effect in the mottled mirror, which reflected Viv's room in all its faded glory. She took in the floral wallpaper that curled at the edges, the old-fashioned iron bedstead in one corner and the frayed rug placed in front of a small iron fireplace. It had to be admitted that Burton Grange was well past its prime — built in the eighteenth century as a grand manor house with extensive grounds but now requisitioned by the War Office to house the twenty or so civilian volunteers who made up the Air Transport Auxiliary in the North Riding village of Rixley.

Mary turned her attention back to her own reflection. 'I wish my nose wasn't so big,' she grumbled quietly.

'It is not big, silly!' Bobbie studied her image in the mirror. 'You'd have cause to complain if you had my sticky-out ears. And on top of that, my toes are all squished.'

'Ears, noses, toeses, schmozes!' Viv blew on her fingernails to dry the varnish. 'Since we're in confessional mode — do you two want to hear my least favourite feature?'

'Yes, please!' Mary and Bobbie sang out in unison.

Viv turned to present her back view. 'It's my der-rière!'

More laughter filled the room and the other two girls sprang to their feet. ' 'Head, shoulders, knees and toes!' ' they chorused with the accompanying actions. ' 'Head, shoulders, knees and toes, knees and toes!' '

'And derrières!' Viv added as she led the charge out of the room, down the wide, bomb-damaged staircase and out into the cold, dark night.

★ ★ ★

A maroon Morris van was parked outside the RAF Aireby venue, its sides emblazoned with the words 'ENSA Roadshow'. Big band music filtered out through an open door of the Nissen hut where the Saturday evening dance was being held.

'See — we're late.' Viv got out from behind the wheel of the borrowed Ford. 'The fun has started without us.'

Bobbie and Mary slid gracefully from the back seat, turning up their coat collars against the blustery wind and clutching their handbags to their chests. As they rushed towards the door, ignoring posters invit-ing recruits to 'Make the RAF Supreme' and insisting that 'Every New Aircraft Needs a Crew', a gang of raucous cadets from the Initial Training Wing jumped out of the back of a Tilly wagon and made a beeline for the girls.

'Here's a sight for sore eyes,' one crowed in loose-jawed admiration.

'Blimey O'Flippin' Riley!' said another. 'Are you three girls real or am I dreaming?'

Viv, Mary and Bobbie found themselves surrounded by smiling, jostling suitors, all dressed in uniform and with brutal short-back-and-sides haircuts, and all smelling of shaving soap and Brilliantine.

Viv sailed on ahead of Bobbie and Mary. 'Make way there, guys. Let the dog see the rabbit.'

'Can I have the first dance?' a tall, gangly youth implored Bobbie. 'Make my night — say yes!'

'We'll see.' She followed Viv inside. 'Let me at least take my coat off.'

'I'll be waiting by the bar,' he promised as he was shouldered aside by two others eager to secure a similar promise from Mary.

'Hold your horses.' Mary fended them off with her handbag. 'Give a girl a chance.'

With the evening already well under way, Viv, Mary and Bobbie were greeted by a swirl of dancers in close ballroom hold — the men in uniform and the girls in bright, shiny dresses, bedecked with silk flowers, pearls and diamanté. From a temporary stage at the far end of the room a stout, young chanteuse with brightly rouged cheeks crooned 'I'll Be Seeing You' into a microphone, accompanied by a four-piece band.

'In all the old familiar places — just as the song says.' Mary turned to find her fiancé, Cameron Ainslie, murmuring the words from Bing Crosby's recent hit song.

'Cameron,' she breathed. There he was, in his flight lieutenant's uniform, waiting for her just inside the door — by far the most handsome man there. And by far the tallest and most distinguished — the most everything! 'You managed to get back from Liverpool in time.' She hadn't been sure that he would; as head of Training Command here at Aireby, answerable only

5

to Group Captain Hubert Norris, Cameron's duties often interfered with his weekends off.

'Wild horses wouldn't have stopped me.' Mary took his breath away, even after all these months of courtship. He thought she looked beautiful in her dark dress, the colour of ripe plums, with a silk spray of lily of the valley pinned to her shoulder strap. Her grey eyes sparkled as she looked up into his face and smiled. 'I'm so glad.'

He smiled back and took her by the arm, leading her to the trestle table where drinks were being served. 'After I finished my meeting I was obliged to show some wireless operators around a Supermarine Walrus — they'd never seen the inside of one before.'

'Say no more.' Mary knew the difficult reputation of the amphibious biplane: a hulking great thing that flapped around all over the sky in crosswinds and was considered by many pilots to be almost uncontrollable. 'I just hope they don't put me in one of those lumbering crates now that we girls are finally allowed to cross the Channel.'

Permission to do so had been a long time coming and had only come into force since D-Day, thanks to the ATA's doughty commander, Pauline Gower, and her deputy, who had pushed hard for women pilots to fly beyond the south coast and into foreign parts.

'No, you stick to your Spitfires.' Cameron turned to the makeshift bar and ordered Mary's Dubonnet and lemonade without having to ask. 'And a pint of bitter for me, please,' he told the barman. 'Anyway, if the met boys in Liverpool have got it right, we're facing a bad winter so there'll be plenty of washout days where we all sit twiddling our thumbs.'

'Worse luck.' Mary preferred to be busy, liking

nothing better than to collect a Wellington (no finesse needed, like flying around in an old railway carriage) from a maintenance unit and fly it up to Lossiemouth, where she would pick up a Dakota (tail wheel-lock positioned under throttle, not, as described in her Pilots' Notes, next to the oil controls), bound for Wolverhampton, then finally (joy of joys) back home to Rixley in a beloved Spitfire. All in one day, mind you, and so from the ferry pool straight back to the Grange, a hot-water bottle and bed.

Cameron and Mary carried their drinks to seats close to the stage. The blowsy ENSA singer had given way to a boy of eighteen or so with straw-blond hair, who began his stint with a lively tune on the piano. The dancers responded to the change of tempo by launching into a daring jitterbug, recently stolen from American GIs who had brought the craze across the Atlantic along with nylon stockings and a seemingly endless supply of chocolate.

'This lot make me feel old,' Cameron complained, though he was only twenty-four.

With a grin, Mary took his drink from him and pulled him to his feet. 'Come on, Granddad — let's dance.'

Soon they were rocking to and fro, tripping the light fantastic and twirling with the best of them. Across the dance floor, Bobbie's gawky but persistent cadet had claimed her and was stumbling around, stamping on her feet and bumping into Agnes Wright and Horace Jackson, two ATA pilots from Rixley whom Bobbie knew well. Poor Agnes was sent flying and had to be picked up off the floor.

'Sorry!' Bobbie gasped at Agnes as her clumsy partner whirled her away again.

'How about the next one?' her cadet demanded when the piano player went into a slow waltz. His hands strayed down to Bobbie's backside as he tried to steer her into a space at the back of the room.

'No ta.' Escaping his clutches, she headed for the bar. 'Lime juice, please,' she ordered, only to find that she hadn't shaken off her dogged dance partner after all. 'Look,' she told him in a no-nonsense way, 'there really is no point.'

'How's that?' The persistent suitor slid a long arm around Bobbie's waist.

She swallowed hard. 'Well, my . . . my young man's not here tonight but I'm afraid I'm already spoken for.' *What a ridiculous, schoolgirlish thing to say!* Bobbie immediately wished that the floor would swallow her up.

'She may be spoken for but I'm not!' Viv rushed in to save her incorrigibly demure friend's bacon. With a wink in Bobbie's direction she yanked the lanky air gunner into the centre of the dance floor and flashed him her most vivacious smile. 'Anyway, live for today — that's what I always say. My name's Vivienne, by the way. What's yours?'

★ ★ ★

'My poor tootsies!' It was Monday morning and Viv had taken off her fur-lined boots and put her sore feet up on the canteen table at Rixley ferry pool. 'I near as dammit got trampled to death on Saturday night.'

Sitting at the same table, Mary cleared a patch in the steamed-up window of the Nissen hut and gazed out at a dismal, foggy scene. She could scarcely make out the small patch of lawn, let alone the two-storey

8

concrete block containing the control tower, ops room and office where the met boys and girls worked. 'Washout,' she mumbled. 'We'll be lucky if we get off the ground before midday.'

Bobbie moved aside a vase of wilting yellow chrysanthemums then laid out a pack of playing cards for a game of patience. The canteen was crowded with bored pilots and ground crew, all waiting for the go-ahead once the weather cleared. 'Open that window,' she suggested to Mary. 'Let in some fresh air.'

'Oh no, please — we'll all f-f-freeze to death!' This was Viv's first experience of a British winter and it was proving very different from the ones she'd recently experienced in California, where she'd worked for a couple of years as a stunt pilot.

'Softie,' Bobbie chided. 'Anyhow, you're Canadian — I imagine winters there are ten times worse.'

'Open or closed?' Mary raised her voice to ask for a general vote.

'Open! . . . Shut! . . . Suit yourself.' Pilots and ground crew came and went, carrying trays with steaming mugs of tea, dishes of porridge and plates of sausage and egg.

'Closed,' Agnes told Mary through a bunged-up nose. 'I'll catch my death if you leave it open.'

'Hey, Agnes!' Viv caught her attention as she passed by. 'I had no idea that you and Horace . . . well, you know.'

Agnes shot her a warning glance then rolled her eyes towards Horace, who was queuing up at the counter with his back turned. 'We're not,' she retorted. 'Not after Saturday night, at any rate.'

'Ooh, tell us more!' Viv lowered her feet and scraped back the vacant seat next to her. The dance at

9

Aireby had ended satisfactorily for Viv, who had had no shortage of partners and who had ended up with a wonderfully handsome flight lieutenant, no less. His name was Brian Wheeler; a square-jawed, smooth-shaven type. He drove a Morgan sports car and spoke with the kind of clipped British accent that Viv had only previously heard on newsreels. He'd been keen to see her again and she'd agreed to let him visit her at Rixley the following weekend.

Agnes sat down and began to tuck into her porridge. She was dressed for action in her Sidcot suit and boots and, like the rest of the pilots, was disappointed by the delay that the bad weather had imposed. 'Horace has two left feet,' she reported sniffily. 'Anyhow, he's not my type.'

'And why's that?' Viv asked.

'He can't keep his hands to himself, for a start.'

'Horace Jackson?' Mary and Bobbie had overheard. They leaned in, eager to hear more from an unusually chatty Agnes, who was normally aloof and generally regarded as a bit of an old maid. 'Never! You don't say!'

Everyone at Rixley viewed Second Officer Jackson as mouse-like and inoffensive. He was slightly built with an already receding hairline — not at all God's gift. Mind you, Agnes herself didn't exude the glamour of someone like Viv. She was a bit too prim and proper, with her scraped-back hair and her long, serious face; a teetotaller who went by the rule book and had a tendency to tell others what to do.

'In any case, I reckon I'm better off not getting involved.' Agnes scraped the bottom of her bowl. 'Men are a distraction when all's said and done.'

Viv smiled broadly. 'A distraction is what men

10

definitely are. And aren't we glad!'

Through the window Mary saw the Rixley operations manager, First Officer Douglas Thornton, emerge from the ops room. He limped heavily across the lawn then entered the canteen to announce an update on prohibited areas. 'Good morning, everyone.'

The room fell silent as Douglas drew a folded sheet of paper from his top pocket. There was automatic respect for this ex-RAF man, once a member of 74 'Tiger' Squadron with four kills and seven hits to his name, now ruled out of further action due to serious injuries and so seconded to the ATA.

'Watch out for extra barrage balloons in Bristol and Liverpool this morning — if we ever get off the ground, that is. Make sure you read everything on this list.'

'What's the latest on the weather?' Bobbie enquired.

'With a bit of luck the fog should clear before midday.' Having pinned his notice to the board next to the door, Douglas queued for a cup of tea then joined Bobbie and the rest of the gang. 'Rain is forecast pretty much everywhere, with the possibility of snow and sleet later on, but not enough to stop us flying.'

'The sooner we're out of here the better.' It was Mary who voiced the impatience that everyone was feeling. Her longing for activity vied with fond memories of her recent time spent with Cameron — in his arms, floating across the dance floor, leaning in and holding him tight. Oh, how she loved that man, with his quiet, clever way of going about things. But now she had to worry about his hankering to be posted back to Bomber Command, which would take him out of his current training role at Aireby and back into the direct line of fire. The transfer would inevitably mean flying missions over France and Germany, seeking out Messerschmitts and Junkers and engaging in dogfights that few pilots ultimately survived. Agnes was right in a way — men did distract. They drew out feelings that were hard to manage and it was only climbing into a cockpit and running through checks before take-off that focused the mind and put Mary back in control.

'How are Jean and the baby?' she asked Douglas with a small, determined shake of her shoulders.

'Both in the pink,' he told her with pride. 'Dorota will be nine months old at the end of November. She's crawling and already getting into everything she oughtn't.'

'Tell Jean we miss seeing her here every day.' Bobbie was aware that Douglas's wife already knew this but it didn't stop her from repeating it. 'Rixley just isn't the same without her.'

'She did the right thing to give up flying, though,' Mary insisted. 'Once you'd decided to adopt Dorota, Jean couldn't justify taking the risk.'

'But it still doesn't mean we Atta girls don't miss her.' Jean had been Bobbie's inspiration — cool as a cucumber up there at 6,000 feet, hurtling along at 400 mph in the latest Spit. *Bloody brilliant at what she did. No one will ever come close; not Viv for all her gung-ho bravado or Mary with her meticulous attention to detail.*

'Drop in at Fern Cottage whenever you like.' Douglas drained his cup then stood up. 'You'll always be welcome.'

He limped off and left them to their own devices — Agnes to her knitting, which she had taken out of a side pocket in her parachute pack; Mary to

12

writing a letter to her soldier brother (*Dear Tom, Where in the world are you? It's been ages since I've received a letter. Are you still somewhere in Europe or have they sent you back to Tunisia? In any case, I hope you're fit and well and managing to cope with whatever Herr Hitler throws at you . . .*) and Bobbie to her game of patience. Viv, meanwhile, with one eye on the slowly dissolving mist, unzipped her Sidcot suit, pushed aside a couple of tables and began her exercises, swinging her arms and twisting her slim, flexible torso, determined to ignore ribald comments from members of the ground crew and working up quite a sweat.

The hours ticked slowly by until, at eleven o'clock, a hiss of static from the loudspeaker above the door presaged the announcement they'd all been waiting for.

'Will all pilots please report immediately to the operations room. I repeat: all pilots . . .'

Then, with stomach muscles tightening and heartbeats quickening, it was a mad scramble to the locker room to pick up helmets, goggles, parachute packs, maps, compasses and whatever else was needed. From there the young pilots took the stairs two at a time up to the hatch where Gillian Wharton, Douglas's efficient secretary, sat at her desk, ready to hand out chits for the day — a de Havilland Mosquito for Agnes for the first time ('Anyone flown a Mossie before? What's she like?'), an Airspeed Oxford for Viv ('Oh no, God help me — not the old Ox-box!'), a Hawker Typhoon for Bobbie.

Rapid words of advice were exchanged on the stairs as pilots came and went. Blue, spiral-bound Pilots' Notes were pulled out of pockets and consulted. Wary eyes were cast skywards at clouds still hanging low

13

over the church steeple in the nearby village.

'Let's see what you've got for me today.' Mary received her slip of paper from Gillian and read the word that always gave her the biggest thrill of all. 'Spitfire!' The very latest type — the excellent Mark 12. 'Bingo!' she cried as she sprinted down from the ops room and out on to the soggy patch of lawn. 'Spit Mark Twelve to Liverpool,' she reported to Viv and Bobbie.

'Lucky you.' Viv was listed as first off Runway 2 in her Ox-box. 'I've to fly the old crate all the way to Southampton then back here in a Wellington. It'll be midnight before I get home.'

'Yes. Oh, Mary, I envy you your little beauty,' Bobbie murmured. 'But go easy on that throttle — they say her back end swings badly if you don't watch out.'

Mary's heart thumped against her ribcage as she sprinted for Runway 1, where she was second in line. *New Griffon engine to replace the old Merlin*, she reminded herself. *Straighten out immediately if swing occurs. Keep a clear head. Let the fun begin.*

14

2

Nothing in the whole of aviation history compared with the inside of a Spit's perfectly designed cockpit. Though Mary was slightly built, the bucket seat was a snug fit and brought her face to face with rows of black dials — forty in all — and within easy reach of the stick. There was a red crowbar fixed to the inside of the door in case of emergency — in theory, one blow from this would smash the Plexiglas canopy to smithereens, allowing the pilot to bail out and parachute to safety.

Mary glanced down at the tarmac, where mechanics Stan Green and Bob Cross made their final checks. Catching her eye, Stan gave her a broad grin and the thumbs-up signal to fire up the engine. *Brakes on, fuel on, idle-cut-off switch off, pre-oiler on for two minutes.* Her excitement calmed to steady concentration as she set the prop to fine pitch and eased the throttle open.

'Clear prop!' Stan yelled up at her.

On with the magnetos then wait for the smell of exhaust fumes, the roar of the mighty engine. There was a three-second jet of flame followed by a shudder. *We're off!*

This was it — no turning back. Bob and Stan took away the chocks then watched Mary taxi towards the take-off point.

Sheer delight, pure heaven! The day might be dank and dismal and the fallen leaves from nearby Burton Wood were dark brown and soggy under the crate's wheels, but Mary knew she was in charge of a beautiful thoroughbred as she went through the motions. *Set automatic trim, open throttle fully, rev to 1,800, give it six pounds of stick. Now or never!*

Whoosh! Mary and her Spit were in the air — just her and her wondrous machine soaring swiftly up towards the unknown. There really was nothing like it; nothing on this earth!

As she flew over Burton Wood she locked her landing gear into a raised position. A glance towards the ground and the thin strip of the runway she'd just left told her that Stan and Bob stood waving her off.

She waved back. Ah, Stan — her loyal, salt-of-the-earth friend.

'Watch out for those barrage balloons over the Mersey,' had been his last words of advice as Mary had scrambled up into the cockpit. 'I don't want to read your name on an accident report tomorrow morning.'

'Thanks, Stan — you certainly know how to buck a girl up!' She'd made a joke of the danger, because you had to and because she knew Stan genuinely cared.

Rising now to 2,000 feet, mist swirled around her cockpit and she could only faintly make out landmarks below. Her map would soon prove useless and she would have to rely on her compass. But thankfully the clouds lifted as she flew west. A railway line directly below glinted in weak sunshine then disappeared into a tunnel. Then came the bare, barren, upturned hulks of the Pennine moors before a change of course southwards. Now it was time to try out the new Spit's ailerons in preparation for landing — surprisingly weighty but responsive, nevertheless — following the coastline and thrilling to the bird's-eye view of the sparkling sea. Mary reminded herself to watch out for barrage balloons as Douglas and Stan had warned.

Sure enough, she spotted at least a dozen of the darned things and was forced to fly further west during her descent so that she came at the Mersey along a narrow corridor of the whale-shaped blimps. She took special care not to snag her wings in the thick wires that tethered them to the ground as she glided down to 200 feet over the dockyard cranes with her engine at zero boost. She followed the steel-grey curve of the estuary then spied the runway and hit the ground with scarcely a bump. Foot on the brake flat to the floor, hold the crate straight, screech to a halt with ground crew to greet her.

Once more Mary conducted her methodical checks before she finally raised the cockpit and stepped out on to the wing. She felt ten feet tall! Exhilarated and grinning from ear to ear as she took off her helmet, she shook out her hair then jumped to the ground.

'Blimey, it's a girl!' one of the eager Liverpool erks cried. 'And not a bad-looking one neither.'

★ ★ ★

Viv's day took her safely to Southampton in the Ox-box then back to Rixley in a Wellington. Truth to tell, she could have flown both blindfolded if necessary, so familiar was she with the old crates' controls and the low churn of their engines. The Wellington, especially, provided less of a challenge than she would have wished, once she was propped up in the pilot's seat with three cushions to enable her to see where she was going. Her wristwatch told her that it was two o'clock in the afternoon, meaning she had just enough daylight left to make it back before nightfall.

The uneventful return flight gave her time to

ponder the state of play in this great war game that was being played out across the globe. Was Germany really ready to fall, as the British newspapers predicted? True, the Yanks had captured Aachen just a couple of weeks earlier and the Allies had recently landed in Athens. The summer had also seen a Russian victory in Belarus and a British one in Burma — not to mention the outstanding success of D-Day and Operation Overlord. Paris was now free, along with Brussels and Antwerp. So far so good, Viv reflected. But Hitler's deadly weapon — the V1 rocket — was causing havoc in London and other major cities.

People said these doodlebugs were vicious little devils — first came the warning sound of them whining overhead and then the heart-stopping moment when the engine cut out, followed by a few seconds' ominous silence before the deadly device dropped to the ground and exploded. What must that be like, Viv wondered — spotting a devilish self-propelled missile overhead, dashing for shelter then waiting and praying for your luck to hold?

And what other horrors awaited besides the V1s? What were the scientists up to behind the scenes in the race to come up with ever more destructive devices? *God knows where and when it will end,* she mused, flying smoothly over clusters of Midlands pottery towns, heading for home and turning her attention to how she would spend her evening.

Enough of the gloomy stuff, she told herself. The only way to get through this hell on earth is to think positively and have as much fun as you can while you're at it.

So this was Viv's mood as she made a perfect landing on Runway 2 then handed her crate over to Gordon Mason, a member of the ground crew who

18

loved to banter with her. He didn't take life too seriously either, sharing Viv's *carpe diem* mentality. He was a good-looking guy from Birmingham with an English mother and a West Indian father — worldly wise and oozing confidence — and more than once he had made it obvious that he believed he was in with a chance with the most glamorous girl pilot at Rixley.

'What do you say we go for a quick drink at the Fox?' Gordon asked the moment Viv stepped out on to the wing of the Wellington, unzipping her sheepskin jacket and removing her goggles and helmet.

'Give a girl a chance to get her feet back on solid ground,' she said and pouted.

'But what do you say?' he pressed.

If anyone could pull off a pair of threadbare RAF overalls it was Gordon. He wore them unbuttoned to the waist with sleeves rolled up, and his 100-yard-dash frame filled out the baggy garment just fine as he stood, hands on hips, waiting for an answer. But Viv resisted temptation. 'Not tonight, Gordon. No offence, but I have things to do.'

'What things?' He offered her a hand as she jumped to the ground. Behind them the Wellington's twin propellers slowed to a halt while Bob, the young apprentice, manoeuvred a heavyweight Amazon lorry into position, ready to tow the bomber into the hangar for repairs.

'Just things,' Viv replied airily, withdrawing her hand as she spoke. Seizing the day didn't include drinking a sweet martini at the local pub followed by a quick kiss and a cuddle with Gordon in the village bus shelter. No — Viv had bigger fish to fry. There was Saturday night's conquest, Flight Lieutenant

Brian Wheeler, for a start — dashing and smiling, dishing out the compliments as if they were going out of fashion. And always in the background was Giles Parseval. Now what on earth should she do as far as he was concerned?

'Follow your heart,' was Bobbie's advice whenever Giles's name came up, which was often because the Parseval family owned Burton Grange and Sir Thomas had recently put his son Giles in charge of running their three far-flung estates.

'The trouble is I don't know what my heart is telling me,' Viv would declare, usually after a couple of drinks in the officers' mess at the Grange. 'It's giving me mixed messages.'

Mary's stock response was more practical: 'Is Giles divorced yet? And can you trust him after what went on earlier this year?'

'I have no clue.' It was true — Viv couldn't be sure about Giles Parseval. She found his urbane manner hard to read. That was the trouble with the English upper classes: you could never tell what they were truly thinking, let alone what they were feeling.

'We'll have that drink another time, then,' Gordon said now with a casual shrug of his shoulders.

Viv could feel the handsome mechanic's eyes following her as she strode away. As a matter of fact, penning a letter to Giles was one of the 'things' on her list.

Dear Giles, she would write. *Thank you for inviting me to your thirtieth birthday dinner this Saturday, the 25th, but I'm afraid I can't attend. I have flying duties that day — I'll be on standby for Priority Ones all weekend, worse luck.* This was stretching a point; in fact, she'd gone to Douglas and volunteered herself for

20

extra duties, but only after she'd received Giles's invite. 'To get me off the birthday party hook,' she'd confessed to Bobbie and Mary, who had shaken their heads sceptically.

'Viv will weaken in the end,' Mary had already predicted to Bobbie in private. 'She won't hold out against Giles for ever.'

'I'm not so sure.' Bobbie remembered that Viv had mentioned more than once the prospect of going home to Canada once the war was over. 'Our Viv isn't one to be tied down.'

Everything's up in the air — literally! Viv couldn't help smiling to herself as she locked away her parachute pack then left the ferry pool to walk home through Burton Wood. Up in the air in Hurricanes and Spits, in Stirlings and Tempests (always pull the emergency exit handle extra hard in this type, according to her Pilots' Notes). Up in the air as regards matters of the heart, too — those fickle entanglements versus the ultimate thrill of piloting the latest plane.

'Well, look who it isn't!' Standing on the terrace at Burton Grange, Brian Wheeler saw Viv emerge from the wood and approach the stable yard at the side of the main building.

With a slight frown, Viv took in the shiny green Morgan parked near by and recognized her handsome flight lieutenant as he bounded confidently down the steps to greet her. 'Brian, to what do I owe the pleasure?' she asked coolly.

'You're not expecting me, I know.'

'Not until the weekend,' she reminded him. 'We said Sunday, I believe.' In Viv's book there was such a thing as being too keen. Showing up six days early clearly fell into that category, so she looked askance

21

at her latest suitor.

'I know, but I thought I'd call in on my old pal Hilary while I was passing. And who else should I bump into while I'm here but your lovely, fragrant self!'

'You know Squadron Leader Stevens?' Of course he did: Brian was part of the old boys' network that had frequented the London clubs in the days leading up to the war. Everyone knew everyone else from shooting parties and similar upper-crust jamborees. 'No, don't tell me — you and our pool commander went to school together.'

'Quite so.' Undeterred, Brian slipped his arm through hers then walked her towards his sports car. 'Fancy a spin in the jalopy?'

'Hmm.' The Morgan was certainly more tempting than a sweet martini in the Fox — sleek and gleaming, with its hood down to show off its tan leather interior. 'Why not?'

Before she knew it, she and Brian were sitting side by side in the nippy sports car, speeding through Rixley village, past the church and a row of terraced houses, past the red phone box outside the Fox and Hounds, then out into the countryside along wet lanes and through tunnels of overhanging trees still dropping the last of their leaves. The sky was tinged red by the setting sun; clouds were edged with gold.

'You're not too cold?' he asked.

'In this jacket? You must be kidding!' Viv turned up her sheepskin collar and settled in for the ride. 'How fast does she go?'

'As fast as you like.' He drove easily at 50 mph, both hands resting loosely on the wheel. When they rounded a bend to be suddenly confronted by an approaching tractor he braked without fuss, pulled on to the verge and stopped.

'She's very smart.' Viv admired the Morgan's dashboard. 'I've driven a Jaguar 100 before but not one of these.'

Brian immediately vaulted out of the car on to the narrow lane then ran round to the passenger side to exchange seats. 'She's all yours.'

Accepting eagerly, Viv was soon behind the wheel, driving at sixty along a straight stretch, feeling the wind blow her curly dark hair back from her face, hearing the splash of puddles to either side until all too quickly the sun sank below the horizon and the fading red-gold light turned dull grey. 'Time to head for home?' she enquired as they entered the outskirts of Northgate, a decent-sized spa town famous for its healing waters.

'Sadly, yes.' Brian told her he had an evening appointment to keep. He took over the driving and on the way back they spoke of engine capacities and fuel consumption. 'I've never met a girl who was so keen on cars,' he confessed as he dropped Viv off in the stable yard at the Grange. 'Have you ever thought of rally driving as a future career?'

She laughed as she hopped out on to the cobbles. 'No thanks; that's not for me. I like cars very much, but I adore planes.'

'You don't say?' Brian leaned back in his seat.

'Yes, I was a stunt girl in Hollywood before I came here. I flew old Blériots, Gipsy Moths, and such like. I even did some wing walking when the need arose.'

'And pretty blasé you are about it too.' Viv went up and up in Brian's estimation. 'It turns out you're a proper little Amelia Earhart.'

'Less of the 'little',' she scolded. 'I suppose you

secretly belong to the school that thinks mere women shouldn't be put in charge of eight thousand pounds' worth of military hardware in case they wreck the crate?'

'You're wrong.' Brian's confident smile wavered as he prepared to drive off. 'I think you Atta girls do a grand job.'

Viv winced again at the hint of condescension then gave a mock curtsey. 'Thank you, kind sir.'

'Touché!' An embarrassed laugh followed. 'I'll see you on Sunday?'

'If you're lucky.' 'Keep them keen' was another of her mottos. Aim to be in the driving seat. 'It turns out I'm on standby for Priority Ones. Telephone me on Friday night to check the lie of the land.'

'Will do.' Brian made a mental note. Viv would no doubt be hard to handle but she would be worth it. 'And if you're busy on Sunday, we can make it another time — whenever you're free.'

★ ★ ★

'My letter to Giles never got written,' Viv confessed to Jean Thornton later that evening.

She'd changed out of her uniform into slacks and a cream polo-neck sweater, flung on her belted camel-hair coat and bright red beret then ambled through the wood to Fern Cottage to drop in on her old friend from the ATA. Now the two young women settled down at Jean's kitchen table for what Jean called a chinwag: a quaint term that made Viv smile.

Jean tilted her head to one side and listened to the sounds of Douglas putting Dorota to bed. She heard the creak of floorboards overhead and his deep voice murmuring softly to their daughter as he laid her in her cot. Satisfied, she turned her attention to her visitor, ready to catch up with the latest gossip from the ferry pool. 'What would have been in the letter if you'd written it?'

'Giles is waiting for an RSVP from me,' Viv explained. She noted that motherhood suited Jean — it had softened her Atta-girl edges and made her more relaxed. She was more gorgeous than ever — her long, fair hair informally yet elegantly pinned up on top of her head to reveal her slender neck. But it was Jean's grey-blue eyes that did it — astonishingly large and softly fringed with dark lashes. 'I received an invitation to his birthday dinner.'

'Whereabouts?'

'At Newpark. His parents will be in attendance so for me it would be like entering the lion's den.'

'You've decided not to go?' It was a long way to the Parsevals' second estate in Leicestershire — a train journey of at least two hours from Northgate — so the distance itself would provide Viv with an ample excuse.

'I haven't decided anything — that's the problem.' The complicated on-off situation with Giles had given Viv some sleepless nights, despite her efforts to put him to the back of her mind. 'If it was just Giles and me it might be different.'

'You'd say yes?' Jean was intrigued. 'You've forgiven him for the cover-up?'

Viv thought carefully before she replied. By 'cover-up' Jean meant Giles's decision to conceal his part in the tragedy that had befallen the Grange housekeeper, Anna Janicki, which in turn had led Jean and Douglas to adopt baby Dorota. 'You think I shouldn't?'

'It's up to you.' Jean was the least judgemental of people but even she found it hard to forgive Giles for his shameful deceit in the spring of that year. After all, a decent man would have acknowledged that he was responsible for getting Anna pregnant. He would have supported her and the baby instead of separating Dorota from her mother and leaving Anna to fend for herself. Jean's tone was distinctly chilly as she went on. 'You've kept in touch with Giles all these months, so you must think he has a decent side.'

Viv nodded then quickly shook her head. It had been made clear to her that Giles wasn't, in fact, the guilty party but he'd sworn her to secrecy and for once she'd kept her promise. 'You think it's better to break off contact?'

'Only you can decide.' Hearing Douglas come down the stairs, Jean looked expectantly towards the stairs.

'Dorota went out like a light,' the doting father reported as he entered the kitchen in shirtsleeves and bare feet. 'Hello, Viv,' he acknowledged with a smile. 'How are you?'

'Swell, thanks.' She quickly switched subjects to what she knew would interest him. 'I hear your little pride and joy has two new teeth?'

'Two beauties,' Douglas answered proudly. Then, glancing at Jean, he came up with a suggestion. 'Why don't I stay here while you two girls escape to the Fox for an hour or two?'

'Are you sure you don't mind?' Jean asked hesitantly.

'No. Dorota's fast asleep. It means I can get on with some paperwork while you're out.'

So it was on with their hats and coats followed by a brisk walk into the village. Viv steered clear of the touchy Giles subject and instead discussed babies with Jean. 'I'm a complete novice on that front,' she admitted, 'though I did help to drag up three kid brothers back in Vancouver. Ask me anything you like about how to remove gum from the seats of pants or the names of any top Canadian ice hockey player.'

'Babies are easy,' Jean insisted as she opened the door into the Fox and Hounds. It was as she'd expected for a Monday night: only a few bandy-legged and cloth-capped farmers propped up the bar; there was hardly anyone in from the ferry pool. 'You just feed them and burp them then change their nappies.'

'So speaks the girl who once out-flew half the German *Luftwaffe*!' Viv reminded Jean of her glory days as a first officer in the ATA, capable of flying Anything to Anywhere, as the saying went. She smiled to herself when she spied Gordon Mason in a smoky corner of the bar, sitting hugger-mugger with Gillian, Douglas's attractive, flame-haired secretary. 'Those two seem to be getting along well,' she observed.

'You know Gordon: he gets along well with all the girls.' After a wry smile Jean asked Viv what she would like to drink then placed her order with Florrie Loxley behind the bar. 'Two Dubonnets, please — with lemonade, if you have any.'

Jean picked up the drinks then joined Viv at a table close to the stone fireplace where a log fire burned. 'It's quiet in here tonight,' she remarked.

The dimly lit bar reminded Viv of a cave. Its ceiling was low and its walls and roughly flagged floor were made of dark grey local stone. A strong wind blew smoke down the chimney and sent it billowing across the room. 'That suits me,' she said with a sigh. 'Sometimes a girl needs a bit of peace and quiet to round off a busy day.'

'That doesn't sound like you.' Jean looked keenly at Viv. 'Is everything all right? And don't just say 'swell'. I know you better than that.'

'No, really,' Viv protested, still unwilling to delve any deeper into the Giles versus Brian Wheeler situation and relieved when the door opened and two familiar faces appeared. 'Look what the wind blew in!'

Bobbie entered, all smiles, with Ray Moore close behind. They both looked windswept, as if they'd just stepped out of Ray's open-topped MG sports car. Ray's cheeks were flushed beneath his flat cap and the collar of his tweed jacket was turned up. Bobbie's hair was hidden beneath a tartan headscarf tied under her chin.

'Fancy seeing you two here!' Bobbie beamed as they came across. 'Mind if we join you for a nightcap?'

Chairs were drawn back and space made. Bobbie went for the drinks while Ray sat down.

'We won't stop long,' Ray promised. 'I drove over from Thresham on the off-chance. My luck was in: I caught Bobbie just after she got back from Ventnor.'

'Isle of Wight — isn't that where Agnes was headed today?' Viv asked Bobbie as she returned with the drinks.

'Yes — in a Mossie, apparently, though I didn't see her.' Bobbie perched on Ray's lap. 'I had one of the new Typhoons. To be honest, I was in danger of nodding off over Northamptonshire until I realized it was due to exhaust fumes seeping up through the floor panels. I reached for my oxygen mask double-quick, I don't mind telling you.'

Viv nodded. 'I had that happen to me recently. They make the exhaust pipe far too short in those crates.'

Ray said nothing but he looked anxiously at Bobbie. He never liked to think of her up there in the air without a radio, sometimes in planes that had been badly designed or patched up and could only limp into a maintenance unit for repair. He worried about her day-in, day-out, and that was the truth.

'We missed you at the dance on Saturday,' Viv mentioned to him before draining her glass.

'There was a meet at Ripon — Ronnie and I didn't get back to the yard till late.'

'Ronnie Evans is Ray's head groom,' Bobbie explained to Jean and Viv.

'Did you win anything?' Viv asked.

'We came second in the two thirty with Rob Roy.'

'Congratulations.' She knew as little about horses as she did about babies, but she was pleased that Ray's training yard was experiencing some success. 'We missed you, though. I was obliged to rescue Bobbie from the clutches of an over-keen admirer. He had the reach of an octopus, I can tell you.'

'I could have rescued myself,' Bobbie claimed archly. She felt herself blush then patted Ray's hand reassuringly. 'Take no notice of Viv,' she told him. 'No one at the dance was a patch on you.'

Viv didn't disagree. Bobbie's beloved was certainly good company and easy on the eye, with wavy dark brown hair, twinkling eyes and straight, symmetrical features that put him firmly in the matinee-idol category as far as Viv was concerned. True, his brilliant smile had been less in evidence of late, what with the stresses and strains of running the business since his father's death, but his devotion to Bobbie was plain for all to see.

'Talking of patches, how's that Border collie of

yours?' Bobbie swivelled round to include Jean in the conversation. The dog had come along with Fern Cottage when Douglas and Jean had first moved in.

'Patch? He's happy as can be. How could it be otherwise? He has the whole of Burton Wood to run around in.'

'And Dorota?'

'Teething.' Though her world now centred almost entirely on home and baby, Jean generally made an effort not to bore her friends with too many details. 'Crawling, almost standing up.' She looked at her watch. 'Talking of whom, I'd better make a move.'

'I'll come too.' Viv gathered her coat and hat. 'We'll leave you two lovebirds —'

But before she'd finished her sentence, a second cold blast of air interrupted her. All heads turned expectantly towards the open door.

'Shut that before all the heat rushes out!' From behind the bar, Florrie barked at Mary and Horace.

Horace hung back but Mary advanced towards the table where Bobbie and Viv sat. She was still in uniform, her forage cap clasped in one trembling hand, her face deathly pale.

Alarm clutched at Bobbie's heart and she nudged Viv and Jean to make them pay attention. 'What is it?' she asked Mary, who shook her head. Her eyes seemed unable to focus and the trembling continued.

'Sit down.' Bobbie jumped up so that Ray could offer Mary his chair.

'Has something happened?' Viv asked with mounting dread.

Jean held her breath, fearing the worst.

Bobbie's mind flew hither and thither — had Mary's soldier brother Tom been wounded or killed, or was it something closer to home? 'Is it Cameron?'

'No, it's Agnes,' Mary said faintly as she sat down. Everything was a blur and she struggled to speak. She drew a ragged breath while her audience waited for more.

In the dreadful, drawn-out silence Horace, whose face was as white as Mary's, shuffled forward. He grasped the back of Mary's chair. 'An accident report went up on the bulletin board at six o'clock this evening. Pilot error, apparently.'

'How bad?' Viv gasped.

The worst. Jean could tell from Mary and Horace's drained, shocked faces.

'Agnes snagged the wires of some barrage balloons over Southampton,' he managed to inform them. 'Her Mossie went up in flames.'

'No time to bail out,' Mary added faintly. 'She never stood a chance.'

3

Agnes's fatal accident seemed to have been due to an elementary oversight: a failure to read the list that Douglas had pinned to the noticeboard, perhaps? Descending towards Ventnor on the south coast of the Isle of Wight, she had flown slap bang into a row of hydrogen-filled balloons that protected Southampton, the major mainland port. The remains of her burnt-out de Havilland Mosquito had been spotted floating in the Solent but of the pilot there was no sign.

The following morning, Bobbie, Mary and Viv gathered in a dazed state in the breakfast room at the Grange. No one had got much sleep, and the tragedy still weighed heavily on their minds.

'By all accounts Agnes had never flown a Mossie before,' Bobbie whispered.

'She's plain sailing provided you guard against under-shooting on landing. Anyway, I don't want to talk about it — it's too sad.' Viv stared mournfully at the uneaten porridge congealing in her bowl.

But Mary wouldn't let it rest. She picked over the facts relating to the two-seater combat plane used as a nuisance bomber to target German U-boats. 'It was a brand-spanking-new crate, straight out of the factory. All Agnes needed to do was read through her Notes.'

'Perhaps she did.' Bobbie was desperate for the accident to have been caused by something other than pilot error. 'I once flew a new crate out of

Wolverhampton. The erks had let me take off with blocked fuel pipes, would you believe? My engine cut out three minutes after take-off and I was forced to make an emergency landing.'

'We might never get to the bottom of it.' Mary's spirits were low but she knew that she, like the others, must battle on. 'I ran into Horace just now. He says Agnes's mother intends to collect her stuff tomorrow. She's taken it hard, as you'd expect.'

A heavy silence followed. No food was touched.

'None of us knew Agnes that well, did we?' It was Viv who led the stuttering conversation forward. 'We didn't include her enough. I feel bad about that now.'

'Don't we all?' A distracted Bobbie spread blackberry jam on to a slice of toast. 'On top of which, if they do put it down to a mistake by Agnes that'll be a black mark against us.'

'By 'us' you mean all female pilots.' Viv took the point. There were always people — mostly men — who belittled their role. Agnes's error would no doubt add grist to their mill. 'Which means we'll just have to go out there and prove them wrong — yet again!'

They fell quiet once more until Douglas entered the room with Hilary Stevens. An expectant murmur rose among the dozen or so pilots sitting at the flimsy trestle tables — it was unusual for the operations officer and their squadron leader to come to their billet at this time of the morning in what looked to be an official capacity. Hilary, the taller and slimmer of the two, with an upright bearing and immaculately groomed appearance, raised his hand before speaking.

'First Officer Thornton has something to say,' he announced. 'We both feel it's important.'

Douglas cleared his throat. 'More information has

come through from HQ this morning regarding Third Officer Wright. White Waltham received a report from eyewitnesses at Southampton that will materially affect the investigation into her crash.' He paused to let the information sink in and for the buzz of surprise to die down.

'Witnesses report that Third Officer Wright's Mosquito Mark Six ran into a flock of seagulls as she prepared for her Ventnor landing. Her landing gear was already down and she was approaching at roughly eight hundred feet, as per the guidelines. But when she came into contact with the birds it seems her engine suddenly cut out. The Mosquito quickly spiralled out of control and made direct contact with the nearest hydrogen balloon, with fatal consequences for the pilot.'

'Bloody birds!' Viv clenched her fist and thumped the table. 'They wrecked Agnes's crate!' She was angry that something so random had ended the life of one of their own.

Mary drew a deep breath then let out a sigh, picturing those last desperate moments — a flurry of white wings in every direction, a smashed windscreen, gulls sucked into the engine, a few seconds' terrified struggle to regain control followed by oblivion.

'As a result, HQ is likely to rule out pilot error.' Hilary calmly took up the thread. With luck, this would boost ferry pool morale back to its former level, an important consideration in his mind. Of course, it wouldn't bring back Agnes Wright — Hilary doubted that her remains would ever be found and decently buried — but the ATA reputation wouldn't be dented and they could carry on with business as usual. He glanced at his watch: a pointed reminder to his flying

34

crew that it was time to hurry to the base and report to the ops room for duty. 'That's all for now,' he concluded crisply.

Bobbie closed her eyes and absorbed what they'd been told. *Try not to feel anything. We have work to do, a war to win.* With the back of her hand she pushed her plate to one side and stood up from the table. 'Let's go and see what the ops boys have got lined up for us today,' she suggested to Mary and Viv in her light, lilting voice. 'As long as it's not a dratted Wellington, I'll be happy with whatever they chuck my way.'

★ ★ ★

A shabby B and B near Lossiemouth turned out to be Mary's fate later that day. After a long but uneventful flight north in, of all things, a Mosquito Mark 6, which she'd treated with maximum care, her taciturn Scottish landlady had shown her into a small annexe attached to the side of a plain, single-storey house and explained the vagaries of the primitive heating system — a portable paraffin stove in the corner of a dingy, low-ceilinged room where the sole ornament was a carved wooden cross hanging on the wall directly above the iron bed. Lighting came from an oil lamp on the bedside table.

Dear Tom. Mary sat on the lumpy horsehair mattress and made another attempt to write to her soldier brother. *Where in the world are you? It's been ages since I received a letter.* On second thoughts, Tom probably wouldn't be free to write down his whereabouts — it would never be passed by the censors — so she tore the top page from the writing pad and started again.

Dear Tom,

I hope you're fit and well, as I am. It's been ages since I received a letter from you so please write, as I fret about you from time to time. I'm sorry if this sounds like nagging but I am your big sister, after all — the one who darned your socks and ironed your shirts, in case you'd forgotten.

She paused and thought back to their childhood: she and Tom, with their older brother Frank and their widowed father, all crammed together in a two-up two-down in the shadow of the immense woollen mill where their father worked. As the baby of the family, Tom had been spoiled — allowed to plead sickness and stay off school whenever he fancied (amazing how many upset stomachs could be conjured up over the years by one fresh-faced boy). And he had always been able to claim the cream at the top of the milk bottle for his porridge as well as the warmest place by the fire in the poky, smoky living room that let in draughts and kept out the daylight. Frank, meanwhile, had been out of the house from an early age and up to no good: playing truant, stealing cigarettes from the tobacconist's and selling them on at the school gates to gullible ten-year-olds.

In contrast, Mary had studied hard and excelled at arithmetic and drawing. At the age of nine she'd won a national prize for her handwriting, but when she'd brought the certificate and a ten-shilling note home to her father, he'd merely grunted and pocketed the money. The memory galled her even now.

She held back a sigh then sat in the flickering lamp-

36

light, trying to think of other news that she could include in her letter. She wrote about the dance held at Aireby camp, praising the lively young pianist, then including the old chestnut about ENSA standing for Every Night Something Awful.

That will make you smile, I hope. The singer on this occasion was no Vera Lynn, I can tell you. Cameron was my partner in the dancing — who else? I'm dying for you two to meet and hope that it can be soon.

After the war is won and our boys come home. Mary sat, pen poised, before underlining the word 'soon' three times.

She pictured Tom scrapping it out in the heat of the desert or else in Germany, riding high in the gun turret of a Cruiser tank, guns blazing. Then her mind turned as it always did to Cameron. They hadn't talked on Saturday about his future at Aireby Initial Training Camp but she knew that fewer cadets were now being sent there and her fiancé's feet were growing itchier by the day.

Soon! she repeated to herself. *Give us victory before Cameron has a chance to volunteer for a second bout of service with Bomber Command. Deep down, I'm ashamed to admit even to myself that I don't want him to be a hero. No; I want the man I love to be alive at the end of all this — not to go up in flames like poor Agnes.*

★   ★   ★

From White Waltham, where Viv had dropped off an ancient Tiger Moth for training purposes (top speed of

37

101 mph, bless it, with a mere handful of control dials to its name), she found she could easily hop on a train to London at the end of the day. Fancying a broader view of what was going on in the world than she'd experienced lately, she decided she would spend the night there before taking the milk train north, hoping to spend time with her old friend Piers Wentworth.

'Hello, darling. Are you by any chance free tonight?' Viv had begun the out-of-the-blue telephone conversation with a good impersonation of her almost-namesake Vivien Leigh, whose narrow, light voice with its long vowels and clipped consonants was famous the world over. 'It's me!' she'd giggled at Piers's confusion. 'Vivienne Robertson. I had you fooled for a second, didn't I?'

Piers had been glad to hear from her and readily agreed to pick her up at Victoria station.

'In the Jag,' she'd made him promise.

'In a coach and four — whatever Your Ladyship requests.'

Piers and Viv had sailed the Atlantic together in HMS *Kestrel* and partied like there was no tomorrow, for that's what you did when the *Luftwaffe* was using you for target practice and U-boats were likely to sneak up on you at every end and turn.

As Viv's train pulled into the station, she set her forage cap at a jaunty angle and lifted her overnight bag from the luggage rack. Piers was thoroughly good fun so she was looking forward to a pleasant evening. She stepped down on to a sooty platform crowded with service personnel, then shouldered her way between duffel bags, knapsacks and flapping greatcoats to the barrier where Piers waited, as promised. He was just as she remembered him — of medium height and build, round-faced and clean-shaven, dressed in an expensive camel-hair coat topped off with a dark brown trilby and a yellow checked scarf.

'You look marvellous in uniform,' he told her as they embraced over the barrier.

'Tailor-made by a master of his craft on Savile Row,' Viv assured him. 'He took my measurements in person and wrote them all down.'

'Lucky him.' Beaming, Piers waited for her to pass through the barrier. 'Now then, Third Officer Robertson —'

'Second Officer!' she corrected brightly. 'They promoted me in August.'

'Congratulations — but where shall we eat?'

'Where do you have in mind?'

'I know a small place close to where I live, just off Kensington High Street. We can drive there in no time.'

No sooner said than he'd led her to his car and they were off in the Jag through dark, grimy streets, heading west through bomb-ravaged districts where shells of buildings stood out starkly against the moonlit sky and sandbags shored up walls still in danger of collapse. There was little traffic and what few cars there were crawled along with their headlights dimmed.

'Poor old London.' Viv gazed out at the damage. 'What was Fritz thinking, dropping bombs on innocent women and kids?' The worst of the Blitz was over, thank God, but it was all too easy to imagine the whistle of bombs dropping to earth, the deafening explosion, the flare of incendiaries, the crack of anti-aircraft guns, searchlights raking through the night sky.

Piers chatted on as he steered expertly through the

back streets. 'Life goes on,' he assured her. 'We didn't let it get us down. And it'll soon be at an end — before Christmas, if you ask me. Then we'll be hanging up the bunting up and down the land.'

'And I'll be out of a job,' Viv reminded him. 'Out in the cold, with nowhere to go, boohoo.'

'You can come and stay with me any time you like,' he suggested gaily as they pulled up outside a small, smart restaurant overlooking Kensington Gardens. He parked the car then opened Viv's door with a gallant flourish. 'You're always welcome at my place — no strings attached.'

She raised an eyebrow. 'Oh, sure.' Sliding her arm through his, they entered through the revolving doors of the restaurant.

'I mean it.'

He does too. Glancing at Piers's expression, Viv saw that her companion was sincere. It was a relief to realize that he was unlike any man she'd come across, seeming to enjoy her company without expecting anything from her, as two weeks aboard ship had proved. They'd been in adjoining cabins but not once had he made any advances.

Piers was greeted with a respectful handshake by a head waiter, who showed them to a quiet corner. 'How have you been keeping, sir?' he asked Piers in a low, discreet voice.

'Pretty well, thank you, Colin. Yourself?'

'Very well too, thank you, sir.'

The exchange of pleasantries gave Viv the chance to glance around the room at small groups of diners who sat in pools of lamplight at tables with starched white cloths and gleaming silver cutlery. Most were fashionably dressed men in their fifties and sixties.

40

She noticed some gold signet rings and diamond tie-pins, plus a smattering of embroidered silk waistcoats. One fellow diner at a nearby table, who sported a flashy green and pink pocket handkerchief to match his tie, caught Piers's attention and gave a coy, fingertip wave, which Viv's companion returned warily.

Oh! she thought with a jolt of surprise before checking her reaction. But then again, *Oh!* as the green and pink guy's companions responded to his elbow nudges by turning to study Viv with undisguised curiosity and an exchange of muttered observations.

No advances when opportunity had been handed to Piers on a plate — nothing expected except friendship. Now I get it! Viv placed her order and let Piers choose the wine. Her new awareness brought with it an unexpected freedom. So what if Piers was not the marrying kind, as the saying went? That didn't bother Viv one bit; in fact, it was rather intriguing.

'Everyone here seems to know you pretty well,' she remarked casually.

Piers gave her a long, conspiratorial look that confirmed her suspicions. 'You don't mind?'

'Not in the least. It's common as can be in Hollywood, though the studio bosses go to great lengths to hush it up. Anyway, I like you and I hope you like me.'

The wine arrived. 'I do; you're a breath of fresh air,' he assured her over the waiter's outstretched, napkin-draped arm.

'Likewise,' she shot back. 'Really and truly; I mean it, Piers.'

'Are you sure? Some girls run a mile once they put two and two together.'

'Not me. Anyway, you guessed that already — otherwise you wouldn't have brought me here.'

'True enough.' He gave a sigh of relief then raised his glass. 'To friendship.'

'To friendship,' she beamed.

Friendship and fine dining; what could possibly be wrong with that? After a meal of grilled plaice, new potatoes and peas, Piers took Viv dancing at Rainbow Corner in the old Lyons Corner House on Shaftesbury Avenue, where they found an American band in full swing. The dance floor was crowded with GIs and dainty Ginger Rogers lookalikes.

'Home from home?' Piers suggested above the trumpets and clarinets.

'Piers, honey, I'm Canadian not American, remember?' Viv laughed and danced with abandon until her feet ached and her wristwatch told her that it was two o'clock in the morning.

'I have to catch a train home in four hours!' she exclaimed breathlessly.

So Piers whisked her back to his Kensington flat and gave her a bed for a couple of hours. He woke her at five with coffee and toast then drove her again, this time to King's Cross.

'Darling Piers, you're the perfect host,' Viv told him as they sashayed, arm in arm, towards the turnstile. On the platform, busy porters loaded mailbags and empty milk churns on to her train, and steam from the engine billowed upwards to the ornate wrought-iron roof. 'So kind and generous. I've had the best time; thank you.'

'You're very welcome.' He leaned in to accept her kiss on the cheek.

'Really — perfect,' she insisted. Yet something in the pre-dawn comings and goings nagged at her like toothache and flattened her mood. Perhaps she was

42

just tired. Perhaps it was suddenly re-awoken thoughts about poor Agnes.

'Will you sleep on the train?' he asked.

'You bet I will.' She realized that the uncomfortable feeling was guilt for having enjoyed herself so much. 'And now it's back to the real world, I'm afraid.'

To steam and smoke, jaded faces, bombed buildings, blackouts. To parks turned into allotments, blackout blinds at windows, women working in munitions factories, all the young men away at war. A fellow ATA pilot killed.

Piers squeezed Viv's hand briefly then released it. Both were aware that this might be the last time they met.

Back to barracks and to Agnes's mother arriving at Rixley to collect her daughter's possessions. Back to the runway routine — brakes on, fuel on, pre-oiler on, throttle set then, 'Clear prop! Chocks away!'

'Look after yourself,' Piers called after Viv as she strode away. Steam hissed from the train's funnel, porters heaved cases, doors slammed.

She turned and smiled. 'I will,' she mouthed. *Goodbye to a true friend and farewell to a city that had borne the brunt of the* Luftwaffe's *attack.*

Piers smiled fleetingly, tipped the brim of his dark brown trilby then walked away.

★ ★ ★

The Isle of Wight, of all places! On the Tuesday morning Bobbie had received her chit from Gillian and had felt a shiver run down her spine. Worse still, she'd been allocated an old Walrus — the heavy, clumsy crate that was designed to land on water as well as on land.

43

It was a biplane with an enclosed cockpit that swung to left and right on the runway — 'like a bloody waddling duck', according to Gordon when he'd handed the plane over to Bobbie.

'You've checked with Maps and Signals?' he'd chivvied as she'd zipped up her suit and fastened her helmet.

'Naturally.' Bobbie had scanned the lists for any alterations to the position of barrage balloons over Southampton in particular and for any new prohibited flying areas.

'Better safe than sorry,' Gordon had insisted. 'I hear the weather's not looking too good further south.'

'Good Lord above!' she'd exclaimed. 'Please don't go on about it. I've already got the wind up as it is.'

As it happened, the met boys and girls had forecast a clear run. 'Frost is all you'll have to worry about,' Dorothy Kirk had assured her. 'No snow or fog to speak of.'

'Thanks — I think!'

Scatter-brained Dotty had given Bobbie a cheerful thumbs up. 'Good luck.'

Bobbie had grimaced then given herself a good talking-to. *Today is no different to any other day*, she'd reminded herself as she'd hurried with her chit to Runway 1. But she'd climbed into the cockpit of the ungainly Walrus with a sinking heart. Her hands had shaken as she'd gone through her checks but by the time it came to take-off the jitters had steadied and once she'd heaved the crate upwards through a thin film of white mist she'd begun to notice the intriguing shapes of clouds in the distant west and to luxuriate in a blaze of brilliant sunlight from the east.

Heavenly! Bobbie had relaxed and taken in the

44

infinite stretch of blue sky above and the shadow of her plane on the clouds below. *Sheer, unadulterated bliss!* An indescribable feeling of power and freedom had spread through every limb.

And so she had Bradshawed her way in the Walrus from Sheffield to Crewe and from there over numerous smoky Midland towns and Home Counties suburban sprawls, following the glint of steel railway lines into and out of London. After that she'd flown on an arrow-straight course towards the south coast and the dreaded corridor of barrage balloons over Southampton. Holding her breath, she had steered her Walrus safely through the hazard that had claimed Agnes's life, then encountered an unexpected hitch. Her blasted undercarriage lever had stuck and she'd wrestled with it to no avail. *Hobson's choice: shall I belly-flop into the Solent and await rescue or shall I reduce throttle and risk landing without wheels in Ventnor?* Heart a-flutter, Bobbie chose the latter. With much rattling, scraping and screeching — *Damn and blast the old crate!* — she had arrived, sparks flying, but in one piece.

'I didn't fancy a swim at this time of year,' she'd remarked to the ground crew who had rushed a crash wagon to the spot.

As usual, a crisis had been turned into a joke and Bobbie had headed off for a cup of tea and a sandwich in the canteen where she'd asked the glamorously made-up, dark-haired girl behind the counter if she could recommend lodgings for the night.

Glamour girl had taken a stubby pencil from her apron pocket and scribbled an address on a scrap of paper — 10 Seaview Cottages. 'Here you are; it's my twin sister's house. Lorna will look after you, but watch out — she'll talk the hind legs off a donkey given half a chance.'

Duly forewarned, Bobbie had found the house and asked to be shown straight to her room. But Lorna, the spitting image of the girl in the canteen, had showered Bobbie with excited questions and anecdotes, including garbled recollections of D-Day five months earlier followed by far-fetched predictions of imminent victory.

'I'm worn out,' Bobbie had interrupted at last. 'I don't mean to be rude but could you . . . ?'

'Show you to your room? Of course — follow me.' Lorna had sprung up and led the way up two flights of stairs. 'Don't expect anything fancy,' she'd warned.

Bobbie's 'room' had turned out to be a tiny attic with sloping ceilings and no natural light. It had a mattress on the floor and beams so low that she'd had to get undressed standing by the door then crawl on all fours into bed. But at least the sheets had been clean and the mattress comfortable.

She'd slept soundly at first but a vivid nightmare about being hopelessly lost in the labyrinthine corridors at Burton Grange had woken her and she'd found it impossible to get back to sleep. So she'd got dressed in the dark and crept downstairs before anyone else in the house was awake, leaving five shillings for her night's lodgings on the kitchen table then stepping out into the pre-dawn light to be met by cold drizzle and the sound of waves crashing on to rocks at the foot of the cliff.

Wednesday the twenty-second of November. Not a single, solitary star was visible through the veil of clouds. *Alone and many miles from home.* 'Washout,' Bobbie predicted grimly. She walked, head down and

46

with her collar up, along a back lane to the town's main street, hoping against hope to find a café that was open before heading on towards the airfield. But when she came to a telephone box she stopped and searched in her pocket for coins. Then she paused — on second thoughts, no, it was too early to call Ray. Then again, there was a phone by his bed.

Hang it all; she would risk waking him just to hear the comforting sound of his voice!

So she pulled open the phone box's heavy door, inserted a coin, heard it drop and dialled Ray's number.

'Hello?' The voice at the other end was immediately alert. 'Ray Moore here. Who's calling?'

Bobbie pressed a button. She held the receiver hard against her ear. 'Oh, Ray — it's me: Bobbie. I'm sorry if I woke you.'

'You didn't — I'm up and dressed. Is everything all right?' She sounded upset. Perhaps the bad news about Agnes had affected her more deeply than she'd admitted.

'Yes, everything is fine.'

'Are you sure?'

'Yes, I'm on the Isle of Wight.' The faint sound of waves meeting the rocky headland reached her as she stood shivering inside the box. 'The weather's bad — I think I might be stuck here for a while.'

Ray's heart sank. 'You managed the dreaded blimps all right?'

'Yes, thank heavens.'

'Don't fly back if the met boys down there advise against it.' He knew Bobbie too well. Like Viv, Mary and most other ATA pilots, in her eagerness to deliver a crate she wouldn't always toe the official line. She would fly through cloud and even sleet or snow if she saw fit. 'I mean it, Bobbie — they pay you to be safe, not brave.'

'I won't,' she promised half-heartedly. The miles between her and Ray seemed to stretch to snapping point. 'You sound faint. Where are you? What are you up to?'

'I've been up since three,' he replied. 'I had to call the vet to one of the horses.'

'Not Glasgow Girl?' Bobbie hoped that it wasn't her favourite horse in the Thresham yard that was ill.

'No, don't worry. It was Never Say Die. Ronnie's room is directly above the stables so he heard him thrashing about. He thought the horse was colicking but it turns out to be nothing too serious after all. The vet left half an hour ago. I decided to stay up rather than go back to bed.'

'It's so good to talk to you,' she breathed.

'What's up? Are you crying?' Ray thought he could detect a break in Bobbie's voice.

'No — well, yes, if you must know.' He still sounded a million miles away. 'The truth is, I miss you terribly.'

Sweet, sweet girl! 'I miss you too.'

'I love you.' The three words tumbled from her trembling lips. Bobbie held her breath and waited for Ray to respond.

'I know you do. I love you too.' So much that he could have thrown caution to the wind and walked her down the aisle there and then. 'More than words can say.'

Bobbie gave a long sigh. 'That's all right, then.' The miles between them were suddenly as nothing. Love overcame distance — you could carry it with you wherever you went. Knowledge of this swelled

Bobbie's heart to bursting.

Hearing the sound of a door opening and closing near to where Ray stood, followed by a voice in the background, she asked the obvious question. 'Who's there with you at this hour?'

Ray's reply was suddenly guarded. 'Oh, no one.'

She heard the mystery voice mumble, 'Sorry, old man,' followed by the sound of the door opening and closing again. 'Do you have a visitor?'

'Yes, but I'd rather not say.' Ray's oath of secrecy put him in a difficult position. Really, the last thing on earth he wanted to do was to keep secrets from the girl he loved.

'It sounded like Giles's voice,' Bobbie decided. 'Is he staying at Thresham with you?'

'I'm not supposed to let on. Oh, damn it, Bobbie — yes, it was Giles that you heard. He's staying here for a while. But don't tell Viv.'

'Yes, yes; all right.' She heard the pips warning her that her money was about to run out. 'I haven't got any more coins,' she gabbled. 'Quickly, tell me why Giles is there. I promise I won't breathe a word.'

'There was a heck of a quarrel down at Newpark,' Ray explained. 'His father kicked him out.'

'Good Lord above!' Bobbie realized that a Parseval family rift could have major repercussions if it were to continue.

'Remember: keep it under your hat for now.'

'All right, I —' *Pip-pip-pip.* There was a click then the line went dead.

Bobbie frowned and put down the phone. She leaned her shoulder against the heavy door, pushed it open then stepped out into the miserable drizzle. Here was a puzzle to occupy her mind if the morning

49

turned out to be the washout that she expected. What were the whys and wherefores behind Sir Thomas Parseval's decision to eject his son from their Leicestershire home? And why was Giles so keen to keep it secret from Viv? Time alone would tell. Meanwhile, Bobbie shouldered her overnight bag and began walking out through the murky dawn towards the airfield.

4

'Let's hope we don't have many more days like today.' Bobbie voiced what Mary and Viv were both thinking as they sat by the fire in the officers' mess at the Grange. It was Wednesday evening and all three had run into problems on their return journeys to Rixley.

'You can say that again. My train was stuck in Crewe for four whole hours because of fog and wet leaves on the line.' Viv sipped from her glass of ruby-red port. 'I could have walked home in the time it took to get things moving.'

'What about me?' Mary hadn't been able to get off the ground until after midday, then it turned out that the crate she'd eventually been allocated — a battle-scarred Hurricane — had been peppered with bullet holes during a dogfight over the North Sea and had proved a draughty so-and-so to fly. 'I was so numb with cold I couldn't feel my feet on the rudders when I came in to land.'

'Here; have my seat.' Viv moved out of the chair nearest to the fire.

'Well, you wouldn't believe the sprog I had with me today.' Bobbie's return from Ventnor in a Faithful Annie — an Avro Anson — had been equally trying. It had involved flying north with a trainee pilot from Aireby whose sole job had been to crank the Anson's undercarriage up after take-off then down before landing — 150 turns of the handle each time, no less. 'Poor lad; he went on and on about how out of puff he was.'

51

'Why do we put ourselves through this?' Mary asked with a loud sigh. She was relieved to feel the direct heat of the fire on her face and hands. 'If we had any common sense we'd have joined the Land Army and done our bit for our country with two feet firmly on the ground.'

'Yes — up to our knees in mud,' Bobbie pointed out. 'Out in the fields in all weathers — no, ta very much!'

'Amen to that.' Now that she was on her feet, Viv took a look around what had once been the drawing room of the grand house. Reminders of its former glory were easy to pick out: the high ceiling with elaborate cornices, two glinting chandeliers and in particular the Adam-style fireplace around which the girls had gathered. But some of the furniture was second-rate — brought in when the War Office had taken over the property from the Parsevals — and entirely out of keeping with the original building. Breaking away from Bobbie and Mary, Viv wandered over to the bar where she found Ernest Poulter, the Grange handyman, chatting to Gillian Wharton, Douglas's Girl Friday. 'I hope I'm not interrupting anything,' she said pointedly as the pair fell silent.

Gillian papered over the awkward silence by rushing into some nonsense about her preparations for Christmas. 'It's only just over a month away,' she gabbled. 'I've crocheted three cotton doilies: one each for my ma, my grandma and my aunty. But I've no clue what to give Dad.'

'Tobacco pouch?' Viv suggested. 'What's your opinion, Ernest? Should you like something to keep your pipe tobacco in as a Christmas present?'

Ernest gave a small cough and looked away.

Viv was nettled. 'What's up? Was it something I said?'

The handyman cleared his throat. Viv was one of his favourites among the girls at Rixley, though he had to admit she was too lively for some tastes. 'Don't mind us,' he advised, taking her quietly to one side before mumbling in her ear. 'We don't mean any harm.'

'So why are you cutting me out of the conversation?'

'We were trying not to upset you,' he explained. 'We were talking about Mrs Wright — Agnes's mother. She came from London on the train, all the way to the Grange, but she went off again before you got back.'

'I don't follow.' Glancing at Gillian, an uneasy feeling grew in the pit of Viv's stomach. 'How would that upset me?'

'Oh, for heaven's sake — let's not beat about the bush,' she snapped. Gillian looked crisp and smart in a white blouse with neat bows at the neck and cuffs. She launched into a rapid account of the bereaved mother's visit. 'Mrs Wright said we were all to choose something of Agnes's that we wanted to remember her by — anything at all.'

Viv narrowed her eyes. 'And?'

'She gave me first pick. I had her autograph book. It was either that or her silk scarf with the horseshoes printed on it.'

'I still don't get it.' Viv looked from Gillian to Ernest then back again.

'I didn't think to hold something back for you — or for Mary and Bobbie, for that matter. I'm so sorry.'

'Oh.' Viv felt the tug of mixed emotions: a twinge of regret versus a fluttering sensation of so-what? Things were only things, after all. 'Poor woman,' she managed to murmur.

'I know — we all felt so sorry for her. But it was very nice of her. She gave a tearful little speech about how much Agnes loved being in the ATA. She wanted us to know how proud she was of her.'

'I wish . . .' Viv began faintly before guilt robbed her of her voice and she stopped.

'Don't we all?' Gillian commiserated.

Too late now. The unexpressed regret hung in the air as Viv went to share her thoughts with Mary and Bobbie. 'I just heard something that breaks my heart,' she told them. 'Mrs Wright gave out some of Agnes's things — scarves and such like. I'm afraid we three missed the boat on that one.'

'If only I'd made more effort . . .' Bobbie followed Viv's earlier line of thought.

'Yes, if only we'd been nicer and included Agnes more,' Mary agreed. It truly was a bitter pill to swallow.

'We will in future,' Viv vowed, wiping a rogue tear from her cheek as she sat on a footstool close to the fire. 'If they send us a replacement for Agnes, we'll make darned sure to welcome her with open arms.'

★ ★ ★

'All right, you two.' Early next morning Bobbie joined Mary and Viv outside the bathroom at the end of their corridor. All stood shivering in their night things, clutching their sponge bags and towels. 'We need to talk about Christmas.'

'Really; do we have to?' Mary was not in the mood.

But Viv was more enthusiastic. 'Yeah; this'll be my first British Christmas. Will we have turkey with all the trimmings?'

As Gillian emerged from the bathroom and made her way down the corridor, Bobbie shook her head. 'More likely chicken, if rationing allows. But the thing is, it's not Christmas dinner we need to organize — it's the entertainment.'

'Now you're talking.' Viv stood aside to let Mary take Gillian's place in the bathroom. 'Will it just be the usual ATA mob, or will the RAF be involved as well?'

'Which would you rather?'

Viv adopted a playful stance, one forefinger resting on her chin. 'Hmm, let me think. Do I prefer playing pass the parcel in the officers' mess with you and Horace or tripping the light fantastic with the boys in air-force blue? No offence, but . . .'

Bobbie laughed at Viv's comical conundrum. 'Precisely. So this is my idea —'

'Speak up so I can hear what you're saying,' Mary sang out through the gap in the bathroom door.

'Aha, so now she's interested!' Viv cried. 'What's it to be, Mary — parlour games or jitterbugging under the mistletoe?'

'My idea,' Bobbie continued, 'is to ask Hilary if we can open up the empty room next to the library and invite the Aireby contingent to an evening's entertainment with ENSA. We can deck the room out with paper chains and balloons. We could even decorate a tree if we can find one.'

'There are plenty of young spruce trees growing near Fern Cottage.' Mary came to the doorway with her toothbrush at the ready. 'We can ask permission to cut one down.'

'Jitterbugging it is, then,' Viv said with a wink and a

mischievous smile.

'I'm sure ENSA will send us a band, provided it's not too late notice,' Bobbie explained. 'And Cameron will put in a good word at Aireby on our behalf. We'll say the invitation is intended to return the favour the RAF did us last Saturday.'

'But will Hilary allow us to throw a party here at the Grange?' Mary wondered. 'Won't he have to ask Giles's permission first?'

It was on the tip of Bobbie's tongue to tell them that Giles was currently in exile at Thresham, therefore such a request would go direct to Sir Thomas at Newpark. She stopped herself just in time. 'The Parsevals can't say we don't deserve to enjoy ourselves,' she insisted. 'And what harm can it do to open up the old place to some music and jollity? It will be Christmas, after all.'

'It's not us you have to convince,' Viv reminded her.

'So you agree that it's a good idea?' Bobbie checked.

'It's champion — and I wish you the very best of luck.'

★ ★ ★

Happiness was as fleeting as sunshine in the dark days of November. Mary was aware of this as she sat beside Cameron during their Friday-night drive to Highcliff.

'I've booked us a room,' he'd told her soon after he'd picked her up from the Grange. 'I hope that's all right?'

As far as Mary was concerned he might as well have said, *I'll fly you to the moon.* The prospect made her dizzy with excitement: a room with a double bed and no one to disturb them. 'Is it the same hotel as before?' she asked.

'The very same.' Cameron had chosen it for that reason — somewhere familiar, where the receptionist didn't look for a wedding ring and gave them their best double room overlooking the sea. He glanced sideways at Mary, sitting forward in her seat, dressed in her dark green coat and narrow-brimmed hat, gripping her handbag with the expression of a child about to embark on a ride on Blackpool's Big Dipper: scared but anticipating the thrill ahead. How young she looked and how full of life.

'The same room?' she added.

'Yes.' Their first time had been Mary's idea; she'd been the one to suggest a hotel: the best in High-cliff, please. No ifs, no buts — she'd wished for them to find a room and spend the night together. And it had been miraculous to Cameron to realize that she'd wanted to seal their love; that what had begun with respect for each other and the roles they each played at Rixley had slid softly and imperceptibly towards something deeper and more physical. He remembered that look of hers — the same one that he saw now — her chin up, eyes gleaming with determination and excitement. 'You're a wonder to me, Mary Holland. I hope you know that.'

'I don't know why.' After all, she was the mill girl who had fought her way from the bottom rung of the ladder to somewhere around halfway; from ATA driver through the conversion course to third officer: an actual pilot qualified to fly Class Ones and Twos, including the famous, fabulous Spitfire. 'I'm not that special.'

'Oh yes you are.' Approaching Highcliff, Cameron could make out the silhouetted ruins of an ancient church straight ahead and hear the crash of waves at the foot of the cliff. 'To me anyway.'

And Mary knew that this was all that mattered. Every time they snatched these moments together, she saw in Cameron's clear grey eyes how genuine his love for her was.

Look at that handsome profile, she thought as he slowed the car for them to contemplate the moonlit ruined arches and crumbling, ancient walls. *See the way his hair is swept back from his forehead and imagine the smoothness of his skin, the tenderness of his touch.*

Cameron pulled on the handbrake then switched off the engine. 'Silence,' he murmured.

They gave themselves plenty of time to take in their surroundings; to feel awe at the immensity of the star-lit sky and take comfort in the warmth and cosiness of their metal and glass cocoon.

'How can two people who are so different have so much in common?' Mary wondered aloud.

'We're only different on the surface — deep down we're the same.'

Mary smiled as he took her hand. 'Both shy,' she agreed.

'Until you get to know us. Then we come out of our shells.'

'Both down to earth and honest.'

'To a fault,' he agreed. Cameron's forthrightness got him into hot water on occasions. 'I've had to learn to be less blunt.'

'I wonder what people at Rixley really think about me flying their precious crates.' It seemed to be the occasion for delving deep beneath the surface. 'Do they still look at me and say, 'She's a jumped-up lit-tle so-and-so. Why doesn't she get back where she belongs?' '

'No, they don't.' Cameron spoke with conviction. 'Hilary, for one: only the other day he dropped in at the Training Wing and I overheard him describing you to Brian Wheeler as one of the best pilots he had.'

A frown creased Mary's brow. 'Then why do I always feel I have to prove myself to him?'

'Hilary's not one for dishing out the compliments — that's why.' Her insecurity ran deep; it was part of her. Yet it only seemed to make her more determined. 'Unlike me,' Cameron went on. 'I'm happy to sing your praises, to tell anyone and everyone that your flying is on a par with any of the boys in my old squadron — your touch, your timing, your judgement are second to none.'

'But you're biased,' she pointed out before suddenly softening with a smile and a squeeze of his hand. 'Sorry, it's hard for me to accept compliments — they embarrass me.'

'Talking of my old Bomber Command pals . . .' Cameron paused and gazed down apprehensively at the ruby-and-diamond engagement ring sparkling on Mary's left hand. Supposing what he was about to tell her were to ruin everything — their night in the hotel, the weeks, months, perhaps years ahead?

'You've reapplied for active service.' She finished his sentence for him. Here was the moment she'd feared.

'Yes.' There; it was out in the open. 'I had to, Mary. There are boys I know still up there scrapping it out with Jerry on a nightly basis. It's not right for me to go on twiddling my thumbs behind a desk.' His voice was earnest, begging for her to understand. 'It's not been an easy decision.'

'I've been dreading it for months,' she admitted, with a lump in her throat. 'Seriously, I don't know if I can stand the strain of knowing you're going to be involved in bombing missions again. And anyway, don't you think you've already done your fair share?'

Cameron shook his head. 'That's not how it works and you know it. I could just as easily say the same thing to you — that you've done your bit and you should step back and let Viv or Bobbie carry on taking the risks. What would you say to that?'

Mary had no answer. She withdrew her hand and let her head fall forward, imagining the night-time forays over Europe: the drone of engines, enemy sightings — Junkers or yellow-nosed Messerschmitts — the crack and boom of anti-aircraft guns from the ground below.

'It won't be for long,' he argued. 'Hitler's well and truly on the run. We'll have this mess sorted out in a matter of weeks.'

The constriction in Mary's throat grew worse. 'What if we don't?' she whispered.

'We will.' His hand tapped the steering wheel as he gazed out at the ruins and listened to the crashing waves.

His mind was made up. There was no changing it. So she must swallow her fears and back his decision. 'You're right; I know you are. We will beat them, and sooner rather than later.'

'That's the spirit.' It was the only way to think. Belief was what kept you going through the hell of war. 'A few more weeks — months at the most.'

Mary blinked away tears. 'When will you leave Aireby?'

'Just over a week from now — Monday the fourth;

60

once I've handed over the reins to Brian Wheeler. He's a clever chap so it shouldn't take long for him to learn the ropes.'

She felt the news settle on her shoulders like a heavy weight; she must brace herself to bear it and go on bearing it for heaven knew how long. *Nine days*.

'We still have the weekend ahead of us,' she said quietly. Stars were infinite, the moon a thin disc of silver against a black sky.

'Shall we drive on?' Mary's sad resignation hurt him more than anything; for a moment he almost wished that she'd kept on arguing, been angry and broken off with him, left him free to risk his own neck without having to consider anyone else. But no, forget that — her love was precious, a shining star to see him through the whole bloody business.

'Yes, let's.' Turning in her seat, she reached out and brushed a hand against his cheek. 'We have to make the most of the time we have.'

'To the hotel, then?'

She acquiesced and they moved on slowly. Once they reached the seafront promenade, Cameron stopped the car once more. 'You're sure?' he checked.

They were the same two words that he'd used for their first time, the same calm, loving gaze.

'Never more so.' His latest decision meant that they were unlikely to spend Christmas together. 'We'll make it an early celebration, minus the tree lights and tinsel.'

He smiled back at her then eased the car forward until they came to their hotel, set back from the road behind a laurel hedge. Its clean, straight lines, flat roof and white exterior denoted a modern, sophisticated style that carried through into a reception area with a gleaming glass-topped desk behind which stood a fashionable young woman in a smart black dress.

Cameron gave the receptionist his name, which she checked off in a ledger, allowing Mary to admire a large clock in the shape of a sunburst hanging on the wall behind the desk and banisters fashioned like a ship's rail leading up green-carpeted stairs. When the woman handed Cameron their room key, Mary felt her heart skip a beat.

'Thank you. We'll find our own way,' Cameron said as he pocketed the key.

Then he linked arms with Mary and they went up the stairs together, remembering to turn right at the top and count the doors to either side of a short corridor until they came to their premier suite overlooking the promenade. Producing the key, Cameron held it aloft. 'The key to the magic kingdom.'

With a bright smile, she snatched it from him then pushed him lightly to one side. The key turned easily in the lock and she sailed ahead, flinging her handbag on a chair by the window then quickly taking off her coat and hat. 'I'd like a bedroom like this after we're married,' she announced. 'Emerald satin for the eiderdown, two bedside cabinets with glass tops and wall lights in the shape of seashells.'

'You don't want much!' He laughed in surprise. Colour had come back into her cheeks and her eyes sparkled.

Mary put her arms around Cameron's waist and landed a series of kisses on his cheeks as she spoke. 'A modern gas cooker (kiss) and cabinets on the kitchen wall (kiss, kiss). The latest settee for the living room with a radiogram in one corner (three kisses). Let me see, what else?'

'A nursery done out in pink?' he suggested.

She frowned and pouted. 'What if we have a boy?'

'One pink room and one blue room,' he decided.

Fairy-tale wishes transported them both into a world without war, where what mattered was the colour of paint and shopping for furniture. Smiles and laughter took them circling towards the bed where Cameron lifted Mary off her feet then gently lowered her on to a sea of green satin. He lay beside her, suddenly serious.

'Promise me you'll remember this moment,' he begged. 'Carry it with you. Never let it go.'

'Never,' she promised. Danger, which had been banished to the depths by their dreams of the future, now threatened to resurface. *What if . . . ?* She drew him close and kissed him urgently. His lips were warm and her body against his remembered the touch, the feel, the shape.

And they lived in the moment with love and longing, with tenderness, with no thought for the past or the future — only for the present and the gift of love.

Remember this. Remember how much I love and adore you. Bodies intertwined, two souls rejoicing.

5

'Surely you're not planning to cycle in this weather?' Gillian watched Bobbie wheel a bike out of one of the empty stables at the Grange. 'I can hardly see a yard in front of me; the fog's that bad.'

It was nine o'clock on Saturday morning, and a real pea-souper had descended over much of England overnight. Gillian had donned her coat and heavy woollen scarf, intending to walk into Rixley village to post letters, but the bad weather had persuaded her to change her mind.

'It's all right; there'll be no traffic on the roads,' Bobbie assured her. She was wrapped up in her sheepskin flying jacket and leather gauntlets, ready to set off for Thresham, and she wasn't about to let a bit of fog stop her.

'What if you run slap bang into a wall?' Gillian pointed out possible cycling catastrophes. 'Or tumble into a ditch, or take the wrong turning to wherever it is you're going and end up in the back of beyond?'

'That's right: look on the bright side.' Bobbie stooped to check that the bike's tyres were fully inflated. 'Ray's expecting me for lunch so I don't want to let him down. Anyway, you're usually in the know. What's today's forecast?'

'This fog should lift,' came the quick reply. 'By eleven o'clock this morning, as far as they can tell.'

So, seeing some sense in delaying her departure, Bobbie reluctantly leaned her bike against the wall and went with Gillian through the boot room at the side of the house, up some stairs into the main hallway where she made a telephone call to the racing yard to say she would be later than planned.

'Join me in my room for a nice hot cup of tea,' Gillian proposed as she led the way up to the first floor.

'Wait; my mother sent me a food parcel earlier this week.' Bobbie detoured into her own room and emerged with a round tin containing home-made shortbread. 'Shall I invite the others?' she suggested, before remembering that Mary had gone away with Cameron for the weekend and that Viv would already be on standby at the ferry pool for a possible Priority One — not that anything would be getting off the ground any time soon. 'No, never mind,' she murmured as she followed Gillian into her room, where there was an electric kettle and a tray set out with a teapot, caddy and cups.

Soon the pair sat with their fingers curled around hot cups of tea and munching shortbread, bemoaning the dismal weather and trying to cheer themselves up with thoughts of Christmas.

'Won't we all be glad to have a few days away from here?' Gillian said with a sigh. Even off duty she looked well turned out, with perfect waves running through her short red hair. She was wearing a beautifully knitted light blue jumper teamed with navy-blue slacks.

'We surely will.'

Ever positive, Bobbie brought her companion up to date with her plans for a Christmas celebration. 'We're organizing a party here at the Grange. Well, more of a dance, really. I asked Hilary first thing this morning if we could open up the room next to the library — the one that's not used at present. I must have caught him at a good moment because he promised to consider it. Once he backs the idea, getting the go-ahead from the Parsevals shouldn't be much more than a formality, fingers crossed.'

'A dance?' Gillian perked up at the idea.

'Yes; with a band. We'll invite the boys from the Training Wing. It'll be very jolly.'

'What date are we talking about?' Gillian instantly began to plan her outfit.

'I'm thinking it should be on the twenty-third.'

'Why not Christmas Eve?'

'It's a Sunday; we wouldn't get a licence for alcohol — so that's why not. Anyway, most of us will be at home with our families by then.'

Bobbie had finished her tea and was eager to depart, fog or no fog. 'Let's agree that Saturday is the better day. Pass the word around — all being well, we'll put on a Christmas knees-up here at the Grange; best bib and tucker all round.'

Leaving Gillian to decide exactly what she would wear down to her fanciest suspender belt and brassiere, Bobbie dashed back to the stable yard to collect her bicycle then quickly set off down the front drive to join the road leading to Thresham. Fog still shrouded the trees and hedgerows, but plucky Bobbie cycled on through wet countryside where all sounds were deadened — the low, wheezing cough of a cow standing in a farmyard, the rumble of a tractor engine, the clatter of a carthorse's hoof kicking at a stable door. She concentrated on the way ahead, avoiding potholes and making sure she took the correct turnings until, with three miles still to go, the fog began to clear and she could distinguish the crooked outlines of hawthorn trees lining the grass verge and the shadowy shapes of roadside barns and farmhouses.

At last! Bobbie breathed more easily and began to anticipate the moment when she and Ray would meet. They would kiss and the world would spin. They would embrace and get lost in smiles and more kisses. She cycled harder and picked up speed, feeling the ground flatten out as she approached Thresham. By the time she arrived, the mist had melted away to reveal the single-track lane leading to the yard and the sedate, symmetrical Georgian manor house beyond.

Bobbie's excitement rose another notch as she entered the immaculate yard. At the sound of her approach, horses' heads appeared at stable doors and a lad in a green polo-neck jumper and brown britches paused as he wheeled his barrow towards a muck heap in the neighbouring field. He seemed to be new there and looked uncertain about how to greet her. There was no sign of Ray.

'He's in the house,' Ray's second-in-command, Ronnie Evans, informed Bobbie in a gruff, business-like way as he emerged from one of the stables. He gave no greeting and went about his business without comment.

'No he isn't — he's here!' Ray had cut short a telephone call to run down to the yard. 'I saw you arrive. I wish you'd let me come and pick you up. You shouldn't have had to cycle all this way.' Aware of Ronnie's cool eyes on them both, Ray resisted the urge to fling his arms around Bobbie.

'No, I knew you would be too busy.' Flushed from her long ride, with her hair and cheeks damp from the mist, she experienced a flash of disappointment. *No embrace; not even a kiss.*

'Rob Roy has cast a shoe. Do you want me to organize a visit from the farrier?' Ronnie interrupted brusquely. He was a small, slight man in his fifties; an ex-jockey who had worked for the Moores for twenty years. Tact was not a quality he nurtured and he would be the first to acknowledge that he was better with horses than with people.

'Yes, go ahead,' Ray told him as he caught Bobbie by the elbow and whisked her towards the narrow arched gateway leading to the house.

'And by the way, Philip wants to work more hours here on the yard.' Ronnie tilted his head towards the lad returning with the empty barrow.

At the mention of his name the new man glanced in their direction. He looked to be in his early twenties and was too tall to be a jockey. Bobbie thought he was rather clever-looking, with steel-rimmed glasses and sharp features.

'What about his forestry work?' Ray asked. 'Doesn't that keep him busy?'

'He reckons he can fit us in.'

'Well, we can do with extra help. Ask him to come back tomorrow.'

Bobbie detected hesitance in the air — both Ronnie and Ray spoke quickly in an undertone while the man called Philip hovered uncertainly. 'Who's that?' she asked with a backward glance as Ray hurried her out of the yard.

'Philip Benson. He was called up at the start of the war but he refused to go. He's a committed conchie.' Out of sight of onlookers, Ray slid his arm around Bobbie's waist.

'A conchie?' The word had bad connotations — Bobbie was aware that conscientious objectors were much vilified as shirkers who were either lazy or degenerate. *What sort of man refuses to fight for his coun-*

try? the saying went. *Does he agree with Hitler? Doesn't he care who wins this war?* 'You don't meet many who admit to that,' she remarked.

'Philip's family are Quakers.' Ray made it clear that he'd rather not talk about his new employee. Now that he had Bobbie all to himself there was no need to hold back his emotions. 'Have I told you lately how much I love you?' he asked as he stopped her in front of the house and wrapped his arms around her waist.

'Not since the crack of dawn on Wednesday,' she replied between kisses. 'When I was cold and miserable, standing in a phone box a million miles away.'

'Well, nothing's changed — I still do.' Ray's smile transformed his face. The olive-toned skin around his eyes crinkled and his lips parted to reveal even white teeth. Whatever his worries and despite the difficulties of his past, he felt nothing but joy when he held Bobbie in his arms and gazed into her eyes.

★ ★ ★

'There's no point in you hanging around any longer,' Douglas had told Viv by mid morning. 'Even if the fog lifts here in the north, the Priority One we're waiting for won't be able to get off the ground in Bristol. That's according to Fred Rowe in the met room.'

Viv had accepted the experts' forecast and reluctantly returned her parachute pack, helmet and goggles to her locker before leaving the ferry pool and trudging back to the Grange. It turned out that she'd cancelled her weekend social activities for nothing.

'What brings you back so early?' Gillian queried as she crossed paths with Viv on her way out to Rixley.

'Washout,' Viv muttered ruefully. At this rate

there would be no flying and no fun either. And so, left with time on her hands — always a bad thing in Viv's book — she changed out of her uniform into a sweater and corduroy trousers, tied a red bandanna around her head and went off in search of her old buddy Ernest.

First she knocked on the door of his storeroom at the bottom of the terrace steps. No reply. Then she tried the boiler room where the handyman was often to be found tending the antiquated heating system, shovelling coke into the furnace to heat a vast copper boiler to a background accompaniment of clunks, gurgles and squeaks. No luck here either. Perhaps Ernest was in the vegetable garden?

Sure enough, Viv found the handyman with his sleeves rolled up, raking leaves towards a pile of fallen branches and other garden refuse. The vegetable plots surrounding the unlit bonfire were mostly dug over for the winter, except for beds of cabbage and Brussels sprouts.

'Need some help?' Viv offered. She seized the rake before the older man could object then went on to tease Ernest in her usual way. 'Sit down on that bench, my friend. A guy your age should take things easy.'

He gave a guttural laugh. 'I might look like I'm past it to you young things, what with my gammy leg, but I'll have you know I'm not ready for the scrap heap yet.' He pulled his pipe and tobacco from his pocket. 'But feel free. I'm happy to just sit here and watch.'

'You do that,' she encouraged with a wink.

Ernest lit up and puffed away while Viv worked under his supervision. 'That's right; pile the leaves nice and high. Don't disturb the branches — I've stacked them so the air can get underneath. You need

70

that to get a good blaze going. By the way, why aren't you off gallivanting with that RAF chap I spotted you with earlier in the week? It's your day off, isn't it?'

'I was on Priority One,' she explained. The sodden beech leaves gave off a mouldy, earthy smell as she scooped them up by the armful and tossed them on top of the bonfire. 'Anyhow, why should I gallivant anywhere? Can't a girl stay home and read a book once in a while?'

'Some girls can.' Ernest's sceptical tone indicated that he didn't regard Viv as one of them. 'Talk of the devil,' he remarked with a tilt of his head towards the arched gateway.

And there stood Brian Wheeler, legs wide apart, hands in blazer pockets, yellow silk cravat at his throat.

'Like a bad penny,' he joked as he approached Ernest and Viv. 'Always turning up when I'm not wanted.'

A flustered Viv flung down her rake and tried to tuck her wayward hair under her bandanna. Then again, why the hell should she care how she looked? So she stood, hands on hips, and waited.

'I took the trouble to pick up the telephone and speak to Fred Rowe first thing,' Brian explained. 'Yes, I know — we RAF chaps are thick as thieves.'

Viv's truculent expression remained. 'We said I would call you if I was free, remember?' The hands stayed on the hips, the face bore a frown.

Ernest tutted quietly in the background. Viv was too sharp for her own good sometimes.

But Brian's confidence wasn't in the least dented by Viv's apparent lack of enthusiasm. A breeze disturbed a wavy forelock, which he brushed back casually, showing off a gold cufflink set into his starched cuff. 'I've come to offer you another drive in the jalopy.

71

Come on, Vivienne — you know it's an offer you can't refuse.'

Viv noticed that the cufflink was fashioned into the shape of a miniature Spitfire — very classy. But the guy's arrogance in assuming that she would just drop everything presented a perverse challenge, allowing her the opportunity to skilfully tip the balance of power to one where she would start to pull the strings. 'I did say I would call you,' she repeated, head to one side, looking at Brian without blinking. 'But since you're here, I suppose I might consider your offer.'

That's more like it, Ernest thought.

'Here and at your service.' Brian turned up the charm knob to full. 'We can go wherever you like — we have the whole day and evening ahead of us. We can drive then have a meal, go to see a film . . .'

Viv glanced down at her sweater. 'I'll have to get changed first.'

'By all means. I'll wait inside the house while you do that.' Offering his arm, he nodded briefly at Ernest then gallantly escorted Viv out of the garden. 'Truly, you don't mind me showing up unannounced?' he continued as they walked arm in arm towards the house. 'I really am rather keen on you, you know?'

'Honestly? You hardly know me.' He was taller than her by three or four inches (always good), dark-haired (styled by a skilful barber, not by the Initial Training Wing short-back-and-sides merchant), had impeccable manners and a nice accent. Viv built up a silent checklist.

They promenaded up the steps and along the terrace.

'But I have every intention of getting to know you better. So I said to myself, why run the risk of standing

72

back while some other lucky chap makes his move?'

A smooth talker (like Giles), probably with a girl in every port (or the RAF equivalent). 'Maybe some other guy already has,' Viv suggested brightly as he held the door open and she entered the house.

'Then that man had better watch out — the Air Force has landed.' Unperturbed, Brian Wheeler grinned and followed Viv inside.

★ ★ ★

All race meetings were cancelled because of the weather but for once Ray didn't mind because it gave him the whole afternoon and evening with Bobbie.

'Let's kick things off with a drink.' Releasing her from his embrace, he led the way into the house and into a living room that bore all the hallmarks of male neglect. A painting of a chestnut thoroughbred, torn in one corner, hung crookedly over the mantelpiece on which stood a bronze statuette of another champion horse and two wax-encrusted candlesticks whose red candles had burnt down and not been replaced. Dusty fire irons lay in the ash-strewn hearth, propped against a brass fender in need of a polish. Two leather sofas were scuffed and stained and discarded newspapers and magazines littered the floor.

'Sorry about the mess.' Ray reacted to Bobbie's disapproving gaze. 'I promise I'll try to do better in future.'

'You need to bring in a cleaner.' Resisting the urge to tidy up, she perched on one of the sofas and accepted the sherry that Ray offered her.

'Dad would never allow one in the house.' His father had been a heavy drinker and too set in his

73

ways to accept help. 'I'm used to living in chaos — I hardly notice it.'

'Still.' On second thoughts, Bobbie thought it best to let the matter drop. Change at Thresham would happen slowly, if at all. She felt the sofa sag as Ray sat beside her and curved his arm around her shoulder. It felt natural to nestle in towards him and rest her head against his chest.

'It's odd,' he confessed after a long silence. 'I've spent most of the week thinking about you — about us. But now that I can actually see you and feel you, everything I was planning to say has gone clean out of my head.' He held her to him more tightly.

'That's all right; I don't mind silence.' One of the things that Bobbie loved about Ray was the smell of him — a clean, sweet aroma of shaving soap and cologne mixed in with hay, horses and the fresh outdoors.

'So how is everything at the Grange?' In fact, he wondered about the atmosphere there since poor Agnes's demise but felt it wouldn't do to ask too directly.

Bobbie knew what he meant. 'We carry on as normal,' she reported quietly. 'Hilary told us that Commander Gower wrote a kind letter of sympathy to Agnes's mother. She described Agnes's time as a trainee at Hatfield where she was said to be keen and quietly confident, very active and attentive. Those were her exact words. But we don't talk about it much at Rixley — it's not the done thing.'

'Yes, I can see why.' It had been the same during Ray's time as a squadron leader in the RAF — his comrades had got out of bed every morning knowing that each day might be their last. Yet they'd joked their

74

way through the day, played cards in the mess and flirted with the girls in the local pub then reported for duty. They'd strapped themselves into their cockpits at night, had tracked down Junkers and engaged in dogfights. Often they'd spotted gunners lying in the bellies of Dorniers or at the rear of the aircraft: men — scarcely more than boys — who would aim machine guns directly at you, close enough for you to see the fear in their faces as they fired their lethal weapons.

This was all in the past for Ray, thank God. Dornier Do 217. Even now he remembered the exact details of every machine flown by the enemy. The Dornier carried a crew of four: pilot, bombardier and two gunners. Wingspan of sixty feet. Attack range 400 nautical miles. Four bomb racks in the bomb bay carrying 550-pound bombs. Such things were indelibly printed on his brain.

How could a man forget?

Bobbie stayed nestled against him on the settee and silence enveloped them once more until the door opened and Giles blundered in.

'So sorry, old boy,' he began. He hadn't known anyone was in the house and had come down from his room in search of a stiff drink. 'Forgive me, Bobbie — I'll leave you two to it.'

Bobbie sat upright with a start and said, 'Giles, please don't go.' In fact, it had taken her a few seconds to recognize him. 'Come in and say hello.'

'No, I don't want to interrupt.' He took an unsteady step backwards. 'Anyway, I'm hardly presentable.'

She took in the details of his appearance. He stooped forward, shoulders hunched, and she spotted bruises on his left cheek in spite of his attempt to keep his face turned away. 'Good Lord, what's happened to you?' When Giles didn't reply, Bobbie turned to Ray. 'Is he all right? Why didn't you tell me he'd been injured?'

'Because I asked him not to.' Giles stayed in the doorway. 'It's a bit of bruising and a couple of broken ribs, that's all.'

'For goodness' sake, you're in pain.' Bobbie sprang from the sofa and cleared magazines from the floor. Then she held out a hand to steady him as he entered the room. 'Tread carefully, come and sit down. Oh, Giles, I had no idea that you'd been in an accident.'

Wincing with every step, he gingerly made his way forward and sat down next to Ray. 'If you don't mind . . . just for a moment, while I catch my breath.'

'Take your time. Let me fetch you a drop of whisky.' Ray gave an apologetic shrug in Bobbie's direction as he went to the drinks cabinet.

'How did it happen?' Bobbie had rarely seen such a dramatic transformation. The Giles she knew was always impeccably groomed and in control, yet here he was, trembling and scarcely able to move. His face was unshaven and his hair uncombed. There was a large swelling on his forehead and close to she could see that the bruising was severe.

'I fell down the stairs,' he mumbled unconvincingly as he pressed his right arm against the injured ribs.

Ray had mentioned a quarrel between Giles and his father. Had the row led to a so-called accident that Giles was keen to conceal? 'Were you at home?' she asked more cautiously.

'Yes, at Newpark.' Giles took the drink from Ray and knocked it back in one.

'So you cancelled your birthday celebrations? Your

76

thirtieth, wasn't it?'

'Yes; not much to celebrate, I'm afraid.' As the whisky took effect and brought colour to his gaunt cheeks, Giles eased himself back against the cushions that Bobbie had positioned for him. 'Thirty sounds awfully grown up, doesn't it?'

Bobbie smiled sympathetically then waited for him to say more.

'It makes a chap assess what's going on in the world: where he's at in his life, and so forth.' Giles paused to clear his throat apologetically. 'Sorry to turn philosophical on you both — especially you, Bobbie. How old are you exactly?'

'I was twenty-two last month.'

'A mere child.' Slowly relaxing against the cushions, Giles accepted a second drink from Ray. 'Listen, Bobbie, I made our friend here promise not to divulge my presence at Thresham.'

Bobbie's eyes widened but once more she was silent.

'But the cat is well and truly out of the bag, so I might as well admit that there was a most awful family row at Newpark, as a result of which the old man has cut off all ties.'

'Good Lord!' She kept up the pretence of surprise for Ray's sake.

'Quite. So here I am at the grand old age of thirty, cast off without a penny, with no visible means.'

'And two broken ribs,' she reminded him.

'Yes, but bones heal.'

'So do family rifts — given time.'

Giles shook his head. The whisky had dulled the pain and loosened his tongue. 'You don't know my father. Once he's made up his mind, he'll never shift. The row was over the offer of a divorce settlement

77

from Nora's solicitors — you remember my soon-to-be ex-wife? She wanted to keep Abbot's Gate, where she's living at present, and I said I was willing to accept that.'

'But your father wasn't?' Bobbie knew that Abbot's Gate was the third and smallest of the Parseval family's estates.

'Not on your nelly,' Giles said with a touch of gallows humour. 'Dad called Nora all the names under the sun, the most repeatable of which was 'gold-digger'. He said he'd rather be dead in a ditch than concede one inch of family property to a woman entirely without scruples, whose only intention in marrying me in the first place had been to get her filthy hands on Parseval land. It may well be true, but you can imagine how it made me feel.'

'I can indeed,' Bobbie conceded. 'But my impression was that it was your father who had helped to arrange the marriage in the first place?'

Giles stiffened. 'Was it Viv who told you that?'

'Yes,' Bobbie confessed. 'We're great chums. We confide in each other a great deal.'

'How is Viv, by the way?' The conversation lurched from one painful topic to another.

'The same as ever: living life to the full.' Bobbie considered her next tactic and decided to pique Giles's interest. 'She stopped over in London earlier this week and met up with an old friend: a chap called Piers Wentworth. Apparently they went to the American club on Shaftesbury Avenue and danced the night away.'

Ray frowned at her and was about to change the subject again but Giles swiftly took Bobbie's bait. 'Anyone would think we weren't in the middle of a bloody world war, the way that girl carries on,' he grumbled moodily. This latest anecdote simply confirmed how quickly Viv had moved on from any interest she might once have had in him.

Good, he's jealous! 'You know how she is,' Bobbie went on. 'She has men falling at her feet wherever she goes.'

'You say you two talk?' Giles shifted position and grimaced.

'Yes, all the time: Viv, Mary and I, and Jean Thornton whenever we get together.' Bobbie let a pause develop, hoping that Ray would have the good sense to stay quiet and let Giles continue.

'Did Viv mention an invitation I sent her?'

'To your birthday party?' Bobbie pretended to search her memory. 'Let's think — yes, I seem to remember she did.'

'I never received a reply. From which I deduced not only that Viv is less polite than I'd anticipated but also that she's entirely lost interest in me. Has she confessed as much?' Giles steeled himself for Bobbie's response.

She rested a hand lightly on his shoulder and looked directly at him. 'Do you really want to know?'

'Yes — tell me the truth.'

'The truth is that Viv isn't sure how she feels about you. For a start, she doesn't even know if your divorce has come through. And she blames you for what happened to Anna Janicki — I'm afraid we all do — which makes it all a little complicated for Viv.'

'I know; I'm not proud of my part in all that.' Giles spoke cautiously. From what Bobbie had just said it seemed that Viv had held to her promise to leave his father out of that particular scenario and for that he

79

was in her debt. *Good girl*, he thought. It must have taken more self-control than he'd previously credited Viv with, not to give the game away.

In fact, the row at home over the divorce from Nora had unleashed many recriminations, with Giles berating his father for behaving heartlessly to everyone involved in the Anna Janicki affair. Insults had been flung, words spoken that could never be taken back.

And then worse had happened . . . Giles pulled himself back from the brink of confessing all that had gone on at Newpark both during and after the argument.

'But you're wrong about one thing,' Bobbie said with conviction. 'I know for certain that Viv did reply to your invitation. I can only suppose that she sent it to Newpark, imagining that's where you would be.'

Giles digested the information. 'I see,' he mumbled.

Bobbie forged ahead with her plan. 'So now that I've set the record straight over the invitation mix-up, why not get in touch with Viv to clear the air? Or I could give her a message if that's easier.'

Giles narrowed his eyes and looked away. 'I don't think so, thank you all the same.'

Why so brittle? Why not drop the formalities and say what you really feel? 'I don't understand,' Bobbie remarked with a touch of impatience. 'What harm could my passing on a message do?'

'I'd rather you didn't.' *A message to say what, exactly? That I've lost position, income, reputation — everything that matters to a man of my standing? That I'm thirty years old with nothing to offer?*

Bobbie heaved an exasperated sigh. 'Can't I even tell her where you are?'

'Most definitely not,' Giles insisted wearily. His

head spun and he felt tired as hell, not up to any further argument. 'I'm convinced that Viv wants nothing more to do with me and that's the end of the matter.'

6

There was a moment when Viv looked in the mirror and almost changed her mind. Yes, she looked perfectly decent: dressed up for afternoon tea in a long-sleeved sky-blue dress and her black peep-toed shoes. Her hair was doing as it was told for once — swept back from her face to emphasize the high cheekbones that other girls envied and to show off her flawless complexion. Make-up — a little but not too much; lipstick to match her carmine nail polish; wearing her grandmother's small gold and pearl earrings that her mother had handed to her on the quayside on the day she'd boarded HMS *Kestrel* and set sail for England.

And yet, with handsome, dapper Brian waiting for her in the entrance hall, Viv felt unsettled. *Why these sudden attacks of the blues — the sort she'd felt when parting from Piers?* she wondered. *Pull yourself together, girl — get out there and paint the town red.*

With a deep intake of breath and a final pat of her glossy hair, she reached for her coat and gloves.

Downstairs, Brian hummed a tune as he poked his nose through various doorways. The officers' mess was a cosy affair, if a little shabby, with faded rugs and chairs and some cheap modern sofas that obviously didn't belong. The bar at the far end seemed well stocked, however. Next to the mess there was a library with floor-to-ceiling leather volumes and long windows overlooking the terrace. An ornate desk took pride of place in the centre of the floor. The large, adjacent room was mysteriously empty — stripped of furniture and carpet and with darker squares on the faded blue walls indicating where pictures had once hung.

'Well?' Viv demanded when she came down to find Brian closing the door on the empty room. 'Isn't that an ideal space for a Christmas shindig, complete with ENSA band?'

'It's big enough, certainly.' Bloody hell, the girl practically shimmered in the dim daylight. She wore a tight-fitting blue dress the colour of the Mediterranean Sea in bright sunlight and her smooth, pearly skin was set off by a delicate cream silk scarf. Her hair was practically jet black, suggesting Italian or Spanish blood way back in her family history.

'I'd like to hear a little more enthusiasm.' Handing him her cherry-red coat so that she could slip smoothly into it, Viv adopted her usual bantering tone. 'Don't worry; you boys from Aireby will receive invitations. Make a date in your diary for the twenty-third — the Saturday before Christmas.'

'Has Hilary given the go-ahead?' On with the coat then two long strides ahead of her to hold open the heavy door.

'Nothing's definite yet but it soon will be.' A sudden thought struck her so she smiled winningly.

'Especially if you and Cameron are willing to back the idea from your end.'

'The twenty-third of December, you say?' Luckily the weather was clearing up nicely as he and Viv walked out under a sky that was less grey than earlier, with a weak sun doing its best to peep through. 'In that case Group Captain Norris will be home on leave and Cameron will be long gone — it'll be my shout and mine alone.' Brian felt Viv pull back questioningly at the bottom of the terrace steps. 'Didn't you know? Cameron's applied to rejoin Bomber Command.'

She shook her head. 'Mary didn't say.'

'It's a recent decision to hand over training duties to yours truly. Sorry, perhaps I've jumped the gun?'

'Poor Mary.' Viv pictured the weeks — perhaps months — of agonized suspense that lay ahead for her brave friend and she had to brace herself to withstand the wave of war-weariness that hit her with full force. 'You weren't to know,' she assured Brian. 'Anyway, Mary's spending the weekend with Cameron. I guess he'll break it to her face to face.'

'That's all right, then. Your carriage awaits, m'lady.' Brian picked up the mood again as he strode ahead to open the passenger door of the Morgan. 'Where shall it be: Highcliff or Northgate? Your Ladyship can decide.'

* * *

If only time could stand still. If it were possible to stop the world from spinning, to prevent night from turning into day . . .

It was Sunday morning and daylight crept in around the rim of the blackout blind in Mary and Cameron's hotel bedroom. The sharp, tuneless scream of gulls broke the silence.

They lay together and treasured the moment, watching as objects in the room gradually took shape — Mary's green coat slung over the back of a chair, the shiny, silvered surface of the dressing-table mirror reflecting their bed with its green satin spread.

'Are you happy?' Cameron breathed.

'Perfectly.' If they kept the blind drawn and didn't

move, perhaps the world could be kept at bay for a little longer.

'I don't want to move.'

'Me neither.' *Stop, stop; everything stop! Make the moment last for ever; savour the touch of skin, the warmth, the perfect feeling between us.*

'I will get through the war,' Cameron promised, out of the blue and with strong conviction. 'I have a feeling deep down that everything is going to be all right for us.'

With a drawn-out sigh, Mary tilted her head to see his dear face more clearly. 'I love you.' Three simple words carried an unfathomable depth of emotion.

He kissed her gently on the lips. 'We could get married. What do you think?'

Her heart jolted then raced. 'Before you go away?'

'Why not? In Northgate Register Office, by special licence. Next Saturday. Shall we?'

'In front of witnesses?' Her mind raced along with her heartbeat. To be Mrs Ainslie; to stand at Cameron's side and recite her vows — this is what he proposed.

'Say yes.'

She'd expected them to wait for the war to end — had envisaged sewing a white dress out of silk and organdie, wearing a veil and walking up the aisle with bridesmaids. It hadn't occurred to Mary that it could happen any other way.

'Or would you rather wait?' Cameron lay with one arm resting under her head, side by side with the woman who gave his life its deepest meaning. He felt her heartbeat, watched her beautiful features flicker and change.

'I want to marry you as soon as ever we can,' she

whispered. To wear his ring. To call herself his wife. Even if she were to lose him or if something terrible were to happen to her, they would always have had that precious, diamond-clear moment of saying 'I do'. 'More than anything in this world.'

* * *

The door to Fern Cottage stood open when Viv approached. Overhanging branches dripped steadily on to the soggy woodland path and a thick mist swirled between tree trunks, lending an eerie aspect to the scene. *What fierce creature — bear or wolf — might lurk in the thickets?* she wondered, before reminding herself of where she was walking. This was good old Yorkshire, not the wild pine forests of British Columbia. And there was bound to be a warm welcome from Jean as soon as Viv crossed the threshold.

Sure enough, Jean heard her visitor stamping mud from her boots in the small porch leading into the kitchen. She came to the door all smiles. 'Hello, hello; has Douglas declared another washout?' she enquired in friendly fashion.

'Yes, darn it.' Yet again there was widespread fog and due to the lack of a radio in every crate flown by the ATA, the ops room had made the inevitable decision to cancel all proposed flights for the day. 'That's two wasted days in a row, as far as I'm concerned.' Viv flopped down at the kitchen table while Jean put the kettle on. She voiced the recurring Atta-girl complaint. 'God only knows why the powers that be don't provide us with radios. Do they think our pea-brains are too small to cope with modern technology?'

Jean smiled. 'No — it's more likely that they've

86

already given all the available radio frequencies to the RAF. Anyway, you look out of sorts.' She sat down opposite Viv. 'Dorota's having a nap, so tell me what's bothering you.'

'It's nothing really.' Only that Viv had woken up again with a dreary, unfamiliar sense that she was merely marking time instead of seizing each moment and living life to the full.

'I don't believe you.' Jean studied Viv's face and confirmed that the bewitching sparkle was definitely missing. 'Is this to do with Giles, by any chance?'

Viv shook her head. 'No, why should it be? As far as I'm concerned, Giles Parseval is out of the picture. I turned down his birthday invite, by the way.'

'Not on my account, I hope.' As the kettle began to hiss, Jean got busy with the tea caddy and pot. 'Honestly, Douglas and I wouldn't mind if you were to take up with him again. After all, I've said it before — it really is none of our business.'

Viv attempted a light-hearted reply. 'But Parsevals don't come along singly. They're like wolves — they hunt in packs.'

'So you'd have to hobnob with Sir Thomas and Lady Jane and all that crew?' Jean took the point with a wry smile.

'Seriously, though, I'm out of sorts because of the weather, that's all.' Looking around at the neat row of pans hanging from hooks and the array of blue and white crockery on the dresser, Viv felt a twinge of envy. 'What's it like to live a life of domestic bliss, Jean?'

'For me it's perfect.' Jean had never felt happier or more fulfilled. 'At first I thought I'd miss the flying — the thrills and spills — but I don't. Dorota and Douglas more than make up for that.'

'You're lucky to live here with your little family. You have your future all mapped out, whereas I fly everywhere by the seat of my pants — literally.'

Jean frowned as she sat down once more. 'So if it's not Giles who's upsetting you, it must be some other chap.'

'I never said that.' Quick as a flash and with a hint of defiance Viv rejected the suggestion.

Jean sipped her tea and waited.

'If you must know, I went out with Flight Lieutenant Brian Wheeler from Aireby last night and we had a whale of a time. We went to Northgate, to the Spa Gardens for afternoon tea, and from there we went to the Opera House to see a variety show.'

'Brian Wheeler? That's not a name I know.' Jean drank her tea then playfully swirled the dregs around the bottom of her cup. 'I see romance with a tall dark stranger,' she intoned in fortune-teller fashion. 'I see a cottage in the country and a smart house in town. I see a nursery with three cots —'

'For God's sake, give me a chance to at least get to know the guy!' Viv groaned then laughed.

'But I'm right about the tall, dark and handsome?' Jean quizzed.

'Yeah, as far as looks go Brian fits the bill.'

'But?'

But he's not Giles. The silent admission took Viv by surprise. 'But it's hard to see beyond the Prince Charming act,' she confessed. Brian had said all the right things and hadn't put a foot wrong — he'd held open doors, pulled back chairs and smiled in all the right places. Viv had felt admiring or envious glances cast in their direction as they'd entered a room. *And yet* . . . 'Plus, he doesn't give me space to breathe,' she added.

'Too keen?' Jean guessed. *As any man might be when he sets eyes on you, Miss Vivienne.*

'He won't take no for an answer.'

'Let me call again tomorrow morning,' Brian had beseeched her at the end of the evening. 'We can drive to the seaside — to Highcliff, if you like.'

'Not tomorrow,' she'd said firmly as she'd got out of the car. 'I'm afraid I'm still on standby for Priority Ones.'

'Then I'll telephone you tomorrow evening,' Brian had insisted before driving off without waiting for a reply. 'Au revoir!' he'd called with a cheerful wave.

So damned cocky and sure of himself — still very much in charge.

'You know, when you and I first met,' Jean said slowly, 'I couldn't work you out. You breezed into Rixley without any sign of nerves, ready to fly any crate that was thrown at you. And you bent a few rules here and there, I seem to remember.'

Viv felt her cheeks turn red. 'Ah, Clifton Suspension Bridge.'

'Precisely; you flew clean under it in a brand-new Spit, with me watching you from my Ox-box. I thought, *What in the world have we got here?* You were a whirlwind flattening everything in your path.'

'What are you trying to say?'

'Since I got to know you better, I see there's much more to you than a daredevil pilot and good-time girl.'

'Such as?'

'You're one hundred per cent loyal, for a start. You were the one who went out of your way to help Anna settle in at the Grange and you stood by her when we found out that she'd had a daughter out of wedlock.'

89

'I didn't handle it very well, though.' Viv shuddered when she remembered how certain she'd been that Giles was the villain of the piece — wrongly, as it turned out. 'I act before I put my brain into gear — that's my problem.'

'But you care about people.' Jean's tone was considered. Leaning across the table, she placed a hand over Viv's. 'I'm just saying, with Brian perhaps you need to scratch beneath the surface.'

'To see what lies below the jaunty charm?'

Jean nodded. 'He's in the RAF so he's bound to have witnessed things he wishes he'd never seen . . . He's lost comrades in the course of this dreadful war. Don't forget, people protect themselves in different ways.' Aware that she hadn't expressed herself well, she felt sad on Brian's behalf and fell silent.

'I know you're right,' Viv murmured. 'I ought to give him a chance.'

'Only if you want to.'

'Do I, though?' Or had she had enough of whizzing around in sports cars and of guys with trim moustaches and cut-glass accents — Piers, Giles and now Brian?

'Why not sleep on it?' Jean advised, gentle as ever. 'There's no rush. Whatever you decide to do, as long as you do it honestly, it will all come right in the end.'

★ ★ ★

Sunday morning proved too wet and dismal for a proposed walk around the reservoir with Gillian, so Bobbie retreated to the officers' mess to catch up on some letter writing. She began with one to her mother, thanking her for the food parcel and asking after her

90

father, whose normally robust health had lately been undermined by a severe bout of the flu. She demanded news of the family pets, including her dogs, Rufus and Captain, and of course North Star, her beloved horse. As usual, she included little about her ATA activities, except to say that her services as first officer were still in high demand and that the Rixley crew remained in good spirits so her mother was in no way to worry on Bobbie's account.

After a good deal of thought she decided to write in more depth about her situation with Ray, describing the well-run training yard and yesterday afternoon's exciting ride on the gallops. Once Giles had retreated upstairs to his room, Bobbie had ridden Glasgow Girl and Ray had chosen Never Say Die, a dark bay gelding who was new to the yard. 'You and Pa will like Ray when you eventually meet him,' she promised, crossing the fingers of her left hand as she wrote. 'He's kind and considerate and has overcome many difficulties.'

Bobbie paused, her pen poised over the paper. Would it be tempting fate to admit to her mother that Ray was her one true love? If she chose to write it down, how should she phrase it without sounding impossibly naïve? 'He's the one for me, Mum' or 'I've fallen head over heels'? She imagined a reply sent post-haste on lavender-scented notepaper — 'I'm happy for you, darling, but be sure to look before you leap. We live through chaotic times when many of society's old rules no longer seem to apply. This is important, Bobbie — your father and I strongly recommend that you don't make any decision that you later come to regret —'

'Bobbie — a word.' Hilary popped his head around the door and interrupted the fanciful scene playing

91

out in her head.

'A word' in Hilary's vocabulary was usually code for a reprimand so, despite the fact that it was a Sunday and Bobbie was off duty, she put down her pen and braced herself.

'There's someone I'd like you to meet,' he announced as they joined a tall, ramrod-straight woman in the entrance hall. Dressed in ATA uniform, the newcomer was perhaps thirty-five years old and wore a skirt rather than the more practical trousers. The stripes on her epaulettes indicated a rank of first officer. Her face was long and thin and her short, dark brown hair was parted neatly to one side. 'This is First Officer Peggy Ibbotson. You may have heard of her?'

'Not *the* Peggy Ibbotson!' Bobbie stepped forward eagerly to shake her hand. 'Of course I've heard of you — who hasn't?' The woman was an Air Transport Auxiliary legend: she had been in charge of Ground School Training in the early years of the war, earning a reputation for fierce intelligence and a practical, no-nonsense approach. Then, as the service developed, she'd been chosen to spearhead the search for raw, *ab initio* recruits, citing attributes such as know-how, determination, good judgement and common sense as necessary qualifications rather than a piece of paper to prove that you could pass an exam.

'Peggy, meet First Officer Roberta Fraser.' Hilary sprinted through the formalities. 'Peggy will take Third Officer Wright's place on the rota. Considering her experience, I've instructed Douglas to assign her as many Priority Ones and cross-Channel flights as possible. Her billet will be Agnes's old room. I expect you'll help her to settle in.'

'Of course.' Flustered in the presence of ATA

royalty, Bobbie's smile was too wide, her voice too high. 'Have you come all the way from Hatfield in one day?' she asked breathlessly as Hilary withdrew and she led the new arrival up the stairs. 'You must be awfully tired. Here, let me carry your bag.'

'I can manage.' Peggy held on firmly to her smart leather suitcase. 'I drove across from Northgate and don't feel in the least tired, thank you. I was visiting family there.' She paused on the landing to get her bearings. 'Where do those stairs lead?'

'To the men's quarters on the second floor.'

'And a bomb did this, I suppose?' Peggy gestured towards the broken banister and damaged plaster-work. She seemed critical of the fact that repair work hadn't been carried out. 'When?'

'Just over a year ago. The raid destroyed one whole wing. Luckily this part of the house isn't too bad.'

'But no doubt the ferry pool and the Grange remain targets.' Peggy marched ahead of Bobbie along the corridor. 'Jerry must still have us in his sights. Which is my room?' she asked in the same peremptory manner.

Bobbie pointed out the door.

'Rather a long way from the bathroom, I assume?' Peggy had noticed the panes of frosted glass in a door at the end of the corridor.

'Yes, but I'd be happy to swap.' Bobbie's eager smile met no response.

'No, no; I wouldn't hear of it.' Opening the door to Agnes's room, poker-faced Peggy entered and put down her suitcase, scarcely bothering to take in her threadbare surroundings. 'How many female pilots are billeted here?'

'Four, including you. Plus two ground staff — a

met girl and Douglas's secretary in the ops room. Then there are thirteen men spread over two floors.'

'Nineteen in all. Is the food up to scratch?'

'Yes, very good on the whole.'

'And where do the mechanics, drivers and canteen staff stay?'

'They're stationed in temporary barracks at the edge of the airfield.'

Bobbie's answers seemed to satisfy Peggy, who stood at the window and looked down at craters on the lawn. 'Jerry again?' she quizzed.

'I'm afraid so. We had bomb disposal teams here for weeks following the raid.' A nervous Bobbie struggled to find common ground. After all, Peggy was at least ten years her senior, and her reputation, though impressive, also served to set her apart. 'Why not come down to the officers' mess later on?' she suggested hesitantly. 'We usually gather there after dinner.'

'Perhaps. Now, if you don't mind . . .'

'Of course — I'll leave you to settle in.' Bobbie stepped out into the corridor and breathed a sigh of relief, almost bumping into Gillian as she backed away.

'Who on earth was that?' Gillian hissed. 'I only caught a back view but I got a distinct feeling that she's a woman who's used to dishing out orders.'

'Hush!' Bobbie put a finger to her lips. 'That's First Officer Peggy Ibbotson.'

Gillian gasped. 'You don't say! Isn't she Pauline Gower's sidekick?'

'That's the one.'

'Then I was right: she'll lord it over us, given half a chance. What's she doing here, anyway? Why isn't she at Hatfield, training new recruits?' A tenacious

Gillian pursued Bobbie into the empty officers' mess.

'Hilary wants her to fly Priority Ones.'

'That'll go down well with Viv and Mary.' Gillian tutted sceptically. 'And you too, for that matter.'

Bobbie nodded. 'But we'll do our best not to hold it against her.'

'I need to know more.' Gillian demanded her informant's full attention. 'Is Peggy Ibbotson the dragon she's reputed to be? Exactly how many trainees has she put through the mill? Does she have a husband tucked away somewhere?'

Bobbie turned both palms upwards and rolled her eyes towards the ceiling. 'Good Lord above, I only just met the woman.'

'Then hazard a guess — married or spinster?'

'Not married,' Bobbie decided.

'Aha; you reckon she's turned her back on men in order to devote her life to the Air Transport Auxiliary?' The notion appealed to Gillian, who ran on full-tilt with her theory. 'All Peggy Ibbotson cares about is meteorology and map reading, aeroplane engines and navigation. What's the betting she was best pals with Amy Johnson until that ill-fated bailout over the Thames? On top of which, she belongs to the same social circle as old Pop d'Erlanger?'

Gillian's name-dropping made Bobbie smile. D'Erlanger was the ATA's respected Commodore, who, the year before, had fought alongside Pauline Gower for equal pay for women pilots. 'I expect we'll find out soon enough.'

'Bobbie Fraser, you're no good to me!' Exasperated, Gillian flounced from the room. 'Since you didn't ask any of the right questions, I'll have to go up there and do it myself. Better still, I've spotted Viv out

95

there on the terrace. She's just the person I need. Viv;
hey, Viv — a new first officer has just arrived. She's in
Agnes's old room. Why not go up and say hello?'

★ ★ ★

'I feel like I've been socked in the jaw,' Viv groaned.
'In fact, it's as if I've gone ten rounds with Jack
Dempsey.' She burst in on Bobbie and Gillian in the
officers' mess, dragging Mary in with her. 'You have
to hear this,' she declared as she sat her down in one
of the old leather chesterfields. 'Gillian here tricked
me into having a conversation with poor Agnes's
replacement — the one I swore I'd be nice to. Ker-
pow — the woman had me on the ropes the second I
opened my mouth!'

Gillian failed to suppress a knowing chuckle. 'Why,
what did First Officer Ibbotson say to you?'

'First of all, I didn't have a clue who she was.' Viv
was wide-eyed and stunned after her mauling. 'You
know me, I treat everyone the same way: no airs and
graces. So I say howdy and welcome to Rixley then I
tell her my name. She flings back a one-word question: 'Rank?' Ker-pow! 'Flying hours?' I tell her six
hundred; a hundred and fifty in Canada, two hundred
in California, the rest here. 'Distinct danger of com-
placency.' She sums me up in seconds. 'An inclination
not to stick to the rules.' I'm down on the canvas but
not out.' Viv mimicked a boxer's stance. 'I come back
at her with a southpaw — what gives her the right, et
cetera?'

'Oh, you didn't!' Bobbie groaned. 'She's only the
ATA's most experienced instructor.'

'Yes, but I don't know that, do I? How come she's

96

judging me, I say again. I tell her, 'As it happens, I'm the least complacent pilot around because I'm determined to see this war through to the end, not get shot to pieces or end up in the drink.' '

'Did she believe you?'

'Well, if looks could've killed.' Viv lowered her hands then flopped exhausted into the nearest chair. 'Out for the count, that was me.'

Gillian turned to Bobbie. 'Is First Officer Ibbotson really that bad?'

The name brought Mary to the edge of her seat. 'Not *the* —'

'The very one,' Bobbie interrupted. 'And here we are, vowing to be nice to whoever was sent to fill Agnes's shoes.'

'Count me out,' Viv grunted. 'That woman and I are chalk and cheese. There's no way we're ever going to get along.'

'And meanwhile, Cameron and I are to be married next week.' Mary couldn't contain herself any longer. Happiness burst from her, lighting up her features as she shared her joy. 'We've decided to go ahead and do it before he leaves Aireby.'

'Good Lord!' Bobbie sprang from her seat to hug Mary.

'Congratulations!' Gillian followed suit.

'That's terrific news!' Viv circled the group until she found space to link arms and join in the hug. 'Where and when exactly? What will you wear? Oh, Mary, I'm so happy for you I could cry!'

7

Yet again there was yellow fog everywhere, with not a breath of wind to disperse it overnight, so on a miserable Monday morning the Rixley pilots woke up and looked out of their windows with sinking hearts.

Breakfast at Burton Grange was a gloomy affair. There was little chatter over porridge until Mary ventured to suggest that the weather must soon improve, allowing them to get off the ground before midday.

'It's in the shipping forecast,' she insisted. 'I heard it on the wireless before I came down.'

'I only hope you're right.' The short days and long nights of late November continued to be a trial for Viv. Noticing Peggy's arrival, she frowned and fell silent.

Peggy acknowledged Bobbie and Viv with the slightest of nods. She joined the queue behind Horace then introduced herself crisply before helping herself to sausage and eggs at the counter.

'Brrr! I swear the temperature just dropped ten whole degrees,' Viv muttered as Peggy seated herself at the opposite side of the room. 'A cold front just swept in.'

Bobbie hushed her and Mary threw her a warning look. Peggy glanced in their direction then proceeded to slice through her sausages with quick, precise movements.

'Jeez, she's performing surgery on her breakfast!' Viv reported sotto voce to Bobbie and Mary. 'Her knife's a scalpel —'

'Hush!' again from Bobbie.

'Don't be so mean.' Though the newcomer's manner might seem off-putting, Mary thought it better to reserve judgement. She finished her porridge and when she returned her empty dish to the serving hatch she made a point of passing close to Peggy's table. 'I'd be happy to show you the short cut to the ferry pool,' she volunteered. 'It's a five-minute walk through the wood.'

'Very good, Third Officer . . . ?' Peggy ran an observant eye over Mary's uniform.

'Holland. Mary Holland.' *Soon to be Ainslie!* 'I'm pleased to meet you.'

Peggy put down her knife and shook the extended hand. 'Thank you, Mary. I appreciate the offer.'

'There's no rush to get there. We'll have to wait for the fog to lift before we're given the all-clear.'

'Quite right. It will give me a chance to get my bearings, so to speak. What time shall we meet?'

'In fifteen minutes? I'll wait for you by the main door.'

'I'll be there,' Peggy agreed before returning to her breakfast.

★ ★ ★

She arrived on the dot, wearing a sheepskin jacket over her uniform, carrying thick gauntlets and a canvas haversack containing goggles, map and compass.

Her face looked pale and pinched in the early-morning light. 'Lead on, Macduff,' she told Mary with a stiff smile.

So they walked briskly along the terrace then across the stable yard and through a narrow gate into Burton Wood. By the time they came to Fern Cottage,

Peggy was quizzing Mary about her ATA experience and how she came to convert from driver to pilot.

'My fiancé, Flight Lieutenant Cameron Ainslie, persuaded me to apply for the conversion course. Corporal mechanic Stan Green backed him up. I would never have thought of it if they hadn't suggested it.'

'They believed you were capable.' Peggy raised her finely arched eyebrows and scrutinized Mary's face. 'Why would you never have thought of it for yourself?'

Mary blushed. 'I didn't think flying was for girls like me.'

'The ATA is for everyone,' Peggy insisted with more force than Mary had expected. 'Men and women, young and old, able-bodied or otherwise. Background doesn't come into it — that's the glory of it.'

'I know that now. And I'm glad I did it — I love what I do with all my heart.' As they walked on and came within misty sight of the Nissen hut barracks at the edge of the airfield, Mary grew bolder. 'What about you? Did you always know that you wanted to take to the air?'

'Not at all, though I've always had excellent coordination skills — and that, as you know, is one of the essential requirements. I was a hockey player for my county in my youth. After school I joined the civil service, hoping to travel. However, when the war started I was as anxious as anyone to do my bit and through a personal connection I learned of Pauline Gower's work recruiting female pilots. I applied because I thought it was a most worthwhile job.' Peggy's language was measured and fluent, with perfectly formed sentences and pleasing cadences.

Her self-assurance made Mary nervous once more. 'And you've never looked back?'

100

'I don't regret my choice, if that's what you mean.' Peggy brought the conversation to a gracious end. She let Mary lead the way between the huts then stopped by a hangar where ground crew were working on a Lancaster. Deciding to introduce herself to the ferry-pool engineers, she bade Mary farewell and went to inspect some obvious damage to the bomber's fuselage. 'You can get this crate shipshape again, I take it?' she demanded of Stan's busy apprentice.

Hearing an unfamiliar voice, Stan himself crawled out from under the plane's belly. His overalls were filthy, his face smeared with black engine oil. 'Not a chance,' he informed Peggy warily. 'One engine's completely jiggered and most of the landing gear went AWOL somewhere over the North Sea. We'll have to dismantle her and save what we can for spares.'

Peggy frowned. 'How did it happen? Did the pilot file a full report?'

Bossy and snooty, just like my old headmistress, was Stan's snap judgement. 'I wouldn't know.' He adopted a deliberately vague air. 'You'd have to ask First Officer Thornton. He's in the ops room — across the lawn and first door on your left.'

'Thank you, I will.' Instead of walking on, Peggy made a point of entering the hangar where she found a Blenheim and two gleaming Spitfire Mark 9s. Without asking permission she climbed up on to the wing of the nearest Spit and eased herself into the cockpit, where she sat and studied the dials.

'What the heck?' Bob clambered down from the cockpit of the Lancaster and peered after Peggy. His sallow face showed a mixture of surprise and irritation. 'She can't just wander in there willy-nilly.'

'She can and she has.' Stan didn't question Peggy's

101

authority. 'I reckon she's got First Officer written all over her.'

'Where's this crate bound for?' Peggy called in a loud voice. 'I see she's equipped with PR cameras and extra fuel tanks, so I'm supposing it must be somewhere in Europe.'

'It says here she's going to Italy.' Stan followed her into the cavernous hangar to read through a list pinned to the back of the door. 'That's if the fog clears and we can get her off the ground.'

'Quite.' From the narrow padded seat Peggy pictured the reconnaissance aircraft climbing towards the sun with her at the stick. She imagined the kick of the engine as she banked to port, the flash of sunlight on the wing, the simple bliss of piloting the aerodynamically perfect machine. 'Italy,' she repeated softly. Then she climbed out of the cockpit and slid nimbly to the ground. 'Thank you,' she told Stan. 'I'm reliably informed that the fog will be gone by mid-morning. Wheel her out for refuelling — make her a top priority, if you please.'

★ ★ ★

That same morning, all the talk in the Rixley canteen centred on Agnes's replacement. 'Is Hatfield winding down the training programme?' Bobbie gave voice to a theory that seemed to explain why Peggy Ibbotson had been released from vital duties there.

From his seat next to a steamed-up window, Horace pricked up his ears. 'That would be a jolly good sign,' he pointed out. 'It'd mean there's an end in sight.'

The buzz of conversation quietened as everyone tuned in to a major preoccupation among pilots

102

and ground crew alike. Peace might be on the horizon — before Christmas, if they were lucky. Then there would be no more dodging the doodlebugs or scrapping it out in Greece — Gordon would hightail it back to his family home in Jamaica and driver Olive Parsons declared she would return to Bolton and set up in a taxi business.

'Why else would Peggy be transferred here?' Bobbie stood in the canteen doorway, arms folded and staring out across the lawn towards the control tower, noticing that the mist was slowly but surely clearing.

'Hasn't anyone thought to ask her?' Horace asked.

Viv flicked idly through the pages of a magazine. 'Horace, honey, you met the Cold Front at breakfast. Seriously, you'd risk a case of frostbite if you got too close.'

'I didn't think she was all that bad when I walked in with her,' Mary objected. She tilted her cup and swirled its contents. 'Remember she helped us Atta girls get where we are today, with equal pay and now the right to fly across the Channel.'

Viv suspected that Mary's fast-approaching marriage persuaded her to see everything through rose-tinted spectacles. 'It wouldn't hurt her to drop the frosty act,' she insisted. 'As for cross-Channel flying — I'll believe it when it happens.'

The hiss of static on the Tannoy system told everyone that an announcement was imminent. Conversation stopped dead and a jolt of anticipation ran through the room.

'Will all pilots please report immediately to the operations room.' Gillian's crisp voice came through loud and clear. 'I repeat: will all pilots report immediately . . .'

Stationed by the door, Bobbie was first to exit the canteen and sprint across the lawn. She felt the customary churning sensation in her stomach, the tightening of nerves and an increased heart rate. 'By the way,' she whispered to Viv, who was close behind, 'we got a definite yes about the Christmas party.'

'The Parsevals have agreed?' As they raced up the narrow concrete stairs to the ops room, Viv checked her pockets for log book, Pilots' Notes, map and compass.

'So it seems.' At the head of the stairs Bobbie was distracted by the fact that Peggy had beaten them all to it. The newly arrived first officer stood to attention by the hatch, receiving her chit from Gillian, reading it then quietly going about her business.

'What type did she get?' Bobbie asked Gillian as she too received her handwritten chit.

'Spitfire.' Douglas's secretary made it clear she was not allowed to say more.

'Lucky beggar.' Bobbie took in the information scrawled on her small piece of paper: Class 5 four-engine bomber; a Wellington, no less — to RAF Benbecula. She was a heavy crate that would require total concentration. 'I had my fingers crossed for a Spit myself.'

'What's the betting Peggy pulled rank?' Viv imagined the new arrival having a none-too-quiet word in Douglas's ear. She edged towards the hatch. 'Don't tell me, Gillian — she's bagged the photo reconnaissance model tucked away in Hangar One.'

Without saying a word Gillian turned the list that she had in front of her so that Viv could read it.

'Would you credit it? Peggy's been given the PR Spit all the way to RAF Brindisi.' Viv breathed out heavily. 'How come? That's what I want to know.'

'Jammy beggar.' Mary had come up behind Viv and could see how peeved she was. 'But it's not worth making a fuss over.'

'But this is the first foreign flight out of Rixley and Douglas goes and gives it to Peggy. It's just not fair.' Viv's instruction for the day was to fly a Hurricane to Ventnor. She was third in line for take-off on Runway 2.

'This is wartime — nothing's fair.' Mary carried on trying to reason with Viv as they went downstairs together. 'They've given me another Mossie to Carlisle. Those crates give me the jitters after what happened to Agnes, but I can't say anything — I just have to fly what I'm given.'

'You're right.' Out on the lawn and on their way to the locker room, Viv managed to curb her resentment and concentrate on the task in hand. 'It may not be technically foreign but at least I get to fly across the Solent in one of the latest Hurricanes.'

'There you are, then.' Seeing Bobbie emerge from the locker room with her parachute pack, Mary encouraged Viv to go on ahead, then she stopped for a quick word with their friend. 'What type and where to?'

'A Wellington to Benbecula, worse luck. It's in the Outer Hebrides — the back of beyond.'

'But it's your neck of the woods. Might you stop off and see your family on the way back?'

'Fat chance,' Bobbie replied with a dismissive snort. Then without thinking she went on to describe her plans for the evening. 'I promised Giles I'd do my best to get over to Thresham and help him unpack properly. Oh!' She stopped when she saw Mary's puzzled expression. 'Damn it,' she muttered. 'Forget I said that.'

At that moment Viv emerged from the locker room with a look of bewilderment. 'Did you say Giles is at Thresham?'

'No — yes — that is . . .' Bobbie was like a jerky clockwork toy about to run down. 'Oh, good Lord; me and my big mouth!'

'Giles is at Thresham?' Viv repeated incredulously. 'How long have you known this?'

'I wasn't supposed to say.' Bobbie's face turned bright red. 'Please don't ask me any more.'

Viv screwed her eyes tight shut. When she opened them again she directed her anger away from what she saw as her friend's betrayal and on to the man himself. 'Trust Giles to put you on the spot, Bobbie. That's typical of him — creeping around behind everyone's back. As if we give a fig where he is or what he gets up to!'

'Obviously I would have told you if I'd been allowed.' Feeling bad for both parties, Bobbie did her best to explain. 'Giles isn't at Ray's place out of choice. He had some kind of argument with Sir Thomas.'

'What about?' Viv both did and didn't want to know. A part of her wanted to be done with Giles — to cut all ties — but curiosity got the better of her. 'Come on, you might as well spill the beans.'

'The row was over Giles's divorce — money and property, apparently. I don't know the details but the fact is that Giles came out of it with two broken ribs.'

Viv couldn't stop her imagination from running wild. 'Sir Thomas and Giles had an actual fight?' she cried. 'There were fisticuffs between father and son?'

Aware of time passing and the fact that Peggy's

106

Spitfire had been towed out on to the runway, Mary placed a hand on Viv's arm. 'This will have to wait.'

'And I've already said too much.' Bobbie's crate was next out of the hangar. 'But before I go, you're wrong about one thing, Viv. You think Giles doesn't care but he does. No, listen to me — he's in poor shape right now, not able to leave the house. It seems to me he's drinking too much and bottling everything up. So why not use this time to build bridges?'

'Because I'm convinced he doesn't want me to. Why else would he be so keen to keep his present where-abouts hidden from me?' Viv put on her leather hel-met and fastened the strap tight under her chin. *Life is a fog. Feelings flit in and out like leaves scattered by the wind.* 'And because . . .' Leaving the sentence unfin-ished, she lowered her goggles and strode off.

Bobbie sighed and looked questioningly at Mary.

'She definitely will get in touch with Giles,' they chorused. 'She won't be able to help herself.'

★　★　★

Peggy prepared for take-off in the specially adapted Spit. The marvel of engineering had always fasci-nated and excited her in equal measure and she knew everything there was to know about the aluminium-alloy, steel, rubber and Perspex construction of this already legendary aircraft. There was no need for her to check her Pilots' Notes — the airspeed indicator was to the extreme left of the instrument panel, the climb and descent indicator dead centre close to the fuel and oil pressure dials, above the turn and bank indicator. Quickly she felt for the undercarriage lever low on the right-hand side.

'You've double-checked for oil leaks?' she asked Stan before lowering the beautifully designed bubble-type canopy. The Spit's oil seals were a recognized and ongoing problem.

He gave her a thumbs up then applied a final flick of his duster to the prop and ailerons. 'It always pays to fly a clean bus,' he mumbled to no one in particular.

'Nose-heavy on landing in certain conditions,' Peggy reminded herself out loud. But mainly if the runway was puddled, and with a bit of luck Brindisi would be dry.

'She's all yours,' Stan yelled above the slow beat of the propeller and the throaty purr of the engine. He slid to the ground and joined Bob at the rear of the crate ready for chocks away.

'Watch out for turbulence.' Peggy gave herself a second reminder. 'We're bound to hit at least one lump of cloud between here and the south coast.' In which case, the crate would lurch and she must keep a close eye on the altimeter to avoid losing height. On the plus side, the Spit had an impressive history of seeing off North Sea raiders and protecting troops over Dunkirk. Pilots talked without exaggeration of her engine's remarkable song at full throttle and of her effortless speed and manoeuvrability. Like a gymnast of the skies, she could jink and turn on a sixpence and practically stand on her head if necessary.

'Contact!' Peggy yelled a final instruction to the erks on the ground. *Here we go*, she told herself. Chocks were away and the runway was clear so, with one last glance towards the control tower and with the lightest of touches on the controls, she rolled away — gathering speed and sliding along the smooth concrete surface, almost gliding until a gentle pressure on the stick got her off the ground and skimming over the trees of Burton Wood. More throttle increased the revs. She gathered yet more speed and quickly gained height — over Rixley village with its toy houses and St Wilfred's Church directly below, over Burton Grange and on over the rolling, empty North York Moors. Soon she would achieve maximum speed — an incredible 100 miles per hour faster than any bomber in existence. Up, up through the grey clouds with tingles of exhilaration thrilling through her body, she kept a constant lookout for the yellow-nosed Messerschmitt — they were renowned for pinpointing then pursuing and bringing down these aerial reconnaissance aircraft, whose work was so vital to the Allied progress in Europe.

Up to 6,000 feet and well clear of the clouds, she relaxed a little, allowing herself to bank to starboard then swoop down and soar again into the clear blue yonder, heading for sunny southern climes.

Now there was no going back, whatever the weather. Peggy must rely on map and compass, calculating speeds with pinpoint accuracy. If she got a glimpse of the ground through the cloud it would be a bonus — the grey sheen of a reservoir or the black patchwork of an industrial town.

She smiled at the memory of her beloved Keith, who used to insist on calculating his route according to the number of cigarettes he chain-smoked during a flight. A certain number of minutes per fag multiplied by air speed had allowed him to work out exact distances and he was seldom far wrong. Peggy would nag him to cut back on his smoking but his devil-may-care excuse had always been that his homespun method of navigation was more accurate than any other.

The Spit Mark 9 had been Keith's favourite crate, due mainly to her superior rate of roll; a flick and a half-roll plus a rapid pull out of a dive could shake off Jerry in a trice. Only once had a German bullet fired from behind pierced the Perspex hood and caught Keith by surprise. However, he'd shrugged it off and continued his love affair with the easy-on-the-eye, lean-bellied crate.

'Keith.' Peggy murmured his dear name as she cleared a bank of cloud and caught sight of the English Channel glittering below. She'd done it — left Blighty behind. The way ahead was clear. She flew on over the thin strip of water patrolled by miniature-seeming warships, over busy shipping routes where Keith had made his final flight.

Look up, not down, she told herself firmly.

In July they'd transferred Keith from flying Spits to piloting one of the very first jet planes procured by the RAF. It was a powerful Meteor 3, capable of an engine speed of 16,500 revs per minute. Only the most experienced pilots had been trusted to fly the state-of-the-art machine. He was in his Meteor directly over the Isle of Wight when three Me 110s had appeared, guns blazing, out of thick cloud. There'd apparently been no radio warning of their presence.

'Look up,' Peggy repeated through gritted teeth, though her whole body trembled. The coast of Normandy was in sight.

The three Messerschmitts had fired tracer bullets; hundreds of red fireflies had torn through the jet plane's fuselage, exploding in puffs of black smoke. Fuel tanks had ignited into a wall of flame, leading to certain death.

110

Back in Hatfield, Peggy had received a telephone call from Keith's squadron leader. The news of her husband's fate, plainly delivered, had ripped through her body as painfully as any bullet. She'd prayed that her dearest boy had been hit and had spiralled down into the sea in a matter of seconds; that he had not suffered. To disappear cleanly in the midst of life was the best that could be hoped.

She'd been eight months' pregnant with Rosie. On their wedding day two years earlier Keith had given Peggy a memento in the shape of a silver bluebird pin, which she wore without fail on the inside of her lapel.

Now he was down there somewhere, invisible under the cold grey surface.

'I flew here to tell you that Rosie is beautiful,' she murmured to her beloved as she soared on towards the French coast. 'She has your eyes and my mouth. She is perfect in every way.'

8

Given the filthy weather they'd experienced recently, it was inevitable that Mary should run into fog during her flight north. Her dilemma was whether to climb over it or to do the sensible thing and return to Rixley. She chose the former. After all, the Mossie FB Mark 6 was fast and light and extremely manoeuvrable for its size, which was twice that of a Spit. The main thing she had to watch out for was tail buffeting at speeds between 240 and 255 mph — a situation that would cause problems with the control column. So she climbed high and fast, aware of her increased fuel consumption and praying that she'd made the correct decision. Sure enough, she emerged from the fog at 3,500 feet then relied on her compass to hold her course.

Meanwhile, her mind ticked over the various technical issues presented by the twin-engined 'Wooden Wonder'. She'd read in her Notes not to use the Mossie's rudder aggressively at high speeds and to be on top of aileron control at low speed. The optimum choice was to cruise at 200 mph — all of which meant that with luck she should reach her destination in under an hour.

Once she'd landed the plywood and balsa crate in Carlisle, the rest of her day was as yet unknown. But, flying calmly above the weather gave Mary time to let her thoughts drift towards Saturday's wedding. 'Wedding!' She said the word out loud with a sense of wonder.

She'd spoken to Cameron late the previous night and heard that the ceremony was actually going ahead. 'Luckily the register office in Northgate has a gap for us at eleven hundred hours,' he'd explained. 'We need witnesses. I take it you'd like to have Viv or Bobbie?'

'Can I bring both?' she'd said in a flash, before asking Cameron who he had in mind.

'Douglas and Jean would be my first choice,' he'd replied after a brief pause for thought.

They'd discussed it as if they were choosing from a menu in a restaurant — the beef sirloin or the pork chop — matter-of-fact, practical and calm.

'Can you believe it?' he'd breathed, once the decisions were made. 'On Saturday we'll be Mr and Mrs Ainslie.'

'You've remembered to buy a ring?' Mary had ventured. *A ring, an actual wedding ring!*

Cameron had assured her that everything was in hand — all they had to do was get themselves and their witnesses to Northgate at eleven.

'Mr and Mrs!' She repeated the words over and over as she flew. They'd agreed they would both be in uniform and that afterwards they and their witnesses would have lunch in the Spa Gardens, after which they would head off to the Regal Hotel on the outskirts of town; just the two of them, newly married, to spend twenty-four hours together before Cameron had to return to Aireby to pack his belongings. His posting with Bomber Command was with a squadron based in Essex — a world away, as far as Mary was concerned. She knew nothing of the county other than the necessary information about RAF stations, ferry pools and maintenance units based there. Her heart ached at the thought of their imminent separation.

Then suddenly, as she eased back on the throttle and reduced speed in readiness for landing, she flew slap bang into a major problem: her visibility went from nigh on perfect to practically zero. What on earth . . . ? Ah yes, her descent had brought her into contact with freezing fog and her entire cockpit canopy was instantly coated in a thick sheet of ice. Mary had only moments to decide what to do. Jagged splinters of white frost obscured her view but a glance at her altimeter told her that she was down to 300 feet and so committed to landing as planned. But how could she achieve this without a view of the runway? There was only one thing for it: she must open up the hood. With her left hand on the stick and with flaps fully down, she fumbled with the clasps until the hood flew back and she experienced a blast of freezing air and a blinding flurry of white flakes. Wiping her goggles with a gloved hand, she leaned sideways to see a rocky ravine directly below. Beyond that there was an area of flat ground and three clearly visible runways bordered by admin buildings and Nissen huts. More pressure on the stick, less throttle. Mary fought to keep the ailerons under control and felt a shudder run through the crate as she swung it to port. The land rose to meet her. Snow whirled around her head. With a terrific bump followed by a violent bounce, her wheels hit the ground. She felt a split second of relief before the Mossie threatened to flip forward on to her nose. Mary fought again for control and won. Bringing the aircraft to an unlovely halt, she slewed sideways across the runway.

Too close for comfort. Short of breath and shaking from head to toe, she clambered down from the cockpit. *In future, keep your mind on the job,* she scolded herself as she brushed ice from her Sidcot suit. *Pay attention to conditions or you won't make it through to Saturday. There'll be no register office, no wedding — full stop!*

★   ★   ★

Talk about far flung! Bobbie's Wellington taxied smoothly to a halt on the runway at Benbecula. It was an RAF base for aircraft carrying out patrols of the Atlantic. The small Hebridean island overlooked the wild ocean: a last bleak outpost of civilization before the waves and wind assumed mastery.

There was just enough useable ground on Benbecula's west coast to accommodate a runway and it had been a tricky landing. But when Bobbie stepped down on to the tarmac to be greeted by the sound of waves lashing the shore and by a friendly ground crew who were full of praise for her handling of the heavy crate, her mood was buoyant. And when she opened her mouth to reveal her Scottish roots, the compliments came faster than ever.

'A wee lassie — who'd have thought it?'

'How tall are you? Not much more than five foot four, I bet.'

'Never mind; you handled that crate beautifully.'

'Come on, lassie — let's take you to the ops room and get you logged off.' A sergeant mechanic — a bald fatherly type with crooked teeth and thick glasses — took charge and led her towards the administration block, where she signed the necessary forms. He took her from there to a warm canteen and made sure she had everything she needed — egg and sausages with a good dollop of mashed potato. 'Take your time,' he told her. 'There's a Flying Fortress B-17 waiting for you in Hangar One but we have to wheel her out and run final checks first.'

Bobbie knew of the mighty four-engined Boeing but had never flown one. She would have to check her Notes carefully before take-off. 'Any words of advice?' she asked the mechanic, who had told her that his name was Bill.

'She's damned heavy,' he warned, watching Bobbie tuck into her sausage and egg. 'Tough as old boots, though. I've known Jerry slash one to pieces with ack-ack fire but she was still able to limp home. This one's getting on a bit. She has thirteen guns, one in the Plexiglas nose. Two bomb racks, four engines. Not exactly nippy when intercepted — she's not built for speed. She needs to be flown straight and level. What else?'

'Similar to a Lancaster?' Bobbie had thirty hours' experience of flying Avro's heavy bomber.

'Shorter range.' Bill admired the Scottish lassie's enquiring mind and plucky attitude. 'But yes, pretty similar. You won't have any trouble with the Fortress if you've flown a Lancaster.'

'Plenty of them,' she assured him, washing down the food with strong, hot tea.

Satisfied that Bobbie knew what she was doing, Bill left her in the canteen and went to supervise the final checks on the Boeing. From the window she could see the erks wheeling out her giant crate against a glorious backdrop of sky, hills and sea. A strong breeze blew wind-torn clouds in from the west and she watched them skim the hilltops — creating a strong tailwind on take-off that she must remember to take into account.

116

Meanwhile, there were magazines to flick through and time to let her mind wander back to her favourite subject — Ray.

She recalled his low voice giving her encouragement as they'd ridden on the gallops at the weekend. 'Not too much rein — that's right, tighten them up until we reach that copse of alders. Now let her go full steam ahead.'

She remembered the speed and exhilaration, the sound of hooves thudding into soft earth, the glory of riding Glasgow Girl with Ray on Rob Roy at her side.

And after that they had spent an evening together — with no sign of Giles, who had taken himself off to his room. There had been a roaring fire and a chance to curl up again on the sofa.

'Sometimes I can't believe my luck,' Ray had whispered, firelight flickering across his features. 'You're the girl of my dreams, Bobbie. I never ever thought I'd meet someone like you.'

Oh, his soft, loving voice, the upturn of his mouth at the corners set against the sadness she sometimes glimpsed in his dark brown eyes. That was the thing about Ray — he was a man of contrasts: often teasing and funny, occasionally prone to dark moods. And last night, with his arms around her, sitting in the twilight, he'd tuned into his serious side.

'You scare me half to death,' he'd confessed. 'Well, not you exactly but what you do.'

'You mean flying?' she'd responded cautiously.

Ray had nodded. 'I've been there myself,' he'd reminded her. 'I know what it's like to be eight thousand feet up and have Jerry appear out of nowhere, all guns blazing.'

'But it hardly ever happens to ATA pilots.' Bobbie

had done her best to reassure him. 'We only come across the occasional fighter plane who's flown off-course and they usually leave us alone when they see we're not armed.'

'But look what happened to Agnes,' he countered. 'Anyway, it's not just that. There's the winter weather to contend with and a hundred and one other things that can go wrong.'

'It's best not to think about it,' she'd counselled, her heart heavy as she'd foreseen where this was leading.

Ray had ignored the advice. 'How can I help it? Here I am on the ground: a bloody useless onlooker. Every time a plane flies overhead I wonder where you are at that moment — what dangers you're facing and whether or not you're safe.'

'I'm good at what I do,' she'd insisted. 'I don't take risks.' They'd both known this last assertion wasn't strictly true.

They'd gone round in circles, with Ray ever more gloomy and Bobbie increasingly unsettled until he'd come out with what he'd been meaning to say from the start. 'I have no right to ask, but might you consider giving it up for my sake?'

Bobbie had given a long, low sigh and searched his face for signs that he would reconsider his request.

'It's not fair, I know.'

'No — I understand.'

'When you're in the thick of it, you tell yourself you're invincible.' Ray had remembered all too well the bravado that had been necessary to set out on nightly RAF raids before his near-fatal crash — before the doctors had interrogated him and declared him unfit to serve, before they'd written LMF in big, thick capital letters on his file. Lack of Moral Fibre — no

118

good to man or beast. He'd recalled the shame and humiliation of being sent home to Thresham as mentally unfit. Yet here he was, practically begging the girl he loved to abandon her flying duties and save her own skin. What kind of double coward did that make him?

Bobbie had longed to calm his fear. She'd tried to stroke it away with her fingertips, to kiss it away with her lips. But it had still been there when she'd left Thresham on a promise that she would consider what Ray had said.

'Please be careful,' he'd begged. 'Whatever you do, come home safe.'

Back in the air, smoothly away from Benbecula in the Flying Fortress and heading home to Rixley, Bobbie let the engines drown out unsettling memories of the weekend. She concentrated on pulling up the landing gear, on ailerons and rudder, altitude and speed. By God, she was a beast of a crate! Heaving her into the air took every ounce of Bobbie's strength and all her concentration. But she succeeded in reaching 3,000 feet, flying straight, level and not too fast, as the sergeant mechanic had advised — proving that a slim girl of twenty-two could handle a Class 5 and was able to calculate distance and direction with pinpoint accuracy. She would deal with wind, rain, snow and whatever the return flight threw at her. Sitting upright at the controls, thinking quickly, making adjustments and on constant lookout for the next hazard, Bobbie flew across the Scottish border towards Carlisle and all points south.

★ ★ ★

119

'I have a bone to pick with you.' Shortly after her return from the Isle of Wight, Viv collared Hilary in the officers' mess. She approached the bar and came straight to the point. 'How come the last pilot to arrive at Rixley is the first to bag a cross-Channel flight?'

Out of uniform Hilary retained an air of authority that casual sweater and corduroy slacks couldn't disguise. A flicker of irritation appeared on his clean-cut, aquiline features. 'Chits are assigned by the chaps in the ops room,' he reminded her.

Viv perched on the stool next to his. 'Gin for me please, Ernest,' she told the handyman who was standing in for the usual barman. 'That's as may be.' She didn't deviate from her challenge to the man in charge of the whole shooting match. 'But you can't tell me you don't have a say in what goes on there. The ops boys need to think about it from our point of view — sure we respect what Peggy has done for our organization, one hundred per cent, but you have to admit that today's chits were hardly fair. She got to fly a PR Spit all the way to Italy, for God's sake.'

'Noted.' Hilary sipped at his whisky.

'Is that it?' Viv tapped her fingertips on the bar top.

'What else do you want me to say?'

'What's your opinion — was it or was it not a case of Peggy pulling rank?'

Lord, Viv was a terrier! Once she got hold of a topic she never let go. 'As I say, I wasn't directly involved, but from what I know of Peggy — and she and I have been friends for a number of years — she isn't the type to pull rank, as you put it. Douglas would have made this morning's decision based purely on experience.'

'Looks like I'm banging my head against a brick wall, then.' The gin slid down easily. Viv glanced

120

around the mess to see Bobbie ensconced in a fireside chair chatting to Gillian and Horace. 'But the thing is, Hilary, we girls compete daily for types — who gets what, and so on. It's only fair that we all have an equal shot at flying a Spit or a Hurricane — and the chance to fly across the Channel, for that matter.'

'And I'm sure Douglas takes that fully into account.'

'Normally; yes, he does.' Viv decided to ease off. 'Sorry, Hilary — you're off duty. I expect you wish I'd change the record.'

'I'm always on duty,' Hilary came back at her. 'It's the nature of the job. And I have taken on board what you say. But you must understand that although healthy competition for types is all well and good, it's not right to launch a personal attack on a first officer, especially someone of Peggy Ibbotson's standing.'

Viv frowned but said nothing.

'I mean it, Viv. Your job is to make any new pilot here feel welcome.'

'I would have if she'd let me.' She recalled her vow to be nice to Agnes's replacement then remembered with crystal clarity that Peggy was the one who'd started trading insults — an inclination not to stick to the rules, blah-blah.

'I've heard differently.'

'Why — what's been said?'

'That you were quick to invent a disparaging nick-name for her.'

Jeez, the walls had ears! 'You know me — I was only kidding.'

Hilary finished his whisky then stood up with the air of someone who knew more than he was prepared to say. 'Peggy's been through a lot lately — she's had a rough time of it; so go easy on her, please.'

121

Knowing by his manner that it was pointless to ask for details, Viv bit her tongue and ducked her head in silent acknowledgement.

'Thank you; I appreciate that.'

Leave me hanging, why don't you? she thought as her commanding officer made a quick exit. *What kind of rough time exactly? And what's behind Peggy's famous* froideur? *Don't tell me there's a bruised and battered heart beating inside that upright frame and the Cold Front is human, just like the rest of us.*

★　★　★

A note was pinned to Mary's door when she got back to the Grange after a long train journey back from Carlisle. She was cold and damp, looking forward to a soak in a hot bath then bed, so the sight of the note addressed to Third Officer Holland in Hilary's handwriting caused her to sigh and wonder what she had done wrong this time.

She put down her haversack then unfolded the paper. It read:

Immediately on your return please report to me in my room.

Thank you,
Squadron Leader Stevens

A glance at her watch told her that it was ten minutes past ten — surely too late to bother him. But then again the note was clear — *Immediately on your return . . .*

Better get it over and done with, Mary thought as she trudged up the stairs to the men's quarters and knocked on Hilary's door.

'Come!' he barked.

She went in, expecting a dressing-down for some misdemeanour or other — an error in one of her logbook entries, perhaps. Or maybe he'd been notified about this morning's clumsy, frost-bound landing? She hovered in the doorway, hands clasped in front of her and shaking all over from a mixture of weariness and anxiety.

'Ah, Mary — there you are.' Hilary put down his book then got up from his fireside chair. His expression gave nothing away.

'I'm sorry it's so late,' she began.

'No matter. Are you all right? You look tired.' He gestured for her to come closer to the fire.

A sudden thought struck her. Had Hilary got wind of Saturday's wedding? Was he about to raise unforeseen objections? The trembling increased and she began to feel dizzy. The sloping ceilings of the attic room seemed to close in and dark shadows in alcoves and corners darted towards her. Instead of joining him by the fire, she grasped the door handle to steady herself.

'Please come and sit down.' Sensing her anxiety, he grew more insistent. 'Let me get you a drink. I can offer you whisky or dry sherry.'

'Nothing, thank you.'

It was time to put her out of her misery. 'I'm afraid I have bad news.'

Cameron! Mary's head whirled. She tried to speak but no words emerged.

'It's about your brother, Private Thomas Holland.'

Not Cameron, thank God! Mary held tight to the handle, scarcely breathing, waiting for more.

Hilary took an envelope from the low table beside his chair. 'The postmaster delivered this telegram to the Grange late this afternoon. I assured him that I would deliver it to you in person.'

The flimsy paper inside the blue envelope was creased. There was a dirty thumbprint at the top, covering the word 'priority'. The typed words danced over the white surface. Mary tried to focus and read:

Dear Miss Holland,

May I be permitted to express my sincere sympathy regarding the sad news concerning your brother, Private Thomas Holland. On 15 November 1944 the regiment in which he served was active in an Allied assault close to Berlin and nothing further has been heard of him since.

    You may be aware that in a number of cases of service personnel reported missing in action, some may eventually be identified as prisoners of war, and I hope this can provide some comfort at this difficult time.

The words 'missing in action' seared themselves on Mary's brain without immediately making sense. She had to reread the telegram then think it through — Tom had been caught up in fierce action deep in enemy territory and had disappeared. No one knew where he was now.

Your brother's effects have been collected and will be forwarded to you in due course through the appropriate channels. Once again please accept my deepest sympathy . . .

As Mary read to the end she felt a constriction around her heart, pressing so hard she felt sure it must stop beating.

Without asking a second time, Hilary handed his stunned officer a glass of whisky. That Mary was taking the news hard was to be expected. 'There is hope,' he reminded her gently.

She stared back at him, her eyes dark and unseeing.

'Shall I fetch someone — Bobbie or Viv, perhaps?'

'No.' With robotic movements, Mary put down the untouched whisky then carefully folded the telegram and put it in her pocket. 'Thank you, sir.'

'Will you speak to Cameron?'

'Not tonight.'

'Are you sure?'

'Yes — it's late. I'll telephone him first thing tomorrow morning.' Still in a daze, she drifted towards the door. For now it was as much as she could do to find her way to her room. That phrase — missing in action — fluttered inside her head like a thousand bats in a dark cave.

'Go straight to bed,' Hilary recommended as he watched Mary walk unsteadily along the corridor and down the stairs.

Bed, sleep, oblivion. Tomorrow she would be able to make more sense of what had happened.

I'll ask Douglas to take her off the rota, Hilary decided as he closed the door. Shock was often delayed. He couldn't risk it kicking in while Mary was in mid-air,

125

in charge of a valuable crate. *God, damn and blast; the stress of it all!* Hilary poured himself another generous double and downed it in one.

9

'Of all the times for this to happen!' Viv commiserated with Mary. It was three days since Mary had received the news of Tom's disappearance and both Viv and Bobbie had anxiously watched the drastic effect that the telegram had had on their friend.

'Yes; how are you feeling now?' Bobbie was in dressing gown and slippers, sitting cross-legged on Mary's bed while Mary perched on her dressing-table stool and a barefoot Viv paced the floor. Bobbie had been away from Rixley overnight and had flown in from Belfast earlier that evening. She'd run into Viv in the ferry-pool locker room and together, despite the late hour, they'd decided to visit Mary in her room.

'Hilary won't put her back on the rota until he's satisfied she can cope,' Bobbie had observed on the walk home. 'In a way it's a vicious circle — the more time Mary has to twiddle her thumbs and think about what might have happened to her brother, the worse she gets and therefore the less likely Hilary is to let her fly again.'

So, following their earlier resolve, Bobbie and Viv had changed out of their uniforms then knocked on Mary's door.

'Let us in,' Viv had insisted. 'We're like the Wise Men — we come bearing gifts.'

'No gold or frankincense, though.' Bobbie had tried to shore up Viv's cheeriness. 'Only Ovaltine and shortbread biscuits — I'm afraid it's the best we can do.'

So Mary had unlocked the door and listened to the trials and tribulations of their respective days — battling winds of up to 50 mph over the Pennines in Bobbie's case, experiencing frozen leaves on the runway and ribald comments from the erks in Lossiemouth for Viv.

'You'd have thought they'd never seen a girl in a Sidcot suit before,' she complained. 'You could've heard the wolf whistles a mile away.'

Gradually the frown etched into Mary's face softened. The gentle waves of conversation had lapped at the edges of her fears and when Bobbie asked her how she was feeling she was able to share her concerns. 'I'm worried sick,' she confessed. 'In my eyes, Tom will always be the baby of the family. I can't even begin to picture what he must have gone through since the war started. And now this!'

'You'd no idea he was in Germany?' Bobbie had heard recent reports on the wireless that Tom's Yorkshire Regiment had been tasked with making a further push towards the German capital.

'No idea at all. I haven't heard from him in months — neither has Dad.'

'You've spoken to your father?' Viv picked up on the unusual event.

'No, Dad refuses point-blank to use the telephone. He doesn't trust what he calls a newfangled contraption — he's afraid it'll blow up in his face. But I spoke to Mr Embsay who runs the corner shop at the end of our street and asked him to find out if Dad had received the same telegram. It turns out I'm the only name Tom gave as his next of kin when he joined up so there was no telegram for Dad. I've had to pass on the news in a letter.'

128

'It's a lot of responsibility for you to bear,' Bobbie murmured. 'Especially with the wedding so close.'

'The day after tomorrow.' Viv counted on her fingers on Mary's behalf as she continued to pace. 'Thirty-seven hours, to be exact. You and Cameron still plan to go ahead, I guess?'

'We did think about calling it off,' Mary reported. 'Cameron said he would understand.'

'You've got a man in a million there.' Bobbie sighed.

'Don't I know it? So I decided I wanted to go ahead regardless. Was that selfish of me?'

The forlorn question and Mary's pale, anxious face brought Viv to a full stop by the blacked-out window. 'Jeez, Mary — how can you even think that?'

'No, it's not in the least selfish. You two deserve to be happy.' Putting herself into Mary's shoes, Bobbie knew exactly what she would do. 'If Ray were to ask me to marry him, I'd be down that aisle like a shot.'

While Viv raised an eyebrow and looked askance at Bobbie's naïve eagerness, Mary felt the band of anxiety around her heart begin to ease. 'Thank you — that makes me feel better. It'll mean the world to have you both there at the register office with me.'

'We wouldn't miss it for the world.' Viv resumed her restless walking, hands thrust deep in her dressing-gown pockets. Her tousled hair fell carelessly over her forehead. 'Your wedding is the high point in the build-up to the festive season, second only to the Christmas party.'

'Viv!' Although Bobbie knew she was joking, she feigned outrage. 'Talking of which, I spoke to the lady in the ENSA office yesterday and she said our luck was in: they can definitely provide entertainers for the twenty-third.'

'Jugglers?' Viv suggested airily. 'Acrobats, a fire-eater, a ventriloquist?' Seizing a sock from Mary's bed, she thrust her hand inside and used it as a primitive dummy. 'Gottle o' geer!' she mimicked without moving her lips. 'Bottle of beer,' she interpreted in her own voice.

'Good Lord, woman!' Bobbie leaped up and wrestled the sock from her. 'Be serious for once in your life. ENSA promises to send a band with a pianist and a drummer, plus a singing duo.'

'Of which variety: male or female?' Mary wanted to know.

'One of each — Dolores May and Leonard Fraser. They're recently back from entertaining our boys in the Far East, God bless them.'

' 'Bluebirds over the White Cliffs of Dover', 'We'll Meet Again' . . .' Viv reeled off a couple of patriotic favourites. 'Are there really any bluebirds in Dover?'

'No, it's poetic licence.' Bobbie uncrossed her legs then stifled a yawn as she reached for the empty mugs. 'Have you any idea when you'll be back on the rota?' she asked Mary.

'As soon as I can convince Hilary that I'm ready.' *Perhaps tomorrow*, Mary thought. *If not, then definitely Monday.*

'We're all feeling the strain, if the truth be known.' Bobbie had yet to give Ray a response to the all-important question: to fly or not to fly? The weekend was looming; an answer would be required. Meanwhile, Viv was still dithering over Giles.

'Speak for yourself!' Viv was first out of the door and heading for her own room. 'I'm happy as Larry, whoever he is!'

'*Was*,' Bobbie corrected. 'Larry Foley was a bare-knuckle fighter. He's dead now.'

'So no longer happy, then.' Viv waltzed off without a backwards glance.

Bobbie and Mary laughed. 'Good night,' Bobbie told Mary softly. 'And sleep well. We'll see you tomorrow at breakfast.'

★　★　★

'I've told Hilary that I deem it unwise to invite the RAF cadets to the Christmas party.' Peggy's announcement in the Rixley canteen next morning caused a crackle of hostility as strong as an electric current throughout the room. She stood behind Bobbie and Viv in the queue, her brow puckered into a frown, her grey eyes cold as steel.

'Happy Christmas to you too,' Viv muttered under her breath as she shuffled forward and Bobbie bore the brunt of Peggy's unwelcome opinion.

'But the invitations have already gone out,' Bobbie objected.

'They can be withdrawn if Hilary so chooses.' Peggy ignored the ongoing ripple of indignation. 'My reasons are twofold. Firstly, many of the trainees may have been posted to their various squadrons by then. The few who remain will be on sentry duty and such like. It will therefore be vital for them to remain in the camp. Secondly, I'm not the only one to perceive an ever-increasing risk of an enemy attack on the training school, not to mention here at the ferry pool.'

'Why, what have you heard?' Bobbie acknowledged that Peggy might have access to secret information that the run-of-the-mill Atta girl did not.

'Nothing specific.' The brusque tone didn't soften

at the sight of anxious faces at nearby tables.

'Her Ladyship had best not put the wind up everyone if she's got no proof,' Stan muttered to Olive, while ostrich Horace buried his head in a newspaper and Gordon and Bob began a loud conversation about tomorrow's football match at Elland Road.

'Then we can't be sure, can we?' Bobbie inched towards the counter.

'Certainly, we can't be sure of anything in this day and age,' Peggy went on. 'But Hitler is desperate and he's throwing everything he's got at the RAF. Winning the war in the air — that's the crucial thing as far as the Führer is concerned. Ergo, any poorly camouflaged ferry pool becomes a prime target.'

Ergo? Viv hunched her shoulders in disgruntlement. *Give us uneducated chumps a break, lady!*

'Out of interest, what was Hilary's response?' Bobbie had met bluestockings like Peggy before and they didn't intimidate her. After all, they'd been frequent visitors to her family estate as wives and companions of the men who came to shoot grouse; modern women who expressed controversial opinions about the sport's cruelty or about the British government's policy of appeasement towards the Third Reich.

'He took my point and now it's up to him.' Peggy reached the counter and ordered a cup of tea. Obviously the forthright expression of her unpopular view hadn't gone down well but that had been no reason for her to hold back. Clearly the ferry pool was a target, as she'd pointed out to Hilary. 'It's happened before and it will happen again,' she'd insisted. She'd advised him to ensure that as many crates as possible were taken off the runways and stored out of sight in the hangars. 'We must be extra vigilant, Christmas or no.'

'What a killjoy.' Viv sought out Mary who had just been given the news that she was not to return to flying until Monday.

As the public announcement system crackled into life, Mary had to agree that a Christmas party without the RAF might prove a damp squib. 'Fingers crossed Hilary won't change his mind.'

'Will all pilots . . .'

Viv popped up from her seat like a jack-in-the-box. The scramble for the door involved a loud scraping of chairs, some pushing and shoving and a robust use of elbows. Peggy's long stride meant she was first out of the building, closely followed by Viv and Bobbie.

Twenty-seven hours to go. Only Mary remained in the canteen, picturing the moment when she would become Mrs Ainslie. Would Cameron feel as nervous as she did? she wondered. Would there be a similar knot in his stomach and the same dreamlike feeling of unreality? *Take a deep breath,* she told herself. *Keep busy. Put your worries to one side and prepare for the biggest event of your life.*

★   ★   ★

Prince's Street in Northgate was a major thoroughfare lined with imposing stone buildings with steps leading up to entrances and solid, impressive porticos. The register office stood opposite the library and next to a bank on one side and a small park on the other.

Cameron stood on the steps with Douglas and Jean. It was a quarter to eleven on Saturday the second of December and as yet there was no sign of Mary, Bobbie and Viv.

'She'll be here,' Jean assured him when she saw Cameron check his watch for the umpteenth time. She wore her best teal-blue two-piece in honour of the occasion, with a matching felt hat that had a small crown and a trilby-style brim.

Despite the reassurance, a nervous Cameron ran through all the things that could go wrong — the car carrying the bridal group might break down or get a flat tyre or skid on black ice. What else? An air strike on Rixley wasn't totally out of the question, though admittedly not so likely during daylight hours. But, God forbid — Mary might actually have decided the whole business was too rushed and changed her mind at the last minute!

'She'll be here soon,' Jean promised, though she too peered anxiously up and down the street. 'At least the weather is in our favour,' she commented. The sky was cloudless blue, the air crisp and clear.

'Jean's right, old chap — no need to worry.' Douglas stood to one side as a small wedding party emerged from the register office.

The groom wore a private's uniform and a wide, somewhat gormless grin. The blushing bride was in pale green, carrying a spray of pink carnations. They were surrounded by family and friends, all smiling broadly. There was much back-slapping between the men and happy sniffles into handkerchiefs among the women as the noisy group processed down the street.

Cameron's mouth was so dry he found it hard to swallow. The minute hand on his watch moved agonizingly slowly. It was ten to eleven and there was still no sign of Mary.

* * *

'What's the hold-up now?' From the back seat of Olive's Air Transport Auxiliary Ford, a fidgety Bobbie tried to find out the reason for the latest delay.

'Stray sheep on the road,' Olive reported phlegmatically.

'Typical!' Viv wound down her window and leaned out. Sure enough, there were half a dozen sheep wandering aimlessly from one grass verge to the other. 'Toot your horn, Olive. Make them shift.'

In the front passenger seat Mary's heart beat rapidly. They'd set out from Rixley in good time but they'd been stopped for ages at a level crossing, waiting for two goods trains to chug slowly by — and now this. The silly sheep skittered and barged clumsily across the road, seemingly determined to make them late.

'Shall I hop out and shoo them away?' Bobbie offered.

'No, stay where you are.' Olive turned down the suggestion with her customary bluntness. Instead, she gave a blast on her horn, which scared the sheep into tottering across a ditch and clear of the road. Then she pressed the accelerator pedal to the floor and roared away.

'A quarter to eleven,' Mary said faintly.

A minute later Olive crested a hill that gave them a clear view of their destination. Northgate was spread out below them: rows of terraced houses, a cluster of church spires, with large civic buildings and broad streets at the centre. She sped on down the hill, across a cattle grid that rattled. Then she gave way at a road junction, impatiently tapping the steering wheel as a coal lorry trundled by, then on again.

Scarcely breathing, Mary took a powder compact from her bag and flipped it open to check her appearance in its small round mirror. She patted her already immaculately styled hair.

'Don't worry — you look very smart,' Bobbie told her.

'Adorable,' Viv confirmed.

Ten to eleven. How far away was Prince's Street? Why was the traffic so bad? Mary slipped the compact back in her bag and snapped it shut. 'Oh Lord,' she gasped, 'what if we're late?'

★ ★ ★

'That's it — we might as well go home.' Cameron had convinced himself that Mary had backed out. He felt a dull certainty that the wedding was never meant to happen.

Three boys in school blazers and short grey trousers scampered down the library steps carrying books under their arms. A tramp wearing a battered bowler hat poked around in a litter bin outside the bank. Olive's car sailed into view.

'Here they are!' With a sigh of relief, Jean ran on to the pavement and waved.

In an instant everything accelerated from slow motion into rapid action. Cameron and Douglas disappeared into the building. Olive braked and the car doors flew open. Mary, Viv and Bobbie stepped out on to the pavement. Jean grasped Mary's hand and hurried her inside, to be met by a strong smell of furniture polish and linoleum. There were several doors leading off from a hallway whose walls were painted cream and green. A dowdy, middle-aged woman carrying a clipboard emerged from one of the rooms.

'Miss Holland?' she enquired.

'That's you!' Bobbie gave the bride a shove forward.

Mary found herself in a small room with a window overlooking a courtyard. The walls were plain cream. Cameron stood beside Douglas, tugging nervously at his cuffs. The registrar retreated behind a small desk then motioned for Mary to come forward. Another shove, this time from Viv, got her where she needed to be — standing next to Cameron.

The registrar began the brief proceedings in a light, sing-song voice. Cameron took hold of Mary's hand. He smiled steadily at her during all the time that he answered the formal questions. When it came to Mary's turn, despite her rapid heartbeat and shaking hands, she spoke clearly. She smiled back at him and drew courage from his steadfast gaze. Then it was time for the ring, then the signing of the register. The scratch of the pen nib over the stiff paper was a sound that stayed with Mary for a long time afterwards, as was the sight of the flourish at the end of Cameron's surname, the tail of the 'e' becoming a downward and backward curve that underlined his whole signature. With a sense that all was complete and as it should be, she wrote her own name in a plain, bold script.

The registrar blotted their signatures before offering the document to each witness in turn. Then she uttered her congratulations and shook hands with the happy couple.

'As simple as that,' Cameron whispered as he and Mary walked arm in arm out of the building. No fuss; just straightforward and quick. They were Mr and Mrs Ainslie.

'For ever and ever, amen.' Viv was close to tears. How come such a brief, functional ceremony had moved her so deeply? She hadn't expected it and wondered at the strength of her feelings.

'They're made for each other,' Bobbie whispered, her heart bursting with happiness for the newly married pair.

Douglas produced a camera to take photographs of Mary and Cameron, arms linked, smiling out at the world — Mary happy, trim and immaculate in her blue uniform, her pilot's stripes and wings on full display; Cameron upright with his head held up and shoulders back, his short hair neatly parted, as smart and proud as could be.

'Jean, come and stand beside Cameron,' Douglas instructed. 'Bobbie and Viv, get in the picture next to Mary. Stand still, everyone. That's right. Now look this way. Say cheese!'

★ ★ ★

'How jolly!' Bobbie beamed across the table at Cameron and Mary.

The wedding party sat at a corner table in the busy restaurant at Spa Gardens. The interior of the Victorian building was a fantastical creation of intricately patterned tiles, wrought-iron pillars and domed glass ceiling, set off by real palm trees in ceramic pots as large as beer barrels. Elderly waiters in black jackets and long white aprons wafted discreetly from table to table, serving a luncheon of cold meat sandwiches from silver salvers.

'And how pleasant to have something to celebrate for a change.' Douglas sat with his arm resting along the back of Jean's chair.

'So you recommend marriage, do you, Douglas?' Viv had taken off her jacket. She'd eaten her fill and now leaned away from the table, balancing on the back legs of her chair.

'Yes, if it's to the right person.' His arm slid smoothly on to Jean's shoulder.

Smiling self-consciously, Jean leaned in towards him.

'Marriage, a family, a thatched cottage with roses around the doorway?' Viv created a chocolate-box picture. 'When should we expect to hear the patter of tiny feet?' she asked Mary and Cameron.

'Steady on.' Cameron gave a good-natured laugh. 'Give us time to catch our breath.'

To spare Mary's blushes Bobbie turned to Jean with a new topic. 'Who's looking after Dorota today?'

'Gillian was more than happy to help out when I told her the reason,' Jean explained. 'She sends her congratulations to the happy couple, by the way.'

Sitting next to Cameron, Mary was content to let the conversation wash around her. She was hardly aware of what was said, only that she was surrounded by smiling faces. When she glanced down and saw the gold ring on her third finger it almost looked like someone else's hand.

'You're quiet, Mary,' Bobbie observed as their waiter removed empty plates.

'I'm too happy to speak,' she whispered. Euphoria was the proper word for how she felt: as if she were floating six inches above the ground, surrounded by golden light.

'And we're overjoyed for you.' Lunch was over and Bobbie nudged Viv, giving her a sign that now was the time to make themselves scarce.

Viv took the hint and jumped up from her seat. 'Come on, you lot — Cameron and Mary have better things to do than sit here chatting with us.'

'No one would ever call you subtle.' Bobbie grumbled about Viv's innuendo as goodbyes were exchanged and the group dissolved.

Viv was first out of the restaurant and on to the street. 'Listen, honey, if I only had twenty-four hours before my new husband went off to war, I know where I'd want to spend it and who with.'

The reminder of Cameron's new posting sent a shiver down Bobbie's spine. Until now, amidst the nerve-tingling build-up to the ceremony and the hearty celebration afterwards, they'd all managed to put his imminent departure out of their minds. She glanced over her shoulder at Cameron shaking hands with Douglas and Jean, then wishing Mary all the happiness in the world. 'Let's hope they won't be kept apart for long,' she murmured.

'Yes, let's hope,' Viv agreed. 'We have to hang on to the idea that we're entering the final stages of this bloody mess, otherwise none of us Atta girls would ever ferry another crate from A to B and no RAF guy in his right mind would set out on nightly bombing raids over Germany.'

'You're right there.' Bobbie watched Cameron whisk Mary off to his car — him with his arm around her waist, her with her hair blown sideways by the wind, not looking back.

The sun still shone, though cool afternoon shadows lengthened and it would soon be dusk.

'So far, so good,' Douglas commented as he put on his forage cap then fumbled in his pocket for his car ignition key. The night before, in the dark, warm intimacy of the bed he shared with Jean, he'd expressed some of his reservations — that marriage in general

140

ought not to be hurried into, that Cameron's decision to rejoin Bomber Command had put the couple under extra pressure and that fear of what might lie ahead could be behind their rush to the register office.

Jean had persuaded Douglas otherwise — she said she knew true love when she saw it and that's what Cameron and Mary had. 'It may have been organized in a hurry but I don't blame them,' she'd insisted. 'Tomorrow's wedding lets the world know how much they adore each other. You remember how that feels?'

'Perfectly,' he'd admitted. 'It feels as if it's meant to be, that you've been waiting all your life for that moment of saying 'I do'.'

'Exactly.' Point proven; no more needed to be said.

Still, everyone understood that happiness was beautiful and as fragile as a butterfly's wing. And now Jean, Douglas, Bobbie and Viv shared a moment of silent apprehension as they stood on the pavement on the shady side of Prince's Street and watched Cameron and Mary drive off down the hill towards the Regal Hotel.

10

'It said on the wireless this morning that Churchill is about to stand down the Home Guard.' Bobbie made conversation as Viv drove them to Thresham the following afternoon.

Viv acknowledged that this was yet another good sign. 'Disbanding Dad's Army must mean that the government can see light at the end of the tunnel. But poor old Ernest won't know what to do with himself once it's stood down.'

They both knew that the Grange handyman was proud of his role as a corporal in the Home Guard, despite the fact that his coarse khaki uniform reeked of mothballs and the buckle, buttons and boots were all in need of a good polish.

'Watch out — cyclist ahead,' Bobbie warned.

Resisting the temptation to overtake on a bend, Viv braked. 'I can't believe I let you talk me into coming today,' she complained, her fingers drumming against the steering wheel.

'You talked yourself into it — remember?' Knowing that Viv had access to Olive's car for the day, Bobbie had cunningly asked her for a lift to the training yard. Viv had quickly acquiesced to dropping Bobbie off at the end of the lane, so long as she assured her there was no risk of running into Giles.

'Done!' Bobbie had agreed.

'I mean, he definitely won't want to talk to me, given that he didn't even want me to know where he was,' Viv had insisted. 'On the other hand, I want to be free to come and go as I please. So yes, I'll drive you there to prove it.'

'According to Ray, Giles is slowly but surely on the mend.' Once they'd overtaken the man on the bike, Bobbie recognized a landmark ahead: a tiny church on the crest of a hill surrounded by an ancient, over-grown churchyard. 'Almost there,' she said in a light, casual tone. 'Yes, Giles's ribs are improving bit by bit and his bruises are fading nicely.'

'La-la-la!' Viv sang to block out Bobbie's voice. 'Not interested. Don't care.' She slowed down again, this time for a couple of pheasants that rose from the overgrown verge then flew low across the road, their rich brown and green plumage glinting in the sun. After that the road was clear, and Viv picked up speed until Bobbie pointed to a straight, narrow lane with high hedges leading off to the left.

'This is it,' she said.

Viv slammed on the brakes and took the turn-ing with a screech of tyres. She scanned the rolling hills and smooth horizon. 'I don't see any training yard — or any house, for that matter.'

'They're hidden away in a dip. Why not come and take a look?'

Viv noticed in her overhead mirror that the man on the bicycle had taken the same turning. 'We've got company,' she remarked to Bobbie.

Bobbie glanced over her shoulder at the tall, thin figure in a tweed jacket, brown britches and flat cap. 'Oh yes, that's Philip Benson. He works for Ray part-time.'

'And this, I take it, is the famous yard.' Viv arrived at some double gates leading to a brick archway and a glimpse of stable doors beyond. A hundred yards further on, in a raised position, she spied a substantial old house overlooking a formal garden with overgrown shrubs and empty borders. 'What do you say I drop you right here?'

'How will you turn around?' Bobbie asked. 'You can't reverse all the way back down the lane. Wouldn't it be better to drive into the yard and drop me off there?'

Viv leaned out of her driver's window to wave the cyclist past. He acknowledged her courtesy with only a slight dip of the head. 'Thank you to you too,' she muttered sarcastically. 'Not a very friendly guy, is he?'

Bobbie shrugged. 'I don't know much about him except that when he's not working for Ray he works for the forestry people. Oh, and he's a Quaker. He believes in peace, not war.'

'Don't we all?' Viv frowned as she slowly made her way into the yard. 'I've read about these Peace Pledge people and I wasn't convinced. Who do they think will stand up to Hitler if they refuse?'

'Search me — you'd have to ask Philip. And I suppose forestry work is important in its own right.'

Viv and Bobbie were too preoccupied with the conscientious objector to notice other activity in the yard. As Philip propped his bike against the cart-shed wall and stooped to remove his bicycle clips, Ronnie came down from his lodgings above the stables. The head groom exchanged a few words with Philip then went back up the steps. Meanwhile, Ray led Never Say Die from a paddock into the yard. When he spotted Bobbie sitting next to Viv in Olive's car, he tethered the horse and ran to greet them.

'Look at you two all done up in your Sunday best!' he cried as he flung open Bobbie's door. 'How was

144

the wedding yesterday? Are Cameron and Mary truly hitched? Come on, both of you — come up to the house and have a drink.'

'Thanks, but I won't stop,' Viv told him hastily. 'I don't have time.'

Meanwhile, Ray called for Philip to join them. 'Of course you have time,' he contradicted. 'Bobbie, tell Viv to come up to the house. Philip, you're in charge of the yard today. Ronnie's got the flu.'

'Yes, sir, so I gathered.' Philip's light voice added to the impression of a clever, self-conscious type that Bobbie had observed the first time they met. The words emerged from lips that scarcely opened when he spoke but the effect was precise and respectful. 'Shall I muck out first then bring the rest of the horses in from the paddock? After that I can move on to tidying the tack room.'

'No, the weather's good so the horses can stay out longer this afternoon. Deal with the tack room first, please.'

'Yes, sir.' Philip, who had scarcely looked at Bobbie and Viv, walked away quickly.

He really is a bundle of fun. Though she was predisposed to dislike a man who refused to serve his country, for once Viv kept her opinion to herself. 'I really won't stop for that drink,' she told Ray, pressing the clutch and putting the car into reverse.

At that moment Giles emerged from the cart shed, wrapped up in a thick blue overcoat and fawn checked scarf. 'Am I the reason?' he asked with a hint of amusement.

Viv's foot slipped from the clutch. The car jerked and the engine cut out. *Don't dare smile at me!* She was furious with herself for stalling the engine and

145

with Giles for simply existing. 'Don't flatter yourself,' she replied as her cheeks burned bright red.

'So you're not avoiding me after all?'

'No, you got that all wrong,' Viv shot back. 'You're the one who's been doing the avoiding.'

'Mission accomplished.' Bobbie winked at Ray as they linked hands and left the yard. It had happened exactly as she'd hoped. She'd discussed it with Ray beforehand and Ray had promised to ensure that Giles would be around when Viv and Bobbie arrived. Now all they had to do was to leave the two of them to battle it out.

At a second attempt, Viv succeeded in finding reverse. *Of all the cheek — Giles smirking then trying to shove all the blame on to me!* She'd forgotten how infuriating the man could be. 'Step aside,' she warned as she swung the Ford towards the exit.

'Run me down, why don't you?' Unable to move quickly because of the injury to his ribs, the car bumper came within inches of his legs, causing him to stumble back against the wall.

'Oh my God!' Viv slammed on the brakes. 'Giles, are you OK? I didn't . . . I mean, I forgot . . . Oh, Jeez!'

A groggy Giles brushed himself down. 'No harm done,' he assured her as she jumped out of the car and rushed towards him. 'Honestly, I'm fine.'

'God, your face!' He was in quite a state, with lacerations to his forehead and blue and yellow bruising to his left cheek. 'Bobbie tried to convince me that you were on the mend.'

'She's right — I am. If you think this is bad, you should have seen me straight after the event.' Damn it; something happened to his heartbeat whenever Viv came near. She had the effect of making it race like

146

an express train so that steam practically came out of his ears.

'And your ribs?' she asked.

'Better, thanks.'

'I am so sorry.'

'For what? For almost running me over or for ignoring my party invitation and breaking my heart?' Though Bobbie had explained how Viv's reply had gone astray, he decided to tease her nevertheless.

Viv frowned suspiciously and stepped back. 'Same old Giles,' she muttered. 'Always kidding around.'

He followed her to the driver's door and held the handle to prevent her from getting in. 'Who says I'm kidding?'

'You don't have to — I can tell by the look on your face.' It was the curl of his top lip, the smile behind his grey eyes that did it. But Jeez, despite the injuries, Giles Parseval had classical good looks — symmetrical, straight features, a strong jawline, thick sandy hair . . . How bloody annoying that the guy was so stubborn and arrogant yet so downright handsome! 'Now, if you don't mind . . .'

But Giles refused to step aside. 'Aren't you going to ask how I got these cuts and bruises?'

'Don't tell me — you went ten rounds with Joe Louis.'

'Not quite.' Common sense was telling Giles to let Viv go on her way, but a rush of blood to his head battered such logic into submission. 'Guess again.'

'OK, a little bird tells me that you fought with your dad.'

Giles's raised eyebrows acknowledged this as fact. 'Did the same little bird say that I walked out of New-park, never to return?'

147

'Not exactly, no.' Viv was dubious. 'Surely it'll blow over; whatever 'it' was.'

'Not this time, I'm afraid.'

How serious was he now? she wondered. She did know one thing for sure: that he was standing with one arm pressed to his ribs and his breathing was fast and shallow. 'Oughtn't you to sit down?'

He nodded.

'Come on; get in the car.' Leading him carefully by his free arm, she eased him into the passenger seat then went and sat behind the wheel.

What now? Giles waited for Viv to take the lead.

'I do want to know what happened — but only if you cut out the jokes.' Did she really, though? Wouldn't it be better, clearer, easier just to keep her distance? In her mind she had a straightforward choice: put bluntly, it was between getting sucked back into the Parseval family mess or forgetting all about Giles and seeing out the war on the arm of debonair Brian Wheeler.

'You're sure?' Giles glimpsed the shadow of uncertainty in her expression.

'Yes, damn it!'

'Then drive.'

Almost without thinking she started the engine. 'Where to?'

'I don't care. Anywhere you like.'

★ ★ ★

From the house, Bobbie and Ray watched with satisfaction as Viv drove off with Giles.

'You enjoy playing Cupid, don't you?' With a wistful smile Ray pulled Bobbie away from the living-room window. The room was in its usual state, with even more crumpled newspapers than last time scattered across the leather sofas and empty glasses littering the low table in front of the fire.

'I want Viv to be happy,' Bobbie confessed.

'My impression is that she already is.' Whenever Ray crossed paths with the Canadian girl her mood seemed buoyant, her actions lively and impetuous.

Bobbie cleared a space on the sofa for them both. 'Don't let the good-time-girl act fool you. Deep down Viv is as mixed up about what she wants out of life as any of us.'

Ray sat down beside her, ready to tackle the big issue of his and Bobbie's future together. All week he'd been turning things over in his head: how long would this heady mutual attraction last and were Bobbie's feelings for him deep enough for her to give up her role with the ATA? It was an enormous ask, he knew.

'So what do *you* want out of life?' he asked now, sitting some distance away so that he could see her face clearly.

'I want *us* to be happy.'

'As simple as that?'

'Yes.' Only it wasn't at all simple — not after their last conversation. She felt a tension between them that hadn't existed before. 'Don't look at me like that,' she pleaded.

'Like what?'

'As though you're trying to read my mind.'

Ray bit his bottom lip. There was no point going over the ground they'd already covered so he quickly brought things to a head. 'What's it to be, Bobbie: me or the Air Transport Auxiliary?'

A flash of panic ran through her, swiftly followed by anger. 'Why does it have to be a choice?'

'You know why. I can't stand the not-knowing. It gnaws away at me and every day it gets worse, not better.' He felt a force within pushing him towards a steep precipice from which there was no backing away. Why, oh why, was he so lacking in resilience? What made him unable to put Bobbie's wishes above his own?

'I'm sorry to hear it.' She looked at him with tears in her eyes. 'In one way it would be easy for me to set your mind at ease and say yes, I'll give up flying. But my head is telling me otherwise.'

Her words pushed him to the brink. He glanced around the untidy room at the torn painting, the ashes in the grate, the empty glasses, which suddenly came to represent his inadequacy. Even the superficial things in life slipped from his control.

Bobbie sensed Ray's despair. 'Listen to me,' she pleaded. 'If I left the ATA before the job is done I would live the rest of my life knowing that I had let everyone down. People would look at me and see someone who didn't have the guts to stick it out to the end.'

'By 'people' I suppose you mean Hilary?'

'Yes, and Viv and Mary, and all the other Rixley pilots. Besides, you don't know how hard I fought to join the organization in the first place. My father was dead set against it — he only allowed me to train because I convinced him that it wasn't a direct-combat role. And now he and Mummy are so proud . . .'

As Ray watched the tears form and then spill down her cheeks, guilt and shame enveloped him. 'I'm sorry. Damn these jitters of mine — you'd think by now I'd have got over them.'

'Oh, my dear, dear man!' Though nothing was

resolved, instinctively Bobbie slid across the sofa then put her arms around his neck. 'Nothing is simple when all's said and done. I know full well what you've been through and I don't blame you for feeling the way you do. But if you can just hang on with things as they are for a few more months — weeks even?'

Ray let his head rest on her shoulder. He longed to stay in her arms for ever.

'You know that I love you,' she murmured through her tears. 'And I'll never stop loving you, whatever happens.'

★   ★   ★

Viv and Giles left the training yard without knowing where they were headed, only aware that fate might have been given a helping hand in the shape of Bobbie and Ray.

'How come you were there when Bobbie and I showed up?' Viv asked as they headed for open moorland. 'Ray press-ganged me into supervising the new lad — what's his name?'

'Philip.'

'Yes, the conchie. Apparently, Ronnie has a bad dose of the flu so Ray reckoned I could make myself useful by keeping an eye on the hired help. How about you — what brought you to Thresham?'

'Bobbie needed a lift.' It felt odd to be chatting normally, even smiling at the trick their friends had played. 'Actually, she's been nagging me for ages: why didn't I write to you or make a telephone call?'

'And why didn't you?'

'Too complicated.' Meaning the whole tangled mess surrounding Giles's divorce, not to mention

Anna Janicki's tragic suicide. Viv took a route that ran along a ridge separating two wide valleys, giving them a powerful feeling of being on top of the world under a blue sky and in a clear light that picked out every detail of some strange rock formations to either side of the road. 'So anyway, you were about to put me in the picture as far as the row with your dad goes.'

'Hold on to your hat — it's quite a ride,' he warned. 'One that ended up with me out on my backside. I won't go into the he-said, I-said rigmarole, but suffice it to say —'

'Wait — it's the he-said, you-said part that I'm interested in.'

Smoothed by centuries of rain and wind, mounds of weathered rock stood out starkly against the sky-line. They were surrounded by a sea of dark brown heather.

'Very well. I said that I was willing to give up all rights to Abbot's Gate if that meant the divorce came through straight away and Nora renounced any other claim. Father refused. I'm afraid it came to blows.'

'Between the two of you?' Viv found it impossible to imagine stern and dignified Sir Thomas scrapping it out with his son.

'Hardly. He pays people to do that sort of thing for him.'

'Jeez!' Viv's eyebrows shot up.

'Exactly — as you so eloquently say: Jeez! Of course, I have no firm proof, but what happened the day after the argument was more than coincidence.' Giles hesitated. Viv would be the first person to whom he'd talked openly about this and he couldn't be sure what she would do with the information.

'So what did happen?' She shuddered as she

152

imagined a dark alleyway where men lay in wait, followed by the sounds of punching and kicking, of ribs cracking.

'You'll keep this close to your chest?'

'I won't tell a soul,' she promised.

'Well then, there's a disused stable block behind the house at Newpark where we keep the cars and tractors. I had the bonnet of my Austin up and was tinkering with the spark plugs. Somehow a handbrake was released on one of the tractors — I didn't see by whom. It rolled forward down a ramp. My back was turned and suddenly I found myself pinned to a wall, unable to move.'

With a sharp intake of breath, Viv steered the car on to the grass verge where she parked then stared at Giles in horror. 'For Christ's sake, you could have been killed!'

'Yes — I'm afraid things got a little out of hand.'

'Seriously! But even if it was only meant as a warning, it was a damned risky way of going about it.'

'You know my father,' he said quietly. 'He doesn't do anything by halves.'

'Why aren't you angry?' she demanded.

'I am.' Giles stared at one of the smooth, whale-shaped boulders.

'You don't sound it.'

'Or rather, I was. Now there's no point in feeling angry or anything else, for that matter. What's done is done.'

'Who found you?' Viv reverted to the scene of the so-called accident, picturing Giles pinned against the wall and calling out for help.

'My mother's driver — a new man called Dexter.' Giles chose his next words with care. 'He happened to be in the stable yard at the time. Luckily he's a strong chap who could shift the tractor just enough for me to slide clear.'

'Don't say another word.' She put her hands over her ears. 'Let me get this straight — your mother's driver 'happened to be' on the scene. You're saying that your mother was in on this?'

He shook his head. 'No. My father's the one who employs Dexter and you know what they say: he who pays the piper . . .'

'But did she stick up for you during the row about the divorce?'

There was a long pause. 'You also know my mother,' he said more quietly than before. 'To cut a long story short, after the accident I spent three days in hospital with a punctured lung but as soon as they agreed to discharge me I returned to my home sweet home . . .'

'Don't,' she begged. 'We agreed: no jokes.'

'. . . where I packed a suitcase, left a forwarding address and drove up to Thresham. Shortly afterwards I received a telegram from my father informing me that I was, under no circumstances, ever to return to Newpark. I was to be written out of the will and would be obliged to pay for my divorce without his assistance. I was on no account to try to contact my mother.'

'That's downright vicious,' Viv muttered.

'My father's priorities have always been questionable,' he reminded her.

'Damned right.' Sir Thomas's conduct during the Anna Janicki scandal had been utterly ruthless. 'I say again — why aren't you mad as hell? If I were you, I'd want to get even.'

'But you're not me.'

'OK, I'm sorry.' Suddenly contrite, she put a hand on his arm. 'Is it really true? Did your old man cut you off completely?'

'Without a penny,' Giles confirmed. Viv might as well understand where he'd ended up, even if it had the effect of making her run a mile. 'No money, no means of earning any, nowhere to live.'

'So what will you do?'

'I won't stay at Thresham longer than I'm obliged — it wouldn't be fair. Anyway, Ray and I would drink ourselves into an early grave if I did. So perhaps I'll put myself forward for the army or the RAF if they'll have me. Not the navy, though; I'm seasick at the very idea.'

'You can't do that.'

'Why not? I'm not over the hill at thirty, am I?'

'But I don't want you to.' Viv tightened her grip on his arm.

'Honestly?' Giles studied her face. 'I didn't think you cared.'

'But I do,' she said softly. 'There; that's God's honest truth — I care about you, Giles Parseval, so please think twice about going off and getting yourself killed.'

11

'You will be all right?' Cameron sat behind the wheel of his car, forcing himself to speak. He'd parked next to Hilary in the stable yard at the Grange, dreading the moment when Mary would step out.

'Yes,' she answered in a faint whisper. They'd scarcely talked since the drive back from North-gate, each clinging to precious moments from the previous twenty-four hours — the scratch of the pen nib on their marriage certificate, happy faces of friends around the table at Spa Gardens, shy smiles exchanged as they'd entered the bridal suite at the Regal Hotel.

'Will this do?' Cameron had been concerned about the heavy, high-Victorian style of furniture and faded curtains; it seemed nothing had been altered since the Regal had been built fifty years earlier.

Mary had scarcely noticed her surroundings. All that had mattered was that she was now Mrs Ainslie. 'Everything is absolutely as it should be,' she'd murmured. 'It's perfect.'

And the night had been just that — every minute, every second. They'd closed the door on the world and made tender love. They'd woken before dawn and loved again in the warm, white nest of the four-poster bed, surrounded by shadows cast by the lamp on the bedside cabinet.

Then daylight had crept into the room and with it the realization that Mary and Cameron's brief honeymoon was coming to an end. She'd sighed as she'd watched him put on his flight lieutenant's

156

uniform (*so handsome*) and the sight of Mary sitting at the dressing table brushing her soft brown hair had moved him almost to tears.

'I won't cry if you don't,' she'd bargained as she'd battled to control her emotions.

And this was how they'd managed as they'd packed their bags and walked along the wide corridor, taken the antiquated lift down to reception and accepted the congratulations of an elderly porter who'd carried Cameron's kitbag to their car.

'Did you remember to give him a tip?' Mary had asked as they'd driven off.

'Two bob,' Cameron had confirmed. 'Was it too much?' he'd asked in response to her look of astonishment. 'I could always go back and ask for some change.'

He'd made her laugh and it was a sound that he would carry with him in the days ahead — the laughter of Mary Ainslie; *his* Mary!

Her heart had been sore during the drive, so full of conflicting feelings that she feared it might burst. She'd stared straight ahead without seeing, imprinting on her memory the way Cameron spoke — the exact timbre of his voice when he said 'Will this do?' or 'Was it too much?': ordinary words but packed with significance — accompanied by that endearing look, that intimacy, which he shared with no one else on earth.

And now they sat in the stable yard, trying in vain to hold back time.

'You will be all right.' Cameron repeated the sentence; this time it was not a question. 'We both will. Dearest, we'll be together and we'll be happy. You do believe me, don't you?'

157

Mary basked in the certainty in his eyes. 'Yes,' she murmured. If she had faith in anything in this dark world it was in the promises that her new husband made. 'You'll telephone me as soon as you arrive at your new billet?'

'I will.' Cameron was headed for RAF Worming-ford, six miles north of Colchester. It was a large airfield that was home to almost three thousand British and American personnel, and his main job would be to attack weapon-launching sites near the Pas-de-Calais as well as to escort Allied bombers to German industrial sites. Both were risky endeavours that would involve low-level flying in the face of heavy ground fire, but he'd taken care to conceal this from Mary. 'And you'll keep me up to date with events here?'

'I will,' she echoed.

'Let me know if you hear more news of your brother, Tom.'

She nodded.

'There is hope, you know.'

'Yes.'

'He'll probably sit out the rest of the war safe and sound in a German POW camp.'

'Yes,' she said even more faintly. Seconds ticked by; each one a torment. It was almost noon. A light rain began to fall.

'It's time for me to go.'

Mary swallowed hard. 'Telephone me.'

'Every day.'

His voice, his face, his certainty — these things would carry her through the coming weeks. 'I love you,' she said. She kissed him softly on the lips then got out of the car.

'I love you too, Mary.'

158

She saw her new husband mouth the words through the rain-spattered windscreen. Then he started the car and she rushed up the steps and out of sight so that she didn't have to watch him drive away.

★ ★ ★

A glance at Mary as she dashed up the bomb-damaged staircase told Peggy that Cameron and Mary had said their goodbyes and that it had been a difficult parting. The girl's head was bowed to hide her tear-stained cheeks and when she saw that she was observed she averted her face.

Peggy stood aside to let Mary pass. She would have refrained from speaking except that Mary stumbled on the top step and Peggy put out a hand to steady her.

Mary grasped the banister, unable to speak.

'Come,' Peggy urged. 'Dry your tears. Be brave.' *Poor child.* Taking a handkerchief from her pocket, she offered it to Mary.

'I might never see him again.' Words poured out after weeks of pent-up anguish. 'I love him so much; I couldn't bear it if . . .'

'Yes, my dear; you could.' Peggy put an arm around Mary's shoulder and led her along the corridor. 'One thinks one can't but if the worst were to happen, you would find the strength to carry on.'

Mary sobbed uncontrollably. 'I can't help it — I'm sorry.'

'It hurts to say goodbye.'

'Essex is so far away.' Gradually Cameron's words of comfort — *You will be all right* — floated to the surface. She must stop crying and pull herself together to show Peggy that she could cope. She broke free

159

then opened the door to her room. 'Thank you,' she mumbled through her tears.

'That's right; chin up.' Peggy watched Mary square her shoulders and raise her head. 'Hope for the best, my dear; it's the only way.'

For the first time, Mary looked her helper in the eye and was surprised by what she saw. Peggy's stern features had softened and her cheeks were flushed with emotion.

'You're right,' Mary said with a sigh. 'Hope for the best.'

'And perhaps fix your mind on practical affairs.' After Keith, Peggy had found solace in mundane tasks — maintaining order amidst the chaos of loss by tidying the kitchen, washing one's hair and above all by preparing for Rosie's birth. She'd gathered items for a layette. Peggy's mother in Northgate knew what would be needed: baby linen and blankets, a cradle, tiny knitted jackets (her mother again), terry towelling nappies; things that Peggy had so far taken little interest in.

'Come home,' her mother Marjorie had urged immediately after Keith's death. Home to Westville Avenue, to comfort and ease.

'Go home,' Pauline Gower had insisted. 'Be kind to yourself for once, my dear Peggy. Hatfield will manage without you.'

So she went to Northgate for Rosie's birth (a long and complicated labour in a top-class nursing home) and stayed with her parents during the weeks that followed. She doted on her beautiful baby with her dark curls and tiny, perfect fingers and toes. The ache of loss had eased and Peggy had declared herself fit to return to ATA duties — not at Hatfield HQ but

160

at nearby Rixley ferry pool. It was agreed that Rosie would remain with Marjorie. As a matter of fact, Peggy had been about to set out for Northgate when she'd come across Mary in distress.

'Get back to flying as soon as you're able,' she advised gently.

'I will. I'm back on the rota, starting tomorrow,' Mary informed her.

Peggy nodded. 'Good. We pilots are essential here — every single one of us.'

Mary thought of the Hurricanes, Tempests and Spitfires hidden away inside Rixley's two enormous hangars. She pictured Stan, Gordon and the rest of the ground crew crawling over them even now, spanners and wrenches to hand. Tomorrow morning she would put on her Sidcot suit then gather with her fellow pilots in the canteen and wait for the Tannoy announcement — 'Will all pilots please report . . .'

'I'll be ready,' she promised with fresh determination.

'Very well.' Satisfied, Peggy backed away. 'Will I see you at breakfast tomorrow?'

'Most definitely.' Back to business, papering over the cracks and putting on a brave face.

Mary braced herself for action as she closed the door and heard it click. She had two shirts to wash, shoes to polish, a button to re-sew on to the waistband of her trousers.

Meanwhile, Peggy hurried along the corridor and down the stairs. She imagined Rosie asleep in her cot, her grandmother dancing attendance. The sweet smell of soap and talcum powder awaited her; long eyelashes curling on to rosy cheeks, the softness of her baby's skin.

* * *

What next? When all was said and done, Bobbie still couldn't be sure how Ray would deal with her decision to continue with her role in the ATA.

He'd pleaded long and hard. Couldn't she transfer to non-flying duties? Surely she'd prove as useful in the met office or the ops room as she was in the air?

Bobbie had listened and reasoned, explaining that her training and flying experience were vital cogs in a machine dedicated to the defeat of Hitler.

Then why couldn't she take up a training role in Hatfield or White Waltham, where she would capitalize on all that acquired knowledge? He wouldn't mind being separated from her for a time, as long as she stayed firmly on the ground.

'They're winding down the training programme, that's why not. Look at Peggy Ibbotson.' Bobbie had pointed out that even someone with Peggy's vast experience was no longer needed in a training role. No, the absolute priority was to ferry as many fighter planes and bombers as humanly possible to the south coast and across the Channel to Calais, where the crates would be on standby for a final assault.

Round and round in circles Bobbie and Ray had gone, moving from the house to the training yard, where they'd helped Philip to muck out the stables then bring in the horses until eventually they'd run out of things to say.

'You know how I feel,' Ray muttered after all the horses were safely stabled for the night.

Glasgow Girl reached out over the door to nudge Bobbie's arm with the soft tip of her nose.

'I have no treats to give you,' Bobbie told the gen-

162

tle-natured thoroughbred. She turned her pockets inside out to demonstrate, mindful of the gathering dusk and a light rain that had begun to fall. 'But you do understand?' she asked Ray.

'I do.' Deep down he knew he was in the wrong and it was a miserable state of mind to be left in. But what was the use of saying sorry yet again? So instead he gave a final, defeated shrug.

Bobbie, too, realized that they'd reached a dead end, leaving them with a choice between reversing out and beginning the arguments all over again or one of them doing a complete U-turn, a manoeuvre that for now seemed impossible. 'Please don't hold it against me,' she said quietly.

'How can I?' Standing in the damp yard under a darkening sky, Ray felt his spirits tumble to rock bottom. 'Is it all right for me to ask Philip to drive you home?' he asked brusquely. 'I'd do it myself but I have a list of things to get through.'

Bobbie winced then gave a brief nod. 'Of course. I wonder what happened to Viv and Giles.'

'They could be anywhere, knowing them.' Ray beckoned the junior groom. 'You know the way to Rixley?' he enquired as he offered him the key to the MG.

'Yes, sir.' Philip took the keys with studied indifference then waited for further instructions. He noticed the bad atmosphere between his boss and the visitor.

'First Officer Fraser needs a lift. You can keep the car overnight — I shan't be needing it.' In an effort to disguise his bitter disappointment, Ray grew increasingly offhand. 'You know where I am,' he told Bobbie.

Then he was gone, striding out of the yard towards the house, head down and hands thrust deep in his

163

trouser pockets.

'All set?' Philip opened the passenger door of the MG. He showed no curiosity about what, if anything, had gone on between the two of them.

'As I'll ever be.' After giving Glasgow Girl a farewell pat, Bobbie got into the car, feeling as if all the life had been drained out of her. Who knew — perhaps this might turn out to be her last visit to Thresham?

'I know of a quiet back road to Rixley,' Philip mentioned as he pulled out of the yard. 'It's a short cut around the back of the reservoir.'

'That's fine.' Whichever, whatever — Bobbie really didn't care.

They drove in silence past the church on the hill before Philip took a sharp turn left along a meandering, single-track lane. By this time it was raining heavily, causing the windscreen wiper to work overtime.

Bobbie glanced at her watch. 'What time were you due to finish work?' she asked above the swish and squeak of the wiper.

'Ten minutes ago,' he replied in his usual guarded tone.

'Oh dear — I'm sorry.'

'It can't be helped.' Driving Bobbie home would mean that Philip would miss the evening gathering at the Friends' Meeting House in Highcliff.

Bobbie decided that by striking up a conversation with the unconventional stranger she might divert herself from the painful problem of Ray. 'How are you enjoying your work on the yard?' she asked as the car crested a hill and Rixley reservoir hove into view — a flat, grey sheet of water set in wooded countryside some five miles distant.

'I like it well enough.'

'Have you worked with horses before?'

'No, never.'

'So it must take some getting used to?'

'Not really. The trick is to stay calm and not do anything in a rush.'

'I agree.' Horses did pick up on a person's mood and they especially sensed if you were afraid of them. 'I've been around them all my life.' A sudden pang of homesickness pierced her at the thought of her own dear North Star at home in the Highlands, unridden since her departure.

'I find it works well as a general principle for living, too.' Patience and fortitude were bywords in Philip's community of a dozen or so Friends. Both qualities were sorely tested during wartime.

Bobbie's brow creased into a thoughtful frown.

Philip had a strong, self-assured presence; everything he said seemed succinct and well considered. 'So you never lose your temper?' she queried.

'If I do, I try not to show it.' He drove in the way that he spoke — with care and confidence, scarcely reacting when an approaching car forced him off the narrow lane on to the grass verge. 'I've been taught to forgive my enemies,' he explained.

'That's all very well, but it must be hard at times.'

He glanced sideways at her. 'You mean while there's a war on?'

'Exactly. What I want to know is: how can you forgive men like Hitler and Goering?'

Philip thought before he answered. 'If I can't forgive, then it's important to offer the other cheek.'

'And let them walk all over us!' Bobbie was incredulous. 'That's what would have happened if Mr

Churchill hadn't taken charge. First Poland, then France, Italy and the whole of Europe.'

Again there was silence.

'What do you say to that?' she demanded with unusual vehemence.

'I say that I stick by my right to refuse military service. It's a question of conscience; I believe in freedom of thought.' The measured answer was not intended to inflame. 'I do my bit as a civilian for the Forestry Unit, like most people who join the Peace Pledge Union.'

'And what does that involve?' She tapped her fingers against her thigh, resolved to bring her emotions back in check. Rain drummed on the canvas roof of the convertible and its wheels splashed through deep puddles, sending up waves of spray to either side.

'We plant trees, for a start. We clear undergrowth and cut bracken under the supervision of the Home Guard. At this time of year there's less to do; that's why I'm lending a hand at Thresham.'

'Pacifists like you come in for a lot of stick,' Bobbie observed.

He nodded. 'If I didn't do the forestry work I'd face a court martial and probably prison.'

'No, I meant that other people must make it hard.'

'You could say that.' Philip thought for a while. 'Here's an example: only yesterday I was there when Wilf Cranston, a new lad in our community, was refused chocolate by our local shopkeeper even though he had the coupons. That's the sort of everyday thing.' What he left out was the shopkeeper's verbal blast when he'd accused Wilf of being a shirker and a coward, ending with the prize insult: 'I know what I'd do with you, you little bugger; I'd put you in front of a

166

firing squad without batting an eyelid — that's what I'd do.'

'We have to accept that everyone's different,' Bobbie conceded. 'But I believe with all my heart in what I do — ferrying crates for the ATA. As a matter of fact, it's caused a recent falling-out between me and Ray.'

Philip acknowledged her confession with a nod but chose not to pry further.

'I do try not to judge others.'

'You did, though — just then, when you questioned me over Hitler.'

Bobbie blushed. 'Did I? Yes, I suppose I did.'

'Don't worry; you're not the first and you won't be the last. In any case, I've enjoyed talking to you.' It was true: Philip had appreciated Bobbie's lively questions and was by no means blind to her good looks. What red-blooded male could be? Her pretty face constantly changed expression as she talked, flitting from disbelief to thoughtfulness in the blink of an eye. Besides, there was an innocence about her that he found intriguing.

They soon reached the reservoir and took a road that followed its eastern edge. They had a rain-soaked view through the bare trees of the man-made dam and pumping station before they climbed a steep hill to Rixley village. Shortly after that they turned through the front gates of Burton Grange.

Philip's first view of the bomb-blasted manor house took him by surprise. 'When did this happen?' he asked as he took in sections of toppled masonry and missing roof.

'Over a year ago. Jerry destroyed an entire wing that was in use as a convalescent home. The ATA got off lightly by comparison.'

'What was the real target? The ferry pool?'

'Either that or the reservoir; no one's sure.' Bobbie preferred not to look back to that awful time. She asked Philip to pull up in the stable yard then swiftly got out of the car. 'Thank you and I'm sorry to have put you out,' she said.

'Not at all.' He returned her friendly smile. 'The rain's coming down like stair rods. Hurry up inside before you get soaked.'

'I already am.' She laughed as the cold rain trickled down her face. 'Thanks again.'

'Go!' Philip urged.

He sat and watched her as she ran, still laughing, up the steps then disappeared. Would he see her again at Thresham? he wondered. Perhaps not, if Ray's earlier brusqueness was anything to go by. Either way, he would remember First Officer Fraser as a brave, bright spark of life; the type you didn't often come across in a divided, war-weary world.

★ ★ ★

Viv had driven Giles as far as Highcliff, where the land ended and the sea took over.

'Where to now?' she asked.

Giles looked out across the harbour of the busy fishing port at trawlers at anchor and at rowing boats bobbing in the choppy water. Heavy rain partly obscured the view, blown in by ominous black clouds. 'There's nowhere to go — you've already brought me to the ends of the earth.'

'Honey, this is one dismal little corner of a big, exciting world,' she contradicted. 'And I should know; I've lived in California, where the sun shines seven days a week.'

'And the streets are paved with gold?'

'No, but the sky is filled with galaxies of new stars — of the Hollywood variety. Clark Gable, Humphrey Bogart, Fred Astaire — give me a name and I've probably seen him in the flesh. Why, I was once a stunt pilot in a movie starring Gable, the King of Hollywood.'

'And look at you now — cooped up in a borrowed car next to a washed-up member of the English gentry without a penny to his name.'

'Boohoo!' Viv struggled to maintain the flippant tone. 'Washed-up and with a hulking great chip on his shoulder. How attractive is that!'

'I have no idea. How attractive is it?' The swelling waves and the roar they made as they smashed against the jetty made him uneasy, bringing home his own powerlessness. 'Not very, I should imagine.'

Viv gave him a sharp look. 'What now — are you fishing for more compliments? I've already said that I'm fond of you — most likely a big mistake on my part.'

'Fond isn't my favourite word in this context. You can be fond of an elderly aunt or a pet dachshund.'

'Are they the funny little ones with the short legs?'

'Viv . . .' Giles interrupted then stopped abruptly.

'What?' She picked up on the effort he'd been making. His face was pale and the strain showed in his creased brow.

'I'm tired. Can we please go back?'

'To Thresham? Yes, sure.' Reversing away from the water's edge, she managed to avoid stacks of lobster pots and other paraphernalia as she turned the car then stayed in bottom gear as they ascended a steep hill lined with small workers' cottages. Soon the sound of the waves receded, replaced by rain hammering down on the roof. 'I'm sorry if I've worn you out with my nonsense,' she said.

'Not at all; you've been your usual entertaining self.' Exhaustion crushed him to the point where he could barely speak.

'Anyway, take it easy. I'll have you back to Ray's place before you know it.' On reflection, Viv was pleased to have been set up by Bobbie. She felt that the air had been cleared, even though Giles insisted on keeping up certain pretences. 'I'm glad we're friends again,' she told him. Glancing in his direction, she saw that his eyes were closed and his head rested back against the seat. *Damned fine profile*, she thought. *Exactly the right proportions with that straight nose and high forehead*. A girl could fall for that profile alone if she weren't careful.

'I didn't hold out much hope of it happening,' he admitted without opening his eyes. He felt the car sway around bends and heard the engine work hard as they rose up another steep hill. 'I was convinced that I'd wrecked my chances with you over poor Anna.'

Whoa! Viv's heart gave a lurch at the sudden switch of mood. *Confession time!*

'Looking back, I realize there were things I could have done differently. I knew what my father had been up to and I hated the fact that he refused to take responsibility. Yet I let him pack Anna off to Rixley after the baby was born.'

'Dorota,' Viv interrupted. 'Anna's baby's name is Dorota. And Jean and Douglas have vowed to give her a wonderful life, just as Anna wished.'

'They're good people,' he said wearily.

'The best.' Was that it? Was Giles through with the serious stuff? But no.

'I'm in your debt,' he continued doggedly. 'You kept your promise not to drag Dad into it. I appreciate that.'

'Your name's been mud as a result,' she reminded him bluntly. 'Anyhow, I didn't do it for Sir Thomas's sake. And not for yours, either. It was your mother I was protecting.'

'Me too.'

'So it's a pity she didn't take your side during this latest spat.'

'Spat' didn't cover it. Strange that he should quibble in his head over the meaning of a word when what he really wanted to do was to get to the heart of what he was feeling. 'Mother never goes against my father,' he reminded Viv. 'She knows it doesn't pay.'

Viv saw that they'd reached the church on the hill close to Thresham. 'Seriously, Giles; what will you do now?' she wanted to know.

He opened his eyes slowly. 'Good question.'

'I mean it. Listen, the Ministry of Food must be crying out for people with your experience of land management. Why not approach them?'

'Thank you for that vote of confidence,' he said with a short, sharp laugh.

'Giles, you are infuriating!'

'Thank you.'

Approaching the training yard, Viv prepared herself for a brief, indecisive farewell. *Adios, au revoir, adieu.*

Giles eased himself forward, ready to step out into the rain. But instead of opening the door he leaned sideways and kissed Viv on the cheek. 'Sorry — spur

171

of the moment,' he muttered.

Viv felt the brush of his lips against her skin. She leaned into him and kissed him back — lightly on the lips. 'Don't be sorry,' she whispered.

There was a moment when time stood still and neither knew what to do. Then Giles got out of the car. He turned up his collar and hurried towards the house.

'Whoa!' Viv said out loud as she turned the car around. 'Did that really happen?'

'Ray!' Giles opened the front door and called from the entrance hall. He took off his wet coat and hat. 'Where are you?'

Perhaps his friend was relaxing in the lounge in front of a nice warm fire. 'Ray, old chap — I have some surprising news.'

Giles opened the door to complete disarray. Ray had flung his jacket on the floor and kicked off his shoes into the hearth. Smoke billowed out from the blocked flue and Ray himself lay spreadeagled and senseless on one of the settees.

'For Christ's sake!' Giles tried to shake Ray awake then wrenched an empty whisky bottle from his grasp. 'Wake up, man!'

Ray groaned. With eyes still closed, he rolled and fell clean off the settee. He stayed motionless on the floor.

'God, what a stinking, awful state!' Giles retrieved Ray's jacket and flung it over him as a blanket then he opened the flue. 'You can stay there until you come to your senses,' he decided. 'And don't look to me for sympathy when you wake up with a filthy rotten head. You'll only have yourself to blame.'

12

'Here, this will cheer you lot up.' Viv bounced into the officers' mess at the Grange and thrust a magazine at Mary, who was sitting with Bobbie and Jean in the bay window. 'There's an article in there about the duo we've booked for our Christmas party.'

Mary glanced at a glossy photograph of an exceptionally good-looking couple in evening dress. A caption underneath read, *Dolores May and Leonard Fraser, the ENSA stars pictured after their recent return from a triumphant tour of the Far East.*

'What makes you think we need cheering up?' Jean asked. She'd arrived full of news from Fern Cottage about Dorota's latest exploits and had been in the middle of relating how the baby had pulled Patch's tail for one thing, and for another, she'd crawled into the cupboard under the stairs then refused to come out.

'It says here that Dolores is sweet sixteen,' Mary read from the article. 'They say she has the voice of an angel; that she could well be the new Vera Lynn.'

'Lucky us.' Bobbie did her best to pull herself out of the doldrums she'd been in since her last visit to Thresham. 'If the rest of the band is anywhere near as good as these two we're in for a whale of a time.'

'But we haven't given any thought to how we'll smarten the place up,' Viv realized. 'Where will we get our Christmas decorations from, for a start?'

'We'll make them ourselves,' Jean and Mary replied as one.

'We can collect holly from the woods for a big Christmas wreath,' Jean added.

'And hang some mistletoe,' Bobbie suggested. 'And no one will notice if we cut down one teeny-weeny spruce tree in Burton Wood, will they?'

'I'll pretend I never heard that,' Ernest grumbled as he shuffled by clutching a pint of beer.

'Have the Parsevals left any tinsel and tree decorations in storage anywhere?' Viv wondered.

'That's a thought!' Mary jumped up with a gleeful grin. 'Come with me.'

Viv followed her out of the house and along the terrace, across the stable yard then up some stone steps to the old grooms' loft, which was full of lumber from a previous era.

Mary headed straight for a large cardboard box in a far corner of the dusty room. 'Look what I came across one day when I was rummaging around.' She opened the box to show Viv a tangle of silver tinsel. 'I thought nothing of it at the time.'

Viv knelt and sorted through the box's contents. She found dozens of shiny baubles and some electric fairy lights hidden beneath the tinsel. 'Some of these glass balls have shattered but most are OK,' she reported.

With satisfied grins, Viv and Mary carried the box back to the house and into the mess.

'Abracadabra!' Viv announced as she delved deep then held up a cluster of tree decorations.

Jean and Bobbie gave exclamations of delight. Within seconds all four girls were involved in disentangling coloured lights and rescuing the delicate baubles.

'Small things occupy small minds,' Hilary muttered

174

dismissively as he observed the excited goings-on. He sat at the bar with Peggy, looking as if he carried the weight of the world on his shoulders.

'Don't be too hard on them,' Peggy advised. She'd always liked Hilary — going back to the time when he and Keith had gone to RAF training school together — but she had to admit that at times he lived up to his curmudgeonly reputation. After all, as commander of the ferry pool it was his responsibility to look after morale.

Hilary knocked back his whisky. 'You've changed your tune.'

'Have I? Yes, I suppose I have.' Since getting to know the Rixley Atta girls a little better, Peggy had begun to see them as individuals with all their quirks and differences. In particular, she favoured Mary, who, with her doggedness and quiet resilience, represented all the best qualities of the ATA. 'I've been thinking about the Christmas celebrations,' she continued. 'I'm afraid I was rather a sourpuss when we first discussed it.'

'About the Aireby contingent? Yes.' Hilary recalled the awkward conversation.

'Well, I'm glad you ignored my advice. As long as Flight Lieutenant Wheeler consents, I believe it will do everyone good to celebrate the festive season together.'

'And consent he does,' Hilary confirmed. In fact, Wheeler had responded with surprising alacrity to the formal invitation for his men to attend.

'Not that we should ignore the ongoing risk to each and every ferry pool across the land.' Peggy tempered her endorsement with a strong dose of caution. She turned her back on Viv and the small group of exuberant girls and spoke confidentially. 'You've no doubt heard from HQ about the recent raid on Hatfield and nearby Colchester. No casualties, thank heavens, but it means we must all be on our guard.'

'Essex is right in the thick of things,' Hilary reminded her, failing to notice that Mary had come to the bar to order more drinks. 'More than we are here, at any rate.'

Overhearing the name Essex, Mary immediately tuned in.

'Jerry carries out bombing raids there on a nightly basis — he knows that if he knocks out RAF Wormingford he disables the entire 343 Squadron, not to mention . . .'

Instant fear clutched at Mary and shook her slender frame. She gasped then turned away from the bar.

Peggy noticed her reaction. 'Hush!' she warned Hilary, but it was too late.

Mary fled from the room in blind terror.

'What?' Slow to respond, Hilary turned round on his stool in time to see the door swing shut behind Mary. 'Oh Lord,' he groaned.

'I'll go after her,' Peggy decided. She followed speedily and caught up with Mary as she ran upstairs.

She laid a hand on her arm and forced her to slow down. 'Wait a moment, please.'

Mary seemed hardly aware of her surroundings. Essex, and Wormingford in particular, were said to be prime targets — the realization filled her with dread.

'You've heard from Cameron?' Peggy enquired calmly. When Mary nodded she guided her along the landing. 'That's good. All is well?'

'I've spoken to him every day since he left,' Mary confided.

176

'His billet is comfortable?'

'Yes, as far as I know. He's not allowed to go into detail.'

'Obviously not.' Careless talk cost lives — the propaganda message intended to safeguard national security had been drummed into every citizen since the start of the war. 'He's well, though?'

'He says he is.' Mary felt the terror recede and along with it the breathlessness that she'd experienced.

'Well then.' Peggy noticed colour returning to Mary's cheeks. 'Why not go back down and help your friends to get ready for Christmas? It will do you good.'

Mary swallowed hard. 'Yes, I will. Thank you.' She gathered herself then turned around.

'You're very welcome.' It was hard, so *very* hard, for a recently married girl to carry the burden of knowledge that Mary did — after all, she was a young woman who flew unarmed crates from A to B on a daily basis, who had been unlucky enough to be on the receiving end of ack-ack fire and to witness aerial attacks in person. Peggy knew only too well the perils of flying these expensive and vital pieces of military equipment. She sighed then retreated to her room.

'Mary, there you are.' Bobbie greeted her friend's return to the mess with a bright smile. Tree decorations had been laid out neatly on a low table and she, Jean and Viv had been making further plans. 'Jean has earmarked a tree for us growing close to Fern Cottage — a spruce tree that's just the right height, with nice even branches. She's promised to show it to us tomorrow morning during our walk to the ferry pool.'

'And you're just in time to help us choose our song,' Viv declared as she made a space for Mary to sit beside her. 'We've decided to provide some of the entertainment ourselves. How's your singing voice, Mary? What's your favourite song?'

* * *

Early on a bright, frosty morning in the first week of December the Christmas tree was chosen.

It was pointed out by Jean who carried Dorota, all wrapped up in coat, knitted bonnet and mittens, and declared to be perfect by Bobbie, Viv and Mary.

They said a cheerful goodbye to Jean and Dorota then hurried on through the wood, remarking on tracks made by foxes across a clearing covered by a sprinkling of snow and wading through deeper drifts in their thick, fur-lined boots. Arriving at the ferry pool, they made straight for the canteen, convinced that take-off would be delayed for at least an hour because of the snowy conditions.

Viv stopped at the entrance to kick lumps of the white stuff from the soles of her boots. 'Bobbie, Mary and I are agreed,' she announced as she entered the noisy room. ' 'Swinging on a Star' will be our party piece at the Christmas concert. Clear a space, everyone — we're about to launch into our first rehearsal.'

'That's the first I've heard of it,' Horace grumbled to Stan as Viv organized the pushing aside of tables and chairs. 'Aren't we supposed to have a proper band?'

'According to reports, yes, we are.' Stan decided not to complain — if the girls wanted to sing, he for one was in favour.

'I've never even heard of 'Swinging on a Star',' Olive chipped in. 'Who sings it?'

'You've never heard of the most famous song of the summer?' Viv mocked the ATA driver's ignorance. 'It's only sung by Bing Crosby in *Going My Way*. Surely everyone knows that.'

' 'Sung' is pushing it a bit.' Gordon had sat through the film at the cinema in Highcliff and reckoned that Crosby's voice wasn't up to much. 'Groaning, more like.'

From the queue at the counter there was a wide range of opinion — from 'I like that tune — it's nice and catchy' to 'It's not a patch on 'White Christmas' '.

'It's a happy song,' Bobbie insisted once the space was cleared. 'And, come to think of it, it's appropriate for us Atta girls because we reach for those stars every time we climb into a Spitfire. Everyone join in the chorus if you know it.'

'What have I let myself in for?' Mary muttered under her breath to no one in particular.

Viv, meanwhile, stepped up on to a chair and asked for quiet. 'In the movie Bing plays the role of a priest. The song is all about bettering yourself, not being happy with accepting things as they are. According to him, we should all aim to be swinging on a star.'

'Hip, hip, bloomin' hooray!' a cynic called out. 'That's all very well for a man with a million dollars in the bank.'

'Ignore him.' Bobbie followed Viv's lead by climbing on to the chair next to her. 'Come on up here, Mrs Ainslie — you have a lovely voice, you can lead us.'

In for a penny . . . Mary reluctantly mounted a third chair and cleared her throat.

'Get a move on,' someone called.

There was a hush; knives and forks stopped scraping plates and cups remained in their saucers as Mary began. When she closed her eyes the tune and lyrics came naturally to her, as did the sentiment behind the song. No one should hate going to school. With education, a person could become whatever they wanted; they might all end up carrying moonbeams home in a jar if they tried hard enough.

Lost in the song, she failed to notice the circle of attentive faces. It was only when Viv and Bobbie joined her in the chorus that she opened her eyes and paid attention to her surroundings.

Stan stared at her with rapt attention while Gordon tapped his feet and nodded encouragement. Even Horace and Olive smiled. After two more verses Mary had everyone on her side.

'Blooming marvellous!' came the cry at the end of the final chorus. 'Well done, Mary. Bravo, Viv and Bobbie.'

Bobbie jumped down from her chair. 'We'll be even better on the night,' she promised.

'We'll have had more time to rehearse and there'll be a band behind us.' Viv bobbed a quick curtsey then jumped down to hug Mary and Bobbie.

They were still basking in the crowd's approval when Gillian came in with the latest met report. 'Relax, everyone,' she announced. 'No crates will take off from here for at least two hours until the ground temperature rises above thirty-five degrees. Gordon, Stan, Bob: we need you to man the snowploughs — orders of First Officer Thornton.'

'Brrr!' Viv pretended to shiver. Seeing Peggy come up behind Gillian, she almost made a wisecrack about the real Cold Front blowing in. Better not, she thought. *Hilary says I have to show more respect and of course, I always do as I'm told!*

The next day Viv came home to a letter pinned to her door. She'd had another frustrating day of yet more delays and eventual detours due to bad weather. Her hop to Wolverhampton in an ageing Lancaster had turned into a marathon after she'd been forced by more snow to fly east and eventually bring the crate down on a grass strip in the wilds of Lincolnshire. The bumpy landing had involved some loose nuts and bolts rattling around the floor of the cockpit followed by a blast of freezing air from a mysterious source. It was only when she had glanced down at her feet and spotted a missing floor panel that she'd understood why she'd almost frozen to death. Afterwards, she'd had to resign herself to a railway journey back to Rixley that had involved three changes of train with long, cold waits in between. Now, finally, she was home and the last thing she wanted to deal with was the note on her door.

'Bathroom's free!' Bobbie called from the far end of the corridor. Viv looked like she would benefit from a nice warm bath. 'Who's the note from?' she asked as she approached, towel and sponge bag in hand.

'It's from Giles.' Though the envelope was sealed, Viv had recognized the confident handwriting and noted from the absence of a stamp that the letter had been hand-delivered.

'Intriguing — let me know what it says.' Bobbie floated on along the corridor, humming the chorus to 'Swinging on a Star'.

Viv tore open the envelope. 'It says he wants to see me, damn it!' she called after Bobbie.

'Of course he does.' After the drive Viv and Giles

had taken on the previous Sunday, Bobbie wondered how there could be any doubt. 'But the point is: do you want to see him?'

'No — yes — I honestly don't know.' Scanning the letter's contents she saw that Giles proposed getting together as early as the next day. 'I've already arranged to see Brian,' she explained to Bobbie. 'Don't look at me like that — I'm a free agent; I can see who I like.'

'Certainly you can.' Bobbie rolled her 'r' and raised one eyebrow.

'I can!' Viv insisted defiantly. 'Anyhow, what about you and Ray? I haven't heard the lowdown on you two recently.'

'There is no lowdown.' Suddenly crestfallen, Bobbie continued on her way.

'What do you mean?' It hadn't occurred to Viv that something had gone wrong between Bobbie and Ray. 'You're seeing him this weekend, aren't you?'

'I don't think so.' Allowing herself to be guided into Viv's room, Bobbie's defences collapsed and she was soon in tears. 'You see, Ray asked me to make a choice between him and flying.'

'And you chose flying? Good for you!'

'I know it's hard for him, having to sit by and watch me take risks.' Bobbie used her towel to dab at her eyes.

'But to force you to choose . . . !' Viv was lost for words. 'Look at Mary and Cameron — they're in the same fix yet neither would dream of doing what Ray's just done to you.'

'But I know he loves me.'

'No, wait. A man who truly loved you wouldn't force you into a choice like that. He would leave your wings unclipped and let you fly free — literally.' As Bobbie broke down once more, Viv softened. She lowered her voice and sat her friend down on a seat by the window. 'Easier said than done, I know.'

'But you're right. Ray should never have put me in that position. Only, he's had such a tough time. He lost a brother, you know.'

'When? How?'

'Two years ago. Frank was killed during a dogfight over Singapore.'

'The brother was a pilot in the RAF?'

Bobbie nodded. 'Before that Ray lost his mother, and now his father has gone too.'

'Yes, but still. Is there a chance that he'll come to his senses and see how unfair he's been?'

'In theory, yes; he's admitted as much. But he of all people knows what we're up against, up there at thirty thousand feet. He told me his nerves won't stand it any more. I'm hoping that he'll get over his jitters but I really don't know if he will.' In truth, Bobbie had been on tenterhooks for days, during which there'd been a deafening silence from Ray.

Viv thought for a while. 'What do you say we two drive over to Thresham tomorrow morning?' she said at last. 'That way I get a chaperone when I meet up with Giles and you have a chance to thrash things out with Ray? Two birds with one stone.'

Slowly Bobbie nodded. 'I say yes,' she agreed.

'Swell.' Taking off her sheepskin jacket, Viv flung it down on the bed. 'Now, if you don't mind, I want to grab that hot water before someone else beats me to it.'

★ ★ ★

183

The meeting between Viv and Brian had been set up by phone earlier that week.

'Have a drink with me,' he'd suggested on the Tuesday. 'Anywhere you like — just name the time and the place.'

So, to keep it low-key, Viv had chosen her local: the Fox and Hounds. 'Eight o'clock this coming Friday. I'll see you there.'

She'd regretted the arrangement almost as soon as she'd come off the phone. *My heart's not in it*, she'd realized. How could it be after her long talk with Giles on Sunday and the brief kiss that had brought it to a conclusion?

That kiss! It had been the slightest of touches yet it had sent her heart racing. There was something about the man that had got deep under her skin, making her rerun in her mind exactly what had been said and how she'd felt when he'd said it. *Am I swayed by his good looks?* she would ask herself, 10,000 feet up in a Fairey Swordfish, battling crosswinds and poor visibility en route to Bristol. *Would I take his side if he weren't so darned handsome? Is he the playboy that he first appeared or the wronged husband, victim of Nora's machinations? Or perhaps both?* She would ask herself these questions as she unzipped her Sidcot suit and returned her parachute pack, helmet, goggles and map to her locker. *Weakling or dutiful son? Coward or hero?*

Viv had kept her doubts to herself and gone on as normal. She was still the life and soul of any situation — sometimes putting her big foot in it, sometimes being the rock upon which her friends relied. Sure, it was an effort but it was what others expected of her.

Now, though, the time had come to enter the lion's

den — or rather, the Fox and Hounds. Viv got ready with a sinking heart. She dressed down for a change in a royal blue sweater and black slacks under her red coat and beret. A touch of make-up, that was all. Then she walked into the village at half her normal pace, dragging her feet as she passed Fern Cottage, tempted to knock on Jean's door and tell her outright: 'Giles and I have kissed — what do you think of that?'

Resisting the temptation, she walked on to the pub; Brian's Morgan was parked in the yard. She went in and found him sitting at the bar, exchanging yarns with a group of farmers. He stood out from the tweed-clad locals in his smart blue blazer and yellow cravat, his thick dark hair slicked back and the cuffs of his white shirt starched and immaculate.

'Hello there, Miss Vivienne!' he greeted her loudly as he beckoned for her to join him.

She noticed that he'd grown a David Niven moustache since she'd last seen him. Somehow it irritated her (it had a ginger tinge and besides, how long must he have spent in front of a mirror to trim it so neatly?), but she forced a smile and joined him. 'Hello, Brian,' she said as he kissed her cheek (absolutely no thrill; nothing at all).

'What will you drink?'

'Whisky, please.'

'Whisky for the young lady,' he told Florrie, drawing up a stool next to his. 'Sit,' he said, patting it complacently. 'You look marvellous, as usual.'

Viv took off her beret and unbuttoned her coat. 'I've had an exhausting few days,' she confessed with a loud sigh. 'Have you ever been to Lincolnshire, Brian?'

'Many times.' He sipped from his glass.

185

'How come it's so flat?'

'Not your cup of tea, I take it?' Viv was comical when she pulled a face. She didn't care about being ladylike; it was one of her many charms.

'I prefer Yorkshire or Lancashire — anywhere with hills.' The way they were going they'd be dragging through all the English counties from Northumberland to Cornwall, giving them scores out of ten for hilliness. 'The Lake District is swell, too.'

'And what have you been flying?'

'An old Lancaster, worse luck — practically dropping to bits.'

'Not a patch on a Spitfire, eh?'

'No; they're chalk and cheese. How about you — how was your day?'

'Group Captain Norris and I attended a meeting in York — just routine; nothing of any interest. I spent most of the afternoon anticipating our little tryst.'

'This is a tryst?' Viv tilted her head to one side. The walls of the tiny, dark snug seemed to confine her and she was forced to raise her voice to be heard over the raucous conversations of the farmers and an assortment of personnel from the ferry pool.

'Why, what would you call it?' Brian asked with a knowing wink. 'Other than a cosy, romantic rendezvous, leading to who knows what?'

OK, time to come clean. Viv took a deep breath then lit the blue touchpaper. 'Try not to read too much into this little get-together,' she cautioned.

'Yes, yes — early days,' Brian said smoothly.

'I mean, perhaps we could cut out the romantic bit.' Eyeing him steadily, she took a small sip of whisky.

His eyelids flickered but the smile didn't waver. 'Friends, eh?'

186

'Yes — friends. I'm sorry if I've given you a different impression.'

'You certainly did,' he said, a touch unpleasantly. The smile slowly faded.

'How did I?'

Brian cleared his throat then spoke out of the corner of his mouth. 'A girl doesn't get into a chap's car unescorted unless —'

'Unless what?' she challenged. Good God, was the guy still living in the nineteenth century?

'Forget it.'

'No, tell me what you mean. Are you saying that taking a ride in your car was a green light for other, so-called 'romantic' things?'

'I'd say so; yes. If we're getting down to brass tacks, you were definitely flirting with me from the off.'

Behind the bar, Florrie pricked up her ears. Someone had been too big for his boots and was about to get his comeuppance.

Viv put down her glass and raised her hand like a traffic cop. 'Whoa there! You were the one who came on to me with your flashy car and your shiny white smile and slicked-back hair. No doubt about it. I only had to turn around and there you were, pretending it was Hilary you'd come to see, or else you were on the phone bugging me.'

'I see.' Brian's voice was quieter, his eyes narrow. 'Tell me something, Vivienne: if you knew I was so keen on you, why not make it clear that the interest wasn't reciprocated?'

'Because, frankly, I wasn't sure; but now I am.' Snatching her handbag from the bar, Viv slid down from the stool. 'I'm sorry, Brian, but that's how it is.'

Good for you, love! In the background sour-faced

Florrie applauded silently. These smooth RAF types thought they could sweet-talk any girl they wanted, but Viv had put him in his place. 'Same again?' she asked Brian as the fiery Canadian pilot turned on her heel and exited.

'Yes; make it a double,' Brian ordered. *Bugger it! Damn and bloody blast!* He'd teach Miss Vivienne not to show him up in public. Down went the whisky in one. He rapped the empty glass on to the bar and ordered another. He'd wreck her damned Christmas celebrations by keeping his cadets away from Burton Grange on the 23rd. Yes; that's what he'd do — first thing tomorrow he'd invent an excuse to withdraw the permission that Norris had granted — not a single trainee would be given leave and that would be that.

*   *   *

'Nay, lad — that won't do.' Back in action on the Thresham yard after his bout of flu, Ronnie gave Philip a stern reprimand. 'Never stand behind a horse while you're grooming him — he'll kick you to bits if you do.'

Philip stepped quickly to one side then went on brushing Glasgow Girl with smooth, even strokes.

'And you!' Ronnie yelled across the yard at the new lad that Philip had brought with him. 'What's your name?'

'Wilf.' The one-word answer from the stocky youth contained a touch of surliness.

'Who told you to bring Rob Roy out of his stable?'

'I did.' Philip stepped in quickly. 'As soon as I've finished grooming Glasgow Girl I was planning to move on to him.'

'And what's this knot supposed to be?' Ronnie's temper didn't improve when he strode over to examine Wilf's amateurish handiwork. 'This isn't how you tether a horse. You do it like this.' Pushing the lad aside, he demonstrated swiftly. 'Are you another of those conchies?' he barked.

'Yes, sir, I am.' Wilf stood with shoulders squared, ready for whatever insult Ronnie flung his way.

'You live at Highcliff with him over there?' Ronnie's hackles were well and truly up. Things on the yard had gone to pot this last week. No feed had been ordered while he'd been poorly and the tack room was a proper mess. Now, in his wisdom, his boss had decided to bring in another useless lump whose experience with horses was nil.

'Yes, sir.'

'You work for the forestry lot?'

'No, sir. I'm with the land drainage team.' Wilf avoided looking Ronnie in the eye. Sure, the wiry head groom was only half his size and Wilf could probably knock him flat with a single punch, but it wouldn't do to give him any cheek. For a start, it was against Quaker principles.

'While the rest of the lads your age do your fighting and dying for you?' Contempt oozed out of every pore. 'You're happy with that, are you?'

'I signed the Pledge, sir.' With his eyes fixed on the grey Austin parked in the cart shed at the far side of the yard, Wilf did his best not to react.

Ronnie grunted and turned away in disgust, just as a black Ford entered the yard. He didn't know at first who the dark-haired driver was but he recognized Bobbie in the passenger seat and prepared himself for another disruption to routine.

189

Bobbie waited for Viv to park then she stepped out of the car. 'Hello, Ronnie; how are you feeling? Better, I hope. Hello, Philip.'

The studious-looking groom stepped back from Glasgow Girl to return the greeting. 'Hello, miss.' She'd come back, then — he hadn't been sure that she would.

'Call me Bobbie, please. And this is Viv Robertson. She works at Rixley with me.'

Viv shook hands enthusiastically with each of the three men. 'Hi again, Ronnie; it's a lovely day, for a change. Hi, Philip. Bobbie's told me all about you on the drive across. Hi, Wilf; that's a good strong handshake you have there.' Once she'd done the rounds she allowed Bobbie to draw her to one side.

'Giles and Ray must still be up at the house,' Bobbie muttered as the three grooms went back to their work. 'They probably saw us arrive.'

'OK, we'll play it cool and let them come to us.' Viv tried not to let her nerves get the better of her. Steering well clear of the horses, she had time to take in further details of the training yard on this, her second visit: the loft above the cart shed well stacked with hay bales and the open door into the tack room through which she spotted rows of saddles, bits and bridles.

Bobbie was uneasy. What if Ray *had* seen them and chosen not to come down? She took refuge in petting Glasgow Girl, standing to one side as Philip wheeled an empty barrow into the stable and showed the novice Wilf the basics of mucking out.

Viv didn't even like the smell of horses, let alone the way they rolled their eyes at you and bared their teeth if you went too near. They were so darned nervy and unpredictable; no, give her a nice modern crate to pilot any day of the week.

'Well, I never.' Giles emerged from the tack room after what felt like a decent interval. He'd been in there doing a stocktake when the girls had arrived — making himself useful around the yard while he decided on his next step in life. He hadn't as yet offered himself as a land manager with the Ministry of Food as Viv had suggested. Instead, he'd been caught on a hook of indecision that made him veer wildly from wanting to flee to far-flung parts by volunteering for the Foreign Legion (if there currently was such a thing) to joining the plodders in the Home Guard (ah, no; too late for that). He had, though, made contact with a solicitor over his divorce from Nora and pressed for movement on that front. 'What brings you to Thresham, Second Officer Robertson? It's certainly not your love of the equine species; I know that for a start.'

'Spot on,' she agreed. 'Actually, I hoped to see you.'

'And here I am.'

'Yes, here you are,' she echoed. Giles seemed almost back to his old self: no longer stooping because of his damaged ribs and with a brighter expression. The bruising to his face had faded, too. 'How come?'

'You mean, why haven't I moved on yet?' He might have known that Viv wouldn't beat about the bush. 'There are a number of reasons.' Drawing her into the tack room, he lowered his voice. 'One is that I'm keeping a close eye on Ray,' he confided.

'Why — is he ill?' Viv glanced over her shoulder to see that Bobbie had already left the yard and was making her way to the house.

'Not ill exactly,' Giles prevaricated.

'What then? Come on, Giles — spill the beans.'

'I'm afraid Ray isn't in very good shape.' All week

191

Giles had watched his friend struggle. On some mornings Ray would fail to put in an appearance before noon and when he did he would still be the worse for wear from the night before, which meant he'd failed to return telephone calls or to pay bills necessary to keep the business ticking over. And on the few occasions when he had made it down to the yard he'd done nothing but criticize. Either Philip had saddled up the wrong horse for Ray to take up on to the gallops or else Ronnie had forgotten to bring in the farrier to give Never Say Die a new set of shoes. Ray had even overlooked the fact that he'd agreed to interview a potential new lad and had accused young Wilf of trying to steal tack when he'd come across him on the yard on Thursday afternoon. He'd sworn at him and threatened him with the police until Philip had intervened.

'Are you sure he's not ill?' Struggling to make sense of what Giles was saying, Viv wondered if she should seek out Bobbie to warn her. 'What are you not telling me?' she demanded.

'If you must know, Ray has been drinking more than is good for him.' There; awkward as it was to tell tales against a friend, the cat was out of the bag.

'Oh, Jeez!' Yep; Viv had better go after Bobbie. 'Wait here,' she told Giles as she dashed from the tack room and headed up the path.

Viv's sudden sprint across the yard made a startled Rob Roy strain at his lead rope and another of the horses — a chestnut mare — kick at her stable door. Ronnie swore under his breath.

'No, that's not a good idea.' Giles was hot on Viv's heels, catching up with her halfway up the garden path leading to the house. 'Best to let Bobbie find out

192

for herself.'

'Is Ray drunk right now?' Viv wanted to know.

Giles shrugged. 'I haven't clapped eyes on him this morning. Listen — wait a few minutes then we'll go in and find out the state of play.'

'It's not a game,' Viv protested. Hearts could be broken, lives ruined.

'I know it's not. I'm as worried as you are.' He told her that they would hover on the front terrace and bide their time. 'Believe me, it's best to let Bobbie and Ray sort this out between themselves. All you and I can do is stand by and be ready to pick up the pieces.'

13

Ray had considered making a quick exit. He'd watched from the bedroom window as Bobbie and Viv had driven into the yard and had experienced an urge to scuttle out through the back door then cut across the copse up on to the gallops where he would lie low until the girls had left.

A glance in the mirror told him that he was scarcely presentable. He ran his hand over the rough stubble on his chin then made an attempt to straighten his thick dark hair. At least this morning he could stand upright and walk in a straight line if necessary.

What to do? Bobbie would be here within minutes. No time to shave or to get properly dressed. Ray glanced down at his creased shirt and bare feet. How could he possibly face her in this state?

But then the idea of sneaking away from his own home, and from the woman he loved, filled him with hot shame.

She would be at the front door any moment. Quickly he ran a comb through his hair then put on some socks. His head hurt like hell when he bent forward — as if a drummer was bashing out a hasty retreat. He heard a knock on the door. Must he really go down and face her? What if he just stayed here in his bedroom and waited for her to go away?

Bobbie raised the lion-head knocker and knocked a second time. 'Ray?' she called, standing back to get a better view of the upstairs windows. She'd stayed in the yard just long enough to see Giles emerge from

194

the tack room and engage Viv in conversation before taking matters into her own hands — she'd seen Ray's MG in the cart shed next to Giles's Austin so she knew he must be in. And if he was nowhere to be seen in the yard then he must be up at the house. 'Ray, where are you?'

There was no reply and Bobbie's heart sank into her boots. This had been a bad idea — she should have talked to Ray on the telephone and tried to iron out their differences. Instead, she'd agreed to Viv's more impetuous course of action and now here she was in the flesh, not knowing what her reception would be. She was about to turn away when the door opened.

'You didn't call,' Ray croaked, his voice barely more than a whisper.

'No — I thought I'd come and talk to you in person.' There were dark circles under his bloodshot eyes and he was unshaven, standing with his shirt open at the neck and with his cuffs unfastened. 'Shall I come back another time?'

'I waited for you to call.' Grasping the edge of the door and uncertain whether or not to invite Bobbie in, he stared at her face for signs of why she'd come. Was it to end things once and for all? Yes, that must be it — Bobbie had had enough of him and was here to tell him so.

'Ray Moore, how long do you intend to keep me standing outside in the cold?' Good Lord above, what was wrong with the man? Was he ill? Or had his anger over her decision hardened his heart against her? 'Are you going to let me in before I freeze to death?'

Ray stepped back and let the door swing open. Bobbie was wearing a green beret and red tartan scarf tucked into her sheepskin flying jacket. She looked boyish and determined. Resentment rose to the surface — all bloody week he'd waited to hear from her. 'Why didn't you call?'

'If you don't stop going on like a broken record I'll go away and never speak to you again.' Unshaven and red-eyed at ten in the morning — of course, he was hungover; what else? 'Is there any coffee?' she demanded. 'Or will we have to make do with tea?'

Striding across the hall and entering the untidy kitchen, Bobbie quickly put a kettle on to boil then lined up cups, teapot and sugar. 'Milk?' she asked in a businesslike way.

Ray shuffled into the pantry and returned with a full pint. He set it down on the table with an unsteady hand. 'No need to look at me like that,' he muttered bitterly. 'And before you ask — yes, I've been drinking. And yes, I know that's what did for my dad — he lost his grip because of the whisky and now I'm following in his footsteps. Like father, like son.'

Bobbie poured the tea. 'There's another new lad on the yard,' she commented as if she hadn't heard. 'I gather Philip found him for you?'

'Are you listening to me?'

'Wilf doesn't strike me as the usual conchie,' Bobbie went on. 'He and Philip are made from different moulds. Philip is my idea of someone whose religious principles genuinely stop him from fighting, whereas first impressions of Wilf are that he's likely to fall into the lazy shirker category that we all complain about.'

'Bobbie?'

'Yes, I'm listening,' she said calmly. 'And all I can say is that it's a good job I didn't try to speak to you if you've been drinking yourself silly all week. And another thing: why was it up to me to call you? If you'd been so keen to talk to me, you were perfectly capable of picking up the phone yourself.'

Ray sat down heavily at the table. 'I was afraid to,' he admitted. 'My head's been in a muddle. I couldn't think straight.'

'Oh well, whisky would help to clear your mind, you may be sure.'

'Sorry,' he mumbled as he buried his face in his hands.

With an exasperated sigh she leaned across the table to grasp both of his hands and place them flat on the table. 'What good is your being sorry to either of us? You're not the only one who's been in a state over this. I've been through it over and over in my mind, tossing and turning and hardly able to get any sleep. Who's in the right here? Am I being selfish for going against what you want or are you putting too much pressure on me to give up doing what I love? I can't decide.'

'I bet the girls at Rixley are on your side,' he said with a cynical shrug.

'As a matter of fact, yes they are. But then I have a mind of my own and I remembered Jean and what she sacrificed to be Dorota's mother. She was the best pilot we had bar none and she loved flying those Spitfires more than anything in the world. But she made her decision: it wasn't worth taking the risk once the baby came on to the scene. She gave up flying overnight. Now I ask myself: why can't I make that sacrifice for you?'

Ray curled his fingers around hers. 'That was different,' he had the decency to acknowledge.

'Thank you; yes, it was. I realized that. The fair comparison is with Mary and Cameron — they carry on doing what they have to do to help win the war in spite of just getting married. Mary can hardly bear it but she knows she must, for her country's sake.'

'You make it sound simple.' What Bobbie said brought the problem into focus for Ray but it didn't make him feel any better. It just proved what a selfish bastard he was capable of being.

'No, I don't. It's the hardest thing. And who knows, maybe Cameron and Mary have been through what we're going through and they've had this very conversation. They love one another and want to spend the rest of their lives together, making a home, having children.'

'Is that what you want?' Ray caught at a straw of hope.

There was a long pause. 'Eventually, yes.'

'With me?' Ray grasped Bobbie's hands more tightly. He hardly dared to believe it but she looked so fresh and lovely and sounded so sincere.

It was the biggest question Bobbie would ever have to answer; it would be so easy to say yes to because she loved Ray and knew he was a good man, but he was also one who might lose his way in life. Yes because she loved to nestle against him and yearned to be with him even when they were miles apart. But no: not if he went on feeling sorry for himself and sulked and turned to drink.

'I see.' He pulled his hands free and scraped back his chair. 'You don't have to say anything; I can tell by the look in your eyes.' Her silence was like a knife to the heart.

'I haven't said no.' She sat as still as a marble statue and made no protest as Ray strode towards the door.

He halted, came back and sat down again. 'What if

I promise not to drink any more?'

Bobbie studied his face. 'It won't be easy — you do know that.' Not with his father's behaviour as a life-long example and not with Giles in residence as his drinking companion.

Ray leaned forward to place his fingertips against her lips. 'And what if I never say another word about your flying?'

'Promise?'

'I swear to God not to mention it again.'

Bobbie closed her eyes and took a deep breath.

'I can be better,' he pleaded. 'I'll roll up my sleeves and get back to work, do everything in my power —'

'Wait,' Bobbie said. 'Don't promise me the world if you can't hold to it. That would be worse than not promising anything.'

'I see that. We'll take it day by day — is that better?'

'And you must make these changes for yourself, not for me.' A calmness came over Bobbie similar to the one she felt whenever she sat at the controls of a complicated new fighter plane. In spite of the risk, in spite of the danger, she knew what she had to do. 'What I'm saying is: let's spend a little time apart and see what happens.'

Ray's heart thudded. 'How much time?'

'Between now and Christmas,' Bobbie told him gently. 'If all goes well, I'll see you at the Christmas party. Until then, you will get on with your life and I'll get on with mine.'

★　★　★

Bobbie emerged from the house to find Viv and Giles waiting for her.

'Well?' Giles didn't hide his concern. 'Have you and Ray had a bust-up?'

Bobbie shook her head then briskly led the way to the yard.

'OK, so did he go down on one knee?' Viv naturally supposed that it must have been one extreme or the other.

'Neither.' Bobbie's decision had left her trembling, yet at the same time she felt sure that she'd done the right thing. Now it was up to Ray. 'Listen, Viv, why don't you and Giles spend the rest of the morning together while I take the car back to Rixley? You can drive her home after lunch, can't you, Giles?'

'With pleasure,' he agreed as they re-entered the busy yard where Philip wheeled barrows of muck to the dung heap, Wilf used a hose to fill water troughs and Ronnie saddled up Glasgow Girl.

'Hey, before you go, aren't you going to give me the low-down on you and Ray?' Viv pulled at her arm.

'Maybe later.' In escaping from Viv's clutches, Bobbie stepped backwards and bumped into Wilf, accidentally jerking the hose from his hand. The hose writhed and water sprayed across the yard, drenching Philip and drawing more black looks from Ronnie. 'Sorry; my fault,' Bobbie mumbled.

Wilf accepted the apology with bad grace then picked up the hose and went on with his work. Philip, meanwhile, ducked into the tack room in search of a towel.

'I'll see you later,' Bobbie said to Viv, who had found it difficult to keep a straight face.

'That was like a scene from Laurel and Hardy,' she giggled.

'Not so funny if you were the one who got half-drowned,' Giles pointed out. 'Go on, Bobbie; make yourself scarce before you do any more damage.'

Once he and Viv had watched Bobbie start up the car then drive away, they were left with a decision about what to do and where to go. Giles thought they should pop back to the house and check on Ray, 'just in case', which they did and discovered him in the boot room at the back of the house dressed in a thick Aran sweater and corduroy britches, pulling on his riding boots. There was a quick, manly exchange of 'old chap' and 'spiffing', which amused Viv and during which they established that Ray was all set to take horses up on to the gallops with Ronnie, leaving Giles and Viv free to do whatever they pleased.

'I'll see you later, old chap,' Giles told Ray as they clapped each other on the back then parted.

'No rush,' Ray assured him. He had much to prove and was determined to make Bobbie proud. This morning was just the start.

So Viv and Giles set off in the Austin and followed a roundabout route to Maltby Bay. It was one of Viv's favourite fishing villages — with its higgledy-piggledy red-tiled roofs and a tall, narrow pub teetering on the edge of the tiny harbour, as quaint as anything you'd see in a guidebook. From there they drove to Highcliff and stopped on the clifftop, close to the site of a ruined church.

'Did you know that in the olden days Highcliff was home to some of the most notorious smugglers and highwaymen in the whole of England?' Giles was intent on entertaining his passenger with tales of derring-do. 'There's a veritable honeycomb of hidden tunnels leading from the beach to the cellars of various inns in the neighbourhood and many a swashbuckling, moonlit fight took place between smugglers and excise men, if the local history books are to be believed.'

'Giles.' Viv leaned her head back against her seat and smiled invitingly. 'That's swell, honey. History is all very well but wouldn't you much rather kiss me?'

* * *

During her short drive home from Thresham, Bobbie did her best to calm her jangling nerves by looking ahead to her working week and by planning more details of the forthcoming Christmas party. She must remember to get in touch with the local ENSA office and check what time the band would arrive on the 23rd. Would they need refreshments and a room in which to change their outfits? Come to think of it, would it be necessary for the Grange to provide a piano, considering how difficult it would be for the entertainers to transport their own?

Her head was full of such busy thoughts as she pulled up in the stable yard.

'Park over here.' Ernest directed her to a corner spot, next to a gleaming black limousine that Bobbie failed to recognize. 'Mind you don't scratch that paintwork,' the handyman cautioned as he dodged in front of her and guided her into the narrow space. 'Forward a bit. Stop. Right hand down. Forward a bit more.'

'Why? Whose car is it?' Bobbie spotted a chauffeur in the Bentley: a man with a rugged profile that looked as if it had been carved out of stone. She got out carefully then walked with the handyman up the steps on to the terrace.

'It belongs to Sir Thomas,' Ernest muttered through gritted teeth, as though he would reveal more if he were allowed.

Thinking little of it, Bobbie said a quick goodbye and went ahead into the house where she saw Peggy in conversation with a small, haughty-looking woman with a pale powdered face, arched eyebrows and pinched red lips. The stranger's fitted two-piece costume emphasized her slim frame; her matching hat sported a delicate veil that dipped stylishly over one eye.

'Ah, Bobbie — just the person!' Peggy waved her across. 'You've been billeted here at the Grange a good deal longer than I have. Perhaps you could help with Mrs Parseval's enquiries.'

For a few moments Bobbie was confused. She'd never come across a Mrs Parseval — only Sir Thomas's wife, Lady Jane, who anyway looked nothing like the current visitor. So she walked slowly across the hall, weighing up who this might be.

'Mrs Nora Parseval, may I introduce First Officer Roberta Fraser.' Peggy ran through the formalities. 'Mrs Parseval was asking me who was in charge of housekeeping at the Grange in the absence of any resident housekeeper. I had to admit that I really had no idea.'

Nora Parseval? Bobbie still couldn't fit her into the picture. But then, wait a second — hadn't Viv mentioned the name in the context of Giles's divorce? Her eyes widened in astonishment; was this indeed the soon-to-be ex-wife?

Bobbie studied the visitor's appearance. She was a woman of around forty with carefully arranged black hair beneath the maroon velvet hat. Her make-up was impeccable and she reminded Bobbie of no one so much as Wallis Simpson, the American divorcee who had stolen the heart of King Edward VIII.

'Well?' Nora Parseval asked impatiently. 'Does a daily come in from the village now that the Polish woman is gone?'

Mention of Anna caused Bobbie's eyes to widen still further. *Let me get this straight,* she thought. *Giles's estranged wife is deliberately bringing up the subject of the poor girl whom Giles made pregnant, who was driven to kill herself rather than endure the agony of watching her illegitimate baby being given away to strangers.*

'Speaking of whom,' Nora continued without a flicker of emotion, 'I suppose you were here at the time of the unfortunate incident?'

'I was,' Bobbie said faintly.

'You weren't the one who discovered that the girl had done away with herself?'

Bobbie swallowed hard then turned uncertainly to Peggy, who looked increasingly uncomfortable.

'Perhaps it would be better to ask Hilary about present housekeeping arrangements,' Peggy suggested.

Nora brushed the idea to one side and continued to talk directly to Bobbie. 'My initial enquiry was a mere pretext, as I'm sure you realize. Frankly, I don't give a hoot about cleaning arrangements; I'm more interested in discovering what you know about the Polish woman. Did she ever mention my husband, by any chance? And did Giles show any particular interest in her unfortunate circumstances?'

Peggy cleared her throat then drew herself up to her full height. 'I really think you should talk to Squadron Leader Stevens about such personal matters,' she said in her authoritative tone. 'If you'll permit me, I'll show you to his room.'

Stepping back and watching Peggy lead Nora Parseval up the stairs, Bobbie shook her head in disbelief. The cheek of it; for Giles's wife to come here and fish for facts that were no doubt intended to help in her divorce proceedings. And how come she'd been able to borrow Sir Thomas's car and chauffeur? The reason for that was a mystery that perhaps Viv would help her to solve. Meanwhile, Bobbie put the unpleasant encounter to the back of her mind.

* * *

Many kisses later and after lunch in Highcliff's Anchor Inn, Giles drove Viv home.

'You really are the most surprising girl,' he confessed as they came to the first cottages on the outskirts of Rixley village. Clouds had thickened during the course of the day and now hung low and dark over Burton Wood.

'In what way?' Viv took in the familiar landmarks that reminded her that she was in the heart of the English countryside: the red telephone box outside the Fox and Hounds, the ancient church surrounded by crumbling gravestones and, last but not least, the pair of stone lions guarding the front entrance to the Grange.

'Your willingness to tackle any challenge, for a start. I haven't come across many girls who ran away from home to join a flying circus.'

'That's because you've led a sheltered life.'

'It's true — I have. But not any longer.' Giles drove past the main entrance and skirted round the side of the estate. 'Seriously, though — I'm amazed that you should want anything to do with me now that I'm penniless.'

'But you won't always be,' Viv insisted. 'You'll soon be back on your feet. And you know something — I'd far rather you made your own way in the world than rely on you-know-who.' She let him know in her usual direct way that this was a subject she felt strongly about.

'I'm touched by your faith,' he confessed as he drove under the archway into the stable yard. 'What the . . . ?' The sight of the Parseval family Bentley parked by one of the stables made him slam on the brakes.

Viv lurched forward in her seat. She too recognized the limousine but refused to be intimidated, prepared to back Giles to the hilt if things got heated. 'Well?' she asked him as he sat silent and stony-faced.

'I'd prefer to give Father a wide berth, if you don't mind,' he muttered through gritted teeth. 'There'd be no point . . . it would only lead to yet another row . . . better on the whole . . .'

'OK, I get it. I'll let you make a quick getaway.' Viv jumped out then set off towards the steps. 'Oh, I almost forgot.' She turned and ran back to Giles's car. *Open your window*, she mimed.

He wound the handle and received a flurry of kisses from her. 'Go!' he said at last.

'One more!' One peck on the cheek turned into half a dozen. Then laughing and breathless, she turned again and took the steps two at a time, only stopping when her way was blocked by a man in a grey chauffeur's uniform and a small, well-dressed woman decked out in snakeskin shoes and handbag, crimped hair and a neat velvet titfer that was the height of fashion. Turning for a final wave at Giles, Viv dodged sideways in an attempt to pass.

At a nod from the woman the chauffeur laid a heavy hand on Viv's shoulder.

She twisted out of his grasp indignantly. 'Say!' she protested. 'What the heck do you think you're doing?'

Down in the yard, Giles stepped quickly out of his car. He slammed the door but didn't come up the steps.

'Why, Giles,' the woman called in a superior, sneering way, 'I see you prefer the younger woman these days, just as your father intimated.'

He advanced slowly. 'Nora, what are you doing here? It can't be a social visit, surely?'

'How perfectly charming of you,' she retorted without deigning to look at him. Instead, she inspected Viv from head to toe. 'Let me see. Hmm, Giles, you do still go for a brunette and she's extremely pretty, I'll give you that.'

'Hey, lady!' As Viv stepped towards the visitor, the chauffeur intervened once more until she pushed him away. 'Call off your gorilla. I know who you are; you're the gold-digger who married Giles for his money.'

'I'm Giles's wife, certainly.' Nora was unmoved by the insult. 'Come and join us, Giles. I was explaining to Hilary the difficulties your recent disappearance created for me — solicitors' letters returned unopened, and so forth. In the end I was obliged to travel to Newpark to talk with Sir Thomas in person. As it turns out, he was most obliging. He made a point of telling me that you offered little if any resistance over his decision to turf me out of Abbot's Gate.'

An angry flush crept up Giles's neck. 'Not now, Nora.'

She was undeterred. 'The name Anna Janicki also entered into our conversation,' she reported almost casually. 'Adultery was mentioned as additional grounds for our divorce. I came here to find out more.'

'Cut it out.' Viv still had to wrestle with the chauffeur as she spoke. 'Giles never touched Anna. It was —'

'Not now!' Giles repeated fiercely. He fought hard to resist the urge to grab hold of Nora and wring her scrawny neck. 'Liaise with my solicitor if you must,' he told her as calmly as he could. 'And tell Dexter to step away.'

'Or else what?' Nora was unperturbed by the turn of events — in fact, she seemed amused. 'Will it be pistols at dawn or something more tawdry and appropriate to the twentieth century — fisticuffs down a back alley?' Nevertheless, she instructed the chauffeur to step back from the fray. 'You see, my dear,' she explained to a furious Viv, 'in my world, a soon-to-be divorced woman must fight for her rights. Surely you can appreciate that.'

'I see that you mean to get your full pound of flesh,' Viv muttered. 'By the way, did Sir Thomas also mention that he's cut Giles off without a penny? No, I didn't think so.'

A flash of anger had altered Nora's previously immobile features. 'Since when?' she demanded of Giles.

'Since you insisted on keeping Abbot's Gate as part of the settlement.' Giles saw no reason to hide the truth. 'That was beyond the pale, as far as the old man was concerned. Naturally he'll do anything in his power to prevent giving up a square foot of Parseval land.'

'He's left you with nothing?' As the implications

filtered through, a deep frown settled on Nora's face. 'He's disinherited you?'

'Completely,' Giles confirmed. 'So you see, there's nothing to be gained by coming here and digging the dirt in an attempt to extricate more money from me.'

'We'll see what my solicitor has to say about that.' Nora's brain worked overtime. 'We'll aim to prove that the disinheritance is merely a tactic to avoid a proper settlement.'

Giles took a deep breath. 'I wish you luck,' he commented. 'The real proof will be in my bank balance, which currently stands at zero.'

'So it's back to Newpark, I guess?' Viv filled the hostile silence with a remark aimed at Dexter, the guy who was so handy around cars and tractors. 'You'll be well placed to fill your boss in on what's happened here.'

Meanwhile, Nora was in sly retreat. 'Of course I'm happy to negotiate with your father. I'll suggest that if Abbot's Gate is the stumbling block perhaps we can find a way around it. We could settle on a market value, a cash equivalent. Then all three Parseval properties would be left intact.'

'He won't stump up the cash,' Giles predicted. 'In fact, I doubt that he could.'

Nora refused to believe him. 'I can talk to your mother for you.' She proposed a different tactic. 'Lady Jane won't agree to your being pushed out of the fold for good.'

The thought of his wife acting as peacemaker brought an ironic smile to Giles's lips. 'You have no idea,' he muttered under his breath. Let Nora do whatever she liked, for all the difference it would make.

'What now?' Viv challenged Nora directly. Now

that she was able to put a face to the name Nora Parseval, any possible shred of jealousy melted away. Jeez, this was one bitter and twisted little lady.

'Now we drive back to Newpark.' Nora shifted her handbag into the crook of her elbow. The impossibly arched, tweezered eyebrows remained in place and the look in her glittering, dark brown eyes was glassier than ever. 'Let the negotiations continue,' she concluded as she glided down the steps with Dexter close behind.

Frowning deeply, Giles accompanied Viv up on to the terrace. 'I'm sorry. What must you think of me?' he said with a dejected sigh.

'I don't think anything bad,' she assured him. 'Quite the opposite. As for Nora and that Dexter guy . . . !'

'Quite.'

Down in the yard a car engine started then tyres rolled over the cobbled surface, growing fainter as the Bentley drove away.

'But it's not over yet,' Giles warned. 'There's bound to be more to come — a lot more.'

Sliding an arm around his waist, Viv walked with him into the house. 'So we'll be ready,' she said softly. 'Pistols at dawn it is.'

14

'These damned V1 strikes are getting worse.' Horace sat in the breakfast room at Burton Grange commenting on an article on the front page of his newspaper. 'The Waffen-SS is currently targeting Antwerp and they don't care who they kill with their bloody missiles. Women and children are fair game as far as they're concerned.'

Bobbie, Mary and Viv sat at a nearby table. A lethargic Sunday morning atmosphere hung over the usually active Atta girls, all dressed in casual slacks and sweaters and each wondering how best to fill their day off.

'Apparently those missiles are guided by gyroscopes and can carry one tonne of explosives,' Horace continued. 'Mr Churchill has been forced to own up to a direct hit in New Cross last month — a hundred and sixty dead from a single explosion.'

'But it's not all doom and gloom,' Bobbie pointed out. 'I heard on the wireless this morning that Russia and France are meeting in Moscow to sign a new pact, which is all to the good.'

'And the Yanks are making progress in Japan; on Iwo Jima to be precise.' Viv, too, knew that it was important to keep abreast of good news as well as bad.

'And closer to home, yesterday I managed to talk to Mrs Warboys, the woman in charge of the local ENSA group.' Bobbie was eager to share her small piece of positive news. 'She says that the band will arrive with their own instruments, including a piano. They'll be travelling from Scarborough in a van and will be here in good time for the party to begin at half past seven prompt.'

'Great. So we've sorted out the tree, the decorations and the band.' Viv ticked off items on her fingers. 'Now all we have to do is polish up our version of 'Swinging on a Star' and make the all-important decision about what we're going to wear to impress the RAF.'

Horace glanced up from his newspaper. 'I wouldn't go counting your chickens if I were you.'

Bobbie pushed away her plate then rocked back in her chair so that she had a better view of their resident Jeremiah. 'What do you mean by that?'

'Yes, come on — spill the beans.' Viv pulled an impatient face. 'Such a bundle of joy,' she muttered under her breath to a distracted-looking Mary.

Horace made a feeble attempt to squeeze out of the tight corner he found himself in. 'Nothing. Forget I said it.'

'No, Horace — if you know something we don't you'd better spit it out.' As the person who'd done the most to put arrangements for the party in place, Bobbie forced the issue.

'It's like getting blood out of a stone,' Viv muttered.

Mary smiled briefly without speaking. She studied her fingernails then picked up her spoon and stirred her untouched bowl of porridge.

'Horace?' Bobbie badgered.

'All right; if you must know I happened to bump into one of the Aireby instructors at the Fox last night.'

'Who exactly?' Viv demanded. She had a bad feeling about what might be coming next.

'A flight sergeant in charge of training wireless

212

operators — I don't know his name. Anyway, he happened to mention the twenty-third.'

'Why, what did he say?' A glance in Viv's direction told Bobbie that she was equally rattled.

'There's a rumour going round the camp that it's all off. The RAF boys won't be allowed to come after all.'

'That's ridiculous!' Bobbie cried. 'They've already said yes to it.'

'I'm only saying what I heard.' Horace made it plain that he thought Bobbie and Viv were making too much fuss. 'Anyhow, the room's not that big — we'd have been squashed like sardines on that dance floor. On top of which, we Rixley lads would have been short of women to dance with. We'd have propped up the bar and got squiffy instead and the whole thing would've ended badly, mark my words.'

'We'll see about that.' Without waiting to hear another word, Bobbie got up from the table and made a beeline for the door, joined soon after by Viv.

'What are you going to do? Speak to Hilary?' Viv asked as they ran up the stairs.

'You bet I am,' Bobbie shot back. 'The Aireby officers can't change their minds at the drop of a hat. It's just not on.'

'You're dead right, it's not.' Viv and Bobbie charged up a second set of stairs to the attic floor on a mission to save Rixley's Christmas — and woe betide anyone who tried to stop them.

* * *

'Is there any news of your brother?' Peggy had sought Mary out soon after breakfast, having noticed that

213

she sat quietly by herself after Viv and Bobbie had dashed off.

'No, nothing.' Mary was reluctant to talk. In fact, she'd been setting out on a solitary walk around the reservoir when Peggy had intercepted her at the edge of Burton Wood.

Peggy was sensibly dressed against the cold in fur-lined boots and her flying jacket. 'It's a nice morning — do you mind if I join you?'

Mary shook her head, though she would have preferred to walk alone.

'I read recently that the Germans have set up many new POW camps, which suggests that they're holding more and more prisoners. Fingers crossed that your Tom is one of them.' As they walked into the shadow of the trees, Mary's lack of response caused Peggy to think again. 'Perhaps you'd rather I didn't tag along?'

'No — please.' Mary apologized for her rudeness and they walked on. Their boots crunched through white frost and their breath made clouds of steam in the crisp, clear air. 'I haven't spoken to Cameron for two days,' she admitted after a while.

'I see.'

'He usually calls me.'

'At a prearranged time?'

'Yes, as long as we know our rotas in advance. If not, he telephones me first thing in the morning, once he's back from his bombing mission and before I set off for the ferry pool. But not this morning.' The break in the pattern was proving torture for Mary — every minute of not hearing intensified her fear that Cameron's plane had been brought down over enemy territory and he'd been forced to parachute clear or worse.

'It doesn't do to dwell,' Peggy insisted. 'I used to

find in your situation that the best way to cope was to discover things to do that took my mind off the problem.'

Surprise caused Mary to break her stride. 'You too?'

'Yes indeed; my husband, Keith, was in the RAF.'

'Was?' Mary echoed shakily.

Peggy nodded without offering any further explanation. 'It's preferable at such a time to choose an activity that is entirely under your control. Sometimes I would read a good book. At other times I would take a walk in the fresh air as you are now — I usually found that most beneficial.'

'I'm sorry; I didn't know you'd been married.'

'How could you, dear? I deliberately chose not to talk about Keith. It alters people's perception of one and the very last thing one wants to do is to invite pity.' Even speaking her late husband's name tore at Peggy's heart and magnified her sense of loss. But she decided that sharing such confidences with Mary in the seclusion of the wintry woods might help the younger pilot through this difficult time.

Mary knew that it was best not to probe. She felt privileged that this dignified, respected member of the ATA had chosen to confide in her even a little bit.

'Why not come to Northgate with me later today?' Peggy suggested suddenly as they emerged from the wood and caught their first bracing sight of Rixley reservoir — a smooth expanse of steel-grey water edged by pebble beaches strewn with pale driftwood, with the long, straight dam bordering its far edge. 'It would be a pleasant diversion for you to meet my family if you feel up to it.'

Peggy's concern felt almost maternal to an anxious Mary. They weren't quite of different generations, though not far off, and the prim and proper first officer bore no resemblance to the memories Mary held of her real mother: an unassuming, prematurely ageing woman who had lived her short life at her selfish husband's beck and call. 'Kathleen, fetch my pipe and slippers', 'Kathleen, run to the shop for an ounce of baccy', 'What's for dinner?', 'Where the bloody hell is my best shirt and why isn't it ironed?' Perhaps it was the very difference — Peggy's cleverness and independence — that drew Mary to her now. 'Thank you; I'd like to come,' she replied as they turned and retraced their steps through the shadowy wood.

★ ★ ★

'I've just had a visit from Bobbie and Viv — it seems there's a snag over those invitations to the Christmas do,' Hilary confessed to Peggy when he came across her on the terrace overlooking the front lawn. 'I'd appreciate your advice.'

'Make it quick,' she told him. 'I'm about to set off for Northgate.'

'Rumour has it that there's been a change of heart at the Aireby end. I don't know the details but suffice it to say that permission for the cadets to attend may have been withdrawn, which of course would not go down well in either camp.'

Peggy took the point. 'Our girls would feel badly let down. I've come to see that the success of this party means more to our girls than I at first realized.'

'You can say that again. What ought to be a small boost to morale might in fact prove the opposite — a damp squib, so to speak.'

'I agree. There's been a good deal of anticipation

and planning for this event, which has raised spirits considerably.'

Hilary pulled out a silver cigarette case and, having offered one to Peggy, lit up then inhaled deeply. 'I'm out of my league in matters of this sort,' he confessed. 'Personally I'm more inclined towards the bah-humbug view of Christmas.'

'You don't see what all the fuss is about?'

'Precisely.'

'So you're asking me what I think you should do.' Peggy glanced at her watch. Where had Mary got to? she wondered. 'Firstly you should get on the blower to Hubert Norris first thing tomorrow to see whether or not the rumour is true.'

'And if it is?' Narrowing his eyes, he directed a thin plume of blue smoke into the clear air.

'Then you should ask him if he has had a hand in the change of mind and if so on what basis. For all we know there may be a perfectly valid reason.'

'Quite right,' Hilary agreed. His attention was caught by the distant drone of an aeroplane that made him scan the sky for signs of its approach.

'It would be a shame, however.' Peggy, too, was distracted. Trained to establish the identity of a plane based on the sound of its engines, she grew more alert. 'What does that sound like to you?'

'Some type of medium bomber?' Hilary continued to scan the sky.

'A Junkers,' Peggy agreed, and felt a cold shiver run down her spine. 'With any luck, just the one.'

'Yes, there she is.' He spotted the German plane approaching from the east, flying low and fast towards them. 'You're right — a Ju88 by the look of it.'

Even from a distance Peggy recognized the enemy

aircraft's less than elegant shape — particularly the heavily framed cockpit and the belly gondola built to contain a machine-gunner. 'Long-range reconnaissance type,' she elaborated as the aircraft drew near and she spotted the black cross against a white circle on its wings and fuselage and a white band painted close to the tail. 'I expect there are a couple of cameras positioned in the rear fuselage — if you ask me, he's after pictures of the ferry pool.'

Hilary agreed. 'He's flying directly over as we speak.' All thoughts of the Christmas party were dismissed as he ground out his cigarette. Such a sighting was rare and was a definite cause for alarm. 'If he's long range, at least he won't have bombs on board,' he muttered, sprinting along the terrace towards the stable yard where his car was parked. 'I'll drive over there and find out as much as I can from the ops boys,' he shouted over his shoulder.

Peggy shuddered at the sight and sound of the powerful Junkers flying much too close for comfort. She feared this might be the first of many such enemy recces, which might explain Aireby's decision to cancel all leave on the 23rd.

The roar of twin engines gradually faded and by the time Mary came out on to the terrace, there was no sign that anything was amiss.

'I'm sorry — I got held up,' she explained, her face flushed with excitement. 'I had a phone call from Cameron.'

Peggy put her concerns about the Junkers to one side, smiled warmly and patted her arm. 'Apology accepted. You must be very relieved.'

'I am.' The call had come just after lunch, as Mary had been getting ready for her outing with Peggy.

Cameron had been stranded near Calais overnight; it was top secret. Bad weather had played a part. He'd known she'd be worried and he was most awfully sorry. All was well.

'I can breathe again,' she said. The familiar feeling of having a steel band clamped around her chest had disappeared and she could suck air deep into her lungs.

'Come,' Peggy said. 'Now you can enjoy our afternoon together in the knowledge that your brave husband is safe and sound.'

★ ★ ★

Spur of the moment didn't always pay off, as Viv found when she arrived unannounced at Thresham on Sunday afternoon, hoping to see Giles.

'Not here,' Ronnie reported in his offhand way. He gave a hollow cough — a hangover from his bout of flu — then carried on pitching fresh straw from a cart into one of the empty stables.

'What's a girl to do when she has a spare afternoon and no one to play with?' Viv said with a sigh. The yard seemed to be experiencing a lull between bursts of activity, with horses in their stables grazing peacefully at hay nets and no sign of anyone to talk to except the uncommunicative head groom, dressed as always in corduroy britches and polo-neck sweater. *He probably sleeps in the darned things,* Viv thought. 'Where is everyone, by the way?'

'Mr Parseval went out with Mr Moore. Philip and the other new lad are on their tea break.'

'Do you know where Giles and Ray went?' Viv had an idea that she might follow them but a shrug from

219

Ronnie proved no help so she amused herself by poking around in corners of the yard that she hadn't visited before. First she inspected the old cart shed and was intrigued by a rusty array of old farming implements hanging from a wall. She recognized a scythe and a pitchfork, but some of the other metal contraptions with sharp spikes and blades looked like instruments of medieval torture. Then she climbed a ladder into the hayloft and sat contentedly for a while among the sweet-smelling bales. Hearing voices below, she descended the ladder to find Philip and Wilf emerging from the tack room to swill their tea mugs under a tap.

She greeted them in her usual bright way. 'Hi, you two; how are you doing?'

Philip smiled back. 'We're doing nicely, thank you.'

Appreciating his civility, Viv followed them into the tack room where they began to tidy away their tea things.

'Frankly, I'm curious about the Quaker thing. I came across Shakers and Amish in California. Are you anything like them?'

'Similar to Shakers,' Philip confirmed. Here they went again: treading a familiar path, giving explanations that were bound to be questioned then in all likelihood rejected. Still, it had to be endured. 'We sing and read from the Bible; we don't sit around in silence like most people seem to think.'

'And are you teetotal? I read that somewhere.' Viv fingered the supple leather of the bridle hanging from a nearby hook. *Teetotal, plainly dressed and opposed to fighting, obviously.*

As she spoke, Wilf brushed past her, head down and with an air of impatience. Philip, however, was more obliging.

'We don't touch alcohol but we do like chocolate,' he told her with a smile that almost developed into a wink. 'God has no objection to the cocoa bean, as far as we know.'

'Say; that's funny.' Viv laughed. 'I suppose He does object to war, though?'

'To violence of any kind.' Philip treated Viv to one of his long, cool stares. 'The use of violence always creates more problems than it solves. 'A good end cannot sanctify evil means; nor must we ever do evil, that good may come of it.' William Penn said that nearly two hundred and fifty years ago and I hold to it still.'

The patter failed to convince her. 'Yes, but most of us have a big problem with Herr Hitler steamrollering across Europe without anyone trying to stop him.'

'As I tried to explain to First Officer Fraser the other day, Quakers resist by peaceful means, by talking and sharing our values and helping others towards the inner light.'

Was the guy serious? 'In an ideal world, yes, that would be swell. But in the real world it's not enough.' Aware of Wilf still hovering in the doorway, she turned to him. 'I have a point, don't I?'

'Don't ask me,' he replied uneasily in his deep somewhat uncouth voice. He seemed uncomfortable under Viv's scrutiny and quickly stepped out of sight.

'Your friend's not the talkative type, is he?'

'You must excuse Wilf. He only recently joined our community so he's still finding his feet.'

'Duly excused.' She came to the conclusion that no one would win the argument between her and Philip. 'I guess we'll never see eye to eye,' she acknowledged. '*You'll* never in a million years agree with me ferrying these crates around the country for the RAF to use and, likewise, *I* don't see how your turning the other cheek could possibly work.'

'Unless you came to one of our meetings,' Philip said as a parting shot. 'Then we might get somewhere.'

'Seriously — is that a genuine invitation?'

'Visit us in Highcliff any time,' he confirmed. 'You can't miss us — we gather most evenings for our meetings at the Old Court House on Market Square.'

★　★　★

Westville Avenue was a wide, tree-lined street in a quiet suburb of the affluent spa town of Northgate where Mary and Cameron had celebrated their wedding. It was a million miles from the cramped, crooked mill town where Mary had grown up. Instead of narrow streets lined with terraced houses, North-gate sported crescents of stylish Edwardian residences surrounded by spacious gardens largely given over to vegetable growing and with nice new cars parked in paved driveways.

Peggy's mother and father stood at the door to welcome their daughter.

'There you are!' Marjorie Shepherd stepped forward with a smile. Tall and slim like her daughter, her grey hair was styled in a straight bob that had been fashionable in her youth and she was dressed in a mustard-yellow two-piece teamed with a dark green blouse and pearl necklace. Life had treated her well, as her unlined face and healthy complexion showed. 'Come in out of the cold.'

Timothy Shepherd waited in the wings until everyone was inside. He was smaller and rounder than his wife, with a bald head and heavy-rimmed glasses, dressed in a comfortable cardigan and slacks. 'I looked after Rosie single-handed this morning while your mother went to church,' he informed Peggy proudly. 'Happily we both emerged unscathed.'

Flustered by her surroundings, Mary scarcely took in what was said.

'Thank you, Daddy.' Peggy took off her coat and encouraged Mary to do likewise. 'I'd like you to meet my fellow ATA pilot,' she told her parents. 'Mary, this is my mother, Marjorie, and my father, Timothy.'

'You can call me Tim,' he encouraged. 'Everyone does.'

'Well?' Peggy looked eagerly around the sitting room they'd just entered. 'Where is she?'

The large, light-filled room was warmed by radiators. It had a bay window overlooking a lawn with fruit trees. The furniture was softly upholstered and the pictures on the walls depicted old-fashioned sailing ships and sunny rural scenes.

'She's upstairs,' Marjorie replied.

'Asleep or awake?'

'Awake the last time I popped in.'

No sooner said than Peggy had vanished from the room.

'We're so proud of Peggy and what she's achieved,' Timothy said, beaming at Mary as he ushered her further into the lounge. 'For her to do so well at Hatfield then to return to her duties so soon after Keith's tragic death — it takes genuine courage.'

Mary nodded her agreement. Peggy's father's words confirmed what she'd already gathered: that Peggy was a recent widow, who had dealt with her grief by continuing to carry out her duties in the ATA.

'We're biased, of course.' Marjorie sat Mary down in a settee by the window. 'I'm so pleased she's made a new friend at Rixley. Tell us about yourself, Mary. What made you want to be a pilot?'

'With the ATA.' The genial Timothy picked up the thread before Mary had time to answer. 'The Always Terrified Airwomen — that was the old joke, wasn't it? Well, my girl, you and others like you have jolly well gone and proved them wrong.'

Mary's head spun as she turned from one friendly face to the other. There was too much to take in, surrounded by cushions and footstools, by expensive knick-knacks behind the doors of a glass-fronted cabinet, by gilt-framed oil paintings and tasteful arrangements of dried flowers in copper jugs. And where had Peggy got to?

'Well, Mary?' Marjorie urged. 'I expect you were a tomboy as a child, just like our Peggy — always climbing trees or playing cricket?'

'I have two brothers — so, yes,' Mary managed to reply before Peggy returned, cradling in her arms a plump baby with curly black hair. The child was wrapped in a white crocheted blanket, awake and alert to what was going on around her.

'This is my daughter, Rosie,' Peggy informed Mary in a voice as soft and smooth as silk as she sat next to her on the settee.

'She's . . . lovely.' Mary's mouth fell open in stunned surprise. No single adjective was good enough. The baby was adorable, beautiful, helpless, contented and perfect. As for Peggy, not only was she a recent widow but a mother too! Rosie turned her head to gaze at Mary with big, brown eyes fringed with dark lashes. And just look at that mass of curls! 'Really and truly, she's absolutely smashing.'

'She is.' Rosie's grandfather smiled broadly. 'We're pleased as punch that Peggy trusts us to look after her precious girl.'

'She's developed a rash,' Marjorie informed her daughter. 'The nurse assures me that it's too early for Rosie to be teething but not to worry; I just have to keep her clean, dust her off with talcum powder and change her nappy every two or three hours.'

Peggy held her baby daughter to her chest and rocked her gently. Rosie's rosebud lips made a popping sound then she raised a tiny hand to touch Peggy's cheek.

'I see from the ring on your finger that you're married,' Timothy said to Mary. 'Do you have any children?'

'What a question,' Marjorie remonstrated. 'Mary is nowhere near old enough to consider having babies.'

'Not yet,' she confirmed, melting to her core as she observed the tender scene. 'My husband is in Essex at present — at RAF Wormingford. I — we — hope to have a family as soon as the war ends.'

We will live contentedly in a house more modest than this, with a modern kitchen and, if we're lucky, space for a car in a driveway. We'll have a nursery room facing south to make the most of the sun. A golden future together.

15

Later that evening Mary invited Viv and Bobbie to her room. They sat in their dressing gowns, with faces scrubbed clean of make-up, their hair and teeth newly brushed.

'So what's up?' Viv sensed that Mary was sitting on some momentous news. 'Let me guess — you and Cameron are having a baby?'

'No, but you're on the right lines.' Mary hugged Peggy's joyful secret to her chest for a little while longer.

Bobbie hazarded her own guess. 'All right then — Cameron has been granted a few days' leave. You'll be together over Christmas?'

'If only.' Mary sighed.

'You've been promoted to second officer?'

'You've had a letter from Tom?'

'You've won a thousand pounds on the football pools?'

Viv's last wild guess made Mary laugh. 'Not even close. You were warmer earlier on. Who is the last person at Rixley that you'd expect to have a three-month-old daughter?'

'Hilary,' Bobbie said with a light laugh.

'Olive. Horace. Dotty Kirk. Ernest. Florrie Loxley.' Viv shouted out increasingly unlikely suggestions.

'You're miles off. Do you give up?'

'Yes, yes!' Bobbie and Viv threw up their hands in defeat.

'All right then, hold on to your hats — the answer

226

is: it's Peggy.'

Bobbie had been lounging in the room's one easy chair but now she sat bolt upright in amazement. 'Blow me down — you mean Peggy Ibbotson?'

'Yes — there's only one Peggy in this ferry pool, as far as I know.' During the drive back from North-gate Mary had made a point of asking if she might pass on the news about Rosie to her best friends, Bobbie and Viv. Peggy had permitted her to share on one condition. 'Be sure to tell them that darling Rosie has her father's eyes.'

'The Cold Front?' Viv gasped, jumping up from Mary's bed then jigging about the room. 'Peggy has a baby? Who with? Why didn't she tell us? I'd no idea she was even married.'

'Calm down.' Mary was delighted to be the purveyor of good news for a change. 'This afternoon I went with Peggy to her family home in Northgate and met little Rosie. Peggy even let me hold her for a while. Her skin is the colour of a ripe peach and she has the deepest brown eyes — like her father's, by all accounts.'

'Jeez, she kept that quiet.' Viv felt vaguely disgruntled and then had the grace to be embarrassed. 'I got Peggy all wrong, didn't I? I was too busy being jealous that she got the first cross-Channel crate to get to know her properly.'

'Good for you for giving her a chance, Mary.' Bobbie realized that she too had kept her distance.

'I didn't do much,' Mary protested. 'Peggy just took to me for some reason. Anyway, listen — there's more to tell you. It turns out that Peggy's husband was killed during a bombing mission so she's left with a tiny baby and luckily two parents who are willing to

227

look after Rosie while Peggy carries on flying.'

The news brought a more sober mood into the room and the three girls sat down together on Mary's bed.

'Did Peggy explain why she made the decision to carry on flying?' Bobbie had a special interest in hearing the answer. She thought of Peggy and her baby then of Jean and Dorota and finally of her own situation with Ray.

'I did ask her,' Mary answered. 'She said it was to do with proving to herself that she had the strength and willpower to keep going — you know how it is.'

'Only too well,' Bobbie said. 'I've heard tell of a Scottish Atta girl called Beattie Lawrence who got news of her fiancé's ship having been torpedoed in the Med. It was blown to pieces; only three people survived, one of whom drove all the way north to Beattie's ferry pool and delivered the bad news in person. She cried, of course. But next day she was dicing again, flying a crate from her base in Lossiemouth to Bristol then back from there in a Spit Mark Four.'

'I like to think we'd all do the same if it came to it.' Viv spoke from the heart. 'Not that I have a fiancé in the navy to worry about; only my handsome landlubber friend who won't even get his feet wet if he can help it. And don't look at me like that, you two. You both know perfectly well that Giles and I are — how shall I put it? — reconciled.'

'Is that what you call it?' Mary teased. She enjoyed the sight of Viv blushing for once.

'I'm not saying that anything serious — you know — has actually happened. Well, maybe the odd kiss here and there. But mostly Giles and I just talk. Oh, and by the way, yesterday he and I had an interesting encounter with the dreaded Nora.'

'Did you indeed?' Bobbie pricked up her ears.

'Here, at the Grange. Nora brought the Parsevals' driver along — a big, grizzly bear of a man. She was intent on digging up evidence against Giles as regards Anna's baby — to help with her divorce settlement.'

'I bet that was tricky,' Mary commented. 'How did Giles react?'

'He kept his temper. And guess what? In spite of everything he still wouldn't let me implicate Sir Thom —'

Bobbie and Mary stared at Viv in stunned surprise.

'Oh, Jeez!' She saw the cogs in their brains slowly turning. 'No — forget I said that.'

'Sir Thomas?' Bobbie's frown was deep. 'What does he have to do with Anna?'

'Nothing,' Viv said hastily.

Mary shook her head knowingly. 'You mean to say that Sir Thomas — not Giles — is Dorota's father?'

'Stop!' Viv pleaded. The incriminating phrase had slipped out before she'd realized. 'I'm sworn to secrecy — please don't say a word.'

Bobbie breathed out heavily. 'If you say so.'

'Promise me, Mary,' Viv begged.

'My lips are sealed.' But Mary and Bobbie were flabbergasted. All of a sudden the picture built up around Anna's tragic circumstances shifted. Reasons and motives collapsed; the perpetrator was not who they'd thought.

'One thing is certain,' Mary said as the three girls clasped hands and swore secrecy. 'Nothing is ever as it seems.'

* * *

Next morning there was the usual scramble for chits outside Gillian's hatch.

A bleary-eyed Viv stood yawning at the back of the queue, complaining to Mary that she hadn't slept a wink. Meanwhile, Bobbie had reached the front and received her instructions for the day.

Her face lit up and she waved her slip of paper in the air. 'Good Lord, can you believe it? They're sending me across the Channel in the very latest Spit!'

'You don't say.' Horace's expression gave nothing away but he was, in fact, green with envy. Taking his own chit he saw he was dicing with a Faithful Annie — strong and reliable but one of the least exciting crates around. 'It's all right for some,' he grumbled as he watched Bobbie race downstairs at full tilt.

Shuffling to the front of the queue, Peggy found that she'd bagged a Hurricane.

'Where to?' Mary asked her as she descended the stairs at a more sedate pace than Bobbie.

'Southampton.' Peggy was as businesslike as usual, without a hint of the maternal tenderness Mary had witnessed the previous day.

'Watch out for the blimps,' Mary reminded her.

'Thank you, I will. Oh, and by the way, I spoke to Hilary about the Christmas party.'

Viv, who was close at hand, butted in: 'What does he say?'

'That he's prepared to discuss the situation further with Group Captain Norris once he can pin him down to a time.'

'So no final decision yet?' Mary asked.

'Not as far as I know.' In a hurry to collect her helmet and goggles from her locker, Peggy didn't linger. 'Apparently the recent change of heart didn't come

230

from the very top, though,' she called back. 'According to Hilary that decision was made by a Flight Lieutenant Wheeler.'

'I might have known!' As Peggy swung through the door on to the concrete yard, Viv struck her forehead with the palm of her hand. 'This is because I told him that I didn't want to be romantically involved. He's done it out of spite.'

'Bloody hell, Viv; what were you thinking?' From behind her hatch Gillian had overheard her remark. 'I've had my eye on Brian Wheeler for weeks — he's the bee's knees!'

'Yes, bloody hell, Viv.' There was a low chorus of female voices.

'Couldn't you have strung him along a while longer?'

'He definitely seems the type to turn nasty if you upset him.'

'Now look!'

'*Mea culpa!*' Viv continued to beat her brow. 'This is all my fault.'

Mary couldn't help smiling at her friend's woebegone expression. 'What exactly did you say to him when you gave him the brush-off?'

Viv wrinkled her nose in an effort to remember. 'I think he used the word 'tryst' and I objected.'

'Come again?' Gillian queried with an air of mild disbelief.

"Tryst' — who in their right mind uses a silly word like that? Besides, he was sporting a nasty little 'tache.'

'Is that all?' Mary asked, unblinking. Tryst and a moustache hardly counted as hanging offences.

'No, it's not all. The guy accused me of flirting with him,' Viv said indignantly while Gillian burst out laughing. 'I wasn't!' Viv protested. 'It's just that Brian

Wheeler's head is so darned big that he's convinced any girl who so much as looks his way will fall head over heels.'

'Are we sure it was him who turned down our invite?' To Mary it seemed there were various possibilities. 'What if one of the other trainers thought it was a bad idea to let so many cadets out of the camp at one time?'

'No, Peggy said it was Wheeler.' Viv was convinced. 'He's put a spanner in the works and all because I told him to his face *nein danke, mein herr, non merci, niet.*'

★　★　★

'Oh dear, another washout day.' On the Wednesday Bobbie raised the blackout blind in her bedroom to see a six-inch covering of snow on the ground. It smoothed out the harsh contours of the rocky horizon and lay in drifts against low stone walls that made a picturesque patchwork of the rolling countryside — spectacularly beautiful but frustrating as far as getting off the ground was concerned.

She went down to breakfast to find that her fellow pilots had already accepted the weather situation and were taking their time over their porridge and toast and jam.

'There's no rush,' Viv confirmed as Bobbie joined her and Mary. 'Dotty dropped by with the forecast. Snow has fallen across the entire country so she says there's no point showing up at the ferry pool until midday at the earliest.'

'Don't you hate being at a loose end?' Mary tapped the table with her spoon — an impatient gesture that she didn't try to hide.

'Yes, it gives you too much time to think.' Bobbie decided that rather than waste the morning she would tramp through the snow and call in on Jean and Dorota at Fern Cottage. There she would be able to describe Monday's feeling of exhilaration when she'd flown her Spit across the Channel for the very first time; 10,000 feet up in a clear blue sky, soaring above mile after mile of sparkling water, chasing those invisible stars.

Meanwhile, Viv propositioned Mary to join her in another impromptu excursion to Thresham in Ernest's Ford pick-up.

'Whatever for?' Mary was dubious. 'To keep an eye on Ray, for a start. We can report back to you,' she assured Bobbie, who shook her head.

'No thanks; I don't want him to think I'm sending my spies.'

'OK then, I admit that it's Giles I want to see. I have to own up to having let my tongue run away with me on the subject of Sir T.'

'Then why on earth would you want me tagging along?' Mary asked.

'This is me thinking of others for once. Didn't you just say that you hated sitting around twiddling your thumbs?'

'All right — I suppose I'll come.' Reluctantly agreeing to meet Viv in the stable yard in half an hour, Mary drifted off. She went upstairs to put on an extra pair of socks then down to the yard in search of some sacking and two sturdy shovels in case their pick-up got stuck in a snowdrift. 'I'll drive,' she told Viv, who had arrived ten minutes late.

'No, let me — you don't know the way.' Viv climbed into the cab and turned the ignition key then listened to the cold engine's sluggish response as Mary got in beside her. 'You can drive on the way back if you like.'

So they set off at a snail's pace along lanes transformed by overnight snow. All was a crisp, sparkling white — the branches of trees shed light flurries of snowflakes as they drove under them and their tyres crunched over the unmarked surface. The water in Rixley reservoir was frozen at the edges.

'See those ducks!' Mary pointed off to their right. Instead of their usual liquid landing, the small flock of birds found themselves skating on thin ice, wings flapping frantically as they skidded to a halt. Beyond the reservoir, two planes flew steadily from east to west.

'Wellingtons or Beauforts?' Viv tried to guess.

'It's hard to tell from this distance. Definitely ours, though.' Now that she was out and about on this bright morning, Mary began to enjoy the sights. She spotted two deer in a copse of silver birch trees but they'd bounded off before she had time to point them out to Viv. Then they identified animal tracks at the sides of the road — a neat, precise fox trail and something heavier and more indistinct — possibly a badger roused from semi-hibernation.

Before long they ran into one of the drifts that Mary had expected. It was on an exposed ridge about two miles from Thresham where the wind had swept the snow across the road, bringing the pick-up truck sliding to a halt.

'Don't worry — I came prepared.' Mary clambered down from the cab. She took the shovels from under a tarpaulin in the back and together the girls began to dig. 'No slacking — put your back into it, Miss Glamour Puss,' Mary instructed.

'Yes, ma'am!'

It was heavy work but exhilarating — shovelling snow on to the side of the road, pausing occasionally and looking down into the valley or up into a sky marbled with pinkish cloud. Once Mary was satisfied that they'd shovelled long enough, she laid half a dozen hessian sacks under the truck's back wheels. 'To stop us skidding,' she explained. 'Try to get away in second gear and don't use too many revs — go on, do as you're told.'

So Viv followed instructions and eased the truck forward until they were clear of the drift, waiting only for Mary to load the shovels and sacks into the back before they set off again for a mostly trouble-free glide down into the valley.

'Go easy on the brakes,' Mary instructed when the back wheels of the truck shimmied sideways. 'Use your gears to keep your speed down — that's better, easy does it.'

'Honey, you're talking to a girl from Canada,' Viv reminded her with a grin. 'We have snow there like you wouldn't believe.'

'And I'm the girl who joined the ATA as a driver,' Mary countered good-naturedly. Yes, she was glad she'd come after all, and she made a plan to stay well in the background when they got to the training yard, to give Viv and Giles all the time and space they needed.

'What's your opinion of horses in general?' Viv passed the time as they drove the final stretch.

'I haven't had much to do with them, if I'm honest.' Mary had vivid childhood memories of an enormous piebald carthorse employed to pull the rag-and-bone man's wagon (a stringy, skinny, dark-haired man with a thin Woodbine cigarette permanently drooping from the corner of his mouth) and of a sturdy Welsh pony unimaginatively called Dobbin who was used to pull the milk float before Billy Marsh had bought himself an electric one.

'Personally, I hate 'em,' Viv admitted, her heart starting to flutter as they drove into the empty yard — she'd started to call it 'the Giles effect'.

'Well?' she asked as Mary took in her smart surroundings.

'Blimey, these horses live the life of Riley!' The rows of immaculately painted stable doors and the array of shiny bits and bridles visible through the open tackroom door impressed her. The yard was already swept clear of snow and the water troughs were free from ice. When two noble-looking grey horses poked their heads over their stable doors and focused on the new arrivals, Mary saw that their manes were long and silky, their eyes bright and alert.

'You're right there.' Jumping down from the truck, Viv looked around for signs of activity and before long Ronnie emerged from the tack room. 'There you are!' she exclaimed. 'I wondered where everyone had got to.'

'If you're looking for Mr Giles, he's up at the house with Mr Ray,' he informed her while Mary continued to look on from inside the cab. 'The snow was bad over in Highcliff so I'm still waiting for Philip and t'other lad to show up.'

'It wasn't too bad at Rixley. We had to dig ourselves out of a two-foot drift up on the top, though.' Finding that Ronnie was more talkative than usual, Viv beckoned Mary down from the truck. 'I've brought my friend along; Mary Ainslie, this is Ronnie . . . sorry, I can never remember.'

'Evans,' he reminded her.

'Pleased to meet you, Mr Evans.' Mary and Ronnie shook hands.

'You're a pilot an' all?' He looked her up and down then sniffed sceptically.

Unsure of his reaction when she told him yes, she was relieved when Ronnie was distracted by the sound of men's voices growing louder as they approached the yard from the lane.

'About bloody time,' he muttered with a glance at his watch before striding away.

'That must be Philip and Wilf. Don't mind Ronnie,' Viv whispered to Mary. 'Bobbie says his bark is worse than his bite.' She invited her to come up to the house and say hello to Ray and Giles and after a short debate, despite her earlier good intentions, Mary agreed.

The two girls chatted cheerfully as they left the yard. They were confessing the secret envy they'd both felt over Bobbie's cross-Channel flight earlier that week when Viv knocked on the door and Ray promptly answered.

He glanced sharply at Viv and Mary in uniform, with their sheepskin collars turned up to protect them against the cold, then peered past them. 'Did Bobbie come with you?' he asked, more in hope than expectation.

Viv could see that he was on edge but not visibly under the influence. 'No. The weather's a washout this morning so she went to visit Jean Thornton.'

'You'd better come in,' he told them. For a self-deluding moment he'd hoped that Bobbie had relented, and he felt a thud of disappointment in his chest when he learned that she hadn't.

So Viv kicked off her boots and stepped inside while

an indecisive Mary lingered on the doorstep.

'Giles is in the study — second door on the right,' Ray mentioned, reaching for his jacket and cap that hung from a hall stand. 'Mary, why don't I show you around? I was on my way down to the yard, in any case.'

She gave him a relieved smile. 'Three is definitely a crowd.'

So off they went while Viv sneaked into the study and crept up on Giles. Ray and Mary heard his cry of surprise then her inimitable laugh — full throated and uninhibited.

'Those two seem to be getting along like a house on fire these days,' Ray commented as they approached the yard. He fumbled awkwardly with a gate latch then asked the question that had been on the tip of his tongue. 'How is Bobbie, Mary?'

'She's champion.' Mary's reply was guarded. 'More to the point — how are you?'

'Still on the wagon, if that's what you mean. Did she ask you to keep an eye on me?'

He paused by the first stable they came to and absent-mindedly rubbed the nose of its occupant. 'There, there, Glasgow Girl,' he murmured. 'We know you miss Bobbie too.'

'No — this was Viv's idea to stop me from fretting over Cameron.' Mary glanced towards the cart shed from where the clang of a hammer against metal emerged. The sun had started to melt the snow on the stable roofs and there was a steady drip-dripping as a background to Ray and Mary's staccato conversation. She felt sorry for him — it was surely a massive strain to run this business single-handed and for him to have the added worry of knowing that the girl he loved diced with death on a daily basis. 'Bobbie does care for you,' she assured him as they strolled across the yard.

Just then Ronnie came out of the cart shed, hammer in hand, to call at the top of his voice: 'Philip, Wilf — come and lend a hand in here, will you?'

Philip emerged from the tack room while Wilf, who was out of sight but not out of earshot, put down the spade he'd been using to clear a narrow path through the snow from the yard to the muck heap. Mary's back was turned when he entered the yard.

'What's up, Ronnie?' Ray enquired matter-of-factly.

'We have to jack up the back end of the pick-up truck,' the head groom explained. 'I need to take a good look at the axle.'

Wilf caught sight of a small, slight figure in ATA uniform standing in the middle of the yard with her collar turned up, her forage cap tilted to one side. She wore trousers and fleece-lined boots, but even under the heavy clothing he knew in an instant who it was. He stopped in his tracks, panicked, turned and set off at a run.

'What the heck?' Ronnie gave a loud yell as he saw Wilf turn tail. 'Go after him,' he growled at Philip.

Wilf's sudden twist and turn caused him to stumble and pitch head first into a heap of cleared snow. He put out both arms to break his fall then rolled behind the snow pile. Mary turned to watch what was going on. Someone had fallen — she couldn't see clearly who it was because there was a water trough in the way.

Wilf struggled to get up, slipping and sliding on the slushy surface. Philip caught up with him and offered a helping hand.

Tom! A shock ran through Mary that scrambled her senses and made her gasp for air. *Surely not!*

'Blithering idiot!' Ronnie stood, hands on hips. 'He's not right in the head, that one,' he muttered before he hurried across the yard to offer Wilf a piece of his mind.

Tom — how can it be? But yes: Philip raised him to his feet and there could be no mistake. The tousled, unkempt hair was the right colour, and it was Tom's sturdy build, Tom's baby-faced features, Tom's way of ducking his head and squirming when he knew he was in trouble.

'Mary?' Ray queried. She'd turned white as a sheet and, with one hand to her throat, she seemed unable to breathe.

'What's he doing here?' she whispered hoarsely, clutching at Ray's arm.

'Wilf? He's helping out for a while, but to be honest he's not up to much.' Ray watched the continuing tussle as Philip held on to the offender and Ronnie yelled at him. 'I'm starting to think he's more trouble than he's worth.'

Mary held tight to Ray. She shook her head vehemently. *Tom's alive — thank God!*

'What's wrong?' Ray worried that Mary was the fainting sort. 'Do you need to sit down?'

'No.' Still shaking her head, she tried to suck in air. 'What is he doing here? How on earth . . . ?'

'Let go of him,' Ronnie instructed Philip gruffly. 'Now, lad — what are you up to? Come on, spit it out.'

As Philip released his hold, Wilf shied away — he had to get out of there before Mary gave the game away. So off he ran again in a blind panic, this time through the gate and up the path towards the house.

240

16

Inside the study in the main house Giles wasn't surprised by Viv's confession. 'To be honest, I expected you to let slip the truth about Father long before now,' he admitted, while silently worrying about what the consequences might be.

'It wasn't on purpose,' she insisted. 'I was describing Nora's visit to Bobbie and Mary and Sir Thomas's name just slipped out. Have you heard from Nora's solicitor, by the way?'

Giles shook his head. 'They say no news is good news but in this case it simply means that her side is marshalling its forces prior to another attack.'

'And nothing from Sir Thomas and Lady Jane?'

'No, not a dicky bird.'

Their subdued and serious conversation was suddenly interrupted by the sound of a loud shout coming from the yard.

'Come back, damn you!'

'What's that rumpus?' Giles went out into the hall then flung open the front door to investigate. Viv, meanwhile, went to watch events unfold through the study window.

She caught sight of the lad, Wilf, cutting around the side of the house, rapidly followed by Philip and Ronnie. He seemed to be heading up the slope, across country towards the gallops, but snowdrifts hindered his progress. He stumbled, fell, then picked himself up while his two pursuers gained on him. Spotting French doors opening from the study on to a small terrace, Viv found she could open them and join the chase.

'Damned fool!' Ronnie was quickly out of breath. He paused mid-coughing fit and ordered Philip to stay put. Meanwhile, Wilf pressed on up the hill.

'Let the silly idiot go.' As Viv caught up with them, the head groom turned back in high dudgeon towards the yard. 'Do we know what got into him?' he asked Philip.

'I have no idea.' As far as Philip was concerned, Wilf's flight had happened without warning. 'He was his normal self when I last spoke to him.'

'Shall Giles and I go after him?' Viv was aware that Giles was struggling through the snow towards them. At this rate Wilf would get clean away and no one would be any the wiser.

'Please yourselves.' Ronnie washed his hands of the whole time-wasting tomfoolery. 'Lord knows where the simpleton thinks he's going. There's nothing up there except trees and open moorland beyond. It wouldn't surprise me if he got stuck in a snowdrift and froze to death.'

Hearing this, Giles agreed with Viv that they should continue, but just then Ray yelled for Viv to return quickly to the house.

'It's Mary!' he called from the terrace. 'She's trying to tell me something but I can't make any sense of it.'

'That sounds serious,' Viv said to Giles with a small shudder.

'Leave it with me,' he said, setting off up the hill. Wilf was quite a way ahead at this point, about to disappear into the copse at the far end of the gallops.

Viv half-ran, half-slid down the hill towards the house.

'Mary's in a terrible state,' Ray explained as soon as she joined him, caked in snow up to her thighs. He seemed set on joining the pursuit, overriding Ronnie's order and telling Philip to accompany him. 'It's something to do with her brother,' he flung over his shoulder at Viv. 'The one that went missing in action.'

So Viv rushed on, not bothering to take off her jacket or boots as she entered the house the way she'd left it — through the French window into the study. 'Mary?' she called as she went through into the hall. 'Where are you?' There was no answer so Viv opened several doors until she found her friend stranded in an untidy lounge, standing in the middle of the room with her hands over her mouth. She wore the dazed expression of a rabbit caught in headlights.

'What's up?' Viv approached warily and led Mary to the nearest couch. 'You look as if you've seen a ghost.'

'Where's Tom?' Mary managed to say in a barely audible whisper. Resisting Viv's attempt to make her sit down, she pulled away.

Viv followed her to the window. 'Who do you mean?'

'My brother, Tom — where is he?'

'Honey, he's not here. Please sit down.'

As if she hadn't heard, Mary made a rush for the door. 'Tom's run off and I don't know why. We have to find him.'

'That wasn't your brother,' Viv tried to tell her, overtaking her in the hall and blocking her way. 'It was Philip's Quaker friend, Wilf. They live together in Highcliff.'

'I know my own brother!' Mary's frenzied cry rang through the house then her voice returned to its slow, faint whisper. 'He's not dead after all — he's alive. I

243

saw him with my own eyes.'

'OK, but come and sit down.' Perhaps it was best to humour her until she'd had time to calm down. *Is this what grief does to a person?* Viv wondered. *Do they sometimes imagine something that they want to be true?*

'You think I was seeing things but I wasn't.' Mary sat and with a tremendous effort composed herself. 'That was Tom; I swear on my life.'

Viv sat next to her. 'How can it have been? Your brother was reported missing. Yes, we can hope that he was captured and is being held prisoner; but nothing else makes any sense.'

'Don't say that.' It wasn't what Mary wanted to hear so she jumped up then strode restlessly round the room. 'Maybe Tom escaped from the German prison then found his way home.'

'And called himself Wilf and joined the Quakers?' Gently Viv pointed out the absurdities. 'Why would he do that?'

Mary stopped and wrung her hands. 'I don't have the answer. I only know that was my little brother out there in the yard. Tom is alive, and however much you try to tell me otherwise, I'm sticking to what I saw with my own two eyes.'

★ ★ ★

When Giles, Ray and Philip reached the copse, they found that the recently fallen snow made it simple to follow Wilf's trail.

'Footprints — over here,' Giles called after a few seconds of searching.

The others joined him. They kept their eyes peeled and listened for any sound that would lead them to the runaway.

'Obviously Mary's made a mistake,' Ray remarked to Philip as they followed Wilf's tracks. 'She seemed to think that your Quaker chap was someone else entirely.'

There was no response until the three men came through the small wood and out the other side, where they stood on a flat ledge of rock to inspect a stretch of untouched, open countryside beyond.

'What made him run when he saw her?' Philip asked.

'Good point. Something put the wind up him.' Giles picked up the trail once more and he jumped down from the crag into a soft drift of snow that came up to his waist. He struggled out with Philip's help. 'What do you know about this lad?' he asked as they continued to search.

'His grandfather was a Friend in our Highcliff community. But the Cranstons didn't stick around after the First War — they moved away to York to find work.'

'But Wilf wasn't happy there?' Giles forged ahead towards a rocky outcrop a hundred yards along the ridge.

'Evidently not.' Philip preferred to stick to the facts. 'There are different branches of Quakers — some more traditional than others. Wilf came to us because we're seen as more liberal.'

'And what did you make of him when he first arrived?' Ray asked.

'We're taught not to judge.'

The stonewalling irritated Ray. 'But off the record?'

'He's young. He still has a lot to learn.' *Off the record — young and somewhat secretive, ill at ease in meetings.* Wilf had arrived at the Old Court House with only the clothes he stood up in and a small canvas knapsack. He'd talked very little about his past but had knuckled down to any physical tasks given to him — with a notable absence of skill, it had to be said. Philip told Ray and Giles none of this as they continued their search.

When they came to the second outcrop they stopped again and examined a scuffed patch of snow where Wilf had probably stopped to work out his next move. He'd set off again in a new direction, down into the valley and towards another small copse. Giles, Ray and Philip scanned the area and sure enough it wasn't long before they saw movement — a solitary figure dodging between trees.

'There he is!' Ray set off on a fresh mission to corner his quarry. 'Spread out, you two. There's another rocky stretch beyond the wood — with luck we can approach from different directions and box him in.'

The tactic worked. On the leeward side of the hill the snow was less deep and they covered the ground fast, with Giles on the left flank and Philip to the right. Soon they closed in on Wilf, who seemed to have given up by the time they reached him, crouching under an overhang, shivering and with his arm crooked over his head as if by this means he could make himself invisible.

'Get up.' Ray stooped to pull Wilf roughly from his hiding place.

'Go steady, old chap.' Giles saw that the fight had gone out of the boy.

So Ray eased off and allowed Philip to step in.

'Come on, Wilf — let's sort this out. We'll all walk back together. You don't have to explain until you're ready. That's right — come along now.'

By coaxing him in this way, the small group retraced their steps. Wilf hung his head and didn't try to escape, only halting on the gallops when the house at Thresham came into view.

Seeing that he might turn tail again, Giles blocked his path and spoke like a stern schoolmaster. 'It's no good, sonny; time to face the music.'

Wilf allowed them to push him on. He'd almost made it — almost but not quite. After his gargantuan efforts; after the risks he'd taken and the lies he'd told; after that one bad action on the battlefield — still he hadn't made it out of the mess he'd created for himself. And all because of Mary, damn her.

'Chin up, old chap,' Giles advised as they frogmarched him down the hill.

★ ★ ★

'Word from Rixley is that the whole day's a washout,' Viv told Mary in the living room at Thresham. It was just as well — it was almost eleven and Mary was in no fit state to fly. 'I've been on the blower to the ops room. Douglas said not to bother clocking in until tomorrow morning.'

'Wherever can they be?' Mary had refused to move away from the window until Ray returned with Tom. 'Has there been an accident? What on earth's happening out there?'

Viv volunteered to go out and assess events from the terrace, though she did so with a sinking heart. Whichever way she looked at it, there was no happy ending to this particular story — of that she was pretty sure. Outside, a strong sun had set in motion a rapid thaw and the sky was a dense blue, which made the snow on the hills seem whiter still. Focusing on the high gallops, she made out a group of four men so she returned quickly and reported back to Mary. 'It looks like they've nabbed Wilf, so we'll soon sort this out,' she reassured her. 'It'll turn out that your brother has an exact double — that's the logical explanation.'

Mary refused to listen. Instead, she rushed outside and began to run up the hill.

'Oh, Jeez,' Viv muttered to herself. Still, the sooner they got this over with the better. So she too set off to meet the group.

'Here comes trouble,' Giles predicted when he saw Mary and Viv making their way towards them.

Tom stiffened then stopped. Should he invent yet another whopper and swear on his life that his name was Wilf Cranston and that he'd never seen Mary before? Would that wash?

'Tom!' Mary's arms were outstretched and she made a sound somewhere between a sob and a gasp. He'd changed since he'd joined the army — his body had filled out and his lovely thick brown hair had been subjected to the regulation short back and sides. Yet she knew in her bones that it was him.

He was afraid he couldn't bluff his way out in the face of his sister's challenge; his voice would break down and give him away. So he stood rooted to the snowy hillside, awaiting his fate.

Mary flew at him and hugged him without speaking until Viv pulled them apart. Then Mary sobbed and still without saying a word she allowed herself to be led back to the house.

★ ★ ★

'For what it's worth, I think you're doing the right thing.' Jean sat in her Fern Cottage kitchen with Dorota on her lap. She'd listened to Bobbie's reasons for staying away from Thresham and found them sound. 'Hard as it is in the short term, in the long run it'll be for the best.'

Bobbie smiled faintly. 'I knew from the start that Ray has two sides to him. Most people see the dashing, charming Ray, but you only have to scratch the surface to discover something much more complicated.'

'Of course — that's the reason you fell for him — you wouldn't have been interested if charm was all there was.' Jean reached for the rattle that Dorota had thrown on to the floor. She held it behind her back then produced it again as if by magic. 'Where's it gone? Oh, it's there!'

The curly-haired little girl gave a delighted squeal then seized the toy and threw it down again.

'Right now the complications have got the better of Ray,' Bobbie continued. 'Keeping the business going is hard at the best of times, but the war and then his dad dying have made it doubly difficult. There are fewer race meetings, for a start. And then owners complain when their horses don't win. On top of which, Ray can't get rid of the guilt he feels about being forced out of the RAF. It's a heavy burden to be labelled mentally unfit.'

'Yes,' Jean agreed as she continued the game of hide-the-rattle. 'If there's an obvious injury — like Douglas's leg, for instance — people are much more willing to sympathize.'

'But if you can't see the damage — if it isn't physical — often they don't understand.'

Jean stood up and carried Dorota to her playpen in a corner of the room where there were more toys for her to play with. 'Does Ray understand that the way out is not through the bottle?'

'Yes, but I suppose it helps him to forget.' Bobbie's anxiety eased as she shared her worries with Jean. 'I don't think Giles being there helps much either,' she admitted. 'They're both fond of a drink or two, then two drinks turn into three and sometimes four.'

'Yes; why is Giles staying at Thresham?' Jean wondered. 'What made him leave Newpark?'

Bobbie watched Dorota playing with coloured wooden bricks. 'His father threw him out,' she said in a tone that conveyed her disgust. Ought she to reveal to Jean the true story of Dorota's parentage? One glance at her friend's serene, contented face decided her against it, for what did it matter to Jean who the father was at the end of the day? 'You know that it's only twelve days until Christmas?' she reminded her by way of distraction.

'Yes, we're already halfway through Advent. When do you three want to cut down that tree, by the way?'

'Soon.' Bobbie's face grew suddenly glum. 'Did you know that the Aireby boys might not be allowed to come to our party after all? Hilary has promised to talk it through with Group Captain Norris but they're both tied up in meetings a lot of the time. Meanwhile, it's hard for us to plan.'

'I see.' Jean thought her way around the problem. 'Why not go ahead with the tree and the decorations anyway? ENSA is still providing the entertainment, I take it?'

'You mean we should make the best of a bad job, even if the boys don't come?' It did seem a pity, though;

after all, the Aireby boys deserved to have some festive fun as much as the Rixley contingent did.

'Exactly.' Dorota had just used the playpen bars to haul herself to her feet, to Jean's delight. 'Did you see that?' she exclaimed, crouching down to her daughter's level. 'Who's a clever girl?'

Bobbie's frown eased. 'You're right,' she declared as Jean lifted Dorota and cuddled her. 'Our Christmas party will be a success, with or without the Aireby cadets. The three musketeers — me, Mary and Viv — will make sure of that.'

★   ★   ★

'We haven't been able to get a word out of him,' Giles told Viv once they'd convinced Wilf to enter the house and sat him down with Mary in Ray's study. Philip and Ray had gone back to work on the yard. Meanwhile, Giles and Viv had promised to stand by in case of further trouble. 'You saw him; he clammed up the moment Mary flung her arms around him — stubborn as you like.'

'She still swears it's Tom.' Viv kept her voice low. 'I tried to persuade her that Wilf was his double — that it was all a big coincidence — but she wouldn't listen.'

Giles shrugged helplessly. 'All we can do is wait.'

Inside the room, Mary watched Tom like a hawk. She didn't care how long she had to wait for him to open up; she wouldn't budge until he did.

He refused to look back at her, though he felt her eyes burn into him. His only hope was that if he stayed silent long enough, maybe she would go away and leave him alone.

'How long do you intend to keep this up?' she

251

demanded in the end. Even if she had to shake the words out of him, she would make him speak.

There were books everywhere, from floor to ceiling. There was a desk with an open ledger on it and an empty whisky bottle on the mantelpiece next to a small statue of a horse. Tom took in everything except Mary's face — he couldn't bring himself to look in her direction.

'I can wait,' she said quietly. *For however long it takes.* This was conscripted soldier Tom, back from war. It was her baby brother Tom: champion sulker and master of pretence of the 'I'm-too-poorly-to-go-to-school' variety. Memories flooded back.

'Bloody hell, Mary; why did you have to go and ruin everything?' His resistance finally broke down and the angry words spilled out. 'You were always the goody-goody, weren't you?' Always with her head stuck in a book or busy winning prizes. 'And now you're a bloody Atta girl, playing the damned heroine. Well, you never saw what I saw in North Africa. You weren't in Germany, in the thick of it.'

'We thought you were dead,' she said, plain and simple.

'I might as well bloody be!' Resentment surged from deep inside. 'If you hadn't poked your nose in, I would've been all right.'

'Tom!'

He turned from the fireplace to stare furiously at her — thinking she was God's gift in her uniform. The ATA wasn't even a military operation, for Christ's sake!

'Finally you admit that it is you.' Mary remembered his angry outbursts as a child, especially when he couldn't get his way. 'I demand to know what you're playing at.'

'I'm saving my skin, that's bloody what! At least, I was until you ruined it for me.'

'Sit down — tell me about it.'

Tom paced the floor.

'All right then — don't sit.' There must be a key to this if only she could find it. 'How did you come by the name Wilf Cranston?'

Tom halted by the window and backtracked. 'Who says I'm not him?'

'I do.' She returned his stare without flinching. 'And I want an answer.'

'I have papers that say I am.'

'And where did you get them from?'

Mary's razor-sharp question robbed him of his last ounce of defiance. His shoulders sagged and he flopped down into a chair. 'If you must know, I stole them from a dead bloke. There — now the cat's got your tongue!'

She shut her eyes for a moment then opened them again. 'The real Wilf Cranston is dead?'

The word 'dead' unleashed a crystal-clear memory of the deed — Tom's disgraceful act and the point of no return.

In his mind's eye, Bob Jerome lay face up in the mud and Harry Williams tore open the dead man's jacket to steal his wallet. 'Caught in the act,' Harry muttered when he saw that Tom had witnessed what he'd done. No remorse — nothing. And Wilf Cranston had copped it alongside Bob Jerome — the lad from York lay spreadcagled on his back with dead eyes staring and blood dribbling from his mouth. Wilf would never know what Tom did next and with luck neither would anyone else. For that matter, he himself was scarcely conscious of what he did as he searched Wilf's pockets for wallet or watch — anything of any value that he could find. But there was a letter in a brown envelope. Around Tom, deafening mortars exploded and sent trees crashing and black earth showering down. A huddled man choked and sobbed then crawled on aimlessly through the smoke. Harry Williams had gone on to loot another body. Tom silently pocketed Wilf's letter.

Mary demanded more answers. 'You pretended to be him? Why?'

'Simple — Wilf had a letter exempting him from active service. He'd gone back to his Quaker roots and turned conchie. He would have been on his way home to Blighty in two days if he hadn't gone and copped it.'

'I see.' Mary's stomach churned. 'You saw it as your way out?'

'Wouldn't you?' Tom turned on her with renewed rage. 'You don't know what it's like, Mary, when Jerry lets you have it. Landmines exploding, men screaming, the smell of burning . . .'

'I do know,' she argued. 'I've been thousands of feet up in the air with no fuel. I've crash-landed. I've flown through fog and hail and snow — you name it.'

He refused to listen. 'It's not the same. You haven't starved and nearly frozen to death because Jerry has you cornered. No one in their right mind could stick it. Better to walk away, to bugger off no one knows where. After that it's days hiding in ditches, scrounging for scraps of food and you're all on your own, hoping and praying that a letter in your pocket will make the difference between living and dying . . .' His words faded and sobs rose in his throat.

254

Disbelief flowed through Mary. Her brother was a deserter — the worst of the worst. 'How could you?' But there was pity, too. It was all too easy to visualize Tom's desperation amid the chaos of the battlefield. Ray had suffered something similar and it was what she most feared for her beloved Cameron.

'I didn't think,' Tom cried. 'It was hell in that forest. I had to get away.'

'Oh, Tom, they'll send you to prison,' she murmured.

He looked up through his tears. 'Not if you don't tell them.'

There was another severe jolt, a further shock to her system. 'How can we keep it a secret? It's impossible.'

A cunning light appeared through the tears. 'Say you've made a mistake,' Tom pleaded. 'Come on, Mary — you're my sister. You don't want to be the one who sends me to prison, do you?'

Shaking her head and trembling violently, she backed away.

'Why not?' Tom advanced towards her with new determination. There was a way out after all. 'If you keep your gob shut I can go back to Highcliff with Philip. No one will be any the wiser.'

17

'It seems Mary has taken a turn for the worse and Lord knows, things were bad enough for her before.' Bobbie sat with Viv in the almost empty canteen at Rixley. It was Saturday, the weather was fine and they were on standby for two Priority One Waits, due in from Glasgow.

Viv agreed. 'To tell you the truth, the whole thing on Wednesday was pretty strange.' Stirring half a spoonful of sugar into her tea, she sifted through events at Thresham. 'I mean, how come she got it so wrong?'

'She must have been in a really bad way to begin with.' Twice in the last two days Bobbie had attempted to approach Mary and get her to talk but she'd been brushed off each time.

'That's just it — she wasn't.' Viv recalled how energetically Mary had taken charge of digging them out of the snowdrift during their drive to Thresham. 'She was dishing out orders left, right and centre. Even when we arrived at the yard she seemed chipper — right until the moment Wilf Cranston showed his ugly mug.'

For a while they sat in thoughtful silence. Stan and Gordon came into the canteen for breakfast, full of noisy, jokey chat as they sat at the next table, and then Dotty dropped by with an update on the weather.

'There's fog and ice around the west coast of Scotland but your crates got off the ground all right,' she reported to Viv and Bobbie. 'All being well, they should touch down here at nine hundred hours. Then

256

it'll be over to you two to take them on to Ventnor.'

Bobbie looked at her watch. 'That gives us roughly half an hour to get ready.'

'The thing is . . .' Viv drained her cup. 'Mary was in that study with Wilf for ages. What on earth did they find to talk about for all that time?'

'Yes, how long does it take for you to realize you've made the worst mistake of your life?' It was unlike Mary to be so idiotic. 'What did she say when the two of them eventually emerged?'

'Not much. It was Wilf who did most of the talking,' Viv remembered. 'He said he didn't blame Mary for what had gone on — he was willing to accept that she'd made a genuine mistake.'

'So he turned the other cheek, good Quaker that he is?'

'Right.' Neither Bobbie nor Viv was convinced.

'Did he say why he ran away in the first place?'

'He swore he didn't. He stumbled and fell, that's all. Then, before he knew it, he was being shouted at and threatened.'

'Who by?'

'By Ronnie. According to Wilf, Ronnie has developed a habit of picking on him so Wilf got it into his thick skull that the best idea was to stay out of his way until he calmed down. Only then events ran out of control and quickly turned into a full-scale hue and cry.'

'I can just about see that happening,' Bobbie conceded. 'Ronnie can be a wee bit fierce at times. But why won't Mary talk about it? She must know we're not just being nosy — that we genuinely care.'

'Maybe she's embarrassed. It's a darned silly thing — to mistake a total stranger for your long-lost brother.'

'Poor Mary; let's hope it doesn't get her down too much.' Bobbie, like Viv and the other Rixley pilots, was acutely conscious of what even a moment's loss of concentration could do in their line of work. 'Maybe we should try to get her to concentrate on more preparations for the party when we get back — arranging refreshments, rehearsing our song, deciding what to wear, and so on.'

Viv gave her hand a quick squeeze. 'You have a very kind heart, you know that? And talking of the Christmas party and our current problem with the Aireby boys' no-show, I have made a Plan with a capital P!'

'Uh-oh.' Bobbie made a cross with her forefingers, as if to ward off vampires.

'Relax; I won't drag you into it.' Noticing that Gordon and Stan had made their way out of the canteen and across to the control tower, Viv decided that it was time for her and Bobbie to pick up parachute packs and everything else they would need for their long flight south. 'Come on — I'll explain as we collect our gear.'

Bobbie was forced to jog to keep up. 'Don't tell me — you're tired of waiting for Hilary to come up trumps so you plan to go straight to the top yourself; to the elusive Group Captain Norris. You'll seek him here, you'll seek him there, then turn on the famous charm and persuade him to let his cadets come after all.'

'No — far better than that.' As they reached the locker-room door they heard planes flying in: two Spits with zebra-striped wings to denote their role in photo reconnaissance.

'Those two beauties must be ours,' Bobbie said with

mounting excitement. The very sight of them coming into land — so elegant, so light and fast — thrilled her to bits.

'Forget Norris.' Viv grabbed her map, gauntlets, helmet and goggles. 'My plan is to tackle the problem at source — namely Brian 'Call-me-gorgeous' Wheeler. If I play my cards right and appeal to his vanity, I reckon I can get him to change his mind and allow the boys to come after all.'

Bobbie chuckled sceptically as they hurried from the locker room out on to the runway. 'Good luck with that,' she said.

★   ★   ★

For Mary the last two days had passed in a daze. She'd scarcely slept since her conversation with Tom and had eaten hardly anything. The decision to stay silent for his sake had caused her much confusion and agitation, even though she knew she'd done everything possible to make him change his mind — to do the decent thing and give himself up — all to no avail.

'I can't.' Tom had trembled and cried. He'd said he couldn't bear to be sent to prison, that his nerves were shot to pieces because of what he'd seen on the battlefield. 'Chaps died in front of me, Mary. Landmines were the worst. I've seen fellows blown to smithereens. And you haven't a clue what they do to deserters in clink — you have to save me from being locked up.'

He'd strung the disjointed thoughts together between sobs and he'd clung to her arm. In the end she'd said yes, she would protect him, against her better judgement, provided he would knuckle down and do the land drainage work and jobs on Ray's yard

259

without complaining. That moment of giving in and agreeing to cover for Tom had felt like clinging on to a cliff edge with her fingertips, only to let go and plummet down into unknown depths.

Still she'd stuck to her promise and managed to do her job: flying an Ox-box to Liverpool on the Thursday then ferrying a Faithful Annie to Bristol the following day. However, even speaking to Cameron on the telephone had failed to lift her mood.

'How are you?' he asked her early on Saturday morning. Viv and Bobbie had already left for the ferry pool for P1W standby duty and Mary was wondering how to fill her day off without them.

'I'm fine, ta.' Her voice was faint on the crackly line.

'You don't sound it. What's up?'

'Nothing — honestly, I'm fine.' She cupped one hand over the receiver and kept her voice low in case anyone in the hall overheard. Horace passed by in his carpet slippers with a pipe in his mouth and a newspaper tucked under his arm while Peggy collared Hilary as he came down the stairs. 'How's life in RAF Wormingford?' Mary asked the man she loved.

'Busy,' he admitted, without going into details. 'You don't sound yourself — I'm worried about you.'

'No need,' she assured him with false cheeriness. They went on to talk of mundane things — Cameron had just had a much-needed haircut; Mary, Viv and Bobbie had gathered in the blue room on Thursday evening to rehearse 'Swinging on a Star'.

'No news of Tom, I take it?' Cameron asked towards the end of the call.

'None.' She hated herself as she delivered the falsehood in a flat, quiet voice.

'Don't give up hope, dear. And try not to worry too

260

much.' He spoke softly and earnestly, reluctant to end the conversation. But then loud pips told him that his money had almost run out so they said a hasty good-bye.

Clicking the receiver into its cradle, Mary felt dizzy from the enormity of what she'd just done. It was the first time she'd ever told Cameron a lie and it lay heavily on her conscience. Her shoulders sagged as she prepared to go upstairs to her room.

'Good morning, Mary.' Peggy broke off from her talk with Hilary. She looked crisp and businesslike in a pale blue blouse, tailored skirt and black, heeled shoes. 'By the way, I'm taking darling Rosie and my parents for tea in Northgate later today. It would be delightful to have your company, should you happen to be free.'

Mary mumbled an excuse and hurried on. Once she reached the privacy of her own room she sank on to the bed and sat without moving. *Why not confide in Cameron?* she wondered. *He's my husband; I ought to tell him everything.*

I could have said, 'Yes, there's news. Tom is alive. He came back to Yorkshire under false pretences. He made me promise not to give him away.'

Imagine that! Picture Cameron's shocked voice telling me how wrong I was to aid a deserter. 'Report him. Do it now, Mary, without delay,' would have been his instant response.

But Cameron hadn't been there in the stuffy, musty study room at Thresham, listening to Tom's terrified account of the battle in the German forest, witnessing the desperation in his eyes. He hadn't felt a sickening sensation when Tom had admitted to stealing the envelope from his dead comrade's pocket or listened

261

to his petulant justification of the act. Her own emotions had swung violently between condemnation and pity. But Cameron hadn't lived in the family home with Tom as she had — favoured by their stern father but given no guidance over how to tell the difference between right and wrong. How, then, could Cameron be in a position to judge?

Desertion, Mary! She imagined her husband's voice playing on inside her head as she sat staring out at a cold, grey sky. *Call it by whatever name you like but it boils down to the same thing. Tom buckled while his comrades fought on. He fled the battlefield. He turned his back on honour and chose disgrace.*

★ ★ ★

'It's over to you, girls.' Gordon met Bobbie and Viv at the end of Runway 2. He winked as he wiped his hands on a cloth that he tucked into the back pocket of his overalls before sauntering off towards the nearest hangar.

'Not so fast.' Stan approached them in a more serious mood. 'Let me introduce you both to the Spitfire PR11 and tell you all you need to know.'

'Thanks, Stan — we appreciate it.' Bobbie fastened her helmet and dutifully followed him to the nearest crate.

'All these reconnaissance types are fitted with extra fuel tanks,' he explained, demonstrating as he talked. There's a thirty-gallon tank here under the port wing, see? That gives you a two-thousand-mile range. These two have a standard Mark-Nine fuselage.'

'With sliding hoods and five cameras?' Viv enquired. She took a special interest in photo reconnaissance

262

and had taken care to learn the variations of each type.

'Correct.' Stan was impressed by her knowledge of the modified aircraft. 'Different size lenses cover all bases, including high-, medium- and low-level reconnaissance. All gun ports are sealed over to reduce wind resistance and therefore produce maximum speed.' He stood back to let Bobbie and Viv circle their crates. 'Any questions?' he asked once they had finished their inspections.

'Not a single one,' Bobbie told him. 'Shall we get cracking?'

'You bet.' Stan stuck his fingers in his mouth and whistled for Gordon to return. 'Get off the ground as quick as you can to stop her overheating,' he reminded Bobbie. 'There's poor airflow through the radiator duct under the starboard wing.'

'Thanks, Stan.' Without further ado, Bobbie vaulted on to the striped wing and into the snug cockpit. Once she was strapped in and with her parachute pack safely tucked under her seat, she ran systematically through the checks — HTTMP — hydraulics, trimmers, throttle, mixture, pitch. Then PFGG — petrol, flaps, gills, gauges. Finally FUST — fuel boosters, unlock controls, superchargers, tail wheel lock.

'See you when you get back,' Stan promised with a final thumbs up.

'Get a move on!' Viv yelled above the roar of the engine and the whir of the propeller. 'I'm freezing to death down here.'

Bobbie slid the canopy into place. Seconds later Stan and Gordon had removed the chocks and she was ready for take-off.

As Bobbie taxied away, Viv climbed into her own crate. The latest met office report gave visibility of

1,000 yards with a 600 feet cloud cover — the minimum required if you went by the rule book. Not that Viv intended to do that, of course — not with a P1W sticker attached to her chit. If necessary she would forget about contact with landmarks on the ground and fly up and over any lump of cloud she hit.

Stan and Gordon waited for Viv to run meticulously through her checks.

'She's thorough — I don't care what anyone says.' Gordon saw beyond Viv's racy reputation to a pilot who was scrupulous when it came to technical details.

'She loves her crates, does Second Officer Robertson,' Stan acknowledged. He was dying for a cigarette once they got back to the canteen.

From the cockpit Viv watched Bobbie's perfect take-off then signalled to the ground crew for chocks away. Seconds later she rumbled along the runway, picking up speed and feeling the usual surge of excitement. Seeing Bobbie circle the base, she realized that her fellow pilot had decided to wait for her. They would fly south together.

The land beneath Viv's wheels blurred. She increased revs and felt the crate lift. Up she went, gaining height, glancing at piles of dirty snow on the roadsides and at smoke drifting up from chimneys at Burton Grange. Beside her, a hundred feet to starboard, Bobbie flew alongside. The two pilots grinned and exchanged thumbs ups. More revs, more height. Below them, Rixley already looked like a miniature village, while the clouds above swept sluggishly from east to west, carrying rain.

Bobbie and Viv's Spits rose beyond 1,000 feet through dense cloud. Their crates were buffeted this way and that but they fought the crosswind and

264

carried on climbing. At 3,000 feet they cleared the cloud. Above and ahead was perfect blue sky. There, in that moment, banking to port, dazzled by the morning sun, gazing down on a blanket of pure white cloud, there was nowhere on the entire planet that either woman would rather be.

★ ★ ★

After the thrill of flying the PR11s to Ventnor, the return journey in a clapped-out Blenheim was a definite come-down for Bobbie and Viv.

'We've found an oil leak in the starboard engine,' one of the Ventnor ground crew had informed them as they'd signed the paperwork. 'Nothing to worry about — just so long as you're aware.'

And, as it turned out, on top of the oil leak there was an uneven play in the throttle, plus fumes in the cockpit soon after take-off. The elderly bomber had a snag sheet as long as your arm.

'We're a sitting duck if Jerry spots us,' Viv complained as Bobbie slid into the cramped pilot's seat on the left-hand side of the nose and Viv took the place where the RAF navigator would sit. 'We've got about as much oomph in these engines as yon flock of seagulls.'

'She was all right in her day.' For Bobbie, the glamour of landing the PR Spit on the Isle of Wight in front of an admiring ground crew had not worn off and her mood was buoyant. 'Metal-alloy skin, retractable landing gear, two variable pitch props — all quite advanced in the nineteen thirties.'

'But look — you have to reach behind you for the propeller pitch control,' Viv objected. 'Where's the sense in that?' Her seat slid forward unexpectedly as the crate levelled out at 2,000 feet and she rammed her knees against the control panel. 'Ouch! Add that to the snag sheet,' she muttered.

Having checked that she was none the worse for wear, Bobbie began to hum the tune to 'Swinging on a Star'. 'I wonder what the ENSA duo will sing next Saturday,' she mused as they crossed over the narrow channel between the Isle of Wight and the mainland. A weak winter sun struggled through thin cloud as they flew north.

"I'll Be Seeing You'?' Viv suggested another Bing Crosby hit. 'Or how about 'You Always Hurt The One You Love'? That's a favourite of mine.'

'Let's play a game of Name that Hit,' Bobbie suggested with a smile. 'What number did Guy Lombardo sing in April this year?'

Viv rose to the challenge. ' 'It's Love, Love, Love'. Your turn — how about Dinah Shore?'

"I'll Walk Alone',' came the prompt reply. 'Will the band play requests on Saturday?' she went on to wonder.

'They might, if we ask nicely.' Viv's mind flitted towards the execution of her master plan. 'What shall I wear to impress Brian when I drop in on him tomorrow morning?' she asked above the heavy drone of the crate's twin engines.

'It doesn't matter — you look terrific in an oilskin and sou'wester,' Bobbie assured her, coughing as the petrol fumes caught in her throat. She decided to keep a careful eye on the fuel gauge, just in case. 'But wouldn't it be better to wait for Hilary . . . ?'

'Hilary will take for ever.' Viv ran through her argument for Bobbie's benefit. 'I'll remind Brian how

266

popular he'll be with his cadets when he relents. 'Relents' is a good word, isn't it? I'll convince him that it will make everyone's Christmas; hence it will boost — yes, boost — morale.'

Bobbie remained doubtful. 'What does Giles say about this plan of yours? Won't he be jealous if he finds out that you've met up with the dashing Brian?'

Viv's eyes widened. 'Why would I tell Giles? Anyhow, this Aireby visit isn't for pleasure, it's purely business.'

'But what if it doesn't wash with Brian?'

'It will,' Viv promised, sitting back serenely as she imagined returning to Rixley in triumph.

On they flew above the clouds. An hour and a half into the flight, Bobbie opened a side window to let out the worst of the fumes then rapidly closed it again when a blast of freezing air tore the map from Viv's lap and blew it across the windscreen.

'At this rate it'll be dark before we're anywhere near Rixley,' Viv forecast as she unbuckled her harness then leaned forward to retrieve the map.

'No; we should get back just in time.' Bobbie flew at full throttle to cover the miles, judging distances and calculating exactly when it would be necessary to drop down through the cloud cover and spot landmarks ready for landing. 'Ventnor told the ops room to expect us around fifteen hundred hours.'

Later, Bobbie and Viv would discuss whether or not they were less on their guard than they ought to have been. They were chatting nicely about this and that as they approached Rixley and they didn't spot the Dornier until it was too late to take evasive action. It came at them from behind and overtook them at 800 feet, its black cross insignia against a white circle making it instantly recognizable, along with the twin tail fins and stepped cockpit. There was scarcely any time to panic as the *Luftwaffe* pilot made a tight turn and approached them head-on with all guns blazing. Red blobs from the Dornier's MG15 front machine gun arced through the air, vivid in the fading light. The blobs seemed to accelerate as they drew near. Several bullets found their target — the girls' crate shuddered on impact — once, twice, three times.

'*Schnellbomber* — turn hard!' Viv yelled at Bobbie, who had already stamped on the starboard pedal. They were so close to the enemy plane that they could see the grim, determined expressions of the pilot and the gunner next to him, but Bobbie turned in the nick of time, risking a blackout from the speed and force of the manoeuvre. 'Turn again!' Viv cried.

The speedy, easy-to-handle Dornier came at them for a second time, so instinct kicked in, prompting Bobbie to jink rapidly to port in a deadly game of cat and mouse. Glancing sideways, she saw that her port wing was on fire. Damn it. Could she make it to the ferry pool or ought she to attempt a crash-landing? It was too late for parachutes, that was for sure.

'We have to ditch this crate.' Viv voiced what she saw as their only option.

The thin, narrow Dornier flashed past — all fifty-two feet of it. The girls saw the gunner say something to the pilot, who nodded then changed course by veering quickly to starboard and flying on in the direction of the ferry pool.

'If he imagines we're done for, he has another think coming.' Bobbie wrestled with the controls as the fire took hold. The port engine had died. Before long, flames would reach the fuel tank under the port wing.

'Quick, Bobbie — we have to ditch her in the nearest field!'

Viv was right. No sooner said than Bobbie had picked out a suitable stretch of open, level farmland. She pulled hard on the stick. Thick, black smoke from the fire obscured her view but she didn't falter. She cut her remaining engine and in the sudden silence steered the Blenheim towards the makeshift landing strip. As they glided down, black earth loomed up and red flames licked along the wing towards the cockpit. With an almighty bump that threw them both violently forward, Bobbie crash-landed the doomed crate.

Again on instinct, Bobbie and Viv unfastened their harnesses, slid back the hood and scrambled out. Despite their painful bruises, they jumped clear then ran hell for leather down a slope towards a deep ditch at the bottom of the ploughed field. Behind them there was a loud boom and their plane, swallowed by fierce red and yellow flames, exploded into a thousand pieces.

★ ★ ★

Down on the ground, as the day drew to a close, Stan was the last of the ground crew to go off duty. Douglas was still at work in the ops room; Hilary occupied himself with paperwork in the control tower while he waited for Bobbie and Viv to bring in the Blenheim from Ventnor so that he could close up shop for the day.

As Stan slid shut the huge door to Hangar 2, he planned his Saturday evening. It involved a quick wash and shave then a change into his one and only suit, because tonight he was taking a village girl called Ivy to the flicks in Highcliff and he intended to impress. Dark blue suit, white shirt, blue and red striped tie — that should do nicely. Hearing the approach of an aircraft, he glanced up. It was most likely Bobbie and Viv bringing in the Blenheim. But no; this was a different crate altogether — an instantly recognizable Dornier Do 217! With a sharp stab of alarm, Stan sprinted towards the cluster of concrete buildings that housed the ops room and the control tower to raise the alarm.

He'd got as far as the door to the ops room when the first bombs dropped. A startled Douglas dragged Stan inside then up the stairs, past the empty met office and up another flight of stairs to join Hilary in the control tower. Together the three men looked down on a scene of devastation.

One bomb had flattened the Nissen hut canteen and scattered broken chairs and tables in every direction. A second had gouged out a deep crater in the small lawn between the canteen and the building where Hilary, Stan and Douglas stood. The third had been aimed at Runway 2 but missed, tearing up grassland bordering Burton Wood and setting fire to several trees. Personnel came running from their barracks not fifty yards from where the third bomb had fallen.

'Get out there with a crash wagon.' Hilary ordered Stan to contain the fire. 'Find a couple of men to help you. If Jerry comes back — which is likely — take shelter in the woods. Tell the others.'

Stan clicked into action. He raced downstairs and yelled for Gordon and Bob to go with him. 'Everyone else, take cover in the wood!'

Drivers, including Olive and a dozen other off-duty ground crew, paused for a second to look up and see the Dornier make a tight U-turn then approach the ferry pool for a second time. Then, as if at the press of a button, they jerked into action and sprinted for the trees, while Stan, Gordon and Bob jumped in the nearest crash wagon to carry out Hilary's order.

Inside the tower, Hilary and Douglas watched the swift return of the deadly Dornier.

'We're sitting ducks up here.' Douglas knew the best chance of survival was to get down to ground level.

Hilary nodded his agreement and they made their way down the stairs, Hilary bringing up the rear behind Douglas, whose injured leg impeded his progress. 'Stay away from the hangars — they'll be Jerry's prime target.'

Sure enough, the Dornier flew overhead and unleashed a second load. Hangar 1 took a direct hit. There was an enormous boom as the half-tonne bomb dropped through the metal roof and exploded, showering red-hot fragments on to the surrounding area.

Inside the cab of the crash wagon, Stan, Gordon and Bob watched the firework display — splinters of molten metal descended, gas cylinders exploded and fuel tanks were set alight. 'Let the trees burn,' Gordon said through gritted teeth. 'Better to try to save some of what's inside the hangar.'

'Too risky,' Stan argued. 'Lord knows what else will go off with a bloody big bang.' So he steered the wagon towards the site of the burning trees and the three mechanics set to work with hoses to douse the flames.

'Perhaps that's it.' From the door of the Nissen hut

271

used as a store for tinned food, sacks of flour, potatoes and other supplies, Hilary watched the enemy plane circle overhead at two or three hundred feet. Smoke from small fires all around the ferry pool caught in his throat and made him cough.

'They carry four loads.' Douglas was less hopeful. 'He's only dropped two so far.'

But it seemed Hilary might be right. As Stan's team fought the blaze at the edge of the wood and Douglas and Hilary observed the Dornier's course, they saw it change direction. 'Look, he's heading for the reservoir.'

Under a minute later, the Germans discharged four more bombs, and the long, straight dam was successfully breached. Water poured through the gaps in wild, white-foaming streams, soon flooding the valley below. Personnel at the ferry pool heard the muffled explosions and then, to their horror, from their hiding places in the dark shadows of Burton Wood, they listened to the increasing roar of the Dornier's engines.

'Watch out — he's coming back!'

'Duck and pray!'

'Keep your heads down, everyone!'

'It'll be the runways this time!'

Hilary and Douglas heard disembodied voices call out warnings. Hilary checked his watch. 'Bobbie and Viv are due back in the Blenheim. We've got no way of telling them what's happening.' No radio, no nothing! God damn the idiots behind desks who sent pilots up without any means of making contact while they were in the air.

'There's nothing we can do.' Douglas's voice was drowned out by the Dornier's engines. There were two more tremendous whumps as the massive bombs hit soft earth surrounding the airfield, followed by blinding flashes as they detonated. Then disaster: a third bomb hit its target. Runway 2 was torn up.

Hilary watched in dismay. One hangar — and all of the Spits, Hurricanes, Mosquitoes and Mustangs hidden inside it — plus one crucial runway; gone in a flash. All the planning, all the hard work to keep things running had come to nothing in an instant. With deep disgust, he left the doorway into the food store and strode back towards the control tower to telephone HQ.

'No — wait!' Douglas saw that it wasn't over yet. Jerry had dropped only three of his final four bombs. He'd flown over, then quickly circled back towards the ferry pool, his twin engines returning with their menacing roar.

In deep despair, Hilary looked up. The enemy crate was close enough for him to see the black serial number stencilled on its side. Then the housing to one of the bomb bays slid open and the final bomb fell to earth.

Douglas watched in horror. There was an almighty explosion not twenty yards from where he stood. Deafened, he was thrown backwards, clean through the storeroom door. When he got to his feet and managed to stagger back into the open, all he could see through the smoke were flying fragments of concrete and twisted pieces of metal descending all around. On the ground lay the body of the ferry pool commander: one leg bent under his body, one arm flung wide — not moving, possibly not breathing. Smoke swirled, the Dornier's engines grew fainter. Silhouetted figures came running out of the woods, crying out at the destruction they witnessed in every direction.

18

Silence settled on Rixley village. Jerry was gone but God only knew what damage he'd done. People came out on to the pavements and stared beyond the darkness towards a red glow in the sky over Burton Wood. They shook their heads and spoke in low voices — a close shave for them but a bad lookout for the reservoir and the ferry pool, all caused by a lone bomber, who, it seemed, had got clean away.

Meanwhile, Bobbie and Viv ran and stumbled as fast as they were able across fields in the direction of thick black clouds of smoke rising into the still air. But progress, once they reached the wood, was agonizingly slow. At Fern Cottage they came across Jean, standing at the gate with Dorota in her arms.

'Douglas is at the ferry pool.' Fear had almost robbed Jean of her voice and her pale face was rigid with fear. 'He was on duty when the bombs dropped.'

'Stay here with the baby,' Bobbie told her hurriedly. 'We'll be back with news as soon as we can.'

She and Viv ran on. They heard footsteps gaining on them from behind and were soon joined by Mary.

'Was the Grange hit?' Viv asked as smoke drifted and twisted between the trunks of the trees.

'No, thank the Lord.' Mary had been alone in her room when the raid had begun. She'd dashed downstairs and seen and heard it all from the terrace, reliving the attack of the previous year — the same explosions had lit up the sky, the same cold dread crept over her skin, she felt the choking terror as the German pilot had banked and returned to wreak yet more havoc on his helpless victims below. First the ferry pool then the reservoir had been hit, then the ferry pool once more. Flashes of light and deafening booms — all at a distance from where Mary stood but terrifying, nonetheless. Then, in the silence and gathering darkness, she'd started to run — into the wood where remnants of snowdrifts made the going difficult, eventually spying two figures ahead of her and, twenty yards to her left, Jean at her gate with Dorota.

'Douglas was on duty!' a distressed Jean cried for a second time.

'Don't worry — we'll find him.' Mary caught up with Viv and Bobbie.

'Jerry had a go at us as we flew in.' Viv gasped for air. She had an ache in her chest where her harness straps had cut in as they'd crash-landed and a sharper pain in her right ankle. 'Bobbie had to ditch our Blenheim into a field.'

'He left us for dead then had a go at the ferry pool.' Bobbie removed her scarf then tied it around her nose and mouth to protect her lungs from the thickening smoke.

'I know — and after that, the reservoir. I saw it all from a distance.' Mary led the way forward.

'Who else besides Douglas was on duty?' Bobbie asked.

'Hilary,' Mary told them as she ducked to avoid a low branch. 'I saw him leave the Grange around midday.'

'And some of the ground crew would have to be there,' Viv reminded them.

'Stan?' Mary was shocked to realize that her close friend might have been in the thick of things.

275

'I guess so,' Viv replied. 'He said he'd still be here when we flew back in.'

They'd shared enough information — Douglas, Hilary and Stan were all possible casualties and panic clutched at the girls' throats as they battled on, almost blinded by the smoke, until they came to the far edge of the wood where they ran into Olive and two other drivers using heavy sacks to beat down flames that licked through the undergrowth. Beyond the firefighters the three girls made out the silhouetted outline of a crash wagon, its hoses spraying water high into the branches of burning pine trees.

'Anyone killed?' Bobbie yelled at Olive.

'I don't think so,' she replied. 'Luck was on our side.'

More hazy figures emerged from the trees on to the grass area bordering the runways. There were shouts of alarm and anger and also the sound of choking and coughing as some who had sought refuge in the wood bent forward and struggled to breathe.

'You go on ahead,' Mary said to Bobbie and Viv. She split off and ran towards the crash wagon where she found Bob and Gordon manning the hoses. Above the hiss of the water jets she yelled out for Stan.

'Ambulance!' Bob shouted above the hubbub.

A spray of icy water hit Mary's face and fear froze her to the spot. 'Why an ambulance — was Stan injured?' she cried.

'Don't think so,' Bob answered. It had been chaos after the bombs had dropped — people wandering around with shrapnel wounds or coughing their lungs up; everyone in a state of shock. 'First Officer Thornton grabbed him — said he needed him to drive the ambulance.'

276

It seemed that neither Stan nor Douglas was badly injured, thank God, but that begged the question: who was? Mary veered away from the wagon and caught up with Viv and Bobbie who stood on Runway 2 close to a deep crater, trying to make out through the smoke which buildings had been hit and which had survived.

'The canteen's gone.' Bobbie surveyed the smouldering remains — a bomb must have smashed through the roof and the wooden walls had caved inwards. Nothing remained.

'And Hangar One.' Viv saw that the roof there had also collapsed. There was another explosion then sudden flames flared from within the hangar, black smoke billowing out — there was not a hope in hell that any of the planes in there had escaped the inferno.

'Douglas and Stan are both alive,' Mary confirmed as several pairs of car headlights suddenly illuminated the gloom. One vehicle close to the damaged control tower turned in their direction then immediately swung away towards the ferry-pool gates.

'I'll go back and give Jean the good news.' True to their word, Viv limped towards the wood.

'No, wait — I'll go.' Bobbie quickly overtook her. 'I'll get there sooner.'

So Viv gave in to the pain and sat down on the ground, clasping her injured ankle. Olive crouched beside her to check that she was all right.

Mary stood alone on the damaged runway. Jerry had done his job and Rixley ferry pool lay in smoking ruins. Would any fighter plane ever take off from here in future? Would she fly again or was this the end of her struggle to help the Allies to victory? With a heavy heart she made her way towards the control tower, drawn by activity close to the entrance.

'Gently does it.' Douglas gave an order to lift a stretcher over the debris and into the back of a military ambulance. 'That's right; quick as you can.'

Two men slid the stretcher out of sight, jumped in after it then closed the door.

Mary quickened her pace. Was this the ambulance that Stan was meant to drive? She ran to the front of the vehicle to see him, face blackened by smoke, arms braced against the steering wheel, turning his head and listening to orders issued from the back of the vehicle.

'All right, Corporal, drive on!' Douglas ordered.

Stan's ambulance moved away, leaving Mary face to face with Douglas.

'Who?' was all she managed to mumble.

'Hilary.' Douglas closed his eyes and drew a sharp breath.

'How bad?'

'Pretty bad. He might not make it to Northgate hospital. And much as I hate to mention it,' he went on through gritted teeth, 'Viv and Bobbie should have been here by now. I'm starting to fear the worst.'

'No need — they made it through.' Mary was happy to deliver the one piece of good news. 'Bobbie was forced to ditch the Blenheim in a farmer's field, thanks to our German friends — but no bones broken. The crate went up in flames, though.'

'No matter — that's the least of our worries.' Douglas felt a great weariness settle on his shoulders. 'I'd better go. Jean will be worried.'

'Bobbie has gone ahead to tell her that you're safe.'

He gave a grateful nod. 'I'll follow her, then — I've done all I can here for now.'

Mary saw a dark stain of blood on the concrete

278

path. Stooping to pick up Hilary's hat from the doorstep, she dusted it down. 'Shall I take this up to his office?'

'Yes, please.' There'd been a major blood loss from shrapnel wounds to Hilary's legs and lower back. The blast from the exploding bomb must have blown him backwards and he'd landed face up, with his limbs twisted beneath him. Douglas had detected no sign of consciousness before he'd run into the building to telephone for help. 'You should go home too, Mary.'

She shook her head and gestured at the chaos all around. 'I want to stay and help.'

'No — go back to the Grange and rest.' Douglas backed away with a look of dazed defeat in his eyes. 'There's nothing any of us can do until tomorrow.'

Startled by another explosion followed by a burst of flame from inside the bombed hangar, Mary clasped Hilary's hat with both hands. She trod carefully over broken glass and splintered wood, carrying the hat into the building, to Hilary's office where she placed it squarely on his desk beside a scrawled memo dated 16 December, which read, *Re Christmas party: Norris washes his hands of the whole business. Referred me back to Wheeler. Remember to inform Bobbie, etc.*

Mary picked up the sad little note and stuffed it in her pocket. It was impossible to believe that Christmas was almost upon them; stranger still to think that she, Bobbie and Viv had all been so determined to carry on and celebrate as if there was no war, no bombs, no casualties. After all, how much did trees and decorations, entertainers and dance partners matter in the face of such disasters?

Not a scrap, she decided as she walked back out into the smoke and confusion.

★ ★ ★

Dorota was asleep in her cot and Jean sat in the kitchen waiting for Douglas when he finally reached home. All was the same — the blue and white plates were still arranged on the dresser, the flagged floor was uneven, three oil lamps hung from the low beams.

Jean heard him wipe his feet on the porch mat — a familiar sound.

He came in quietly so as not to wake their daughter, asleep in her upstairs room, and experienced the blessing of the plain, warm kitchen and of his wife's face eagerly turned towards him. She stood up and stretched out her arms.

'Here I am,' he said without moving towards her.

The day had obviously taken its toll — he looked ground down and utterly dispirited.

'If Dorota and I were to lose you . . .' Jean's sentence tailed off without conclusion. *Worn out and defeated, poor man.* But what use were words?

'Hilary is in a bad way, I'm afraid.'

She grimaced at Douglas's dry delivery. But then this was how men with his RAF background got by. 'What else?'

'We've lost a hangar and part of a runway.'

'No, I mean — were any others injured?'

'Shrapnel wounds; cuts and bruises — nothing major. Everyone followed orders; there was very little panic.'

'And no warning?'

'None.' Thank God he was home and he could drop the act. 'I wish it were over, Jean — I really do.'

'It will be; soon.' Touching his cheek lightly, she realized how cold he was, so she drew him through

280

the door into the living room with its warm fire.

Douglas sank into the easy chair and loosened his tie. 'They keep saying that we're making progress, that the enemy is weakening. But then this happens out of the blue. One minute I'm filling out chits for Monday, ordering petrol and what have you, and next thing I know we're getting blown sky high.'

'What about Hilary?' Jean sat on the rug and leaned on his lap, gazing up at her husband's grey, exhausted face.

'I honestly don't know, Jean.'

'Is there someone we should telephone — a girl-friend or brothers and sisters?' She realized how little she knew about Hilary's background.

'HQ will do all that. I know he has a brother in the Royal Navy, parents somewhere in Surrey.'

'How dreadful for them,' she murmured.

'I'll drive to the hospital first thing tomorrow and find out the latest. I'll say one thing, Jean: when you see a wounded man laid out like that with blood pouring from him, you do your best — listen for a heartbeat, stem the flow of blood, and so on — and it's only afterwards that it truly hits you.'

'You will cope — I know you will.' Jean loved Douglas and she had faith in him.

'Yes,' he said with a sigh. 'I expect I will.'

★ ★ ★

Bobbie, Mary and Viv returned to the Grange.

'Everything smells of smoke,' Viv remarked as she took off her jacket and hung it on the stand by the main door. 'Clothes, hair, every darned thing.'

There had been a roll-call before they'd left the

281

ferry pool, conducted by Peggy, who had driven back at speed from Northgate as soon as she'd got wind of the raid. Everyone had lined up on Runway 1 in the glare of the crash wagon headlights — all present and correct except for Hilary and Stan. There were six walking wounded among the ground crew with cuts, bruises and some minor burns, but everyone agreed that they'd got off lightly.

'We need a stiff drink,' Bobbie concluded as they shook flakes of ash from their hair. 'Let's regroup in the mess as soon as we've tidied ourselves up.'

As Viv and Bobbie went upstairs to their rooms, Mary seized the chance to call Cameron from the telephone in the hall. When she eventually got through, he told her he was standing by, waiting for further details about the night's mission.

'Did you hear about today's raid on Rixley?' She kept her voice steady so as not to alarm him unduly.

'Good Lord, no! What happened?'

Mary told him the basics in her plain, matter-of-fact way.

'But you didn't come to any harm?'

'No, not a scratch. Everyone's worried about Squadron Leader Stevens, though. And we don't know how soon we'll be able to fly out of Rixley again — if ever.'

Cameron thought through the implications. 'Perhaps they'll transfer you.'

Mary said she hoped not. 'We're a tight little group here. I'd far rather stick with the people I know — especially Bobbie and Viv. And Peggy, too.'

There was another pause. 'Yes — I understand that you want to stay where you are. You say you still have one runway in operation?'

'Yes, but we lost a lot of planes. And there's always

282

a chance that the *Luftwaffe* will be back to finish us off for good.' Besides Hilary, this was Mary's main concern.

'Let's hope not.' Cameron spoke quickly. 'Do you hear that siren? That's our signal to scramble. I have to go.'

Mary's heart skipped several beats. 'Don't forget — I love you.'

'Be careful, Mary,' were his last words before he joined his fellow fighter pilots in the frantic race to climb into their crates and get airborne.

★ ★ ★

'That's better.' Bobbie relaxed with her favourite tipple in a time of crisis — a ten-year-old single malt whisky. She sat with Viv and Mary close to the fire in the crowded mess. The buzz of conversation was all about the day's events — which planes had been lost, how quickly the damage to the runway could be repaired, together with speculation over how much damage had been done to the dam.

Viv revelled in the warmth of the fire, stretching out her bruised limbs and resting her head against the back of her leather chair. 'My neck's as stiff as a board,' she sighed. 'Where's a good masseur when a girl needs one?'

Mary, meanwhile, nursed her concerns in silence.

'I suppose Douglas is in charge now,' Bobbie reflected, staring into the flickering flames as if they could predict the ferry pool's future. 'He'll keep us up to date with any decisions made by HQ.'

'Any news of Hilary?' Gillian came over from the bar where she'd been drinking with Horace. 'Mary,

283

I hear that you saw them drive him off in the ambulance. How bad was he?'

'He was on a stretcher so I couldn't see much. Douglas said he looked pretty bad.' The image of the large, dark bloodstain on the path flashed back into Mary's head and she did her best to conceal a shudder.

A sombre Gillian nodded then moved on.

Gingerly, Viv sat forward in her chair. 'Cheer up, everyone — it could've been far worse. We can still use Runway One and there's a row of bombers lined up for us to ferry in Hangar Two.'

'That's right.' Bobbie agreed with Viv's cup-half-full outlook. 'With Douglas in charge we can carry on, if not as normal in the run-up to Christmas then at least at fifty per cent of our capacity.'

'Without a canteen, though. No more cups of tea on tap, no bacon sandwiches — whatever will we do?' Viv's wail of despair made the others smile.

'Leave it to Douglas — he'll sort something out.' Bobbie downed the last of her drink. 'I vote we spend some of tomorrow smartening up the room for our Christmas party. It needs a thorough clean — plenty of elbow grease required.'

'Count this old crock in.' Viv got up creakily from her chair. 'Oh no, I can't help you.' She suddenly remembered that tomorrow morning was set aside for something important. 'Hush, it's a secret!' she said with a wink.

Bobbie and Mary watched her hobble off.

'What's Viv up to now?' Mary wanted to know.

'Let's just say it has something to do with Flight Lieutenant Wheeler and the problem with the Aireby invitations.' Bobbie tapped a finger against the side of her nose. 'She has what she calls a master plan. Anyhow, it won't stop us from doing the cleaning, will it?'

'No, of course not.' Party plans had been far from Mary's mind until this moment but now she delved into her pocket and pulled out the scrap of paper with Hilary's scrawled memo. She showed it to Bobbie, who read it with a deepening frown.

'So Group Captain Norris still wants nothing to do with it,' Bobbie muttered. 'Typical.'

'Should we warn Viv?' Mary wondered.

Bobbie gave an emphatic shake of her head. 'What difference would it make? Viv's unstoppable once she gets going. Nothing we say or do will prevent our daredevil pal from putting this plan of hers into action.'

* * *

Ray knew that what he was doing was against the rules. No contact before the 23rd — that had been

Bobbie's crystal-clear wish. No contact and no alcohol until then, to prove to her that he could stay on the straight and narrow.

But earlier that evening Giles had taken a call from Viv. 'I say, old man,' he'd told Ray as soon as he'd come off the phone. 'Remember that German bomber we saw fly over Thresham late this afternoon? Turns out it was heading for Rixley.'

At the time Ray and Giles had been dealing with an emergency of their own, but it had paled into insignificance in the face of this fresh disaster. Ray had demanded the details and learned that no one had been killed but that Hilary had been rushed to hospital. 'How are the girls?' he'd asked.

'Viv assured me they're all fine.' Giles had poured

himself a drink and offered one to Ray. 'Sorry, old chap — I forgot,' he'd mumbled when Ray had shakily declined.

Ray had taken himself off to the yard to absorb the news — a direct hit on the ferry pool and some garbled information about Viv and Bobbie's Blenheim getting in Jerry's way, which Giles hadn't been able to get to the bottom of. Ray had paced from stable to stable, distractedly patting the necks of various horses. What did 'getting in Jerry's way' actually mean, for goodness' sake? It had seemed that Viv was reasonably all right — fit enough to make the telephone call, at least. But what of Bobbie? What if there was some vital information that Viv hadn't shared? Might Bobbie even now be nursing a serious injury that Viv had deliberately kept schtum about?

There was nothing for it but to jump into the car and find out for himself. Acting on impulse and without telling Giles, Ray sped out of the yard and on to the Rixley road — empty at this time of night — taking bends at speed and feeling a mounting tension as he neared the village. Only when he was within sight of Burton Grange did he pause to look at his watch. Almost midnight, damn it. Everyone would be in bed.

A curtain in the upper-floor window of the nearest house twitched and an inquisitive face peered down at his car. A pale moon floated clear of a bank of clouds. Perhaps it would be better to turn around — wait until morning to find out exactly what had happened to Bobbie. But no, Ray had come this far and he wouldn't rest until he knew.

So he eased forward along the village main street then entered the grounds of the Grange by the side gate. All was silent in the stable yard but there were a couple of downstairs lights on in the main house so Ray pressed ahead with his plan, taking the steps two at a time then walking swiftly along the terrace, only to find the front door locked. What now? Should he look for signs of life around the back of the building? Peering through a low window and about to beat a retreat, he noticed movement in the hall. He tapped lightly on the pane to attract attention. The door opened and a woman in her thirties, upright and neat in every respect — from the straight parting in her short brown hair to her red quilted dressing gown and down to her fur-edged slippers — answered his knock.

Peggy looked out suspiciously at an agitated young man in a polo-necked pullover, riding britches and boots. 'Yes?'

'I've come to see Bobbie Fraser. My name is Ray Moore.'

'I see. Is Bobbie expecting you?'

'No. But I gather she was involved in an altercation with a *Luftwaffe* pilot.' Shifting anxiously from one foot to another, Ray looked beyond the stranger in the hope of spotting someone he knew. 'If you could just find Bobbie for me — please.'

Peggy's hold on the door knob relaxed. The visitor seemed genuine enough, despite the unusually late hour. 'Come inside and wait,' she told him. 'I'll inform Bobbie that you're here — Ray Moore, you say?'

He nodded. With ever-mounting tension he watched the severe-looking woman ascend the stairs and disappear. He prepared himself for the blow of Bobbie's refusal — she would be well within her rights to refuse to see him and he would be forced to go away with his tail between his legs. But he might at least catch a glimpse of her and see for himself that she was all right.

After what seemed like an age, the severe woman returned alone. *No good*, he thought; Bobbie had indeed said no.

'Bobbie said could you please wait for her in the officers' mess,' Peggy informed him as she ushered him in. 'She'll join you there presently.'

Ray breathed a sigh of relief — he was over the first hurdle. Hovering by the fireplace, he listened out for Bobbie's footsteps, hearing the last embers of the fire settle in the grate. The rows of glasses and bottles behind the bar glinted in the low light — Dutch courage lurked within those bottles, a challenge to Ray's willpower if ever there was one.

'Hello, Ray.' Bobbie entered in her pale green dressing gown. Her feet were bare and her sandy-coloured hair freshly brushed. Her expression was calm, her voice low.

He moved towards her but she held up her hand to stop him. 'I'm sorry — I couldn't stay away.'

She inclined her head warily.

'Viv told Giles that you two had a near miss today. I was driven mad with worry.'

'We were forced to crash-land but we're both here to tell the tale.' Bobbie's heart beat fast and furiously beneath the surface. The mere sight of Ray threatened to melt her resolve. Oh, how she'd missed him! However, what was she to make of the fact that he'd broken his promise? Caught between two conflicting emotions, she waited for him to speak again.

'No need to tell me any more — I just had to see for myself.' She was almost within reach; her skin smooth and clear, her hair soft as down. 'Forgive me;

I shouldn't have come.'

The intensity of his gaze proved too much. 'I've missed you,' she confessed on the spur of the moment, and in spite of her earlier resolve. 'I've been longing to know how you were.'

'I'm well.' What she really meant was, *Have you been drinking?* 'And I'm sober.' Still looking directly at her, he faced his problems head-on. 'I'm getting back on my feet, Bobbie — slowly but surely.'

'That's wonderful.' She felt her cheeks flush with relief. 'I hoped and prayed that you would.'

'I will — I'll do whatever it takes to win you back.'

Ray, my dearest love. 'You never lost me,' she whispered as a tidal wave of relief washed away all barriers. 'I told you before: my heart will always be yours.'

'Really and truly?' *My heart will always be yours*, spoken by Bobbie in that sincere, lilting, musical way — it was everything he could have wished for and more. 'If I lost you I couldn't bear it — you know that. Or if you'd been injured, God forbid!'

'I know.' The agony in his voice cut deep. 'But you haven't lost me. And I'm not hurt.'

'I will prove myself,' he vowed. 'You mean the world to me. I won't let you down. And I'll never question you ever again. You can have all the space you need to live your own life.'

It was as if a cage door had flown open. 'Likewise,' she promised. 'I won't get in your way and you won't get in mine. We'll live our lives like that, wherever fate takes us — together.'

They reached out and held hands, standing silently for a long time until Ray felt Bobbie sway towards him and he clasped her in his arms. Her small, slender body contained such strength and determination.

She was beautiful in every way.

A kiss sealed their future in the flickering firelight. He held her in the silence — there to lean on whenever she should need him but prepared to let her spread her wings and fly.

19

Bobbie and Mary stood in the doorway of the room where they were soon to throw their party. They were armed with brooms, dusters, mops and buckets and dressed in slacks and short-sleeved jumpers for the job in hand. Their hair was covered by brightly patterned silk scarves tied like turbans around their heads.

'It looks grim.' Mary came out with what they both thought — the corners of the unused room were swathed in cobwebs and there were thick layers of dust on the windowsills and skirting boards. The pale blue walls were faded, the parquet floor stained and dull. Yet in less than a week's time this was to be the venue for their Christmas bash.

'Nothing that a good dose of elbow grease won't cure.' Bobbie's optimism carried them forward. With a clank of metal buckets and the swish of wet mops, they began the clean-up operation.

'Need a hand?' Popping her head around the door, Peggy was pleased to see that Mary in particular was in a keep-calm-and-carry-on frame of mind. 'I'm due at Westville Avenue at ten o'clock but I can spare you half an hour.'

So Mary handed her a duster and set her to work.

'I don't see any sign of our Canadian friend,' Peggy commented as she ran the duster along the dado rails. 'Still in bed, I presume.'

'On the contrary.' Bobbie squeezed out her mop. 'Viv is bound for Aireby this morning. She aims to sweet-talk Brian Wheeler into letting his cadets come

291

to the party after all.'

Peggy flipped the contents of her duster out through an open window, grimacing when a gust of cold wind blew the dust back into the room. 'Second Officer Robertson can charm the birds out of the trees if she has a mind to, but I'm not certain that even she will succeed on this occasion.'

'You don't know Viv,' Bobbie replied before a second interruption made her turn towards the door.

Ernest ambled into the room, pipe clenched between his teeth and with braces dangling. 'I wondered what the racket was,' he growled as he surveyed the scene. 'There's an electric floor polisher in my storeroom. Shall I fetch it?'

'Yes, please.' Mary accepted with alacrity then beamed at Stan, who had appeared in the doorway behind Ernest. 'There you are!' she exclaimed with evident delight.

'Yes, here I am — none the worse for wear.' He'd driven over from the ferry pool to deliver the latest news on Hilary and had been attracted to the blue room by the sound of lively chatter. 'How about you, Bobbie? I hear you wrecked a Blenheim for us.'

'The cheek of the man!' Bobbie flicked her mop head in his direction. Stan ducked to avoid being splashed with dirty water. 'I'm tickety-boo, since you ask.'

'Is this where we'll be dancing the night away?' Stan cast a critical eye around the bare room. 'Never mind the spit and polish, what you really need is a nice solid platform for the band.'

'What we need is a plasterer, a painter and decorator and an electrician.' Mary stood, hands on hips. 'Any recommendations, Stan?'

'No, but I can build you a platform, if you like.' Striding down the length of the room, he paced out a couple of measurements. 'How big do you reckon it should be?'

Bobbie and Peggy were sceptical. 'Where will you get the wood to build a stage?' Peggy asked.

'There are some old floorboards kicking around in the grooms' loft and some lengths of four-by-four in one of the stables. I can soon knock one up.'

Mary believed that Stan could accomplish any practical thing he set his mind to. 'A stage is just what we need,' she agreed. She ran after him as he set about fetching the timber and caught up with him in the hall. 'Thank you; I don't know what we'd do without you.'

'Leave off — you'll make a chap blush. By the way, I came over to tell you that First Officer Thornton went to the hospital to visit Squadron Leader Stevens first thing this morning.'

'And?' Mary held her breath.

'The docs say he was lucky — a piece of shrapnel came this close to paralysing him for good.' Stan held up his thumb and forefinger to demonstrate a tiny gap.

'But will he live?'

'They told First Officer Thornton that it's too early to say for sure.'

'Has he come round yet?'

'Just about. Still woozy, of course, and not making much sense.'

Mary thanked Stan again and blew him a kiss then dashed back to the blue room to pass on the news.

Allowing herself a moment of weakness, Peggy shed a quick, relieved tear then blew her nose on a surprisingly frilly lace handkerchief. 'Hilary is a tough old bird — it'll take more than a five-hundred-pound bomb to finish him off.' She attacked the dust on the windowsills with fresh gusto. 'With luck he'll be out of hospital before we know it; but of course there'll have to be a period of recuperation . . .'

Bobbie and Mary listened to Peggy's forecasts without comment. Bobbie's mind was on Ray, and Mary's as ever flitted from Cameron to Tom and back again. She hadn't heard from Cameron today but was hoping that no news was good news — he was probably getting his head down for a few hours' kip after his return from his squadron's latest bombing raid. As for Tom; well, Mary's stomach tied itself into a knot every time she pictured her brother in the study at Thresham, sobbing and begging — a boy broken by the sights he'd seen on the battlefield and stuck deep in the desperate hole that he'd dug for himself.

'Balloons!' Peggy said suddenly as she came to the end of her half-hour stint.

Bobbie and Mary paused and leaned on their mops.

'How many will we need?'

'Four dozen?' Bobbie hazarded a guess. 'What do you think, Mary?'

'Yes; red, blue and white ones — the colours of the Union Jack, you know. Our balloons should be patriotic, don't you think?' Where was Peggy going with this? Mary wondered.

Peggy laughed at their puzzled expressions. 'Daddy used to own a factory that made, among other things, balloons of all sizes, shapes and colours. He sold the business several years ago but he still has a garage full of rubber doorstoppers, elastic bands, balloons — you name it, he has it.'

'Bingo!' Bobbie said softly.

'Hurrah!' Mary clapped her hands.

Peggy beamed at them. 'Splendid! How does ten dozen red, white and blue balloons sound to you?'

★ ★ ★

Viv chose to cycle to Aireby, believing that the fresh air would help to clear her lungs of the smoke that she'd inhaled the day before. She'd forgotten about her sore ankle, however.

'Steady on,' Stan warned when he emerged from the grooms' loft loaded down with planks of wood. 'You'll not get far at that rate.'

Viv wobbled her way across the yard then put both feet down on the ground with a jolt. 'Ouch!'

'Where are you off to?' He came slowly down the stone steps then deposited the planks on the cobbles.

'To Aireby.' Viv dismounted and rubbed her ankle.

Stan dipped into the top pocket of his overalls and drew out the key to the pick-up he'd driven across in. 'Take her,' he offered with a nod towards the vehicle. 'No need to hurry back — I'll be here all day.'

'Swell!' Viv grabbed the key then planted a kiss on his cheek — the second he'd received that morning.

Blimey, I must be doing something right. 'Second gear's a bit iffy.' He rubbed the site of the kiss with the back of his hand as Viv jumped up into the cab.

'I'll bear that in mind, thanks.' And off she went, rattling out of the yard and down the lane in the military truck, out on to the main village street, where who should she see approaching the Grange but Giles in his grey Austin.

'Hi!' she cried as she leaned out of the side window.

'Yoo-hoo, it's me! Didn't you recognize me?'

Giles stopped with a squeal of brakes. He smiled at the sight of Viv, dressed up to the nines in a pert, narrow-brimmed blue hat and matching jacket with a softly frilled white blouse to set it off. 'Where are you off to in that old bone-shaker?'

'Never you mind.' She kept her mission to herself. 'More to the point, what are you doing here?'

Giles tapped the side of his nose with his forefinger — two could play the secrecy game. 'Are you in a rush or can you spare a few minutes?'

'For you, honey, anything!' Jumping down from the cab, she forgot about her ankle once more. 'Ouch!' she said again.

Giles leaped out of the Austin and helped her to hobble to a nearby bench, set against the low church wall. 'Shouldn't you be taking more care after yesterday's mishap?'

Viv resisted his help. 'Jerry may have shot us full of holes but I'm not about to let him slow me down.'

Giles matched her flippant tone. 'So I can't be your knight in shining armour?'

'Not unless you have a castle tucked away somewhere.'

'Not even a cottage in the country with roses around the doorway,' he reminded her with a wry smile. 'Talking of my misfortune . . .'

'Were we?'

'No, but at any rate it seems an agreement between my father and Nora is on the cards.' He grew more serious. 'Even she can see that a portion of nothing is nothing, which is what I currently have. So with me out of the picture, her only option was to negotiate with the boss — namely Father, who, as you know, relies on my silence to protect his good name.'

'So he's not in a strong position.' Viv pictured battleaxe Nora and merciless Sir Thomas going head to head. 'Did she get Abbot's Gate after all?'

Giles shook his head. He turned up his coat collar and took out a cigarette. 'No, Father continued to draw the line at that. He wouldn't budge. But Nora got the Dower House at Newpark — he was prepared to give way to that extent. So there they'll be — Mother, Father and Nora — living on each other's doorsteps, and much good may it do them. I'm still out of the picture, thank God.'

'I'm sorry, Giles.' Viv meant it. *Sorry that your father is so heartless, sorry that your mother doesn't back you, sorry that your ex has a heart of stone.*

'I'm not.' Blowing a thin funnel of blue smoke into the air, he spoke with conviction. 'I'm glad to be free of them. Plus, I have a new plan.'

'Which is?' Expecting him to have contacted the Ministry of Food at last, Viv was surprised to hear something entirely different.

'I'm thinking of basing myself at Thresham with Ray.'

'Jeez, Giles — you don't know one end of a horse from another.'

'What do you mean? I can spot a winner when I see one,' he objected.

A grey-haired verger in a long cassock and wearing steel-rimmed glasses tottered down the church path to open the gate in preparation for the next service. Just in time — the first worshippers began to trickle in.

Viv ignored the curious glances cast their way. 'I mean, you don't ride.'

297

'Granted. But I know how to balance books and I have a good head for figures, which Ray admits that he doesn't. I could take over the ordering of feed, hay, veterinary supplies, and so on — that would be the idea.'

'You two have talked about it?' She began to see the sense of what he said.

'Discussions are under way,' Giles confirmed. 'What do you say to that?'

'It could work,' she said with a satisfied nod. 'I can definitely see you as Ray's right-hand man, as long as you both stay off the booze.'

'But what do you think about me staying in your neck of the woods?' He hid his nervousness behind a fresh cloud of smoke — Viv didn't know it but an awful lot rested on her answer.

She pondered for a long time.

'Take your time,' he said with a touch of sarcasm. Her silence didn't bode well.

Viv herself wasn't sure why she hesitated. She still felt the Giles effect whenever she was with him — the rapid heartbeat and a small surge of joy when he smiled at her or kissed her on the lips. Besides, her respect for him had grown since she'd observed his dealings with Nora and his father. Giles hadn't got lost in a maze of bitterness or anger; quite the opposite — he was looking forward to a new future free from the ties of his dreadful family. And yet she must come clean and tell him that she wasn't sure what part, if any, she might play in that future.

'Giles, honey, please don't make your decision based on the fact that I'll be around for ever,' she said slowly and clearly, with no hint of gamesmanship.

Giles's face clouded over and he braced himself for

298

the rest of Viv's reply.

Don't give the guy false hope without being certain of your own plans, she told herself. Yet when she spoke the words came out all wrong — much too black and white and as if she didn't care about hurting Giles's feelings. 'I'm here now and I plan to stay at Rixley until the war is won if HQ sees fit to get the ferry pool up and running again. But after that — when Hitler has got his just deserts and the whole thing is done and dusted — I have no clue where in the world I plan to be.'

★ ★ ★

Viv knew for certain that her answer was not what Giles had longed to hear — quite the opposite, in fact. She'd seen it in his face: the flicker of hurt followed by what she could only describe as the shutters coming down. His expression had gone blank and he'd been distinctly cool as they'd said their goodbyes and returned to their respective vehicles, not looking back as he'd driven on towards the Grange.

But what's a girl to do? she asked herself as she carried on towards Aireby. It would have been wrong to mislead him. On the other hand, the slam of those shutters had thrown her off balance. *He'll take my answer as an outright rejection*, she forecast with sharp regret. *Giles's pride is hurt — he may never speak to me again.*

Gripping the wheel until her knuckles turned white, she drove the last couple of miles under a gloomy cloud, approaching the RAF camp along a narrow, straight lane until she came to the wide entrance manned by two armed sentries.

One sentry came out of his box as she pulled up at the gate. He regarded her sternly and barked out a demand to know her business.

Bless the boy; he's scarcely old enough to shave. Viv put the Giles problem to one side and geared herself up to achieve her current goal. 'Is Flight Lieutenant Wheeler at home, by any chance?'

'What if he is?' The boy's suspicious reply reflected an uncertainty about his next move.

'I'm here on a social visit.' Viv's confidence didn't waver as she got out of the pick-up. Through the wire fence she could see rows of green huts set at right angles around an open square that was backed by a line of tall, straight pine trees. No doubt the trees acted as a windbreak for this exposed spot. This being a Sunday, the square where the cadets carried out their drills was deserted — the only sign of life was a thin trail of smoke emerging from the chimney of a hut that displayed a sign reading 'Canteen'.

'Brian Wheeler is a friend of mine — he won't mind me dropping by.'

At the sight of the visitor in a kingfisher-blue costume, with the figure and the face of Vivien Leigh, the second sentry emerged from his box. 'I take it you don't have permission?' he queried.

Viv smiled brightly before turning her lapel to reveal her ATA badge on the reverse side. 'Is this good enough for you?'

The two sentries made a great display of examining the badge at close quarters.

'You're one of the famous Atta girls, eh?' The first sentry was duly impressed. 'Lucky you; you fly Hurricanes and Wellingtons. What's your favourite crate?'

'Spitfires,' Viv replied without hesitating.

'We hear Rixley took a direct hit,' the second sentry commented. Boy, the visitor's perfume was quite something — she smelled like a blooming florist's shop!

'We lost one runway and the entire contents of one hangar.' Engaging them in conversation had paid off. Other cadets were emerging from various huts and strolling towards the gate. There were joking cries of 'Hello, hello!' and ear-splitting whistles of approval, bringing still more bored trainees out on to the square. Viv cupped her hands around her mouth and called out. 'Hey, guys — someone run and fetch Flight Lieutenant Wheeler. Tell him that he has a visitor!' She grinned as one cadet ran to do her bidding.

'Are you American?' the first sentry was keen to find out.

'No — Canadian.'

'Are all the girls in Canada like you? If they are, tell them to watch out — I'll be over there in a flash as soon as we've beaten Jerry into a cocked hat.'

Viv grinned and bided her time. Sure enough, Brian soon appeared from a small hut off the main square, recognized her and walked quickly across. He was in uniform so obviously on duty.

'Let her in.' His order was curt and without preliminaries. He waited for the cadets to raise the barrier before speaking again. 'Follow me,' he told her, equally curtly.

'Thanks, boys,' she told the sentries, taking long strides to keep up with Brian. All eyes were still upon her as the two of them disappeared into the office from which he'd emerged.

'What do you want?' Brian asked as soon as they were out of earshot.

Viv took a quick look around the room, noticing an array of notices pinned neatly to a board, a large map of Europe on the wall with all the major towns and cities highlighted, a green metal locker in one corner and a typewriter and a telephone on the tidy desk. 'I came to ask you to change your mind about the party.' Deciding that it was best to take the bull by the horns, she looked directly at him and waited for his reaction. The moustache was gone, she noted — a definite improvement. But she had to admit that his expression was hostile.

'You're wasting your time. The order for all cadets to be confined to barracks on the twenty-third still stands.' Turning his back on her, he transferred a note from his desk on to the board behind him. 'Now, if you don't mind . . .'

'No, listen — it's obvious that this is happening because of the small spat you and I had in the Fox and Hounds.'

He turned with a frosty frown. 'It may be obvious to you but it's not to me.'

'Oh, come on, Brian — why should everyone have to suffer because you and I fell out? Think about it — the Rixley crew are pretty shaken up by yesterday's bombing and we don't have Squadron Leader Stevens to speak up for us.'

Brian's startled look told Viv that he hadn't heard about Hilary.

'He's in Northgate hospital,' she explained quickly. 'We don't know yet if he'll pull through.'

Leaning both hands on his desk, he quizzed her for more information. 'Was anyone killed? What about planes — how many did you lose?'

She told him what he needed to know. 'There's no

way that Jerry will stop us from flying, though. So what do you say, Brian? Will you and your crew help us to make our little Christmas party a big success?'

Thinking silently for a while, he decided on an opportunist course of action. 'That depends,' he said slowly, looking at her through narrowed eyes.

'On what?' Hopefully she saw a chink in Brian's armour.

'On you, Miss Vivienne.' Clearly she wasn't interested in him romantically — she'd told him so in no uncertain terms. But Viv was exceptionally attractive: a girl who would look good on any man's arm, which led Brian to think that it might be worth striking a deal. 'Perhaps I would be inclined to reconsider under certain conditions.'

'Go ahead, shoot.' Oblivious to what was coming, she smiled eagerly.

'Firstly, I will attend the event myself — in my capacity as second in command here at Aireby.'

She nodded cautiously. *So far, so good.*

'Secondly, you will agree to dance the first dance with me.'

'Sure,' she agreed. *Easy — no problem.*

'And the last dance,' he added slyly.

The closing dance at such events was bound to be the slow waltz: a smoochy number that involved clasping your partner in a tight hold. Viv hesitated over the third condition and failed to suppress a shiver.

'Well?' he prompted.

'OK,' she said through gritted teeth, deciding it was a price worth paying for the sake of the Rixley celebrations.

'And afterwards —'

'Hold it!' Viv held up her hand.

'And afterwards,' Brian repeated with cool menace, 'once I've accepted your invitation to the Christmas party, you will then return the favour by accepting mine.'

Jeez, of all the mean tricks . . . ! Viv's hackles rose. 'To do what?' she demanded.

'To be my partner at a forthcoming social event,' he continued smoothly. 'There's a New Year party at my London club — a very smart event. My friends will no doubt be green with envy when we make our entrance.'

'We do what?' she spluttered. Her powers of persuasion deserted her in an instant. Brian Wheeler really was the lowest of the low.

'Otherwise, my cadets stay grounded,' he reminded her. 'So, come now, Vivienne, what do you say?'

★ ★ ★

Giles found Mary in the blue room, observing a member of Rixley ground crew hard at work with saw, hammer and nails. She perched on a high windowsill, ankles crossed and talking excitedly about making a success of the Christmas event; she hadn't noticed Giles's quiet entrance.

'Real singers and a real band,' she enthused while Stan sawed a plank in half. 'Think of that! There'll be a tree with all the trimmings — electric lights and all.'

When Giles cleared his throat to attract her attention, Mary jumped down from her perch with a smile. 'Viv isn't here, I'm afraid,' she reported.

'I know. I stopped in the village and spoke with her.' He talked rapidly to get the thing over with. 'It's you I came to see.'

304

Mary was puzzled. What could Giles possibly want with her? And he seemed unusually grave as he led her from the room.

'In here?' He opened the door to the empty library.

'What is it?' she asked with a tightening of the stomach.

'Sit down, Mary.' Giles pointed to a window seat.

Automatically she did as he said. 'What's the matter, Giles?'

'You remember last Wednesday at Thresham — your unfortunate mistake about your brother?'

'Of course I remember!' She grasped the edge of the seat. *What now?* Her heart beat rapidly and panic welled up from the pit of her stomach as she waited for more.

'There's been a further development,' he went on.

'When? What?'

'Yesterday evening. Mary, why were you so convinced at first that Wilf was not who he said he was?'

'I was being silly,' she said faintly. 'As soon as I talked to him I realized my mistake.'

Giles stared out of the window at the hills in the distance. 'The thing is, I had my own doubts about the chap. He didn't seem . . . well, quite right for a Quaker. Not like Philip, if you catch my drift.'

Mary closed her eyes and held her breath.

'Of course, I was willing to admit I could be wrong. But his behaviour on Wednesday — well, you know.' *Spit it out, man!* He cleared his throat before continuing.

'Yesterday afternoon, while Rixley was under attack, Ray and I were dealing with a problem of our own. The fact is, Mary, the chap calling himself Wilf

Cranston has absconded from the yard with a petty-cash box containing three pounds and eight shillings. Philip was the one who reported him missing. He and Ronnie had searched everywhere before coming up to the house to let Ray know. Wilf and the cash have vanished without a trace and that's the truth.'

Mary opened her eyes and stared at Giles in abject misery.

'Ray and I got Philip to admit that he, too, had had his doubts. In fact, he'd been on the point of getting in touch with Wilf's relatives in York to check up on his background.'

She bent her head. *What to do? What to say? Oh, Tom!*

'I thought you should know,' Giles said gently, sitting beside Mary and putting a hand on her arm. 'Just in case it turns out that you were on the right track from the start.'

20

Mary's unhappiness was compounded when she learned more details from a careful and considerate Giles.

'I believe that Wilf, as we must call him until we can prove otherwise, acted on the spur of the moment. Apparently there'd been a row between him and Ronnie: a storm in a teacup over the careless way Wilf hosed down an empty stable. Angry words and a few blows were exchanged and as a result Ronnie gave Wilf the unpleasant job of tidying up the muck heap while he and Philip rode out on the gallops. When they came back the heap was in a bad state — horse manure was scattered all over the yard. Philip then discovered that the tack room was in similar disarray — bits and bridles had been taken from their hooks and flung on the floor.'

Mary gave a groan. *Oh, Tom!*

'And of course there was no sign of the culprit. A bicycle had been taken from the cart shed. It wasn't long before Ronnie checked the contents of the tack-room locker and found that the lock had been forced and the petty-cash box was gone too.' Weighing the drastic effect that the news was obviously having on Mary against the duty he felt to relate the full story, Giles decided that he must press on. 'Ronnie and Ray threw up their hands and declared that Wilf was a lost cause — good riddance to bad rubbish. So it was left to Philip to search for the miscreant. He drove straight to Highcliff, to the Old Court House where

Wilf had his lodgings. Apparently there'd been a brief sighting of him there by Philip's sister, Pauline. Wilf didn't offer her any explanation as to why he'd come away from work early; he simply collected his belongings — a small canvas knapsack — and cycled away again.'

'Is that the last time he was seen?' Mary made an effort to gather her thoughts.

'There was a possible sighting in Maltby Bay by the landlord of the Harbour Inn. Someone fitting Wilf's description went in there late last night. He stuck out like a sore thumb because he paid for his beer with a crisp pound note, which is unusual in those parts. After that we have no idea where he went.' Giles allowed a silence to develop. He considered breaking the tension by remarking that Wilf's teetotal credentials were somewhat tarnished by his presence in the public house, but decided that Mary was way beyond gallows humour. 'Shall I fetch someone?' he suggested after a while.

In fact, there was no need since Bobbie had come looking for her friend.

'Ah, Mary, there you are; I've been searching everywhere for you,' she exclaimed as she ventured into the library. 'Stan would like to know how high we want the platform to be . . .' Bobbie tailed off as she looked from Mary to Giles and back again.

'She's had a bad shock,' Giles explained as he drew away from Mary. 'Will you tell Bobbie about it or shall I?'

Bobbie moved swiftly towards the window seat to take his place. 'We can sort this out, thank you, Giles.' Waiting for him to back out of the room, she clasped Mary's hand.

'I've done something dreadful,' Mary confessed once the door was closed. 'You and Viv will hate me for it; I know you will.'

'No, we won't,' Bobbie said softly. 'We could never hate you.'

Her kindness brought tears to Mary's eyes. 'I've betrayed everyone. I've let my country down.'

'Mary, it can't be as bad as all that. Come on, spit it out; it'll help to get it off your chest.'

The tears fell without restraint. 'I helped a deserter — there, you're shocked! But it's true; I did it.'

Bobbie held on to her hand. 'Of course I'm surprised. But I'm sure you didn't mean to.'

'Oh, but I did!' The truth forced its way out of Mary's mouth. 'I helped this man of my own free will. And I did it even though I knew it was wrong and it would force me to lie to you and Viv, even to my own husband.'

Bobbie was unable to fathom the mystery. Mary was fiercely patriotic and a faithful friend and wife. 'But why? You're as honest as anyone I know. And you risk your life for your country. Which man made you do such a thing?'

On the brink of her revelation Mary grew suddenly calm. Her tears ceased and she drew a deep breath. 'You know him as Wilf Cranston,' she told Bobbie. 'But his real name is Tom Holland.'

'Your brother?' At last the puzzle pieces slotted into place. 'Dear girl, Tom forced you to lie?'

'No; he begged me. He was desperate. He saw such terrible things in Germany — pals blown to pieces, bodies being looted . . .' Her voice cracked but she took another breath then continued. 'Tom was never cut out for the army; I know that. And he's not the only soldier to have buckled in the heat of battle, Bobbie.'

'I understand — truly I do.' Lack of Moral Fibre: the cruel medical term that had once been stamped on the front of Ray's RAF file echoed inside Bobbie's head.

'Tom was in a daze; he didn't know what he was doing. He stole another man's exemption papers then once he'd done it and started to live a lie there was no way out for him. There never will be; he'll be forced to run away again and again, with the fear of going to prison driving him on. It'll be a miserable, hopeless life. And the fact that I covered it up will stay on my conscience for ever.'

★ ★ ★

Everyone was kind to Mary in the days that followed. Word got around — some at the ferry pool treated her with kid gloves, afraid to broach the topic of Tom Holland's desertion. Others, like Olive, went at it head-on.

'One bad apple doesn't mean the whole barrel is rotten,' she commiserated with Mary over breakfast on the Monday. A large canvas tent had been erected beside the control tower and kitted out as a temporary canteen. 'To be honest with you, at the start of the war my cousin Albert was hauled up in front of the Tribunal for conchies for refusing to attend his medical — it meant an automatic court martial and prison. He's still there, as far as I know.'

Unable to eat the sausages and egg that lay congealing on her plate, Mary gave a thin smile.

'She's right, you know.' Peggy was intent on shoring

310

up Mary's fragile confidence before she flew again. 'Your brother placed you in an impossible position. What you must try to do now is put the whole episode behind you.'

As always Mary trusted Peggy and tried her best to follow her advice. Monday and Tuesday passed without any more word of Tom. A rumour went round that he might have gone to Maltby Bay in search of passage out of the country; perhaps in a fishing boat bound for waters off the Dutch or Danish coast.

'If he's any sense he won't show his face around here again.' Stan trusted — wrongly — that his blunt opinion would comfort Mary. 'I'll knock his block off if he does.'

'You don't look well,' Gillian told Mary as Mary queued to receive her chit on Wednesday morning — the day when flying out of Rixley was due to resume. 'If you carry on not eating you'll waste away.'

All pilots received their chits with quiet relief. After days of inactivity, the clear priority was to get as many planes away as possible — mostly on short hops to RAF bases in Yorkshire or Lancashire, which meant that the majority of pilots would be back at Rixley well before dark.

'We're limping along,' Douglas commented to Peggy as she received her chit — a Defiant to Lancaster. His attempts to get runway repair work under way had come up against many obstacles — there was a nationwide lack of both materials and manpower. Meanwhile, the dismantling of the wrecked hangar was also causing him headaches.

Viv shuffled towards the hatch to receive her own chit. 'Beaufort to Hull,' she informed Mary and Bobbie. 'What do you say we three girls reconvene this

311

evening to cut down our spruce tree?'

'Excellent idea,' Bobbie replied for them both. She picked up her orders for the day — Wellington reconnaissance type to a rural strip south of Sheffield — then waited for Mary.

'Spitfire Mark Nine. I'm going where you're going,' Mary told Bobbie. Even the prospect of flying her favourite crate did little to lift her mood. She cast her mind back to Monday evening and to her painful telephone call to Cameron when she'd given him a halting, guilt-laden account of what she'd done. He'd listened quietly and assured her that it made no difference; he loved her still. But, sensitive as Mary was to every inflection in her husband's voice, she'd interpreted his silences as stern disapproval. That night she'd cried herself to sleep.

'Keep an eye on her,' Viv said in an aside to Bobbie as they headed for the locker room after breakfast.

Bobbie nodded. 'It goes without saying.'

In the event, Bobbie and Mary's day went without a hitch — no lumps of cloud to climb over, no ice on the windscreens or low-lying fog, no dicing with barrage balloons. They, like all the other Rixley pilots, were safely back to base in time for tea. Then it was a quick change into civvies for Viv, Bobbie and Mary and on with stout boots for a night-time tramp through Burton Wood. Mary and Bobbie carried saws from Ernest's shed while Viv led the way with her own saw slung over her shoulder like a rifle as they made for the eight-foot-tall tree that was designated for the chop.

'Ill met by moonlight!' Jean quoted Shakespeare when her three armed accomplices reached the spot. She'd brought along a Thermos flask full of hot tea

312

and an old toffee tin containing two rich tea biscuits each.

'Yes; it's a perfect night for a spot of furtive tree felling.' Viv pointed up at a bright moon and a sky sprinkled with stars before immediately getting down to work. The teeth of her heavy saw had difficulty cutting through the trunk — chewing the wood rather than slicing through it — and she soon stopped to mop her brow, giving way to Bobbie, who in turn gave way to Mary. Eventually the obstinate tree began to lean.

'Timber!' Viv leaped clear.

There was a long creak and several moments of suspense before the doomed tree finally toppled. Viv and Bobbie darted forward to raise it and stand it up straight. 'Well?' Bobbie demanded.

Mary passed judgement. 'Well done, one and all — it's a fine tree.'

'Now for refreshments.' Jean handed out the steaming tea then they sat on two mossy logs, gazing up at the stars.

'I take it Douglas is at home with Dorota?' Bobbie said. No one was in a rush; in fact, they all welcomed a breather before carrying their prize back to the Grange.

'Yes, but he's worn out, poor man.' Jean sipped at her tea. 'There's so much for him to do now that Hilary's out of commission. Dorota and I hardly see anything of him.'

They talked for a while about Hilary's injuries — the doctors had reported a definite improvement but had warned of a long convalescence at a nursing home on the coast.

'I take it that Peggy will step in and ease Douglas's

workload?' This seemed logical to Bobbie, until Mary reminded them of Peggy's family responsibilities.

Jean resigned herself to the fact that Douglas would have to cope alone. 'On the bright side, the Rixley Atta girls are back in full swing, ferrying those crates from A to B.'

'And it'll soon be Christmas.' Nothing got Bobbie down for long; not even a full-scale bombing raid. 'Come along, ladies; this tree won't decorate itself.'

So they said goodbye to Jean then set off for home with Bobbie humming the tune to 'Swinging on a Star', soon breaking into loud song as she strode along. The words involved funny rhymes about mules with long ears and monkeys in zoos — you too could be a monkey or a mule if you refused to go to school.

'Talking of mules,' Bobbie said when she came to the end of the song, 'what answer did Brian Wheeler eventually give?'

Viv grunted. 'Brian may grow up to be a pig,' she complained, cleverly adapting the words of the song.

'So, no go?' Bobbie interpreted the remark.

'Not unless I agreed to become his mistress.' Viv intended to surprise her friends but not for Bobbie to drop her end of the tree in shock.

'Good Lord above! Is that what he said?'

'In as many words.' A party at his London club followed by a night in a hotel — it had been as plain as the nose on her face, and for once she knew that she wasn't exaggerating. 'I was to dance with him on Saturday then go to a New Year's Eve party with him, leading no doubt to you-know-what.' Viv grew surprisingly coy.

'I hope you told him no.' Mary spoke out against the idea. 'What rotten cheek!'

'I didn't give him a direct answer — I said I needed time to think.' Viv had marched out of Brian's office and across the square towards the gate of the training base with a sick feeling in the pit of her stomach. What did Brian take her for? Then again, had it been partly her fault for giving off the wrong signals in the first place, as Brian had originally claimed? Jeez, the whole tryst business was too complicated for her simple brain! 'I'll think about it,' she'd said, while every nerve ending had cried out at the unsavoury idea of being bedded by Brian Wheeler. She hadn't imagined it — she'd been able to tell from his steely determination that this was what he'd intended.

'It's entirely up to you,' he'd called after her. 'Telephone me when you've made your decision.'

'Say no!' Bobbie jumped in to back Mary up.

'Then we kiss goodbye to our cadets.' Viv sighed. The lights of the Grange twinkled between the scorched trunks of the pine trees at the edge of the wood. 'What if I were to call him and agree to his terms then change my mind after Saturday? Would that work?'

'No; deep down, who cares about the cadets?' Bobbie's response came quick as a flash. 'All we care about is you, Viv. Call Brian the minute we get back.'

'No shilly-shallying,' Mary agreed. 'You must tell Flight Lieutenant Wheeler to take a running jump.'

★ ★ ★

The following day snow was once more in the air. A raw wind blew in from the north and put a question mark over flying out of Rixley from its one surviving runway. Peggy was first in line, waiting at the end of

315

Runway 2 in a nimble Spit Mark 5, followed by Horace in a second Spit. Back in the ops room, Douglas juggled weather forecasts, destinations and availability of ground crews. 'Bob Cross and Gordon Mason have gone off sick,' he told Mary, Bobbie and Viv as they queued for their chits. 'We've fallen behind schedule — I'd go and have a cup of tea if I were you.'

So the morning passed in a desultory way until at noon the skies cleared and the three Atta girls got off the ground at last. Once more they flew short hops and were back in time for tea.

'Brrr! My tiny hands are still frozen,' Viv complained as she, Bobbie and Mary gathered outside the blue room. 'I flew a Wellington to Newcastle — she had more holes in her fuselage than your average colander.'

'Let's warm you up with a drink at the Fox,' Bobbie suggested. 'Oh no you don't!' she told Mary, who was about to slink off to her room. 'That includes you, too.'

She made them put on extra layers and don woollen scarves, hats and gloves for the tramp through Burton Wood. Once they reached the pub, she sat them down and went to the bar.

'What's got into Miss Pollyanna this evening? What does she have to smile about?' Viv grumbled as she and Mary sat close to the fire. She noticed that Florrie had arranged small sprigs of holly along the shelves behind the bar — the stingy landlady's solitary attempt to introduce Christmas cheer.

'More to the point, what's got into you?' Mary was always quick to pick up the moods of others. 'Why so down in the mouth?'

'Brian.' Viv's short, bitter answer said it all.

316

'Best to forget about him.' Mary had seen Viv hold the receiver at arm's length during last night's tirade. She'd heard him call Viv words that didn't belong in a gentleman's vocabulary. 'He's not worth losing sleep over.'

'You're right.' Viv accepted the shandy that Bobbie had carried across then she leaned across the table to Mary. 'No news of your brother, I take it?'

'Nothing. Philip still keeps his eyes open for me, but it's as if Tom's vanished from the face of the earth.' Part of Mary was relieved by this but still she fretted over her brother's friendless state — last seen alone in Maltby Bay on a dark, windy night — at the edge of the world and facing a stormy sea, most likely at his wits' end.

'Philip is a decent chap,' Bobbie conceded. 'I might not agree with his conchie views but his heart is in the right place and he works hard. In fact, Ray talks about offering him a permanent position on the yard once the war is over.'

Mary and Viv gave murmurs of approval but the conversation came to a halt when the door opened and a group of carol singers bustled in and a rousing chorus of 'God Rest Ye Merry Gentlemen' filled the room.

' 'Let nothing you dismay',' Bobbie echoed softly.

' 'Tidings of comfort and joy'.' Viv's face lit up at the sight of melodious singers, young and old, their chapped faces glowing in the firelight, their chests puffed out and heads thrust back, mouths making round 'O's as the hymn rose to the rafters.

'Sing 'Silent Night',' a voice from a dark corner of the crowded snug called out once the last notes had faded.

'Make it 'While Shepherds Watched',' a second voice cried.

' 'In the Bleak Midwinter'.'

This third suggestion was shouted down — 'No: too miserable.'

Ignoring all requests, the choir plunged into a lusty version of 'The Holly and the Ivy'.

"When they are both full grown',' Bobbie hummed as she tipped sixpence into the collection tin. 'Mistletoe!' she said suddenly as the tin was passed on to the next table. 'Talking of holly and ivy, that reminds me: we forgot the mistletoe for the blue room.'

'What's the point? There'll be no Aireby boys to kiss,' Viv reminded her with an exaggeratedly glum expression.

But Mary thought they should hang mistletoe anyway. 'Don't worry, we can collect some on the walk back to the Grange.'

"Oh, the rising of the sun . . . And the running of the deer . . .' '

When a second gust of cold air blew into the snug, the girls glanced over their shoulders to see Peggy wrapped in scarf and hat standing in the doorway.

'Over here!' Glad to see her, Mary gestured for their fellow pilot to join them.

Peggy arrived at their table and dusted a covering of snowflakes from her jacket. 'I bring glad tidings,' she announced as she sat between Viv and Mary, giving Mary's hand a special squeeze.

'Let me get you a drink.' Bobbie stood up.

'No, no; I won't stop. I simply came to share the good news — which is this.' Peggy glanced round at their faces: Bobbie was curious, Mary expectant, Viv suspicious. 'I flew my Mark Five into Liverpool today

318

and guess who I should bump into: why, none other than Hubert Norris.'

The girls looked uncertainly at one another.

'Hubert went to college in Cambridge with my husband, Keith.' Peggy took her time. 'As a matter of fact, back in those days we three attended several social events together so today was a perfect opportunity to reminisce.'

'What took Group Captain Norris to Liverpool?' Bobbie asked.

'He was obliged to attend one of those interminable jaw-jaws, as he calls them.'

Viv nudged Bobbie with her elbow to prevent her from asking any more time-wasting questions.

'Hubert was kind enough to offer me a lift back to Rixley in his car. He was most concerned about recent events here. He asked after Hilary and hoped the bombing raid hadn't affected our Christmas plans. He assumed that our party was still on.'

'Jeez; he mentioned the party of his own free will?' Viv sat forward eagerly in her seat.

'Quite so,' Peggy continued at her own sedate pace. 'I assured Hubert that it was full steam ahead with preparations, adding that it was a pity that Flight Lieutenant Wheeler had seen fit to withdraw his consent. After all, what harm could it do for the trainees to join in with our Christmas fun?'

'Yes; what did he say to that?' Viv imagined an insistent drum roll playing in the background; dum-dum-dah-dum . . . Around their table the suspense built.

'Hubert took my point. I explained the trouble that had been taken to organize such an event — liaising with ENSA, preparing the room, and so on.'

319

Viv couldn't contain herself a moment longer. 'You're saying that you got Group Captain Norris to override Brian Wheeler?'

'Precisely,' Peggy informed them with a modest smile. 'Weather permitting, Hubert is perfectly willing for his cadets to attend.'

★   ★   ★

It was eleven o'clock that night when Viv knocked on Peggy's door. Peggy answered it in her demure quilted dressing gown and with her short hair held back by a tortoiseshell Alice band.

'I hope you don't mind.' Viv's approach was tentative. It had taken a lot of nerve for her to do this. 'I could come back tomorrow if you'd rather.'

'Not at all — come in.' Peggy held the door wide open.

Viv stepped inside the bedroom. Everything was in apple-pie order as she'd expected, but what drew her attention was a large framed photograph of a round-faced, dark-haired baby on Peggy's dressing table.

'Rosie,' Peggy explained with quiet pride.

'Yes. She's adorable.'

'Thank you.'

'No — thank *you*.' Viv shifted from one bare foot to the other, clutching awkwardly at the plunging neckline of her lilac silk dressing gown. Humble pie wasn't part of her usual diet but she must go ahead and eat it now. 'That's why I'm here: to thank you for doing what I so spectacularly failed to do — namely getting our party back on track.'

'You're most welcome. I'm only sorry that Flight Lieutenant Wheeler's conduct fell short of what is

320

required.'

'How do you know that?' Viv admitted that Peggy continued to be full of surprises.

'Never mind; I have eyes and ears — let's leave it at that. By the way, I'm told that Flight Lieutenant Wheeler will be otherwise engaged on Saturday evening.'

'Also . . .' Relief made Viv hesitate to catch her breath. Then she careered on at a gallop. 'I came to say I'm sorry — no, hear me out. I'm an idiot; an absolute fool at times. I open my mouth and talk garbage. But Jeez, I was scared of you when you first arrived. You reminded me of my math teacher in high school. I was back to being twelve years old — which is why I talked behind your back and called you names.'

'The Cold Front, as I recall.' Peggy repressed a smile.

Viv's jaw dropped open. 'How did you . . . ? Never mind. I got you all wrong and I apologize.'

'Apology accepted.' Peggy flicked on the electric kettle in the corner of her room then brought out two mugs and a tub of cocoa from a small cupboard. 'And you're by no means an idiot — far from it. In fact, only this morning Douglas and I had a quiet word. Sit down, my dear.' She pulled out the dressing-table stool for her astonished visitor. 'He proposes a promotion to the rank of first officer as a reward for your recent service. I'm in complete agreement — you really are a splendid pilot, Vivienne.'

'Oh, I don't know what to say!' Viv sank on to the padded seat. She would be First Officer Robertson, on a par with an RAF Flight Lieutenant — stick that in your pipe, Brian Wheeler!

'The same will apply to dear, brave Mary,' Peggy

went on. 'She will be promoted to second officer.'

Viv clapped her hands in delight. 'That's terrific! May I tell her?'

'By all means. And here's to you both,' Peggy murmured as she handed the hot chocolate to Viv and they clinked their mugs together. 'And long may you continue to fly — through to the end of the war and for a long time after.'

21

As Christmas approached, the threat of a second bombing attack receded and the weather became the Rixley pilots' main enemy. Viv, Bobbie and Mary woke on the Friday to a thick, damp fog and went down to breakfast in a low mood, predicting another washout day for all.

'We're to stay put at the Grange until further notice,' Bobbie informed Mary, who had come down later than usual. 'Douglas's orders.'

A plan was put in place to gather in an hour to hang streamers and balloons in the blue room. Meanwhile, Viv and Mary would catch up on chores while Bobbie spoke to Ray on the telephone.

At ten o'clock, as planned, the three girls fetched ladders from Ernest's storeroom then lifted out the contents of the large cardboard box of Christmas decorations.

'I bet my bottom dollar it'll never get fully light today.' Viv sat down on the edge of the new platform at the far end of the room to disentangle some fairy lights. 'At this rate we'll be stuck on the ground until after Christmas.'

'On the bright side, it means we have more time to get ready for tomorrow.' Bobbie spoke from the top of a stepladder. She had multicoloured paper streamers looped over one arm. 'Someone hand me some drawing pins.'

There were none available so Mary volunteered to go in search of Ernest, who would surely know where to find some.

'Try my storeroom.' The handyman was taking his time over a mid-morning cup of tea in the butler's pantry. 'They should be on the third shelf from the bottom on the left as you go in.'

So Mary made a foray outside, along the terrace then down into the yard, barely able to see a foot in front of her. She felt her way like a blind man towards Ernest's room, avoiding his pick-up lorry and almost bumping her shins against an empty wheelbarrow that had been abandoned beside it. As she opened the door into the storeroom, thinking that she heard a muffled sound from one of the stables, she paused, turned her head and listened again.

Perhaps she'd imagined it, or perhaps it was a small animal — a fox or a cat — that had taken refuge from the damp and cold.

The sound was repeated — a low cough that was human, not animal. *Drat this fog; I can't see a darned thing.* 'Who's there?' she called.

There was no reply. Perhaps it had been nothing after all. *On my left, third shelf from the bottom,* she reminded herself as she entered the small, window-less store. She felt for a light switch but before she found it, a heavy shove from behind thrust her violently forward. In pitch-black darkness she heard the door bang shut followed by more coughing. The unknown person was in the room with her, bumping into obstacles, blundering towards her.

Mary kept her head. No one would hear her scream — everyone was indoors, keeping warm. Her skin crawled as the coughing stopped and the man — she could tell it was a man by the force of his shove — pushed objects out of his way. She decided she must try to work her way silently towards the door.

The intruder guessed her intention. 'Don't move. Stay where you are.'

'Tom!' The voice was unmistakable. Her heart stopped then raced. Her legs threatened to buckle under her.

'Yes, it's me.'

'Tom, for pity's sake, let me turn on the light.'

'What for?'

'So I can see you — please.' *Tom — of course; who else would he turn to in his hour of need?* Mary swallowed back her shock and worked her way by touch towards the light switch. 'I'm going to turn it on,' she warned.

With the flick of a switch the room was illuminated. Tom stood with his back to shelves that lined the wall, blinking in the light. He was dirty and unshaven, poorly dressed in a thin jacket and a shirt without a collar, with neither coat nor hat. She noticed a bruise on his temple and his knuckles were scuffed from the scrap he'd had with Ronnie.

'I've been holed up in one of the stables,' he muttered. 'I knew you were bound to turn up sooner or later.'

'How did you know it was me?' He wouldn't have been able to see her through the pea-souper fog that had swirled around the yard as she'd ventured down the steps.

'I heard your voice.'

Who's there? Two words was all it had taken for him to recognize her. 'How long have you been hiding here?'

'Since Monday night. Don't worry — I made sure no one knew I was here.'

'Have you had anything to eat? You must be starving.' Tom had the gaunt, hunted look of a long-term fugitive, with his eyes darting here and there to check that they were alone.

'Mary, you've got to help me.' He clutched her sleeve. 'You're the only one who will. Please, Mary.'

She shook her head. 'No, I can't.'

'Wait; let me tell you my side of it. I lost my temper on the Thresham yard, I admit it. I took a swing at Ronnie. We had a fight. But you never saw the way he treated me. He was like a bloody sergeant major — yelling orders, calling me names, giving me the worst jobs.'

'Tom, I can't bear these excuses. You shouldn't have come.' Mary felt wretched as she refused his plea.

'Where else was I supposed to go?' He slumped forward and wrapped his arms around his chest. 'I had nowhere, no one — you don't know what it's like.'

She recalled him as a child — the youngest of three, wheedling and spoiled, always preferring the easy way out. Yet that wasn't the full picture. Tom as a boy had failed to achieve much in school — always near the bottom of the class, sometimes bullied by the bigger boys, often given short shrift by teachers who picked on the ones like Tom who hid away at the back of the class. No real wonder then that he'd grown up to be surly and resentful — a tendency that had run unchecked over the years and brought him to this tragic point. 'I'm sorry that it's come to this. But you have to own up to what you've done. You can't run away for ever.'

He raised his hands to block his ears. 'No one understands — not even you and you're my sister.'

'Oh, but I do, Tom.' Moving forward, she held his

wrists and persuaded him to lower his hands. 'Believe me; I do. I even think there's a name for what you're feeling. It's called battle fatigue. Thirty years ago it was known as shell shock.'

Doubt flickered in his eyes; the same colour as Mary's — grey with hazel flecks — and with the same dark lashes.

'You should see a doctor.'

'How can I? I'm meant to be missing in action.'

'You would have to admit that you're not really Wilf Cranston. That's the hard part, I know. But if you did, then at least Wilf's family would know the truth about their boy.'

'Then what?' In his simple way Tom could only see one step ahead.

'Then the doctors would take a look at you. They can do tests — someone I know who was in the RAF had them done. The doctors decided he'd never see action again; his mind was permanently affected.'

'Did they send him home?' A new gleam of hope entered Tom's eyes.

'They did.' Mary kept back the fact that Ray had gone down in his plane in a blaze of glory and so the circumstances were entirely different. 'Who knows? They might not go as hard on you as you think.'

'Who's 'they' when they're at home?' A suspicious cloud returned to block out the chink of light.

'There's a Tribunal that decides such things.'

'Would they chuck me in clink?'

'It depends on what the doctors decide.' Careful to stick to the facts, Mary held his frightened gaze. 'Even if they did, it might not be for long. In the end, that would be better than running away.'

'No — not if you get me some food and some

proper clothes.' A cunning desperation reappeared. 'And if you give me some money on top of what I took from Thresham I could get clean away.'

As Mary shook her head in exasperation, the door suddenly opened and Ray appeared.

'Mary, what's up?' Learning from Bobbie that flying was off for the morning, he'd driven over to spend an hour or two with her, only encountering the worst of the fog a mile from his destination. He'd parked his car in the stable yard as usual and had been curious to hear voices from the storeroom so he'd gone to investigate. Now Ray looked from Mary to a lad he took at first to be a tramp until he realized that the miserable, shivering creature with his back against the wall was none other than his runaway stable lad.

Ray's arrival clicked the fugitive into action. He made a rush for the door but Ray stood his ground. He grabbed Tom by the jacket lapels. 'Oh no you don't!'

Tom pummelled Ray's chest, to no avail. His assault ended in a new fit of coughing.

'Now then, Wilf — or should I say Tom?' Ray thrust him back against the wall. 'No point in denying it — we all know the truth. Now, Mary, first things first — are you all right?'

She nodded. 'It's a good job you're here. I want Tom to own up but he's not having any of it.'

'Is that right?' Ray took his time to weigh things up. 'Your sister has her head screwed on; you should listen to her.'

Tom tried to wrestle free but found that Ray was stronger.

'You've already caused enough trouble on my yard. Yes, you've got yourself into a jam but no, it's not fair to involve Mary — do you hear?'

Tom squirmed then stopped struggling. 'What's it to do with you? This is between me and her.'

'Wrong — it's between you and your colonel. It's the authorities you'll have to answer to.' Ray relaxed his hold. 'Listen, Tom, I'm not saying that what you've done is right — far from it. But you're only young. You have your whole life ahead of you — there's plenty of time to put things right and make a fresh start.'

'You don't bloody care what happens to me — nobody does.' Tom lashed out a second time but was again restrained. 'You don't understand.'

'Try me.' Ray leaned against the door with his arms firmly folded.

'Talk to Ray.' Mary reached out to touch Tom's arm but he pushed her roughly away.

'Why should I?'

'Because I know what it's like.' Ray's simple words seemed to cut through Tom's anger and gain his attention. 'I've been through it myself.'

'Ray is the RAF friend I mentioned,' Mary explained.

'I've been down in that same deep hole as you — not coping, feeling worthless. Other blokes fought for their country so why couldn't I? Only, my nerves were cut to ribbons — I couldn't go back out there and fly those crates; not for all the tea in China.'

Tom searched Ray's face for signs of a man who was broken and disgraced. Instead, he saw someone unafraid to face up to the shattering events he'd been through.

'On my last mission I got into a dogfight with a Messerschmitt,' Ray continued. 'I was close enough to see the whites of Jerry's eyes — it was either him or me; I was a split second away from going up in flames. Instead, it was Jerry who bought it. I was the lucky one — I only ended up in the drink. The thing is, Tom, when they fished me out I was a gibbering wreck — I wasn't talking any sense and I had no idea where I was. So they took me to hospital and after a while the docs decided I wasn't right in the head. I got a stamp on my file to say so. Then they sent me home.'

'But you got better?'

'Bit by bit. Booze helped me to blot everything out for a while but then I was in danger of it taking over so I'm doing my damnedest to cut it out.' Ray hoped his honesty would guide Tom through. 'It's not easy but I'm getting there. And I'm only telling you this to help you realize that, like it or not, there's only one way out of your present mess: Mary's way. So what do you say — are you willing to give it a go?'

'Maybe — I don't know.' He slurred his answer and ducked his head.

'That's the way forward, Tom.' This time when Mary approached him he didn't push her back. 'Ray knows what he's talking about.'

'What would happen?' he mumbled.

'We'd need to drive you from here to your regimental base in . . .' Ray turned to Mary with a questioning look.

'In Leeds.'

'That's easy. We can take you there in no time and you can own up.'

'Please, Tom.' Watching the fight go out of him and seeing him sag forward like a sack of potatoes, in spite of everything Mary's heart was flooded with compassion and she wanted to gather him in her arms and comfort him as you would a small child. 'It really is the only way. Ray and I will ask for a doctor to examine you. We'll do all we can to make sure they treat you fairly.'

'And you'll begin by saying you're sorry,' Ray instructed. 'Starting with Mary here.'

Tom looked up at the ceiling then down at his boots — anywhere except at his sister.

Ray cajoled softly. 'Come along, son — it's not that hard.'

'Sorry,' Tom muttered. Then, as if a dam had burst, the words poured out. 'I'm sorry for all of it: for what I did to Wilf and for running away, for lying to everyone and stealing that money and for getting you into hot water, Mary. I wish I hadn't, and that's God's honest truth!'

She moved towards him and rested one hand on his. 'Everything will be all right in the long run; do you hear me? You'll take your punishment like a man then we'll get you back on the straight and narrow — a proper job, somewhere decent to live.'

'I'll make sure of that,' Ray promised.

Gradually, with Ray's firm handling and Mary's soft persuasion, they talked a defeated Tom out of the storeroom into the stable yard, where they found Viv hovering.

'Mary, you were gone for ages. What happened to the drawing pins?' Viv saw Ray standing guard over an abject Wilf Cranston-come-Tom Holland, whose teeth chattered and whose body trembled from head to toe. Mary stood close behind him like an attentive Florence Nightingale. 'Jeez,' Viv breathed. 'Now I see what took you so long.'

* * *

331

'Ray was marvellous.' Mary had nothing but praise for him once the deed was done and she had her first decent night's sleep for weeks under her belt. She told Bobbie that Tom had submitted to being driven to Leeds and handed over to the authorities without a word of complaint. 'Ray knew just what to say and do — he couldn't have behaved better.'

Bobbie stood back from the festive tree to which she, Mary and Viv had put the finishing touches. 'Is that so? Ray said that you were the one who made the difference.'

'He's being modest.' Mary fiddled with a tinsel arrangement. 'It was because he was honest with Tom. Lord knows what would have happened if he hadn't come along when he did.'

'It's for the best, as far as Tom's concerned.' Viv cast a critical eye around the room — streamers and balloons were in place, as was the hastily gathered bunch of mistletoe hanging above the doorway. 'Did the guys in Leeds give you any idea of what will happen next?'

'They'll keep Tom in a military prison.' On hearing this the day before, Mary's heart had sunk.

'The lad should count himself lucky,' the bluff military policeman had pointed out. 'You should see what happens to deserters who don't make it back across the Channel. There are hundreds of them. If he'd only got as far as Paris or Naples he'd have come up against armed gangs of the blighters and been press-ganged into helping them to rob supply trains.'

Relieved that Tom had escaped a worse pickle than the one he was in, she'd asked how long they would keep him in prison but received no firm answer. But she had learned that pleading his case successfully in a military court could lead to a suspended sentence.

'Fingers crossed,' she'd whispered to Tom as he was led away between two guards.

'Chin up,' Ray had added.

'It was a hard thing to watch,' Mary admitted to Bobbie and Viv. 'Tom looked so bewildered — it nearly broke my heart.'

'So what do we all say to a small snifter as a pick-me-up before the ENSA gang gets here?' Bobbie's bright suggestion was quickly taken up and they repaired to the mess, where they found a group of like-minded off-duty pilots.

'Just the one drink, otherwise I'll be squiffy before the fun even starts,' Viv predicted, casting cushions aside and plonking herself down in a window seat.

'Right you are — a small brandy, then? And the same for you, Bobbie?' Mary took their orders.

'All set for tonight?' Gillian called from the other side of the room.

'Just about.' Mary went to the bar to order the drinks then learned from Peggy who stood next to her that George the barman was prepared to open up the officers' mess to Grange residents, Rixley ground crew and Aireby guests alike.

'To help the party go with a swing,' Peggy informed her. 'Sadly I shan't be attending. I prefer to spend the night at Westville Avenue with Rosie and my parents.'

'Be sure to thank your father for the balloons,' Mary said, 'and thank you for working your magic on Group Captain Norris.'

'In fact, thank you for everything,' Viv butted in as she came up to help Mary with the drinks.

Peggy blushed and brushed away the praise. 'I'll be back tomorrow on Priority Ones and I expect to hear all the gossip.'

'There won't be much for me to talk about, worse luck.' As the time for the party drew near, Mary had grown resigned to the fact that Cameron wouldn't be there. She would be surrounded by dancing couples with no special partner of her own. No doubt a row of callow Aireby recruits would be on hand instead, to tread on her feet with their big clodhoppers.

'Christmas isn't the same without one's husband around,' Peggy commiserated. 'Still, one must keep one's head up and soldier on.'

If Peggy can, then so can I, Mary vowed as she took the drinks to the table.

'What do you think — shall we get changed before or after the ENSA lot roll up?' Viv, too, was experiencing a touch of the blues. After all, she'd put her heart and soul into making the event a success and yet she feared a main ingredient in the form of Giles would be missing from the mix. Naturally she would bluff everyone into believing that she didn't give a jot — she would waltz and foxtrot, jitterbug and Lindy Hop with the best of them, but would her heart really be in it without Giles to dance with?

'Let's get changed afterwards,' Bobbie decided, ever practical. 'You never know, we might have to help carry instruments from the van.'

Sure enough, when the musicians arrived in their maroon Morris van, the girls' assistance was needed.

'Blimey, how do you manage to fit so much into such a small space?' Mary queried as two men, two women and a variety of instruments emerged from the vehicle into the stable yard.

Most astonishing was the way they manhandled the upright piano out of its back door — down a portable ramp on to a flat trolley.

334

'Easy does it; take care not to knock the corners off,' the older of the two women instructed. She was sturdily built, with carefully curled blonde hair. 'Hello, I'm Elsie Dibb.' She introduced herself to Viv, Bobbie and Mary. 'The chap with the 'tache is my hubby . . .'

Lo and behold, said husband re-emerged from the cramped van with a bass drum.

'Yonder is Leonard.' Elsie pointed to a youngster who was fussing over some marks on the sleeve of his tweed jacket. He was thin as a rake, with slicked-back, black hair and eyes that were too close together. 'Don't let appearances put you off,' Elsie continued. 'When Leonard opens his mouth you could shut your eyes and swear you're listening to Bing himself.'

'No third-rate, end-of-the-pier singers for us,' Elsie's better half assured the girls. He was as stout as his wife and equally cheerful. 'We have only the best singers in our line-up, eh, Dolores?'

The question was directed at a chalk-white, red-haired slip of a girl shivering inside a bottle-green wool coat.

'Dolores is our soubrette,' Elsie informed them. 'They say she's going to be the second —'

'Vera Lynn.' Bobbie finished the sentence for her. 'So I heard.'

'Dolores is her stage name. Back home in Glasgow she's plain Margo Connelly.'

Viv and Mary put their backs into pushing the piano up the ramp with Elsie and Leonard while Bobbie and Dolores carried the drums.

'You'll have plenty of time to get ready,' Bobbie assured Dolores as they struggled on. 'The party room is all set up and there's a separate place for you to get changed.' She'd set aside the butler's pantry for the purpose.

'You're Scottish.' The young singer's pale, pretty face brightened immediately. 'Have you ever been to Glasgow?'

'Have I ever been to Glasgow?' Bobbie echoed incredulously. 'Why, Buchanan Street is my favourite place to shop and there's a tea room on Sauchiehall Street that sells the best fruit scones in the world!'

22

Bobbie had saved up clothes coupons especially for tonight's party — enough to buy a satin halter-neck dress from an exclusive shop in Northgate and a brand-new pair of nylons. The dress was deep purple with a black bead trim. Mary's outfit was one she'd worn before — a floor-length, coral-coloured gown with a gored skirt that would flare out when she danced. Her only jewellery consisted of her two precious rings — one for her engagement to Cameron, the other for her marriage. Viv's look was more eye-catching — a mid-calf black velvet dress nipped in at the waist and with a plunging neckline adorned with diamanté clusters. A pair of glittering earrings completed the glamorous effect.

The girls gathered at half past six in Bobbie's room.

'Do either of you have a crimson lipstick I could borrow?' Viv enquired as she scrutinized her reflection in Bobbie's dressing-table mirror.

Bobbie promptly produced one from the top drawer. 'I say, is this neckline too low?' She'd caught sight of her reflection showing a good deal of cleavage as she'd leaned forward.

'No, it's just right.' Mary assured her that the overall effect was both classy and sophisticated.

After much twirling and many final inspections, the three girls were ready at last. Bobbie went to the window to peek through the blackout blind. 'The Aireby boys should be here soon.'

'Is there any sign of them?' Viv asked.

'Not yet,' Bobbie reported back. 'I can see Stan and Gordon getting out of a car with Olive, and there's a whole throng down on the terrace.' She let go of the blind, a little thrill of excitement running through her veins.

'Did you catch sight of Ray, by any chance?' Viv's attempt to sound casual didn't fool Mary and Bobbie.

'No,' Bobbie replied. 'And what you really mean is, "Is Giles there with him?"'

'No; why should he be?' Viv asked defensively as Mary slipped out on to the landing. She heard the sound of voices from the hall, picking out Douglas and Horace among others. As she stood listening, Gillian emerged from her room in a dress of soft, flattering jade green. She smiled at Viv then descended the stairs.

'I hear the sound of a truck!' Viv's exclamation drew Mary back into the room. 'Maybe I'll take a little look . . . Hurrah, here come the boys!'

The Aireby contingent clambered out of their covered Tilly wagon: a gaggle of gawky, noisy lads intent on having a good night out. There were squawks and raw yelps of laughter as they shouldered their way up the broad steps.

Bobbie glanced anxiously at her watch. 'I'd better go down and see if the band is ready.' She dashed from the room and was soon lost in the crowd assembling in the hall.

'Shall we go down too?' Mary fought to overcome her reluctance.

'No, let's be fashionably late,' Viv decided. *Will he, won't he come?* She wondered about Giles, like a child picking daisy petals — *He loves me, he loves me not . . .*

Meanwhile, Bobbie threaded her way through the

crowd and slipped into the blue room, closing the door behind her. She was greeted by a triumph of riotous colour and silver sparkles. Streamers, balloons and their magnificent tree had transformed the drab space, and at the far end instruments were arranged on Stan's platform.

'Are you all set?' Fearing that her nerves were running out of control, Bobbie began tweaking tinsel and straightening baubles on the tree.

'You've set a lot of store by this party.' Beneath his jovial exterior, Elsie's husband was an observant type with a strong belief in bringing cheer to war-weary troops and all who served.

'I have,' Bobbie agreed. 'We've had a difficult couple of months here at Rixley so it'll do us all good to let our hair down.'

'Well, relax — we won't disappoint.' Sitting at her piano, Elsie began to play a jaunty tune. 'Recognize this?'

'"We're Going to Hang Out the Washing on the Siegfried Line".' Bobbie sang along to the old patriotic number while Leonard and Dolores joined in. By the time Bobbie had opened the door to welcome everyone in, the ENSA quartet was in full swing.

'This is grand!' Gillian was one of the first to view the lively scene. 'Look at that tree, everyone.' She took in the coloured lights then glanced at the mistletoe hanging above the door. 'Stand by your beds!' she warned as the cadets swarmed in.

One jostled to the front and seized the nearest girl — it happened to be Olive, all decked out in crimson satin — and held her in a firm clinch. Another stood under the mistletoe, puckered his lips and invited a similar embrace. 'Come along, girls — I'm yours for the taking.'

'No, ta!' Gillian gave the would-be kisser a wide berth.

Soon the room filled up with eager trainees and Rixley ground crew, and the dancing began in earnest.

'Hello, Jean.' Smiling broadly, Bobbie made her way towards the door. 'I'm glad you could make it. Who's babysitting?'

'A girl from the village; just for an hour or two.' Jean looked lovely in her favourite colour — a rich royal blue. Her fair hair was swept back in an elegant style. 'Where's Viv?'

'Still upstairs, waiting to make a grand entrance, I suspect. Why?'

'I just saw Ray's car pull up outside, that's why. He had someone with him — I couldn't see who.' Before she had time to say more, Douglas came up and guided his wife on to the dance floor.

Instead of rushing outside to meet Ray, Bobbie paused for thought. Could the 'someone' be Giles? she wondered. True he hadn't been invited, but might he have decided to come anyway? If so, Viv deserved advance warning.

So she made her excuses to Stan and Gordon, then rushed upstairs.

'Jean says Ray is here,' she announced to Viv and Mary as she burst into the room. 'Apparently he has someone with him.'

'Man or woman?' Viv demanded as her heart skipped a beat.

'Jean couldn't see. I wondered if it might be Giles.'

'Don't be silly!' Viv spun Bobbie back towards the corridor. 'Giles wouldn't be interested in coming to our little get-together.'

'Says who?' Mary asked.

'I do!' Viv refused to consider the possibility. 'Now, off you go, Cinders! Your Prince Charming awaits.'

Bobbie shrugged then darted off obediently.

'We'd better go and face the music,' Mary said a touch reluctantly.

'Might as well.' Viv tried to slow her heartbeat. 'I truly don't believe Giles will come,' she told Mary with an air of insouciance. 'So you and I will be wallflowers together.'

The duo went downstairs to a dozen admiring glances from their Aireby guests — the ones without partners who had already found their way to the bar then back out into the hall. The quickest off the mark ditched their drinks and presented themselves smartly to the two single beauties who had descended the stairs like angels from on high.

'I remember you,' Viv's cadet told her with a wink. 'You're the girl who came to see Flight Lieutenant Wheeler.'

'That's me.' Blushing at the memory of her ill-advised visit then quickly recovering her composure, she allowed herself to be led on to the dance floor, where the band had begun to play Vaughn Monroe's 'When the Lights Go on Again'.

It was young Leonard's turn to shine up there on the stage as he sang hopeful lyrics about the boys coming home victorious. Couples swayed to the slow rhythm and soon Dolores's sweet voice joined in the chorus and a romantic mood filled the crowded room.

Meanwhile, Mary's clean-cut trainee proved a better than average dancer, and he guided her confidently around the floor. 'I had lessons when I was a kid,' he explained when she complimented him. 'My mum's a ballroom dance teacher. It's embarrassing, so keep it under your hat, won't you?'

Mary smiled and promised to stay silent.

'I see you're wearing a wedding ring,' her young partner observed.

'Yes; I got married earlier this month. I'm Mrs Ainslie now.'

'More's the pity,' he commented as he swept her along.

Meanwhile, Bobbie, having gone outside to look for Ray, found him quietly smoking a cigarette at the end of the terrace.

'To steady my nerves,' he said apologetically as he stubbed it out. 'I never was much good in crowds.'

'Take your time,' she told him. 'At least you're here —'

'And I'm sober as a judge,' he interrupted.

'— and that's all that matters.' Taking his hand she walked with him towards the main entrance. The night was cold and clear, the moon three-quarters full. 'Did Giles come with you?' she asked on Viv's behalf.

Ray shook his head. 'But speaking of Giles, he and I are making firm plans.'

'Oh?' This was the first Bobbie had heard of it and she was intrigued. They came to a halt just outside the door, where strains of a Tommy Dorsey jazz number reached their ears.

'Yes — didn't Viv tell you? Well, things have progressed on that front. Giles is all set to take charge of the yard's financial affairs, which will leave me free to oversee the practicalities — making sure the horses are in tip-top condition, keeping the owners happy, and so on. How does that sound to you?'

'I'd say that was an excellent plan — good for all concerned.'

'You look like the cat's whiskers, by the way.' Bobbie really did look, smell and feel gorgeous, with her hair falling loose over her bare, sweetly perfumed neck and shoulders.

'So do you.' She returned the compliment with a squeeze of his hand. This was the Ray she'd first fallen in love with: a handsome, smiling companion with a twinkle in his brown eyes and no sign of the shadows cast by his painful past.

'Giles and I are determined to make a go of things,' Ray assured her. 'On top of which, Philip has agreed to stay on at Thresham after the war. He'll still live in his Quaker community in Highcliff — his religion is important to him and I respect that. He's willing to cycle over to the yard each day.'

'And is Ronnie agreeable?'

'Perfectly. He says he's not as young as he used to be and could do with an extra pair of hands.' Ray looked apprehensively towards the room where the party was in full swing. 'Normally I'd ask you if you fancied having a drink at the bar before we went in,' he confessed.

'But not tonight!' With a relieved smile, Bobbie pulled him across the hall. The music had changed once more: it was Dolores's turn to steal the limelight with a chirpy rendering of the Andrews Sisters song 'Don't Sit Under the Apple Tree'.

'Quickstep,' Bobbie informed Ray.

'If you say so.' His reluctance soon melted away, however, once he had Bobbie in his arms. Together they flitted across the dance floor, weaving in and out of Stan and Gillian and Horace and Olive. 'You hear

343

that?' he said, with a nod towards the band. 'You're not to go sitting under the apple tree with anyone else but me.'

'If you say so,' Bobbie echoed with a smile.

'You're not to go walking down lover's lane, either — it's in the song.'

'With anyone else but you,' Bobbie agreed. She felt her head float in a woozy way. This was happiness, pure and simple. Tomorrow would be Christmas Eve, then the big day itself. 'Do you have any plans for New Year?' she mentioned as the song came to an end.

He led her to a seat in a quiet corner where he took out another cigarette. 'As it happens, no, I don't. How about you?'

'I expect I'll go home for Hogmanay unless I'm needed here.'

'To Bonnie Scotland?' Ray inhaled deeply and watched Mary separate from her latest dance partner with a quiet, polite thank you and what he interpreted as a sad smile. She joined Viv, who was standing alone close to the stage.

'Yes — I was wondering . . .' Bobbie hesitated then took the plunge. 'I was thinking that you'd be the ideal person to do the first footing for us; it's meant to be a dark-haired stranger carrying a lump of coal for good luck. What do you say?'

He looked at her in astonishment. 'Is this an invitation for me to travel north of the border to meet your family?'

'It is,' she agreed. 'If you can spare the time?'

So bright and beautiful — Bobbie took his breath away. 'I can and I will,' Ray replied wholeheartedly. 'Believe me, First Officer Fraser, I can't think of a single thing that would stop me.'

Across the room Mary asked Viv why she wasn't dancing.

'I'm having a breather, that's all.' In fact, Viv was in two minds over whether to stay or go. There was no point in denying it: there was a big Giles-shaped hole in proceedings. True, she could dance with whomever she pleased and in fact the music alone would have been worth staying for under normal circumstances. The girl's voice was sweet and smooth as honey and young Leonard, though scarcely old enough for his voice to have broken, gave a decent impression of an experienced man about town with his cheeky rendition of 'The Waiter and the Porter and the Upstairs Maid'.

'That's not like you,' Mary commented. 'Come clean — are you sad because Giles didn't come?'

'Trust you to hit the nail on the head.' Viv felt her eyes smart with sudden tears. 'Yes, I guess I am. But it's my own silly fault — the last time I saw Giles I did my usual foot-in-the-mouth trick and now he's obviously avoiding me like the plague.'

'What did you say to him?'

'It's not so much what I said as what I didn't say,' Viv confessed. 'He told me he planned to work as Ray's business manager at Thresham and what did I think of that? I said not to stick around on my account.'

'You didn't!' Mary gasped.

'I did. I told him I had no clue what I'd be doing in six months' time or whenever the war finally ends — and I honestly don't.'

'No more do I,' Mary reminded her. 'Or any of us Atta girls, once the ATA is disbanded.'

'That's true, I guess. In any case, Giles took my answer as a final, once-and-for-all brush-off and I can't say I blame him.'

'But was it?' Mary insisted on knowing.

'No. Once the words were out of my stupid mouth, I couldn't take them back, could I? The damage was done. For a second Giles looked so darned hurt then he clammed up the way he does. End of story.'

'Not quite.' A tap on Viv's shoulder made her turn around. 'You don't get rid of me that easily.'

'Giles, what are you doing here?' Were her eyes fooling her or was he really standing there in his Savile Row suit and shiny dancing shoes?

'I'm enjoying a Christmas shindig like everyone else — if you'll permit me?' In fact, it had only been at the last minute that he'd put on the suit and driven over to the Grange. There'd been an awful lot of indigestible pride to swallow first so he'd arrived late and only just spotted Viv deep in conversation with Mary close to the stage. 'The band is rather good, actually,' he mentioned to Mary before she slipped discreetly away. 'May I have the pleasure?' he asked Viv.

The pianist changed the tempo and Elsie invited dancers to attempt a Lindy Hop.

'Are you sure?' Viv checked with Giles. The modern, uninhibited American dance craze hardly seemed his cup of tea.

'Sure I'm sure.' Taking her by both hands he pulled her towards him then pushed her out again, pulled her in then twirled her with one hand, moving to the brisk beat in what she thought of as his understated English way. When he kicked with his left leg his foot was scarcely two inches off the floor. Likewise when he rocked her sideways it was without obvious effort and after her twirl he caught her smoothly round the waist then began all over again — in, out, kick, twirl

346

and kick again.

'Say; you're not bad,' Viv told him.

'I'm full of surprises.' Kick, twirl, kick.

'You sure are.' When he held her by the waist the full Giles effect came into play — *Whoa, take a deep breath, keep your feet on the ground!* 'For a start, I didn't think you'd come.'

'Neither did I.' He gave her another twirl and then swayed her from side to side. 'But then I thought, it's only a party — nothing more. It's not as if we're committing ourselves in any way.'

'We're not,' Viv agreed hesitantly.

'We're both free agents,' he said above the trill of the piano.

'Sure thing.' The plan that she'd been quietly hatching to go back to Canada to work for an air taxi company suddenly seemed like a truly dumb idea. Why not try for a similar job in England instead? Yes, indeed!

'It'll take me a while to work out how long I want to stay at Thresham.' Kick and twirl, nonchalant as you like. 'Once Ray's back on his feet I might like to move on.'

'The world's your oyster,' she agreed. Boy, were Giles's eyes a brilliant shade of grey — almost blue in certain lights. And he sure knew how to swing a girl around the dance floor.

'But since we're both here in Yorkshire, living within twenty miles of each other, how do you feel about us spending Christmas Day together?'

'Are you serious?' Viv's recent doubts and worries slipped away in an instant. Her eyes lit up.

'Yes; either here at the Grange or at Thresham.' He would leave the decision up to her. 'What do you say?'

'I say yes, please.' As Giles pulled her towards him, she looped both arms around his neck and kissed him. They would spend Christmas together and then who knew? Who even cared? 'Thank you, Giles. And a very Happy Christmas to us both!'

★ ★ ★

Towards the end of the celebrations, when Ray and Giles went outside for a smoke, Bobbie and Viv found vacant seats close to the Christmas tree.

'Congratulations — this is a terrific success.' Viv praised Bobbie's dogged determination in bringing arrangements for the party together. The band played on and couples danced under the streamers and balloons.

'It was a joint effort, don't forget.' Bobbie mopped her damp forehead with a handkerchief. Ray and she had danced the night away. 'You and Mary made all the difference.'

'We had fun, didn't we?' A wistful Viv looked back to the night when they'd felled the tree with a cry of 'Timber!' followed by a jolly tramp through the wood.

'We always do.' With her plan for New Year firmly in place, Bobbie floated on cloud nine.

'And Peggy was a big help, too,' Viv conceded. 'It's a pity she's not here.'

'According to Mary, she'd rather spend the time with her little girl.' Spotting Mary among the dancers with a young Aireby partner, Bobbie gave a sigh.

'What's up, Roberta McFlirta?' Viv followed the direction of her gaze. 'Oh, yeah; Mary's missing you-know-who.'

'If only . . .' Bobbie wished for a magic wand.

'Maybe singing our song will cheer her up.' Viv hoped that the evening would end with a bang when the three girls took to the stage and sang the party to a close.

'Let's hope so.' Glancing towards the door, Bobbie spied Ray and Giles crossing the hall to rejoin the festivities. She jumped up and dragged Viv with her. 'Come on; let's waylay them under the mistletoe.'

Mary noticed Viv and Bobbie make their rapid exit then saw the reason for it: mistletoe embraces and soft kisses were exchanged as the band played another quickstep. When the number came to an end she thanked her partner — a tall trainee wireless operator — and prepared to slip quietly from the dance floor.

'May I?'

Mary felt a tap on her shoulder and spun around.

'Would you like to dance?' Cameron had arrived without anyone noticing. He'd parked his car and come in through the boot room, along dark corridors past the butler's pantry then up the stairs into the hall. He'd stepped back into the shadows when he'd seen Ray kissing Bobbie under the mistletoe then waited until the coast was clear. He wanted this to be a complete surprise for Mary. 'Yes, it's me all right,' he murmured before he kissed her.

Mary closed her eyes. Would he still be there when she opened them again? The answer was an astonishing yes — Cameron in his uniform, a little thinner and more gaunt, stood before her, asking her to dance. 'You managed to get leave?' she whispered.

'Not quite.' He drank in the sight of her in her coral-pink dress, her cheeks flushed, her eyes brimming with tears. She clung to his hand as if fearing that he

349

would disappear into thin air. 'I applied to my group captain for a transfer to Rixley.'

'What do you mean? For how long?' At first she couldn't make sense of what he was saying.

'I volunteered to take charge of the ferry pool in Hilary's absence,' he explained. 'They said yes, go ahead. Rixley needs a chap with my experience while he gets back on his feet — which I'm assured he will do, by the way. In any case, my squadron is about to be disbanded and its pilots sent off in various directions, so it turns out that my request suits them as much as it suits me.'

'You're back for good?' Her husband, the man she loved and had pined for through every moment of his absence, had been removed from nightly bombing missions. He'd been taken off the front line and posted to the relative safety of Rixley ferry pool.

'For a few months, at least.'

Mary gripped his hand then closed her eyes again to absorb the bolt from the blue.

As she did so, Elsie came to the front of the stage to make an announcement. 'Ladies and gentlemen, before we play the last waltz I'd like to invite our three guest singers to take to the stage.'

'Cameron — that includes me.' The room seemed to spin. Mary saw Bobbie and Viv make their way towards the platform. 'Don't go away.'

'I'll be right here.'

'Promise?' Releasing his hand, she rushed to join Viv and Bobbie.

An astonished Viv bent forward to pull Mary on to the stage. 'Am I seeing things or is that Cameron over there?' she hissed.

'It's him.' Mary nodded quickly. There he was, in

the spot where she'd left him, head and shoulders taller than anyone else, beaming at her.

'Explain later.' Hearing the introduction to 'Swinging on a Star', Bobbie quickly lined them up at the front of the stage, ready to begin.

So Mary, Viv and Bobbie faced their audience. They saw a sea of faces — friends and strangers united in seasonal revelry — and they heard the beat of drums and the swinging rhythm of piano bass notes. They picked out Cameron, Giles and Ray from the crowd and performed the song for them, the men they loved.

They sang of moonbeams and starlight, of hard work and hope. Their voices harmonized perfectly. Tonight they stood shoulder to shoulder to celebrate Christmas 1944. Tomorrow, next week, next month and next year, Bobbie, Mary and Viv would be together still, rising through clouds in magnificent Spitfires, Tempests and Hurricanes — taking control of miraculous flying machines and helping their country to victory at last.